The Infidelity Chain

TESS STIMSON is the author of four previous novels, the most recent being the top ten bestselling *The Adultery Club*, and one biography. She writes regularly for the *Daily Mail* as well as for several women's magazines. Born and brought up in Sussex, she graduated from Oxford before spending a number of years as a news producer with ITN. She now lives in Florida with her American husband, their daughter and her two sons.

www.tessstimson.com

The Infidelity Chain

Tess Stimson

PAN BOOKS

First published 2008 by Pan Books
an imprint of Pan Macmillan Ltd
Pan Macmillan, 20 New Wharf Road, London N1 9RR
Basingstoke and Oxford
Associated companies throughout the world
www.panmacmillan.com

ISBN 978-0-330-44521-4

5 7 9 8 6

A CIP catalogue record for this book is available from
the British Library.

Typeset by SetSystems Ltd, Saffron Walden, Essex
Printed and bound in Great Britain by
Mackays of Chatham plc, Chatham, Kent

For my husband,

Erik.

Sometimes you are right,
and I am wrong.

Acknowledgements

I have been helped in so many ways by so many people; but in particular, I owe a deep debt of gratitude to Carole Blake, the most wonderful agent in the world, and Imogen Taylor, my brilliant editor. I am exceptionally lucky to be the beneficiary of their talent and friendship. Thank you for all you are and do.

Both are backed up by superb teams at Blake Friedmann and Pan Macmillan – Oli Munson, Trisha Jackson, Emma Giacon, Ellen Wood, Anna Bond and all the Pan team, you are all amazing. Without you, none of this would happen; this book is truly a team effort.

Dr Jerold Lucey, Professor of Paediatrics at the University of Vermont College of Medicine and Editor-in-Chief of *Pediatrics* magazine, and Professor David Edwards of the Department of Paediatrics at Hammersmith Hospital, provided invaluable information regarding the care of premature infants, and I am extremely grateful to them for their time, advice and kindness. Jerry, you are a wonderful and generous friend. Any errors in the book are entirely mine.

One of the main characters in this book endures frightening and debilitating panic attacks. I would thoroughly recommend the online book *Panic Away!* by Joe Barry (www.panicaway.com), whose simple, effective technique has transformed the lives of so many sufferers.

To Danusia, Michèle, Georgie and Charlie, Sarah, Peter and Jayne, Julie and Tony, Christina, Andrew and Susan, Robert, Grub – thank you so much for always being such marvellous friends, especially when I visit you with such chaos and disruption on my brief trips home. I love you all.

Kisses, too, to my father Michael and WSM Barbi, to my out-laws Sharon and Harry, to my sister Philippa, brother Charles (the original English gentleman), my nephews Christopher, Alexander, William and George: every novelist should have a family like mine.

My children Henry, Matthew and Lily – what can I say? I love you to pieces, though you drive me to drink. If only I could bottle your laughter.

My beloved mother, Jane – I miss you still. You're always in our hearts and prayers.

Above all, to my husband, Erik, for loving me more.

TESS STIMSON
Florida, September 2007
www.tessstimson.com

1

Ella

I've often wondered if adultery runs in the genes, like blue eyes or buck teeth. Am I unfaithful because it's written in my DNA?

The idea appeals to the scientist in me: we're all the sum of our genetic barcodes, no more, no less. See, yes, there it is, nestling between my red hair and tendency towards the pear-shaped (hips, life, take your pick) – there, *infidelity*, clear as day. Biological proof that I can no more stay faithful than shrink a shoe size, however hard I try.

William stirs next to me. He reaches for my breast, and my nipple peaks instantly beneath his touch. His cock jabs my hip, already hard again. I smile. After eight years, we don't have sex that often, but when we do, we get our money's worth.

He rolls on to his back and pulls me on to him; I wince slightly as he enters me. He isn't to know I had sex with Jackson – twice – last night.

As he thrusts upwards, I cling to the brass bedstead for

support, my breasts shivering tantalizingly above his mouth. His lips fasten on my nipple and there's a zig-zagging pulse between my legs. I tighten my grip. William is the more selfish lover; I've learned to take my pleasure from him without asking. Jackson is far more thoughtful: always seeking out new ways to please me, holding himself in check until I've come, sometimes three or four times.

I shunt Jackson out of my head. Contrary to popular myth, women *can* be good at adultery. All they have to do is learn to think like a man.

My clit rubs against William's pelvis, and the familiar heat builds. His teeth graze my breast; swift, greedy bites. I reach between his legs, skittering my fingernails along the inside of his thighs and across his balls. He bucks inside me, hitting my G-spot, and I stiffen, savouring the moment at the crest of the rollercoaster. Then my orgasm breaks over me in sweeping, almost painful, waves.

With one hand, I find the tiny sensitive spot between his balls and asshole, pressing just enough to send him wild. With the other, I reach for my beeping phone.

Only two people would text me this late at night. Jackson, or—

'Shit!' I tumble off William, groping for my clothes.

He slams his head against the pillow. 'Christ. I thought you weren't on call tonight?'

'Emergency.' I hook up my bra, and scrabble under the bed for my knickers. 'I'll be back as soon as I can.'

'Couldn't it have waited until *after* I came?'

I give up on the knickers, and pull on my grey pencil skirt before sliding my feet into a pair of skyscraper scarlet heels. I can only find a single topaz earring; I *hate* losing one of a pair.

Buttoning up my white silk shirt, I lean forward and drop a kiss on his sandpaper cheek. He smells of my sex. 'Happy Valentine's Day.'

William scowls. 'You owe me.'

'Get in line.'

Fifteen minutes later, I ease my toes from the to-die-in stilettos as the lift grinds its way up to the obstetrics floor. There must be another butter-wouldn't-melt little genome tucked away on that adulterous double helix to explain my uncontrollable fetish for pretty shoes. How else to explain the purchase of lust-have red Ginas in a size six (the only pair left – and no, they haven't 'stretched with wear' as the commission-only salesgirl promised) when I've been a size seven all my adult life?

My mother was always perfectly shod. Even when the French bailiffs evicted us from our little *appartement* on the Rue du Temple because my father had stopped paying the rent, her footwear (if not her reputation) was beyond reproach. We might starve as a result, but she could no more resist a new pair of polka-dot peep-toe slingbacks than she could him.

She brought her only daughter up in her likeness.

The lift doors open and I hobble towards the delivery suites, uncomfortably aware of the draught beneath my skirt. Lucy is my best friend, and I love her to death, but I really hope she isn't on duty tonight. I'm used to moral sermons from my mother; she speaks from fingers-burned experience, after all. But Lucy and I have been *les soeurs sous la peau* since we crossed scalpels over a half-dissected corpse as medical students at Oxford. She's the one I go to for a Xanax scrip before I fly. It's not like she hasn't known about my affair for years.

On the other hand, when your husband leaves you for a teenage choreographer (forget semantics: if you're thirty-six, as we are, twenty-three *is* teenage) I suppose it entitles you to take a more jaundiced than jaunty view of other people's adultery.

My mobile rings as I reach the labour ward. Peering through the glass porthole, I realize my patient must still be in the back of an ambulance trapped in stubborn traffic somewhere on the Fulham Road, and take the call.

'Jackson,' I say, 'I'm with a patient.'

'You're at work?'

'You knew I was on call.'

One of the perks of being a doctor (aside from delightful offers from strangers at parties to allow me to examine their thyroids or anal fissures in the guest bathroom, heedless of both the social niceties and the fact that I am a neonatologist) is the ability to stay out all night unquestioned. As paediatric consultant at the Princess Eugenie Neonatal Intensive Care Unit, I owe the hospital six nights on call each month. My husband has always believed it to be seven.

'You've got five minutes,' I tell Jackson.

'That's not what you said last night,' he teases, his Deep South drawl undiminished by nearly a decade in England.

I'm not having an affair because my sex life with my husband is either infrequent or unsatisfying. On the contrary: he's a conscientious lover. Though I have plenty of plausible reasons for my infidelity, I'm not sure that I can find an excuse that actually excuses me.

I shrug on my white coat. 'What is it?'

'I need to talk to you.'

'*Now*? Can't it wait?'

He hesitates. 'I just found this neat motorcycle on eBay, an Indian. The bids end at midnight, and I wanted to talk to y'all about it first—'

I can't help thinking he was going to say something else. 'A motorbike?'

'C'mon, Ell, you know I've always wanted one. It'd make it real quick to get to work. It's all right for you,' he adds, an edge creeping into his voice, 'living so close to the hospital. You're not the one gotta sit in traffic for an hour two times a day.'

'I'm sure DuCane Pharmaceuticals would still—'

'For Chrissakes, Ella! How many times?'

'No one's asking you to raise money for their pills,' I say tightly. 'We all know they're immoral drug-pushing pimps who'll go straight to hell, yada yada. But the research programme is different—'

'Suddenly stem-cell research is OK?'

'Jackson, I'm a doctor. What do you want me to say?'

'You don't have to leave your conscience at the door when you put on your white coat, Ella,' he says bitterly. 'Just your fancy shoes.'

I wish.

'I don't see what my conscience has to do with—'

'I thought you were supposed to be saving babies, not murdering them.'

'Not that it's anything to do with neonatology, Jackson,' I say, stung, 'but since when did messing about with zygotes become equivalent to baling infants with a pitchfork?'

'Stupid of me to think you'd care.'

'Stupid of me to think you'd be able to reason like a grown-up.'

Subtext whirls through the ether. We both know what this is *really* about.

I switch my mobile to the other ear, holding on to my temper with difficulty. Now is not the time to call him out for wanting to break our deal; we agreed from day one: no children. It's not as if the subject is going to go away, I think resentfully.

'Look. I only meant—'

'I know what you meant, Ella.'

It's one of the things I always admired about Jackson (particularly since I lack it myself): his steadfast, unfashionable integrity. A gifted fundraiser, charming, sincere and articulate, he has the kind of likeable persuasiveness that, were he politically minded, could have seen him in the White House (although his incurable honesty might have counted against him, of course). In the past couple of years, head hunters for several prestigious NGOs have offered him six figures and an open-ended expense account to run their capital campaigns or head up their development offices. All have come away disappointed – though only after Jackson has charmed them into donating hefty sums to One World, the lentils-and-hairy-armpit environmental charity for which he works.

It's one of the things that always irritates me about my husband: his rigid, my-way-or-the-highway Southern sense of honour.

I jam my mobile between chin and shoulder to button the white coat over my smart crêpe skirt. There's nothing I can do about the fuck-me red shoes. 'Fine. If you've made up your mind.'

'Think of it as a belated birthday present.'

I close my eyes, suddenly awash with remorse. 'Oh, Jackson. I'm sorry.'

'Forget it.'

'I've been so busy at the hospital – we're under-staffed—'

'I said forget it.'

The silence lingers. How could I miss his birthday? It's Valentine's Day, for God's sake. You'd think I could manage to remember *that*.

Jackson coughs again. 'How's the cold?' I ask quickly; guiltily.

'Actually, I feel kinda lousy, to be honest. I think I'm spiking a fever.'

I suppress a smile. It's extraordinary, the way the same bug affects the male and female immune systems. I should write a paper on it: 'A virus that will just produce sniffles in the female of the species miraculously becomes an upper respiratory infection the moment it encounters macho Y chromosomes . . .'

'Look, Jackson, we'll go out at the weekend, I promise. I'll make up some excuse—'

'Sure.'

'You choose. Anywhere you like.'

'Ycp. Whatever.'

'You'll enjoy it more when you're feeling better any-way.' Then, partly to appease my conscience, and partly because, despite William, despite everything, it *is* still true, I add, 'I love you.'

'Love you more.'

It's our catchphrase, one of those couply exchanges you develop in the early months together and then later cling to, like a lifebelt, out of mingled superstition and hope and fear when the going gets rough.

It is also, in six words, a synopsis of our marriage.

We met in America eleven years ago, at the perfect-storm moment; the one night when I was tired enough, and vulnerable enough, and (let's be honest) drunk enough for a window in my carefully nurtured cynicism to crack and give Jackson time to slip through.

I'd lost my virginity at seventeen (to my thirty-four-year-old tennis coach; the cliché embarrassed me more than being caught *in flagrante* by my grandmother, who'd merely nodded with the quiet triumph of one being proved right). Since then, all the men I'd dated had had just one thing in common: not one was remotely available, and that's just how I liked it.

A part of me knew my behaviour wasn't exactly well adjusted; but the rest of me figured it'd sort itself out when I met the right man.

It wasn't a *coup de foudre* when Jackson Garrett sauntered into the piano bar on Bourbon Street, in the French Quarter of New Orleans, and headed straight over to Lucy and me as if we'd been waiting there all night just for him. Love certainly didn't come into it.

Jackson was – *is* – the most handsome man I'd ever seen. He's got this all-American, dazzling-white movie-star smile, and the kind of skin that looks golden even in the middle of an English winter. Eyes a Tiffany turquoise, with obscenely long lashes and the kind of sparkle that makes your skin tingle and your clothes somehow unbutton themselves. And a mouth so mobile and sensual you have no choice but to throw your anal British reserve to the wind and demand that it kiss you. *Come on, it's my birthday, what are you, shy?* (Looking back, I believe that's where three Hurricanes came in.)

After we came up for air, I grabbed my cigarette lighter and fumbled for my poise, waiting for him to zero in on Lucy. Men always do. Hardly surprising, given her fifties curves, perfect skin and waist-length, old-gold hair; for the first year I knew her, I seriously considered a Sapphic conversion. The universal Law of Attraction, which dictates that people end up with partners of the same degree of attractiveness as themselves, plus or minus one point (unless money or power distort the equation), put Jackson firmly in her league, rather than mine.

But, bending his dark-blond head to mine, he murmured in my ear, his warm breath rum-sweet, 'I always knew you colonialists didn't play fair. I should warn y'all, I surrender easy.'

'I'm no Virginia myself.'

'I'd Nevada thought it.'

'I know there's something rude I could do with Kansas and Mississippi,' I mused, 'but these Hurricanes are stronger than they look.'

His skin smelled of leather and soap and pine trees just after it's rained. There was a quiver in the region of my knickers.

He took the unlit cigarette out of my fingers and guided me towards the door. 'I think we need to discuss the state of this union somewhere else.'

It was obviously never going to be more than a brief holiday fling, since Lucy and I were only down from North Carolina for the weekend. We planned to experience the

'Come as you are, leave different' philosophy of the Big Easy before we graduated from Duke and – her words – went home to London and stuck our heads back up our uptight British arses.

So while Lucy generously waved me on, I went back to his apartment and slept with him (oh, the brazen shame of me!) *the first night*, with none of that tedious game-playing, no-touching-below-the-waist-till-the-fifth-date routine.

Over breakfast the next morning – Creole beignets, fresh fruit fritters and cinnamon sopaipillas; dear Lord, the man could *cook*! – we exchanged some of the personal details we'd neglected in favour of energetic sex the night before, such as our names. Jackson was a fundraiser at New Orleans' Tulane University. When I told him I was studying medicine at Duke, he nearly spat out his (strong, black) coffee.

'I'll be damned. I just got a job at Duke, I'm movin' there in a couple weeks.'

Still aching pleasurably from the night's exertions, I decided Jackson was the perfect rebound lover (there'd been a brief and unhappy dalliance with a married history professor, recently ended and best not dwelt upon): the casual, restorative relationship that helps mend a broken heart after a romantic near-miss, or at least someone to play hooky with while you wait to meet The One. He was not, as he warned me at the time, supposed to be the man I *married*.

All relationships are intrinsically unequal; I'd learned that lesson as a small child. Whoever loves the least has the most power.

Growing up, I'd often wondered why my mother always seemed to be waiting for something that never came. I'd vowed into my pillow, as I listened night after night to my mother sobbing on the other side of the wall into hers, that I would not end up like she had. I would not wait *seventeen years* for a charismatic, faithless man who had no intention of ever leaving his wife for me, who would get me pregnant and not give our child so much as his name, who would die and leave me, at forty-six, not-quite-a-widow in a still-strange land with a nine-year-old daughter to support and no earthly means to do it.

Thrown unceremoniously on to the streets after the untimely death of *mon père*, my mother and I had slept in the back of her ancient green Peugeot for three weeks, living on day's-end baguettes and over-ripe cheese, before she'd admitted defeat and summoned the courage to go back home, beret in hand, to Northamptonshire. Her own father had died without ever forgiving her. Her mother referred to me as 'the French bastard'. It had seemed reasonable to me at the time.

For the next nine years, I'd watched my mother scrabble for scraps of approval from the old witch, struggling hopelessly to atone for her one doomed act of defiance (how she'd ever found the courage to escape to Paris in the first place, I'd never yet worked out). I'd stared into the speckle-backed mirror at my homely reflection, with its unattractive mass of red curls and eyes the colour of weak tea, so different from hers and therefore so clearly *his*, and wondered what she had seen in my father that could possibly make him worth this misery.

As soon as I turned eighteen I fled to Oxford, determined that, whatever happened, I would never depend on a man for anything: love or money.

Jackson had all the hallmarks of a toxic bachelor;

charming, sexy and footloose, he should have broken my heart. But right from the start, and against all reason (even with a streaming cold he was a definite 9½; on my wedding day, with a flotilla of *Vogue* make-up artists, I'd be lucky to scrape a 7), somehow I always knew I was the one in control.

It was no single thing, but a thousand tiny kindnesses. He filled our bedroom with Confederate jasmine because I mentioned that I liked its scent. He stayed up all night testing me before my exams, never taking offence when I yelled at him out of nerves or sheer bloody-mindedness. When I wanted to ski in Colorado, he was happy to take me, even though he hated the cold with all the fervour of a Southern boy who's never experienced a morning frost. Not just keep-the-peace happy. Child-on-Christmas-morning happy. Being with me was enough for him. No matter what I proposed, he smiled his easy smile which scrunched the corners of his blue blue eyes, and said that if it worked for me, it worked for him too.

Our light romance bridged the gap between Mardi Gras and real life with surprising success. We were very different people, and yet we understood each other. We both knew what it was like to suddenly lose a parent at a young age – in Jackson's case, both: his parents had died in a hotel fire when he was eleven, leaving him to be brought up by his brother Cooper, six years his elder. We'd both had to grow up hard and fast, and if our reactions to this hot-housed awareness of the fragility of life were very different – he chose to live for today, I to control tomorrow – we had a shared knowledge of the chaos that lay beneath. We both loved jazz and blues, Gregory Peck and baroque architecture. Jackson adored peaceably walking in the mountains almost as much as I loved the challenge of climbing them; we both relished the thrills of white-water rafting, kayaking and canoeing. Admittedly I missed the bright lights of London, but in those early days we were truly both happiest when we were far from the madding crowd, holed up in a cabin somewhere with just the odd harmless black bear for company.

Of course I loved him; it was impossible not to. He gave freely and asked nothing of me (the talk of babies came much later). He was always there for me, my confidant and companion, my dearest friend.

And I needed him; for many reasons, but most of all to counterbalance the fatal pull I felt towards men I couldn't handle, men who *didn't* make me feel safe. Men like my father, men who would catch me in their riptide and drag me under.

We all marry partly out of fear: of being alone, of dying unloved. Three months after we met I asked Jackson to marry me, knowing that whatever his reservations, he would be unable to say no, because I was afraid of what I might do if I didn't.

Lucy looks up from the nurses' station, where she's skimming a bulky manila folder. 'Nice shoes.'

I hesitate. She smiles ruefully and, relieved at the unexpected *détente*, I smile back.

She hands me the folder. 'Sorry I had to call you in. It's Anna Shore.'

Damn. Anna is one of Lucy's heartsink obstetric patients: thirty-nine, six miscarriages in five years, two of them distressingly late, at nineteen and twenty weeks. This pregnancy is her last chance to have her own child; she and her husband, Dean, have already decided that they cannot bear to go through the shattering cycle of hope and despair again if this attempt fails.

'Remind me. How far along?'

'Twenty-two weeks and six days.'

'Shit.'

I scan the notes, trying to get a read on how developed we think this baby is. It's hospital policy not to save babies of less than twenty-three weeks' gestation; born at the very cusp of viability, their chances of survival, even with our intervention, are minimal. I'm relieved Lucy called me in; William will get over it. This sort of case isn't something I'd want a senior house officer handling in my absence.

'Look, Ella,' Lucy says carefully, 'I'm sorry about going off at you the other day. It was just a shock, running into the two of you like that. Tell William I'm really sorry about the carrot juice. I'll pay for the dry-cleaning—'

'Forget it. At least it wasn't hot coffee.'

'It's just that you know how much I like Jackson, and what with – with Lawrence—'

'Did he agree to counselling?'

She seems to shrink inside her skin, so that suddenly it hangs loose and grey on her bones. 'He's asked for a divorce.'

'Oh, Lucy. Oh, darling, I'm *so* sorry.'

'*Shit*, Ella. Don't be nice to me or I'll lose it completely.' She pulls herself together with a visible effort. 'I know you don't want to hear this, but I'm worried about you. Jackson is such a good man. You two could be really great together. I don't want this thing with William to blow up in your face.'

'It's a bit of a mess, I know, but—'

'Eight years, Ella!'

'Look, all right. It kind of drifted. But it's not like we see each other that often.' I snap shut the file. 'Lucy, you know the score. This is about you and Lawrence, not—'

'Do you love him?'

'Jackson? Or William?'

'Either,' she exclaims, exasperated.

'It's not that simple. Life isn't black and white, you know that—'

'Actually, Ella, some things *are*.' She looks at me sharply. 'It was one thing playing with fire when we were at college, but it's different now. This is real life. I thought when you met Jackson you'd finally got whatever was eating you out of your system. Obviously I was wrong.'

I shift uncomfortably. How to explain in a way that makes any kind of sense? At twenty-five, when I married Jackson, I truly intended to be faithful to him for ever. I thought *wanting* to be in love with him was enough. But within a year, I discovered that getting what you wish for isn't all it's cracked up to be. Beautiful and careless, Jackson never, ever said no to me. But I soon realized he let me have my way less out of love than a desire to slough off responsibility for anything at all. I hadn't married an equal, but an emotional child; and why would I want to have a baby – already an enterprise I felt deeply ambivalent about, given my own parents' staggering incompetence – when I was already parenting my husband?

I'd hoped that moving back to London for my residency would help, that the buzz of the city would somehow jump-start things between us. But then, just a week shy of our third wedding anniversary, I met William.

He wasn't anywhere near as good-looking or charming as Jackson. Twelve years older, tough, cynical, sexist and controlling, he was everything my gentlemanly, easygoing husband was not. And unlike my husband, he just had *it*; in spades.

It was like being hit by a train. The sexual chemistry was tangible, but it was more than that. Meeting him made me realize how much I'd short-changed not just Jackson but myself when I took the safe way out and married him. I morphed into a different person when I was with William, the person I'd always wanted to be: confident, desirable, exciting. He challenged me; being with him was like walking a tightrope – terrifying and exhilarating at the same time. One slip and I could lose him; or, even worse, fall in love.

I never considered leaving Jackson. I married him to protect myself from men like William Ashfield. And I was very fond of my husband. None of this was his fault. But I couldn't face the thought of spending the rest of my life never experiencing anything stronger than *fond*.

William wanted the same as I did: an escape. A chance to play what-might-have-been, without jeopardizing what was.

To my astonishment, tears threaten. I blink furiously, surprised and shocked. I *never* bring my personal life into work.

'Ella, I'm sorry. I didn't mean to upset you—'

'You didn't. It's my problem, not yours.'

'I'm sure you know what you're doing,' Lucy says uncertainly.

'You'd think, after eight years.'

She folds her arms. 'Ella, you're the most self-controlled

person I've ever met, but even *you* can't expect to lead two separate lives and not have them collide now and again, if only in your head. Feelings have a way of coming to the surface, whether you like it or not.'

Lucy is my dearest friend, but she doesn't know what she's talking about. Things are absolutely fine. My life is perfectly organized. It's all beautifully balanced. William and I have the perfect arrangement. Jackson isn't going to find out; nothing's going to go wrong. I'm totally in control.

I jump at the asthmatic sound of the Victorian lift. Instantly, thankfully, my focus is on my patient. *You escape into work and call it altruism*, Jackson said once, in a rare moment of anger. *I call it the coward's way out.*

A flurry of medical personnel wheels a hospital bed from the lift. Anna Shore's frantic husband struggles to keep hold of her hand as the cavalcade steps up its pace. Behind them, Richard Angel, the hospital's chief number cruncher – known, without a trace of irony, as the Angel of Death – strides down the corridor. His fine blond hair is so badly cut it borders on rude. He snaps his fingers constantly at his sides, an irritating nervous tic.

'Shit,' Lucy mutters, 'I meant to warn you.'

'If I might have a word . . .' Angel starts.

Lucy disappears to a private room to examine Anna, while Angel and I glare at each other across the nurses' station. I'm acutely conscious of the fact that I'm not wearing any knickers.

The prognosis is written on her face when she returns. 'The drugs aren't working, Ella. She's in full-blown labour. I said you'd talk to her, and explain what happens next.'

Of course. I'm always the one who has to break bad

news. Lucy's far too beautiful for anyone to believe in her as the bearer of grim tidings. Clearly, awash with freckles and gifted with hideous ginger ringlets and my father's Depardieu nose, I have the right looks for tragedy.

I'm sluiced by a wave of sadness as I go into Anna's room and sit down on the edge of the bed. It's not the fear in her eyes that disarms me; it's the unremitting hope.

'Anna,' I say gently. 'We've tried to stop the labour, but it's not working. Your baby is going to be born in the next hour or so. We've given her steroids, to try to mature her lungs, but we haven't really had much time. She's very tiny, Anna. Not much more than a pound. Do you know how small that is?'

'Half a bag of sugar,' Anna whispers.

'She's so little, darling. Not quite twenty-three weeks. I need to talk to you about what that means, and you're going to have to be very brave. Can you do that for me?'

She glances up at her husband, then nods, her grip tightening on my fingers.

'At this age, we lose two-thirds of these tiny babies during delivery. They just can't cope, sweetheart, their little lungs aren't strong enough. If they do make it, we have to help them with their breathing. We give them something called surfactant, which keeps their lungs from sticking together and makes their breathing easier—'

'What about brain damage?' Dean, her husband, asks fearfully.

'When a baby is born this early, there is a risk she'll have an intracranial haemorrhage – bleeding of the brain.'

'How high a risk?'

'If the baby is really small, about one in three.'

Anna closes her eyes and turns her head away.

God, this never gets any easier. 'That doesn't necessarily mean that the baby will be brain-damaged, Anna. There's only a bad outcome in a small percentage of cases—'

'Wait. Wait. What do you call a bad outcome?' Dean interrupts. 'What are we talking about here?'

'Some type of limited motion, or intellectual trouble at school, that kind of thing.'

'So how long before you know if she's going to be – *normal*?'

'We can't tell with babies this small. I'm sorry, I know it's hard.' I pause, my heart aching as I search for the right words to help them. 'Sometimes when the baby is this little, it can be better to just let her go. Intervention can be very traumatic, for you and your baby, and when the outlook is as uncertain as this—'

'I don't care if she's not perfect!' Anna cries. 'I don't care if we have to spend the rest of our lives looking after her!'

Dean swallows. 'And if she makes it? What then, Dr Stuart?'

'Call me Ella, please.' I sigh. 'Look, Dean, I'm not going to lie to you. There are lots of hurdles a baby this premature has to face, but there's no point giving you nightmares by outlining every possibility. We really need to concentrate on the here and now, not on what might develop later down the line. I want you to clearly understand what's going to happen once we start to deliver your baby, because I may not be able to explain everything at the time. I might need you to make some very difficult decisions very quickly.'

He nods, jaw working as he fights to hold back tears. Jesus, why would anyone want to be a parent and risk going through this? Having a child must be like spending the rest of your life with your heart walking around outside your body.

'If you want us to stop at any point during resuscitation, you just have to say so,' I add gently. 'No one is going to think badly of you.'

Tears seep beneath Anna's closed eyelids. 'I don't care what you have to do. Just don't give up on her. Please.'

I spend the next forty minutes prepping with the neonatal team, acutely aware that somewhere in this hospital another team of medical staff are preparing to abort a baby a week older than the infant we are trying to save. I know the chances are high that Anna's infant will die. I have dealt with a thousand cases just as tragic as hers. Why has this one got under my skin?

Richard Angel is lying in wait for me when Lucy pages me back to the obstetric suite. He glances at my scarlet heels, opens his mouth, then wisely thinks better of it.

'What are you still doing here?' I demand. 'No funny Valentine waiting at home?'

He scurries to keep pace with me, fingers clicking like a skeletal metronome. 'New policy. I expect to be notified whenever there's a borderline neonate.'

'Borderline?'

'You know hospital policy, Dr Stuart. It's a perfectly reasonable—'

'I'm sorry. Did I miss your graduation from medical school?' I hiss. 'Since when have *you* been qualified to determine viability, Richard? Is it just small babies you want to flush down the sluice, or do you plan to tour the geriatric ward pulling plugs, too?'

He looks like he wants to hit me. I watch him struggle

to keep his temper, knowing and not caring that I have just made a permanent and dangerous enemy.

'Someone has to be responsible for the operating costs of this hospital, Dr Stuart. If your department overspends, we have to make cuts elsewhere. One day in NICU costs the same as—'

'Do you expect me to stand by and watch this baby die?'

'This *foetus*,' he stresses, 'is too young to be viable.'

'Check your facts. It's ten past midnight,' I snap. 'Which means that, as of ten minutes ago, this *baby* is twenty-three weeks old and wins tonight's big prize: a shot at life. Now, if you'll excuse me, I have a patient waiting.'

I should be elated. Angel had both probability and statistics on his side. But against all the odds, Anna and Dean's baby – appropriately named Hope – snatched the chance we offered her. She'll spend the next four months in the NICU, a dozen lines snaking into her tiny body; it'll be weeks before she even breathes on her own, but she's alive. A brain scan hasn't shown up any obvious abnormalities, though we have a long way to go before we can relax. The risk of infection with a baby this young is acute. But so far, so good.

Yet the usual high eludes me. I let myself quietly into William's flat a little after four in the morning, my mood oppressed. A sense of unease drags at my heels. For the first time in years, I crave a cigarette.

Pouring myself a glass of tap water, I add four ice-cubes – thank you, America – and tiptoe through the darkened hallway towards the bedroom, wincing like a teenager as the ice clinks noisily in the sweating glass. For a long moment, I stand in the open doorway, leaning against the jamb. Asleep, William looks younger than his forty-eight years, the cynicism stripped from his expression. He is not conventionally handsome; his features are too uneven for that. A faded scar, three inches long, bisects his right jaw, the result of a climbing accident when he was eleven. He still nicks it when he shaves, one of the reasons he sports designer stubble – salt and pepper now, I notice, like his overlong hair. His head is heavy, leonine; when he smiles, his tawny eyes glow like copper. Angry, they darken to the colour of coffee beans. It is impossible to know the extent of his charisma, the force of his sexual energy, until he turns it on you.

I'm not in love with him. I knew from the beginning I couldn't allow myself that – especially after Cyprus. Divorce from Beth was not an option, given her problems, nor would I ever want it. That was never part of our arrangement.

Suddenly weary, I finish my glass of water and strip off my clothes, padding into the bathroom to brush my teeth. I notice my period has started a couple of days early; annoyed at being caught out, I grab an emergency tampon from my wash-bag and make a mental note to pick up a new box from the corner shop tomorrow; or rather, today.

It's four-thirty when I finally slip into bed beside William: too late to pick up where we left off. His alarm will go off in half an hour; despite owning a successful PR agency with a staff of over forty people, William is always the first to arrive at the office, and the last to leave. If I were married to Beth, no doubt I'd do the same. I'm very lucky to go home to a man I can at least respect.

Lucy's words have burrowed deeper than I care to

admit. For the first time in a very long time, I allow myself to think what it might be like to have to live without Jackson. I'm faintly surprised at how much I don't want that to happen. I know full well I deserve to lose him. I've always been very careful to control my feelings for William, to keep our relationship separate in my heart and head; I would never leave Jackson. But I know that would prove scant consolation to him if he ever found out about my affair. It would break his heart; and that would break mine.

I realize the unfamiliar feeling in the pit of my stomach is shame. This is not the kind of wife I ever wanted or intended to be. I've short-changed my husband; not only have I cheated on him, but I've denied him the only thing he has ever asked of me. Would a baby *really* be so bad?

My mobile rings, making me jump. I reach for it as William stirs, recognizing the hospital number on the caller ID. My heart sinks. Baby Hope seemed stable enough when I left the NICU—

But it's A&E on the other end of the line, not the NICU. And when I end the call a few minutes later, I am no longer any kind of wife, adulterous or otherwise.

I am a widow.

March 8, 1997

Chapel Hill Road
Durham
North Carolina 27707

Dear Cooper,

      Well, I'm not dead yet, despite what you must be thinking! I'm sorry it's been so long since I touched base, but it's been a crazy couple months. It'd be easier if you got connected – once you're online you can get these whizzy little electronic letters, they call them emails, maybe you've heard of them?!

    Anyways, I'm back in the Land of Tar; you always said I couldn't stay away from the mountains for long! I'd have called you before I left New Orleans, but everything happened so fast, I didn't have time. My new condo hasn't got a phone yet and the landlord's dragging his heels, so I guess this letter is it for a while.

    The thing is, I've met a girl. Her name's Ella Stuart, and she's the most beautiful woman I've ever seen. She's British (she has this cute accent!) and she's a doctor – well, studying to be one over at Duke.

    I'm guessing you're putting the pieces together right now and shaking your head and wondering what trouble your kid brother's gotten himself into this time, but it's not like that. This girl is the real deal, Coop. There's just something about her; soon as you meet her, you'll know what I mean.

    Anyways, couple weeks ago, first night of Mardi Gras, I went down the Famous Door (you remember, I took you there last time you were in the Easy, you got picked up by that

*transvestite) and soon as I walked in the bar, I saw her.
She's hard to miss, Coop, with this long wild red hair, like
the setting sun, and these big gold eyes that put me in
mind of Lolly's iced tea. She was laughing with her friend,
and right then she turned and caught my eye, and something
just clicked inside of me, like tumblers sliding into place.
I couldn't take my eyes off her. There was a look about her,
underneath all the sass: wary and sad at the same time. She
hides it well, but it's there. You think first off she's tough as
nails, but deep down she's sweet as pie.*

*So there I am, still trying to think of something smart to
say, when Ella just comes up and kisses me! I swear, I could
feel the tingling in my toes for ten minutes afterwards.
What's it called? A coup de foudre, something like that.
When you know the rest of your life is never going to be the
same again.*

*I bet you're laughing your ass off right now out on the
back porch, wondering how your brother has ended up all
misty-eyed over some girl like a lovestruck loon. Well, take
another pull on your Jack, brother, because that isn't the half
of it.*

*Next day, she tells me she's studying at Duke, and I just
come right out and say I've got a job there – don't ask me
what made me do it, Coop, I couldn't tell you, I just knew I
couldn't let her slip through my fingers. So I've spent the last
three weeks calling in every favor I ever chalked up and then
some, and two days ago I got a letter offering me a job in the
Department of Earth and Ocean Sciences, starting Monday!
It's less money than Tulane, but I like the idea of working for
the environment, I've had my fill of capital projects. So I gave
notice, quit my apartment, and drove up here yesterday.*

Now here I am sitting in a rental condo without a stick of furniture but a bed and a chair, wondering if I've gone and made the biggest fool of myself since Old Man Allen caught me buck-naked with Blair in the sawmill!

Thing is, Coop, I'm blown away by Ella, but I'm not so sure she's sold on me, and I don't know what all to do. Not to toot my own horn, but my problem's usually the other way round! I know she likes me, but I'm pretty sure she thought our hook-up was just a weekend fling. How do I close the deal, big brother? She blows hot and cold; one minute she's all over me, and the next I feel like I've got her foot in my ass and I'm being led out the door. I'm guessing she's been screwed over in the past by guys who never did the honorable thing, but the one thing you got to give me is that I say what I mean and I do what I say. If I can get her to trust me, I'll never give her cause to regret it.

Guess this is all part of your famous Karma Credit Plan, right? Payback for some of those hearts I broke along the way. I can't wait for you and Lolly to meet her. She's the one, Coop. I can see us sitting on the swing at Dad's old place by the lake, watching the sun set behind the mountains and knowing I've come home. I want to grow old with this woman, watch our kids grow up together, rock grandkids on my knee like Grandpa did with us. I can't blow it, bro.

I'd better close now, and go unpack some boxes before she comes round. I thought I might find some jasmine – she says she loves the scent, just like Mom used to. Lord, but I still miss her.

Write me soon, kiss Lolly for me, and see about that computer!

    Jackson

2

William

Christ Almighty, the poor bastard was only forty-one. Seven years younger than me. And a damn sight fitter, according to Ella: tennis, cycling, jogging down the Thames towpath at weekends. You're always reading about these health nuts keeling over in their running shorts, perfect specimens of physical fitness (apart from the unfortunate fact that they're dead); but it wasn't the running that gave him a heart attack. A fucking *virus*. Jesus.

It makes you think. Shit, it could happen to anyone; I could be next. Ella says it's not catching, it was just one of those freaky bugs that come out of nowhere, but let's face it, she's a paediatrician, not an immunologist—

'Mr Ashfield, is everything OK?'

I start. 'Sorry, Carolyn, miles away.'

My PA consults her notepad, nipples perking from the air-conditioning. 'Joe needs an answer on the Brunswick proposal. I told him you're still waiting to hear back from

Natasha, said you'd be in touch after the weekend. He's not happy, but he'll live with it.'

'Good. Did Sky get back to us yet about the Malinche Lyon interview?'

'Still waiting to hear. You've got about a dozen messages from Andammon, they're really keen—'

'Not interested. We'll have all our blue-chip clients beating a path out the door if we start representing foot-ballers' wives. Tell them we're not taking anyone else on right now, and give them Clifford's number.'

Idly, I watch her pert derrière wiggle out of the room, then swivel my chair back towards the window, barely noticing the stunning floor-to-ceiling view of Canary Wharf. Funny how you can work towards something for years, and six months later it barely registers.

I can't get Ella's husband out of my head. Which is ironic, given I've been screwing his wife on a regular basis for the last eight years and until he checked into the morgue a week ago I'd barely spared him a thought.

I'm not bloody proud of it; messing about with another man's wife isn't something I take lightly. No question, if Jackson had twigged what was going on, he'd have been quite within his rights to nail my balls to a tree. But in my defence, it wasn't as if I was going to break up the marriage. Perhaps, if it hadn't been for Beth – if she wasn't the way she is . . .

It's always been clearly understood, right from the out-set, that divorce wasn't an option for either of us; all the more so after Cyprus. Ella wouldn't have it any other way.

Still. She was in *my* bed when she found out her husband had turned up his toes. Hardly my fault, but it makes me feel a bit of a prick none the less.

Of course, now she's convinced it would've made a difference if she'd been with him. Says she might have seen the signs; though as I understand it, the whole problem is that there weren't any.

I've never known Ella feel guilty before. She doesn't experience the self-doubt that plagues us ordinary mortals; that kind of confidence is very sexy. Handy, too, for a doctor; if you second-guessed yourself over every life-or-death decision, you'd wind up off your head. But I suppose that kind of hubris catches up with everyone in the end. Even brazen, beautiful Ella.

I rub my hand over my face, trying to dispel a lingering weariness. Haven't been sleeping all that well lately. Beth isn't doing too brilliantly at the moment. I keep hoping she's just missing the boys, that we're not back on the slippery slope, but in the meantime there's a lot of slack for me to pick up at home, and of course Cate is at that stage – mothers and daughters, never easy even in a normal household.

And now Ella. Hard to know how things are going to go there. Suddenly single. Available, after all these years.

I hope she's not going to go getting any ideas about *us*. She seems to be taking it in her stride, as usual, but you never know. Even caught myself playing the old 'What if?' game once or twice. Jackson dying has rather put the cat amongst the pigeons, all in all—

My mobile buzzes. 'Cate,' I exclaim, pleased. An unsolicited phone call from my seventeen-year-old daughter is a rare honour. 'I was just thinking about you—'

'Dad,' she interrupts, 'I think you'd better come home. Quickly.'

*

The house is cold and silent when I open the front door. Instantly, I smell burning. I throw my briefcase on to the hall table and sprint into the kitchen. Inside the Aga are the charred remains of the steak-and-kidney stew I put in it at six o'clock this morning. I slam my fist against the wall. *Damn it, Beth!* I may not be Jamie Oliver in the kitchen, but I was up at sparrow's fart to peel bloody carrots in the dark! All I asked you to do was take the fucking casserole out mid-morning. Is that really too much to ask?

I throw the blackened dish in the sink and run the hot tap, holding on to my temper with difficulty. It's not her fault. *It's not her fault.* But Jesus Christ almighty, it isn't mine either.

Upstairs, Cate's bedroom door is closed. The faint back-beat of music echoes down the hall. I raise my hand to knock, and then think better of it. Cate's pretty savvy, but at the end of the day she's still a child. She should be obsessing over pop stars and clothes and worrying about her exams, not helping me hold it together while her mother falls apart on us. Again.

In our room, Beth is sitting on the edge of the unmade bed in her shapeless pink flannel nightdress, bare feet dangling over her towelling slippers. As far as I can tell, she hasn't moved since I left her here this morning.

Foreboding fills me. I haven't seen her like this for years, not since Sam was small. I call her name, but she doesn't respond. Even when I crouch down in front of her and say it again, she doesn't show by so much as a flicker that she's heard me.

'Beth, baby, come on, you can't do this to me. You have to *try.*'

Gently, I take her chin between my thumb and fore-finger and turn her head to look at me. She blinks, as if I've shone a light into her eyes.

'I know you're in there, darling. I'm not letting you just give up.'

Her watery blue eyes are expressionless, but still lucid, I note with relief.

'Come on, sweetheart. I know you miss the boys, but they'll be back soon as term's over. Sam has an exeat weekend soon, and Ben will be down from Oxford in just a few more weeks—'

'I want to die,' my wife says.

Marvellous. Well, at least she's talking.

'You know you don't mean that.'

'I don't want to feel like this any more. I want this to be over. I want to just not *be*.'

I stand up and switch on the bedside lamp, flooding the room with light. Briskly, I draw the curtains that I flung open this morning. 'That's not an option, Beth. This isn't exactly a party for me, either. But we'll get through it, we always do. Perhaps we need to go back to Dr Stone and get another prescription. Up the dosage.'

'I don't want any more drugs.'

Well, I bloody do. The kind Ben is secretly growing under the cloche by the apple tree in between the tomato plants, so the spiky leaves don't give him away.

'Beth, darling, you must see you can't go on like this,' I say through gritted teeth. 'Look at you: you haven't moved in over twelve hours. You haven't even managed to get dressed or take dinner out of the oven, let alone look after Cate. Sweetheart, you can't even look after yourself!'

Her still-pretty face is a blank mask. I have no idea what – if anything – is going on inside her head. I hate it when she shuts down like this.

I resist the sudden urge to shake a response from her. She can't help it. I have to keep telling myself that.

'Look. If we need to change your medicine, darling, that's what we'll do. I'll take some time off work, God knows how, but we'll go away for a bit, do whatever we have to—'

'Don't you get it?' Beth cries unexpectedly. 'This isn't about the boys leaving. It's not *about* anything. It's *me*. It's who I am. It's not going to change. You can't cheer me up or jolly me out of it with a trip to the seaside. Don't you think I'd give anything not to be like this?' She thumps her thigh with her fist. 'I'd rather be dead than wake up one more morning feeling this way, and the only reason I'm still here is that I'm too much of a coward to do anything about it!'

She buries her face in her hands, and I'm about to comfort her, to put my arms around her as I always do; but for once all I can think of is Ella, who has been my lifeline for eight years; strong, fearless Ella, knocked sideways in an instant by death. I am scared shitless of what it may mean for us, of all that I suddenly now stand to lose.

Fear explodes into anger.

'Death may be better for you, but what about those you leave behind?' I demand. 'What about Ben, and Cate, and Sam? What about *me*?'

'You'd be better off without me.'

To my shame, I don't contradict her. I've soothed and calmed my troubled wife for twenty-one years, biting my tongue and getting on with things. I may not have kept all my vows, God forgive me, but I've stuck with the one that really mattered: she's my wife, in sickness and in health. Even at her worst, even when she doesn't know her own name. I've loved her as hard as I can, in the best way I know how. Of course I've had the odd fling – Christ, I'm only human – but nothing serious, not until Ella. And she made it clear from the start that she wasn't going to leave her husband, so that took divorce off the table once and for all.

But suddenly the well of sympathy has run dry. I'm exhausted from carrying Beth day after day after bloody day. I'm tired of her depression and inertia and sheer relentless fucking *misery*.

'Pull yourself together, Beth,' I say sharply, and walk out of the room.

It started when Cate was born. Beth had always been a bit highly strung, but until then I'd put it down to a mixture of PMT and artistic temperament – we'd met at her student exhibition at St Martin's, where a cousin of mine was also showing. I forget how we got talking. Beth didn't graduate, of course. Ben put paid to that, halfway through her final year.

At twenty, she was seven years my junior, and pretty, in a virginal, girl-next-door way. She had an old-fashioned air about her; it was partly the way she wore her fair hair in a shoulder-length bob held off her face with an Alice band, partly the way she dressed, in cashmere twinsets and pearls – more débutante than starving artist – but more than anything it was the vulnerability in her pale blue eyes. She seemed fragile, damaged, in need of fixing. I was looking for a science project, and Beth Llewellyn was it.

She also fucked like a rabbit. I'd never met a woman who wanted sex as often as Beth; it was all the more erotic for being so unexpected. I'd spent the previous ten years courting bankruptcy with flash dinners and flowers to get girls into bed; now here was this shy English rose practically ripping my clothes off every time I walked through the door.

Stupidly, I'd assumed she was taking precautions. It was only after she'd skipped two periods that she told me, in her artless way, that she'd stopped taking the pill because it made her feel sick. Of course I offered to marry her. I'd been searching for a way to stick it to my bitch of a mother – and she'd never liked Beth.

At our wedding, everyone agreed we made the perfect couple. Admittedly, I wasn't exactly head-over-heels, but we got on well, we were comfortable together – and the sex was frequent, if a little vanilla. I'd never made any secret of wanting to settle down with a nice ordinary girl who'd be happy to look after hearth and home while I went out and earned a crust. No tricky career women for me; I'd had enough of ball-breaking alpha females for one lifetime. I had no intention of ending up like my poor bloody father.

We'd barely brushed the confetti out of our hair when I began to realize that what I'd taken for agreeability was actually apathy; that Beth's acquiescence on every issue – other than sex – came less from a desire to please me than because she simply didn't care. About anything. Ever.

I chose the first house we bought, the furniture we put in it, even the cushions on the bloody sofa. I told myself it was just her hormones – everyone knew pregnant women were serene and unruffled. It was a good thing, surely? Better than throwing saucepans and demanding to know if I was having an affair.

That came when Ben arrived, four months after our wedding. Poor little sod, he must have wondered if he'd been born in Beirut. For his first few months, all we did was scream at each other. She burst into tears when I bought full-fat milk instead of skimmed. I nearly got my nose broken for forgetting to tape *Casualty* when she was at the shops. We smashed more plates than a Greek restaurant.

But between the rows, we screwed our brains out. And when Beth (unsurprisingly) found herself pregnant again when Ben was just nine weeks old, things calmed down once more. Apparently back to her placid self, Beth sat out in the garden rocking Ben in his pram for hours, stroking her swelling belly and seemingly content to immerse herself in motherhood and domesticity.

When Cate was born, I braced myself, ready for the airborne crockery, but it never came. Instead, Beth abruptly slid into a state of listless misery. I'd come home to find her standing at the sink with her arms in the washing up, tears pouring down her cheeks, unable to tell me what was wrong.

It soon became evident, even to an unreconstructed young male like me, that this wasn't your normal baby blues. She wasn't eating, she wasn't sleeping; her moods swung between biting my head off and near-catatonia.

'She's sinking, William,' Clara, Beth's capable mother, warned when Cate was about four weeks old. 'I'm sure you've done your best, but she needs professional help. It's no good sitting back and giving her time and waiting for her to get better. Beth's never been much good at managing her life. You have to take charge.'

Easier said than done. I tried to cut back at work, but I was still getting my fledgling company up and running, and I couldn't afford to sit at home minding the kids while my wife slumped comatose in front of *Neighbours*. I did manage to get Ben and Cate into a nursery two mornings a week at the local parish centre, and hired a cleaner we could ill afford to come in once a week and 'do'. Beth had got better last time; if we could just muddle through for a bit longer, I was sure things would sort themselves out again.

Six weeks later, I arrived home to find the police waiting on my doorstep. There had been some sort of accident – the children strapped into their car seats while Beth ran into the butcher's, a handbrake left off, the car parked on top of a hill . . .

'It's a miracle no one was seriously hurt, sir,' the young cop told me on our way to the hospital. 'Your wife's car crossed four lanes of traffic on the A22, knocked down a garden wall and ended up in an old lady's sitting-room.'

I thanked God the only casualty was the old dear's budgie, which apparently flew out of its cage in the confusion and was eaten by next door's cat, and hugged my children a little tighter than usual when I put them to bed.

'I didn't really want to *hurt* them, William,' Beth said piteously, later that night, 'it's just Cate wouldn't stop crying – then Ben started screaming too, I couldn't stand it any more, I thought if I could just – I only wanted them to *stop* . . .'

Appalled by her admission and secretly ashamed of my

neglect, the next day I took Beth to see a psychiatrist, who diagnosed severe post-natal depression and put her on a course of anti-depressants. When my wife started to refer to herself as the Virgin Mary and took to cleaning out the attic at three in the morning in preparation for the second coming, he switched her to anti-psychotic drugs. She responded by building a pyre in the back garden.

I took her back to the doctor. 'We may need to think about electroconvulsive therapy,' he advised grimly.

Repulsed at the thought of wiring my wife up to the mains, I told him where to stick his Frankenstein therapy. For the next week, I took turns with Clara to watch Beth in case she tried anything else with the children, and ground her pills into her food when I realized she'd been palming them.

Then one morning Clara rang me at work to say she'd caught Beth force-feeding four-month-old Cate table salt, to 'purify her'. Reluctantly, I agreed to the ECT.

For two months, I drove Beth to a private mental health clinic an hour from home three times a week, while Clara and Beth's best friend Eithne minded the children. I sat outside the clinic in my car with my clunking great mobile and attempted to keep my flat-lining business afloat, whilst my wife was anaesthetized, had electrodes glued to her scalp and was electrocuted into convulsions. She'd emerge so confused she didn't even know who she was. I'd drive her back home and put her to bed, thankful that at least the children would be far too young to remember the deranged, gibbering woman who wandered the house at all hours of the day and night in her dressing-gown.

It was the stuff of horror movies, but the ECT worked. Within weeks, Beth started to get better; by the time Cate was six months old, she was almost back to her normal self, albeit a dramatically subdued version.

But the treatment had wiped out huge chunks of her memory, some of which never came back – she didn't remember meeting me, for example, or giving birth to Ben and Cate. It had its plus sides: she forgot she'd loved *EastEnders*, thank Christ. But she became forgetful and uncertain; her confidence, never strong, ebbed to the point where she could be reduced to tears at the thought of entering a roomful of strangers.

Her mood swings were levelled out by a pick 'n' mix selection of anti-depressants and tranquillizers. Occasionally she complained she'd lost her sense of feeling – 'It's like my emotions are numb, William. I don't feel happy or sad, I don't seem to feel *anything*' – but whenever she tried to go cold turkey, the depression would creep back.

Unfortunately, the drugs also wiped out Beth's libido. Not only did she no longer want to have sex; she quite simply refused to.

The impact on our marriage was devastating. I couldn't communicate with my wife inside the bedroom or out of it; if it hadn't been for the children, I honestly don't know if I'd have stayed.

When Cate and Ben were three and four, I came back from a business trip to Dublin (with a rather pretty brunette who couldn't type to save her life; be fair, by that stage Beth and I hadn't had sex for two and a half *years*) to find my wife running through a neighbouring orchard stark naked, giving away five-pound notes to passers-by.

'Well, at least we know what the problem is now,' the doctor observed, diagnosing her with manic depression and writing her a prescription for lithium. 'This should help her get back to her old self. I'm surprised we didn't pick it up before, but it may have been the post-natal depression that triggered it. The drugs she's been on since then would have masked it. I don't suppose you ever noticed any manic tendencies before she got pregnant the first time?'

'Like what?'

'Oh, reckless behaviour, excessive energy, out-of-control spending, that sort of thing.'

'You've just described ninety per cent of my ex-girlfriends, but not Beth. Though she did paint a lot at night sometimes, now I think about it. She'd fill whole canvases at a single sitting, but that's just the way artists work, isn't it? Other than that, I don't—'

'Abnormally high libido?' the doctor asked, scribbling on his pad.

'Ah,' I said.

The lithium enabled Beth to control her moods without turning her into a zombie. Gradually she began to pick up the threads of her old life. Things improved in the bedroom, too, although sex was only ever at my instigation; her wild enthusiasm, it seemed, had gone for ever. Occasionally she still cried over nothing or threw herself into new projects with rather too much energy (the house was littered with half-finished tapestries and misshapen clay pots), but on the whole, if you hadn't been there during the darkest days, you'd never have known anything was wrong. I was confident Ben and Cate would have no memories of their mother as anything other than the way she was now.

And then when Cate was nine, Beth fell pregnant again.

When she went into premature labour at twenty-nine weeks, my first concern was for my wife, not the baby. The pregnancy had been closely monitored; Beth's lithium had been cut back, but not eliminated because of the risk of relapse. All I'd been able to think about since discovering the bloody unreliability of Greek condoms (purchased whilst on holiday in Rhodes) was whether the birth would trigger another psychotic episode.

But when we were led into a delivery suite, and a stunning blonde obstetrician with distracting breasts explained the possible complications, I was seized by a new and terrible fear: that after all the risks we'd taken to ensure his survival, I would lose my new son before he was even born.

'I've taken the precaution of calling a neonatologist down, just in case,' the doctor explained; 'she's one of the best. Your son will be in safe hands with her, I promise.'

Which was how I met Ella.

'I'm married,' she'd said.

'So am I.'

'I'm *happily* married,' Ella emphasized. 'I have no intention of leaving my husband.'

'I'm – married,' I grimaced, 'and I promise you, I've no intention of leaving my wife.'

'In that case,' said Ella, 'what are we doing here?'

'If I really have to explain, then I've just made the second big mistake of my life.'

Her strange gold eyes danced with amusement, crazy red hair spiralling out in all directions. She effervesced with barely contained energy, from the tips of her long, delicate fingers, now tapping a brisk tattoo with a packet of sugar on the Formica tabletop, to the razor-sharp toes of her bizarre purple high-heeled knee-boots (not the footwear one normally expected to see beneath a doctor's white coat). She certainly wasn't beautiful – the large nose and the freckles saw to that – but she was the most arresting woman I'd ever seen. Tall, maybe five-ten or so, she went in and out in all the right places. Her mouth was wide and full-lipped, her smile white and even – if it hadn't been for the idiosyncratic gap between her two front teeth, I'd have said she'd had work done. But it was the knowingness in her eyes that almost had me coming in my pants. This was a woman who knew what – and who – she wanted, and wasn't afraid to take it.

The chemistry between us had been obvious from day one. We'd both known, as we made eyes at each other across Sam's incubator, that as soon as he was discharged and any possible doctor–patient conflict removed (Ella was fiercely protective of her career), we'd end up in bed. The only question was whose.

Six weeks later, I'd picked Sam up from the hospital, taken him home to Clara, kissed Beth chastely on the cheek and turned the car straight back round to the hospital where Ella was waiting for me.

She stood up and hitched a huge leather bag on to her shoulder. 'What I meant,' she said as she threw four pound coins into her saucer, 'was what are we doing *here*?'

I followed her out of the hospital cafeteria, climbed into the black cab she hailed – by stepping out into the middle of the road and raising one autocratic arm, like Boudicca, heedless of the screeching brakes and hail of curses that ensued – and settled myself in the corner so that I could look at her for as long as it took us to get wherever she'd decided we were going.

Ella pulled her bag on to her cinnamon-suede lap and

rummaged around in it. 'Your wife never came to the NICU. What's the story there?'

'Beth has problems. Post-natal depression, bipolar disorder—'

'Yes, I saw that from her notes. But she's getting treatment?'

'Christ, yes. She nearly killed the kids last time round, so this time they dosed her up to the eyeballs as soon as she had the baby. Turns her into a bloody space cadet, which is why she never came in to see Sam, but it's better than—'

'Ah, here they are.' She tossed a small foil packet into my lap. 'Don't think they're time-expired, but you might want to check.'

'Condoms? Shy, aren't you?'

'Sorry. Love babies, but I couldn't eat a whole one.'

'I can't rule out a dose of the clap, but I'm not going to be sowing any seed, if that's what you're worried about. I got the snip the week we found out Beth was pregnant again.'

'All the same.'

'We've had one coffee,' I said, 'and you didn't let me finish that.'

Ella looked me in the eye, picked up my hand and slid it under her skirt. Her hard thighs, bare beneath the suede skirt, parted, and my fingertips brushed the crisp curls of her pussy. *No knickers. Jesus Christ.* 'You're not hiring me to be your children's nanny, William. What are you waiting for, references?'

The cab pulled up at Hyde Park. Ella thrust a couple of notes into the driver's hand as I tumbled out after her into the weak September sunshine, my dick tenting my trousers.

Without speaking, she pulled me into the eerie green shade of a chestnut tree, its leaves just beginning to turn. A few feet away, a mother fed the ducks with her two small children. A jogger ran past, barely breaking stride as a couple of teenagers on rollerblades tore up the pavement.

Backing up against the tree, Ella unzipped my trousers and lifted her skirt. My knuckles scraped against the rough bark of the tree as I gripped her arse with one hand. With the other, I rolled on the condom and plunged my dick into her slick, sticky wetness. Behind me, hooves thudded as a rider trotted past.

I buried my face in her neck, inhaling the scent of seawater, patchouli and fir, and ripped open her violet blouse without troubling with the buttons. She wasn't wearing a bra. Her nipples were as hard as the conkers at my feet.

'Ella, I'm going to—'

'Too late,' she gasped, her body shuddering, 'I'm there already.'

Later, as we walked past pensioners and tourists, I asked her, 'Do we do this again, or was it a one-off?'

'Which would you prefer?'

I stopped, watching the boaters on the Serpentine. Until now, I'd only ever had brief flings with girls I felt nothing for, none of which had lasted more than a few weeks. Once or twice things had got a little messy; one girl, a blonde PA who looked, accurately, like she'd been ridden hard and put away wet, had even turned up at the small bachelor pad I'd bought in Bayswater, a year or two after Cate was born, so that I didn't have to traipse home after a late night out with clients. Much as I'd appreciated the no-strings sex, I was growing increasingly wary of shitting on my own doorstep, and I was terrified that one of the gym bunnies would, sooner or later, turn out to be a bunny boiler.

Clearly I'd been going about things the wrong way. Single women naturally always wanted me to leave my wife, which I had no intention of doing. But a *married* woman, a happily married woman with as much to lose as me . . . A married woman, who got her kicks having sex in the park, who wasn't afraid to take the initiative, who had made it plain she didn't want to rock her marital boat either.

A woman who lifted my hand to her mouth as we stood in the sunshine amid a crowd of people, and tasted her juices on my fingers.

We sat down at a wrought-iron café table near an ice-cream kiosk and, over another cup of coffee, thrashed out the terms of our arrangement. No question of divorce on either side, *ever*; that was a given. Nothing that risked discovery: no phone calls at home, and to the mobile only in the event of an emergency (in eight years, there never had been); circumspect, and limited, emails, to our work accounts only; no personal gifts or photographs of us together. We agreed to meet no more than once a month, both to minimize the risk of arousing suspicion on the part of our spouses, and to prevent either of us become too entwined, or too involved, in the other's life. If either of us ever wanted to walk away, there would be no questions asked, and no comeback.

In another era, Ella would have made the perfect courtesan. Intelligent, witty, accomplished and accommodating, she was good company both in bed and out of it. Always civilized, always controlled: no demands or rows or histrionics. Apart from one little hiccup, that week in Cyprus – swiftly ironed out and never repeated – the arrangement worked perfectly.

I didn't ask Ella about her marriage; she didn't ask about mine. I knew her birthday only because I'd booked the flights to Cyprus. I could tell you her bra size and that she was allergic to strawberries, but I had no idea what really made her tick, and I was happy to keep it that way. It was bad enough having to pretend I cared about one woman's relationship with her mother. I was damned if I was going to do it for two.

We had the perfect set-up. And now Jackson has to die and fuck it all up.

When I get back downstairs, Cate is standing in front of the Aga, warming her bottom as she waits for the dented steel kettle to boil on the hotplate. Her boyfriend, Dan, has his arm wrapped around her waist, his fingers buried deep in the back pocket of her jeans. I want to punch his fucking lights out.

Cate was fourteen when she got her first boyfriend. Ever since she was born, blonde and blue-eyed and utterly perfect, I'd joked – only it wasn't funny – that I was putting her name down for a Romanian convent, and that any boy who wanted to date her would have to go through me first. Shovel or shotgun, I'd tell them. You mess with my baby, you dig your own grave.

I'd show her the drawing on the back of the cheap white wine her mother sometimes drank. 'Look,' I'd say, 'that's what you're going to be when you grow up.'

'A nun,' Cate would nod seriously.

Yet somehow I'd never actually considered how I might feel when she finally brought a boy home, how sick and angry the sight of a man's proprietary arm around her waist might make me. It had never occurred to me that she'd ever look at another man with that gold light in her eyes, turning to him like a flower to the sun, barely sparing a glance for me.

'How's your wife doing, William?' Dan asks concernedly.

Dan is twenty-three. Too old, apparently, to call me Mr Ashfield. Too old to have his hand tucked into my seventeen-year-old daughter's jeans.

How I let Cate talk me into using him for the firm's new logo . . .

'She's just tired,' I say tersely. 'A good night's sleep, and she'll be fine.'

'Dad, she needs to see Dr Stone,' Cate says. She detaches herself from Dan's grasp and busies herself with the tea. 'She's been getting worse since Christmas. He needs to change the pills again.'

Dan drops a kiss on the top of Cate's head. I know he wants to fuck my daughter. If he hasn't already.

Cate drops to her knees as Cannelle pads into the kitchen, and buries her face in the dog's silky golden coat. 'D'you fancy some very burnt stew?' she asks the animal. 'Daddy got up in the middle of the night and made it specially for you, didn't he, Cannelle?'

'I have to go,' Dan says. 'I promised I'd help set up the exhibition. Some of those sculptures are pretty heavy.'

'See you Friday?'

'Cate, I can't. Got to take the first-year life class, remember? It counts towards my teaching credits. Maybe Saturday. I'll call you.'

Cate shrugs moodily.

Dan catches my eye over her head as he leaves, and smiles as if to say, *Women*. But Cate isn't women, *she's my daughter*. I don't want some fucking randy art teacher in ripped jeans and a tight T-shirt – THIS IS BEAVER COUNTRY, for Christ's sake – rolling his eyes at me like we're best buddies: these birds, always trying to tie you down, good for a legover but a bloke's got to sow his wild oats, right? Who the *fuck* does he think he is? If he so much as *touches* her, I'll—

'Dad, for God's sake,' Cate snaps, standing up. 'Get with the programme, would you? I said I need you to take Mum's tea up to her.'

'Sorry, Kit-Cat.' I ruffle her hair. 'Been a long day.'

She scowls and pushes my hand away. 'Leave it, Dad. I'm calling out for pizza, OK? There's, like, *nothing* in the fridge. You said you were going shopping.'

'Pizza's fine. I'll go shopping at the weekend.'

'You'd better. Ben phoned to say he's coming down on Saturday, and he'll pick Sam up from school on the way. You know how much he always eats when he's home, he says the food at Corpus is worse than it was at school.'

'Fine.'

'If you don't get in some burgers and chips, he'll—'

'Cate, I said I'd do it,' I say irritably. 'Look, go and order the pizza, and I'll see if I can get your mother to come down. I don't suppose she's eaten anything all day.'

'She'd have a hard time *find*ing something,' Cate mutters, and flounces out.

I pick up Beth's mug of tea, straightening a crooked picture in the stairwell as I pass. This is all I need right now. Ella's taken it into her head to go off and scatter Jackson's bloody ashes in California or Carolina or wherever it is he comes from, which means it's going to be weeks before I see her again. *If* I see her again. There's no knowing how she's going to feel about us when the shock wears off and this really hits home.

Cate's right: Beth needs to go back to see Stone. We all know the routine by now. If this doesn't get nipped in the bud, she'll sink back into depression, and then – almost worse – the pendulum will swing the other way. She'll be seized by an unnatural manic energy, rushing around the house frantically tidying and painting and cleaning, until she crashes like a jet slamming into the ground. The last time she had a manic episode, she hired a helicopter on my company Amex to the tune of £49,000. Luckily they were very understanding.

'Beth?' I say, glancing round the empty bedroom.

I put the tea on the bedside table. The bathroom door is closed, and I can hear the sound of running water. Maybe she's feeling better, having a shower.

And then I see the empty Valium bottle on the floor.

'Beth?' I rattle the door handle. '*Beth!*'

Christ, she hasn't—'Pull yourself together' – oh dear God, not again, not on my watch, oh Jesus, *no*—

The door gives on the third shove, wood splintering beneath my weight.

At first I think the bathroom is empty. The claw-footed tub is overflowing, the hot tap still running; I paddle through an inch of water to turn it off, swearing as I nearly go arse over tip on the black and white tiles.

For a second, I see her, but I still don't understand.

My wife is lying at the bottom of the bath beneath a foot of water, her blue eyes wide and sightless, and I know instantly she's dead.

3

Beth

I'm not a victim. Dr Stone keeps telling me that. I'm not a victim, I'm a *patient*.

If anyone's the victim in this, it's William. I know I love him; actually, I'm quite sure I love him rather more than he loves me. The problem is that an awful lot of the time, I can't feel it. Which means I can't show it either.

It's the drugs. I don't feel much of anything any more.

'I'm off now, Beth. You'll be all right, won't you, darling?'

Nothing. It doesn't even hurt, these days.

'Sweetheart? Cate's spending the day studying at Dan's, but your mother said she'd pop round later this morning to see how you're doing. And I put a steak-and-kidney stew in the Aga for dinner. You just need to get it out mid-morning.'

If I could choose between another forty-one years of this bleak, soul-destroying emptiness, desolate and stripped of all feeling, or just *not being* at all . . .

'Right. I'd better get going. I'll see you later, then. Don't forget the stew.'

I curl into a tight ball on the bed, and watch the brittle winter sky lighten from black to grey. I've forgotten lots of things, what with the pills and the electric shocks, but I still remember every single detail of the moment we met, laid out before me like a *My Guy* photo-story. The nubby tweed of my skirt, hot and itchy at the waistband; the ladder in my brand-new tights; the gouache abstraction on papyrus I was hanging when he walked into the exhibition hall. I could tell you every word of our conversation, after William stopped to help steady the painting, and steady me. Word for word.

I knew right away he was the one I'd kept myself tidy for. Sometimes I wish I had someone to compare him with, and then I think, Why? What good would it do? If he was worse in bed (although I don't really know what 'worse' is – do you measure in orgasms? Minutes spent in foreplay? Whether he makes you a nice cup of tea afterwards?) then wouldn't I always feel a bit let down, disappointed, like turning up on the second day of the M&S sale and finding all the pretty colours had gone, and you're just left with the sludgy browns and greys? And if he was better, how would it help to know that? I'd simply regret I'd wasted myself on others who weren't quite up to the job.

He was *so* gorgeous. The sheets sizzled when we were in bed together, whatever anyone thinks now. The firm, muscled, hard-bodied strength of him; I'd never seen a man naked before. When he was inside me, it was the only time I stopped feeling alone.

'Mum! Didn't you hear me calling you? Your toast'll be well cold by now.'

Cate puts her head round the door, and then hangs there, swinging on the knob as if she doesn't want to come into the room for fear of catching something.

People are like that about depression. I read a poem, once: 'You are the modern leper, though you do not carry a bell.' I'm treated like an outcast, as if I've brought this on myself through some fault in my character. But nothing I could have done deserves this punishment. I wouldn't wish it on my worst enemy – I live in terror that I've passed it on to my children, as my father did to me. If I'd known beforehand, I'd never have had children at all. No one realized Dad was ill, of course. He was just a flamboyant, hail-fellow-well-met restaurateur who drank most of his profits until my mother left him and he found God (and Lillian); 'It's just Hector,' people used to say, 'such a *character.*'

I've watched Cate closely as she's grown up, far more than the boys; somehow I've always known they'd escaped it. Boys are so much easier to love, anyway, aren't they? Less rivalry. I haven't seen any signs of it in my daughter yet, but then no one did with me, they just thought I was artistic and creative; and then of course Cate was born and—

'Mum, stop staring at me like that, you're like freaking me out.'

Cate's closer to her father; she worships the ground he walks on. That's fine: I hate my mother too.

'Great, Mum, don't talk to me. Like I care. I'm off to Dan's, I'll be back this afternoon. Don't forget Dad's stew or he'll throw his toys out of his pram, you know what he's like.'

A few flakes of snow whirl against the windowpane. Grey outside, grey inside. This time of year, it never really seems to get properly light. How can February be the shortest month? It seems to last a year.

Later, when I wake to a knock at the front door, it's already turned to rain. My mother's sharp voice pricks and pokes through the letterbox. I roll myself in the duvet, its protective softness wound around me like a suit of armour.

Clara ruined my wedding day, just as she ruins everything. Even the name she chose for me was an act of spite. Louisa and Georgia for my sisters; just the one dull syllable for me, the middle sister. Beth. Not Bethany, or Elizabeth, which could have been shortened to so many other things; sassy Liz, glamorous Eliza. Beth, after one of the sisters in *Little Women*. The quiet, boring, mousy one who dies.

I wanted to marry William so much I nearly burst with excitement in the weeks before my wedding day. Nothing could dampen it, not even my mother or the hideous nylon empire-line dress she picked out to hide my 'condition'. (As Clara pointed out: why else would he be marrying me? Although even she didn't guess that a silly goose like me might be capable of doing something so clever on purpose. She doesn't really know me at all.) Her own mother-of-the-bride outfit was stunning, of course. A beautiful Jean Muir in matte gold silk, with sheer sleeves and small silk buttons on the side where it wrapped elegantly around her size-six hips.

The week after she showed it to me, pink with triumph, my father's new wife came round with the same dress (only four sizes larger). She'd already had it altered to fit her short frame, so she couldn't take it back.

Sick with fear and trepidation, I told my mother. 'Never mind,' she said graciously, 'I'll just get another dress. After all, it's your special day.'

A few days later, she returned with an even more beautiful suit from Chanel. 'Did you return the other dress?' I asked, as she twirled in front of the cheval looking-glass.

'Take it back? Of course not.'

'But it's so weddingy! Where on earth will you wear it?'

'Oh, I'll think of something,' Clara said, smiling secretively.

She turned up to our rehearsal dinner in it, the night before our wedding. Poor Lillian spent the evening in tears, knowing she couldn't possibly wear her dress the next day. My mother sat smugly at the head of the table at our reception, full of gracious charm and looking like she'd just swallowed the canary.

It gets dark so early in the winter. Four o'clock in the afternoon, and I'm still curled up in the duvet as the squares of glass behind me slowly darken from grey to black. I can smell burning. I should have gone downstairs and taken William's stew out of the Aga ages ago, but I didn't want to.

The bedroom door thunks as it hits the wall.

'Mum! You can't *still* be in bed! Gran rang my mobile and said you hadn't answered the door— Oh, for God's sake. I'm calling Dad.'

If only I could go to sleep one day and never wake up. I'm not really brave enough for suicide – it seems too calculated to contemplate, too wilful, its effect on the children would be too devastating – but if someone were to do it for me, to just come and flip the off switch . . .

Everyone thinks I'm wallowing in misery and self-pity

out of *choice*. If I had a pound for every time I've been told to pull myself together.

I'm woken again by William on the stairs; I'd recognize his tread anywhere. I force myself to sit up at last. I knew he wouldn't be pleased Cate called him home. I should have stopped her.

'Beth!'

You'd think I could let my husband make love to me, even if I'm not in the mood. But you don't know what it's like. You can't imagine how I feel. Or rather: don't. In the end, I couldn't bear it. All that stroking and touching and kissing and fondling, and I couldn't feel anything. Oh, not literally; my nerve endings hadn't died. But it gave me no pleasure. And that killed William's. I hated that more than anything. The concern in his eyes, the determination to do better, to make it better. Later, the irritation, quickly hidden (but not quickly enough). The *pity*.

'Beth, baby, come on, you can't do this to me. You have to *try*.' He kneels in front of me and turns my chin towards him, so that the light from the hallway gets in my eyes. 'I know you're in there, darling. I'm not letting you just give up.'

Easy for him to say.

'Come on, sweetheart. I know you miss the boys, but they'll be back soon as term's over. Sam has an exeat weekend soon, and Ben will be down from Oxford in just a few more weeks.'

Of course I miss the boys, especially Sam; he's only eight. I didn't want him to board, but William said it'd be good for him, so there wasn't much point in arguing.

Doesn't he understand how much it costs me to do what everyone else takes for granted? Of course I don't want to eat; it just prolongs the agony. If I get dressed, and come downstairs, and go through the motions of living, I'll only have to go back upstairs, and get undressed, and go back to bed so that I can not sleep, and then get up again and do it all the next day. Knowing that it will be exactly the same, that I'll feel exactly the same.

If only the world could be hit by an asteroid while I sleep. No pain, no mess, no family left to pick up the pieces. I want this to be over, I want to die—

'You know you don't mean that.'

I hadn't realized I'd spoken aloud. 'I don't want to feel like this any more,' I mutter, punishing him. 'I want this to be over. I want to just not *be*.'

'That's not an option, Beth. This isn't exactly a party for me, either. But we'll get through it, we always do. Perhaps we need to go back to Dr Stone and get another prescription. Up the dosage.'

The wretched *pills*! Pills to stop me going too high or too low, pills to help me sleep and prevent the paranoia, pills to stop my hair falling out as a result of all the mood stabilizers I have to take. Shake me – I know William wants to – and I'd rattle.

'I don't want any more drugs.'

'Beth, darling, you must see you can't go on like this. Look at you: you haven't moved in over twelve hours. You haven't even managed to get dressed or take dinner out of the oven, let alone look after Cate. Sweetheart, you can't even look after yourself!'

I deliberately say nothing, knowing it drives him mad.

He sighs heavily. 'Look. If we need to change your medicine, darling, that's what we'll do. I'll take some time off work, God knows how, but we'll go away for a bit, do whatever we have to—'

'Don't you get it?' I cry, provoked out of my silence. 'This isn't about the boys leaving. It's not *about* anything. It's *me*. It's who I am. It's not going to change. You can't cheer me up or jolly me out of it with a trip to the seaside.' Why doesn't he get it? *Why*? 'Don't you think I'd give anything not to be like this? I'd rather be dead than wake up one more morning feeling this way, and the only reason I'm still here is that I'm too much of a coward to do anything about it!'

'Death may be better for you, but what about those you leave behind? What about Ben, and Cate, and Sam? What about *me*?'

'You'd be better off without me.'

'Pull yourself together, Beth,' he snaps, and storms out of the room.

I'm stunned. William *never* gets cross with me. He soothes and tolerates and understands me. His pity is almost as hard to bear as his indifference. It's such an unexpected pleasure to be treated normally, to be shouted at, that the tears stop as suddenly as they started.

A crumb-strewn plate and an old Valium bottle fall from the tangle of bedclothes on to the floor as I get up and go into the bathroom. Maybe I'd feel better if I had a bath. Clean, at least.

I strip off my nightgown and stare dispassionately at my reflection as the bathwater runs. The weight's fallen off me in recent weeks, but not in a flattering way; I look like a shapeless, baggy sack of flesh. My fine blonde hair is cut in exactly the same bland style my mother chose when I was six. I'd never hear the end of it if I changed it. It makes me look like a woman from another age – from Clara's age, an age of girdles and aprons and cotton sanitary napkins on belt loops. My breasts sag, my cheeks sag, my stomach sags. *I* sag. I look like what I am: dried-up, used, no good to anyone. I wouldn't blame William if he had an affair. It's been years since we slept together. You'd have to be a saint not to want sex from *some*one.

The bathwater is still only tepid when I get in, so I leave the hot tap running for a bit. I love the feeling of being submerged beneath the water, the outside world muffled and far away. I used to be a good swimmer when I was a child. My PE teacher wanted me to compete in the school diving team, but Clara said I'd never cope with the pressure. My sisters used to count how long I could hold my breath under water, I could do it for twice as long as either of—

Suddenly William is looming over me, his face distorted by the bathwater. I gulp a lungful in shock as he grabs my shoulders, yelling my name. My ribs and hips and elbows and knees bang against the old iron bathtub as he clumsily yanks me out and on to the floor.

'Jesus Christ, Beth, what are you doing? Come on, Beth, stay with me, don't die, please don't die—'

I'm gasping for breath on the fluffy peach bathmat like a landed fish. I slap his hands off me as he tries to check my pulse.

'William,' I pant, when I'm finally able to speak, 'what on *earth* is going on?'

*

Honestly. You have to laugh, don't you? I couldn't help it, every time I tried to explain, I just dissolved again. I don't think the hysterical laughter helped my cause, actually, but by the time I'd got over my giggles, I couldn't be bothered to go through it. I don't suppose he'd believe me, anyway. After all, I do have what Ben would call 'previous'.

'You have to rescue me,' I tell my best friend Eithne three days later. 'They've all but got me on suicide watch. Mother's downstairs now, guarding the razor blades.'

Eithne snorts down the phone. 'An hour in her company, and anyone would want to top themselves.'

'It's ridiculous. Cate gave me plastic cutlery last night and told me everything else was in the dishwasher. Honestly, I'm depressed, not dim-witted. Although,' I add, 'I think the worst is over, for now. All that drama has rather perked me up. I haven't felt this upbeat in months.'

'Beth, darling, I don't want to rain on your parade, but you're not feeling *too* upbeat, are you? Only you know how you sometimes get—'

'I'm not manic,' I say crossly. 'Just full of the joys of spring, that's all. Oh, please, Eithne, they'll let you through the cordon, they're scared of you. I want to go to my studio, see if it's still standing. I thought I might even do a bit of work later.'

'Wonders never cease. OK, you've twisted my arm. I'll be over soon as I've finished soldering my roundhead. But if Clara tries to strip-search me, I can't answer for the consequences.'

I pace the bedroom impatiently, trying not to trip over the heaps of clothes I've been frantically sorting into piles: things to keep, things to throw away, things to donate to

Cate's school spring fête. The room smells of fresh paint, although I'm not sure about the slate green now it's on the walls. It looks rather too much like the bottom of the fishpond. But then I didn't like the primrose either – in places you can see where I didn't give it long enough to dry and it's mingled with the green to look suspiciously like diarrhoea. I don't think William's going to be very pleased when he gets home. He liked the Colefax & Fowler wallpaper we had. Maybe I should have stuck to the taupe I started with in the first place—

As soon as I hear the crunch of Eithne's ancient orange 2CV on the gravel outside, I fly downstairs. Clara, resplendent in a grey wool trouser suit and pearls, stands guard in the kitchen.

'Blue and green, dear,' she reproves.

I glance down. 'Midnight isn't really blue, is it? And these trousers are so comfy.'

She gives me a look she's perfected over the years, one of mingled disappointment and resignation: this is her lot, the daughter she's been saddled with, but she'll stoically pick up her cross and make the best of it. I slink back upstairs and change into a pair of canvas dungarees I know she hates. Eithne will have parked her car by the time I come back down; Clara won't dare say anything if she's there.

It seems my daughter is less encumbered by good manners than my mother.

'God, Mum, you look like the window cleaner,' Cate exclaims when I appear.

They both turn pitying blue eyes upon me. It strikes me again how similar they are. We all share the same polar-pale colouring and blonde hair – a little ashier in Clara's case, these days, and rather too much henna in Cate's, I note, frowning – but I'm not really *like* them. I lack the confidence, the supreme self-belief that runs through my mother and daughter like a stick of rock. Good things fall into their laps because they believe they should. I expect nothing, and am never disappointed.

Eithne marches into the kitchen.

'Come back here, Beth, there's absolutely no need to go and change.'

'But maybe I—'

'Bollocks.'

My mother affects affront at Eithne's robust language. A papery hand flutters to her throat to fiddle with the pearls (third-generation; a coming-out gift to her grandmother from Queen Victoria, if Clara is to be believed).

'Keep low till we're past the fence,' Eithne whispers as she propels me through the back door, 'when you see the barbed wire, run for it.'

Eithne is a kindred spirit. She remembers Spangles and *Jackanory* and *Jackie* magazine. She knows what it's like to go upstairs to fetch something and forget what it was by the time you reach the landing. She understands perfectly that when you bend down to pick up something from the floor, it's only prudent to wonder what else you can do while you're down there. Eithne appreciates what it is to be forty-one and fallible.

She also knows what it's like to have the world think you've gone mad.

We met in my first year studying art at St Martin's – have you noticed how you stop making real friends sometime in your twenties? Friends of your *own*, I mean. After that, it's all about the mothers of your children's friends, or the wives of your husband's colleagues; colleagues of your own, too, I suppose, if you're lucky enough to have a job. But the friends you'd call upon in a crisis, the women you'd ring if your husband left you, or ask to look after your children if you were both killed in a plane crash; you stop making those kinds of friends much earlier than you'd think.

We didn't share many classes; my Fine Arts pathway was 2D, drawing and painting, whereas Eithne was 3D, sculpture and installation; now I think about it, that rather sums us up: compared to Eithne I do seem rather *flat*. But we were next-door neighbours at our hall of residence, and though neither of us really fitted in, somehow we fitted together. I couldn't help dressing like I was going for tea with the Queen, and while Eithne looked the art-student part, with her spiky cropped hair (dark naturally, but pink that first term) and kaftans and piercings and tall, rangy body, well, she wasn't quite as brave and fearless as she made out. Just how damaged, I didn't discover until our second year, when she had a passionate, showy affair with an aspiring actor called Kit Westbrook, which all ended rather horribly when she went round to his flat early one day and found him in bed with her brother.

I was the one who called the ambulance and held her hand when they pumped her stomach, and I was the one who listened to her when she screamed and shouted and wished she'd been left to die.

They called it a nervous breakdown, but I think she'd just turned inside-out with grief. And when she came back from the clinic, she was tougher and brighter and sharper than she'd ever been, and even though she dated like fury, she never – then or since – let anyone get close to her again. All that passion and energy she poured into her art, and long before she'd even graduated, people who mattered were starting to know who Eithne Brompton was.

She fidgets impatiently while I struggle to unlock the door to my studio, a converted folly at the end of the garden that's icy in winter and suffocating in summer. I haven't been here in months.

As soon as the door opens, Eithne pushes past me. She stops abruptly in front of a huge canvas that fills most of one wall, a monotype in blacks, purples and greys.

'Fuck. This is amazing. I feel like Alice falling down the rabbit hole.'

She pulls a charcoal-and-oil-pastel canvas from a rack, dislodging a cloud of dust, and steps back, her head (plum, these days) tilted to one side. 'This is stunning, too. And this. Shit, you've done so many since I was last here.'

'Some of those aren't quite finished . . .'

She whirls round, silver bracelets clanking. 'Look, Beth, why don't you let me arrange for you to exhibit? I'm owed a few favours, it would be so easy to organize a show—'

'I couldn't.'

'Why not? You've got enough art for one. You need to get out a bit. Break free from William. He makes you so damn *help*less.'

'Of course he doesn't. I couldn't manage without him, Eithne. You don't understand. I need him.'

'Yes. And he needs *that*.'

I put the canvases sullenly back in the rack. 'You don't understand.'

'What I don't understand, Beth, is why you keep your

talent hidden away in a mouldy old shed when you could be blazing across the London art scene. And with Sam at school now, you've got time—'

'Cate still needs me.'

'I've never met a seventeen-year-old who needed her mother less. Talk of the devil,' she adds, as Cate appears in the doorway.

Cate's in awe of Eithne, partly because she's scary (even to me, at times) and partly because of her winning the Turner Prize a few years ago and all that that implies.

'I don't mean to interrupt?' she says to Eithne, voice rising in the irritating way teenagers have these days. 'I was just wondering if I could, like, ask you something?'

'*Like* ask me? And how would that differ from *actually* asking?'

Cate turns pink. I know it's mean of me, but I can't help enjoying her discomfort a little. She's always so superior.

My daughter wraps her arms around her narrow torso, ducking her head so that her long hair falls across her face. 'Cate,' I exclaim, as her thin hooded sweatshirt lifts with the movement, 'is that what I think it is in your belly button?'

'She's had it pierced for a year,' Eithne says, 'where have you been?'

'Your father's going to go spare.'

'Only if you tell him,' Cate mutters.

She thinks she's making a point by rebelling. It's not that I'm jealous. I'm just trying to protect her from a world that doesn't treat rebels kindly. You have to keep your head down, and try to fit in. She'll learn.

I wish I had her courage.

Eithne picks up a daguerreotype I was experimenting with last summer. 'What was it you wanted, Cate?'

'Well, it's, like, our – I mean, it *is*,' she amends hastily, 'our spring fête in a couple of weeks, and my class has to organize the charity auction. I was wondering if maybe you'd let us have something, you know, a piece of art, to auction. It's in a really good cause, we're like raising funds for this environmental charity called One World who—'

'I know who they are,' Eithne says coolly, 'I designed their Green Scene awards a few years ago. Who're they sending down?'

'No one. Well, this guy *was* coming, but he died, bummer for him.'

'Caitlin!'

Eithne frowns. 'Jackson Garrett? I read about it in their newsletter. I met him a few times – nice guy. American, married to a doctor. He was only the same age as us, Beth.'

'Oh, dear, how sad. His poor wife must be—'

'So can we?' Cate interrupts. 'Have something, I mean.'

Eithne shrugs. 'Why not? I'll look something out for you and bring it down.'

'I might pop along,' I say brightly. 'To the fête.'

Cate pulls a face. 'Great, Mum. Trash my cred, why don't you.'

'Cate—'

The door slams in my face.

When Eithne leaves, I'm seized by a sudden burst of energy, flinging open shutters and poring over half-finished canvases until it's too dark to see. My mind races all night with images and inspiration; I'm up at dawn and back in the studio before William even wakes up.

For the next ten days I do nothing but paint, filling canvas after canvas with abstract images worked in watercolours, oils, charcoal and gouache, consumed by a burning need to get the maelstrom in my head down on paper before the creative door slams shut again. I don't sleep, I barely eat. Obviously I don't need my pills any more; I'm clearly over the depression at last, thank goodness, so I stop taking them. I'm not manic, just having a few good days, that's all. William tries to get me to rest, but I can't, my brain is on fire, so he leaves me to it, to 'let it burn out in its own time', he says. 'I'll be here for you afterwards, Beth, don't worry.'

I order more paint, more canvases, recklessly putting a professional Nikon camera costing thousands of pounds on my credit card when I decide to photograph black-and-white images on to glass and then paint them. Working with a luscious mocha pigment, I suddenly fancy some Belgian chocolates. Without thinking twice about it, I simply arrange for a box to be couriered from Brussels. William won't mind. Eithne is right, I *am* good, what I'm doing now is some of the best work I've ever done, I *should* let her exhibit my paintings. Why on earth have I been so shy? To think that the fear of being judged stopped me going back to college, when I was one of the best students they'd ever had. Perhaps I should finish my degree, just to prove – I don't know, prove *some*thing.

The studio is soon crowded with canvases, and then I realize that of course it's too small. What I need is something more like Eithne has in London, a huge bright airy space four times the size of my horrid little studio, with plenty of room to spread out. This garden is big enough for an extension – no, we might as well knock down this folly altogether and start again. If we're going to do this, we should do it right. Yes, a big, open studio; if we get rid of William's greenhouse there'll be plenty of room, he never uses it anyway – of course we'll have to move the garage, it's in the way and I need *light*, lots and lots of natural light—

The architect is very accommodating when I contact him and explain what I need to do, and that time is of the essence and money is absolutely no object.

Within days, I'm poring over plans and discussing options. Of course Murray's right when he says that I shouldn't just be thinking about my current needs, I must plan for the future. In that context, cathedral ceilings and a separate photographic loft are actually an economy. There's no point bothering William with it all now, especially given the mood he's in. I've never known him so tetchy. He got *so* cross about the bulldozer earlier (poor Murray, he was very upset about it, after all our hard work), and then rushing off when he got that phone call from work, didn't even stop to say goodbye, it's not like him at all.

No. We might as well wait until everything's finalized, and in the circumstances, a 50 per cent deposit is entirely reasonable – Sam won't be needing his college funds for years yet, and by then I'll have paid him back ten times over: sales from my work will make all this minor expense seem like a drop in the ocean.

I bounce back up to the house in exuberant mood, throwing my arms around my daughter as she messes about at the Aga with the kettle, trying not to notice the way she flinches within my hug.

'Darling, I've had a marvellous idea! I need to go down to Brighton tomorrow, I have to see the sea – I need that colour in my mind's eye, nothing else works, I have to *be* there. Why don't you come too, Cate? We'll have a wonderful time and—'

'Mum, I can't. I've got exams soon, I can't just bunk off.'

She's looking peaky, poor thing. She works far too hard. I know exams matter, but sometimes you just have to take a little time out and enjoy life!

'Of course you do, darling,' I soothe. 'I hadn't forgotten, I just thought you could do with a break. We don't spend enough time together, I miss you, sweetheart, and silly old school will still be there next week—'

'You're not getting it, Mum,' she snaps, washing her hands under the tap. 'I don't want to go to bloody Brighton and see the sea. I'm not five years old, I'm seventeen and I've got to study!'

'All right, darling. No need to get quite so huffy. I just thought it would be fun, I was only trying to help take your mind off—'

'Look, if you really want to help, call Eithne and ask her about the artwork she promised us! The auction's on Saturday and her name's in all the brochures and if she doesn't turn up I'm just going to die!'

'I'm sure she'll—'

'Oh, never mind! I'm going over to Clem's!'

I don't know what's got into her lately. She's been in a funny mood for days; it must be the pressure of her exams.

I call Eithne about the artwork; 'Oh, Christ!' she says, 'I did promise, didn't I? Only I'm in the middle of something, I really can't get away. I don't suppose if I send the bloody statue down in a cab you could take it instead?' And I say of course, because actually, for once, I feel like I *can*.

Obviously I didn't expect to be called on to the stage to present the wretched thing. But on Saturday I'm in such a good mood I don't feel shy at all, so I clamber up the steps at the end of the playing fields with the artwork Eithne's donated, an exquisite (and rather heavy) abstract bronze statue two feet high.

Despite a smattering of polite applause, no one is really paying much attention. Even Cate's whispering furiously with Dan as the bidding gets under way.

The headmistress does her best: 'An Eithne Brompton,' she says gamely, 'surely we have some takers? At the back there? Come on, ladies and gentlemen, it's for a good cause! Now, who'll start me at a thousand pounds?'

The crowd shifts on its feet. It's not that they don't have the money (after all, fees at Cate's school are currently running close to £20,000 a year); but these aren't the sort of people who appreciate art. They just want a nice painting of something they can recognize, trees on a hill, cows in a field. Something that goes with the new curtains.

'Five hundred, then.'

What they need is something to wake them up, get them in the mood, make them sit up and take notice— Of course! Why didn't I think of it before? It's always worked in the past.

I put down the statue and lean into the microphone. 'Come on, everyone. This is an Eithne Brompton. Do you know how much her artwork is worth on the open market? There's a waiting list two years long for commission pieces.'

I catch Cate's eye, and wink.

Then I unbutton my neat navy shirt-waister, whip off my bra and knickers, and, before anyone has even realized what's happening, I'm streaking naked across the playing field.

For a moment, there's stunned silence. Then a roar of enthusiastic applause breaks out, and the bidding for Eithne's statue has reached £4,000 before I'm halfway to the sports pavilion. I'm sure Cate will be thrilled when she realizes how much we've raised for her favourite charity.

I'm just starting to appreciate that it's still only March and actually jolly cold when someone throws a coat over me and whisks me out of sight around the side of the pavilion.

'Dan! Thank you so much, I was beginning to get a little chilly – but wasn't it worth it? Did you hear the bidding – terrific, isn't it? Not that I'm anything terribly exciting to look at, of course, not any more, rather frightening, I should imagine, actually, but I really think I put everyone in the mood, jazzed things up a little – I remember we used to do this sort of thing when I was at St Martin's, Eithne and me, you should have seen us one year at the Edinburgh Fringe—'

And then Dan silences me.

It's not his kiss that horrifies me, warm and smoky and delicious though it is, because after all, the most effective way to shut a woman up is to give her mouth something else to do. But the fact that, with a passion I haven't felt in twenty years, I kiss my daughter's boyfriend back.

4

Cate

'C'mon, Cate. Relax,' Dan murmurs. 'I'm not going to make you do anything you don't want to.'

'I know, but . . .'

He strokes the side of my cheek with the back of his hand, tilts my head and kisses me softly on the lips. It's like being in a movie; I could do this all day.

Then his hand slides up my calf, and I quickly cross my knees so he doesn't get the wrong idea.

'Hey. It's OK, you know. My students won't be here for ages. We're cool.' He drops gentle, nuzzling kisses down my neck; it tickles, and I giggle. 'Just go with the flow, baby. Soon as you want me to stop, say so, and I will.'

His knuckles brush my breast, back and forth, back and forth, and even though I'm wearing a bra and a school blouse and a gross woolly jumper, my nipple goes all hard, and a warm wet feeling spreads between my legs.

'You're so beautiful, Cate,' Dan says thickly. 'Please, can

I just look at you properly? I won't do anything, I swear. I just want to see you. Let me undo your blouse, please. That's all, I promise.'

'I don't—'

'You're not scared, are you?'

'No!'

'At least take off your sweater. That's not going to do any harm, is it?'

Why did I tell him I was a virgin? Talk about red rag to a bull. He's even more determined to get into my knickers now. It's Mum and Dad's fault. First they make me go to a girls' school, and then they send Ben off to board. What's the point of having an older brother if all his hot friends live, like, three hundred miles away? Honestly. Dad wasn't joking when he said he'd send me to a Romanian convent. He might as well have done. How am I supposed to get any real experience when I never meet any boys?

In a private act of defiance, I pull up the hem of my jumper with both hands, feeling unexpectedly sexy and grown-up as Dan's eyes darken and he touches his tongue to dry lips. I struggle to get the sweater over my shoulders, and he helps me, his hands pulling and touching and smoothing a bit more than I need, actually, somehow he's untucked my blouse at the same time, and I know I didn't leave that many buttons undone—

'God, Cate. Feel what you do to me.'

He grabs my hand and puts it on his *thing*. I'm kind of grossed out, but it's cool at the same time. I can't believe how hard it is under his jeans. I mean, *totally* hard, like a bone or something. I squeeze it a bit, just to feel, and he rocks back on his heels and closes his eyes and moans.

'You have no idea how sexy you are, Cate. You're driving me crazy.'

I undo another button on my blouse, just to see the effect it has. He gulps, rubbing his hand against his chin. I can't believe I have this *power* over him, it's a total trip.

I try out this sexy look my best friend Fleur taught me, and daringly unfasten another button, so my shirt falls open to my waist. I'm so glad I wore my new lacy pink bra from Miss Selfridge. I hadn't planned to let Dan see it, exactly, but then, I hadn't planned not to either. God, imagine if I was wearing my period pants – not that it matters, I'm not letting him go below the waist yet, but still. No one feels hot and sexy in their period pants.

I suck in my stomach as Dan's eyes travel up and down my body, and sit up a bit straighter. I wish I wasn't wearing my school uniform. He must think I'm such a baby. I mean, he's twenty-three. His students are older than I am.

He pushes me gently back against the sofa pillows and slides his body over mine, his hands crushing and squeezing my breasts. I like it, but I stop him when he tries to pull them out of my bra. I sort of ache between my legs, and when his knee pushes my thighs apart, I rock my hips a bit against him, as if I'm scratching an itch. It feels really good, like having a hot drink on a cold day.

It's getting a bit warm in here, so I don't mind too much when Dan slips my blouse off my shoulders. My pleated grey skirt has somehow got rucked up around my waist, and I hook one bare leg around his hips as he pulls me close, his hands roaming all over my back. God, this is really good. I must stop in a minute, though. I don't want things to go too far. In a minute, I'll stop him.

He leans up on one elbow, staring at me with such intensity I barely recognize him. Then he dips his head to my breast, and I realize with a gasp of shock and pleasure that my bra has somehow come off, and his lips are on my nipple, *my naked nipple*, I'm naked from the waist up, and his hand is between my thighs, oh God, that's good, I've got to stop now, but that's so good—

'Dan . . .'

His fingers slip beneath the edge of my cotton panties, and they're stroking me *there*, he's touching me *there*! It feels so much better than when I do it, it's hot and wet and heavy and—

'Dan, no . . .'

Every time he sucks my nipples, I can feel a zing down below, oh, God, this is so good, but I have to stop him, I have to stop—

Suddenly he leans back and unbuckles his jeans. I have a brief glimpse of his thing, red and swollen and totally huge, and suddenly all the warm lovely feelings vanish as if someone's thrown a bucket of cold water over me. I struggle up from the sofa, pulling down my skirt and grabbing my jumper from the floor.

'I can't, Dan. I'm sorry, I just—'

'Cate, come on, I'll be careful, it won't hurt.'

I pick up my bra from the floor and clutch it to my chest. 'I'm sorry, Dan,' I mumble, cheeks flaming. 'I have to go home. My mum will be wondering where I am.'

He leaps to his feet, his thing sticking out of his jeans. It looks purple and angry. I can't take my eyes off it.

'Are you kidding me? You can't come on to me like that and then stop! I'm not a fucking robot, Cate!' His expression hardens, and he turns and tucks himself away. 'I can't just switch it on and off like a tap, even if you can!'

'I didn't mean—'

'Christ! This is what I get for dating a kid!'

'Dan, that isn't fair—'

'Nor is behaving like a prick-tease. Do you have any idea how much my fucking balls ache right now?'

All of a sudden, I start to cry. Dan hesitates, then exhales and slowly runs his hand through his hair. 'Look, I'm sorry,' Dan says, as I sniff miserably. 'I shouldn't have pushed you, I obviously got it wrong. I didn't mean to make you do something you weren't ready for.'

He hands me my blouse, waits until I've turned around and put it on, then pulls me into his arms and rubs my back gently. 'You've got to be more careful, Cate. I'm a decent guy, and I stop when I'm asked. But there are some men out there who think that when you set something in motion, you've got to follow through.'

'I'm sorry. I didn't mean to—'

'Yeah, I know. It's OK.'

I hiccup. 'You're not going to dump me?'

'You think I'd do that because you won't sleep with me?' He holds me away from him, his expression serious. 'What kind of man do you think I am? I care about you, Cate. You're beautiful and funny and totally nuts. I love being with you. And besides,' he grins, 'I'm depending on you. Who else is going to keep me on the straight and narrow?'

My breath frosts in the cold March air as I walk home. I'm so embarrassed, I wish the ground would just open up and swallow me. It's not as if I'm saving myself for Prince William or something. Basically I want to get on with it and then I can forget about it – well, not forget about it, exactly, but tick it off the list. Lose virginity, check.

So why does it feel like such a big deal? I mean, Dan's really nice and totally hot, and he's twenty-three, at least one of us'll know what we're doing. Fleur's right, he'd be a great person to do it with the first time.

I wish she hadn't gone back to France last summer. I really miss her. She's so cool, and she knew all these really neat places to hang out after school. Plus, she didn't think I was sad for wanting to study hard so I can get into NYU and be a journalist. The only thing the other girls at school care about is when they'll get into a size zero.

Last year, I gave up chocolate for Lent, like everyone does, but my best friend, Clem, gave up everything containing sugar. *Everything*. Pretty much all food has *some* sugar in it, right? Basically, she had to live on celery and lettuce, so then everyone else in the class copied her. It was like this weird virus. For weeks, no one could think about anything but diets. People were, like, fainting all over the place. The swimming team had a total crisis, because everyone stopped swimming in case it gave them muscles. Girls would sit round me at breaktime and watch me eating an apple – an *apple*, for God's sake – with their eyes totally focused on my mouth, until I couldn't even chew. All they read were stupid glossy magazines with pictures of skinny stars in them, and they'd talk and talk and *talk* about celebrities and what they ate and how thin they were.

Most of them gave up after a few weeks, but a few kept going. Clem even wrote this whole pro-ana blog on her

Facebook page, until Mrs Buchanan, our headmistress, found out and made her take it down.

Dan calls them the girls from St Thinian's. He says men don't like skinny girls, or women who obsess about their weight. He says older women can be really sexy because they're not always worrying about how they look. Yeah, right. Like you wake up one morning and think, *Oh, I'm thirty, I'm just going to let it all hang out from now on.* Total BS.

I should stop thinking about it and just sleep with him. Get it over with.

Dad hates him. Every time he comes over, he gives Dan this laser-beam glare. He's like, *Are your intentions honourable, young man, because if not I'm going to chop up your body and feed it to the fishes.*

It took me for ever to talk Dad into letting him design the new logo for the company. But Dan was really cool, he knew all this stuff about Ashfield PR, so in the end Dad gave in. I wish he'd stop acting like this Victorian paterfamilias, it's so embarrassing.

I think Mum quite likes him, though it's hard to tell with her. When she's acting like a zombie she doesn't even talk to you; you can be like, 'The house is on fire and I just stuck an axe in my foot' and she'll just sit on the bed and like *look* at you and not even move. Or else she can be this nutso freak, painting all night and jabbering on at you at a million miles an hour and doing crazy stuff, like when she decided to knock down the conservatory last summer and build an open-air theatre for this stupid triptych she was doing. Luckily I came home early the day the demolition crew arrived or we'd have ended up with half the house gone. I wish I could just talk to Mum sometimes. I really envy Clem that. Her mother is so normal. You can talk to her about school and boys and stuff and she really *listens*.

But it's thanks to Mum I met Dan in the first place. Like, a few months ago, she'd promised to go to the opening of Eithne's new show in London, but when it came to it she couldn't face the thought of going alone. Dad was too busy, as per, so she dragged me along, which actually wasn't too lame after all because all these cool people turned up, it was in all the papers the next day and everyone at school was seriously impressed. Clem even asked for my autograph; I worry about that girl sometimes.

So anyway, we're in this huge hall, and I kind of left Mum alone for a bit to sneak a quick glass of wine, and when I go back, she's yakking with this guy about art or something, and I'm like, *Wow! he's hot*, and I give him my best smile, but he just keeps droning on about expressionism or individualism or whatever, and I'd had enough by then and dragged Mum away.

Then a week later, I'm at home on study leave and Mum's gone Christmas shopping, and Hot Guy turns up on the doorstep! He'd obviously gone to a lot of trouble to track me down, so I couldn't leave him sitting there. He was actually a lot more interesting once you got him off the subject of art. Anyway, I asked him if he wanted to come to our New Year's Eve party, and he said yes straight away. So that was it, really.

I wish Eithne would send us that statue she promised. I'm going to be *so* dead if she doesn't come through.

I bump open the garden gate and trudge up the drive. I've got a ton of work to do. I shouldn't have gone over to

Dan's. Now I'm going to have to stay up all night if I want to finish that stupid essay on the American Revolution.

Cannelle leaps up to welcome me as I let myself into the kitchen. I give him a big hug, then throw my bag on the kitchen table and put the kettle on the Aga hotplate. I wish we had a proper electric one, like everyone else does. I loathe this crappy thing.

My nerves are totally jangling. I've got a headache, and I'm all achey. It's like PMT, or something. God, I hate being a woman.

Mum bursts through the back door and I jump, spilling hot water on my hand.

'Darling, I've had a marvellous idea! I need to go down to Brighton tomorrow, I have to see the sea – I need that colour in my mind's eye, nothing else works, I have to *be* there.' She swoops me around the kitchen, and I nearly trip over the dog. 'Why don't you come too, Cate? We'll have a wonderful time and—'

I prise her off me. 'Mum, I can't. I've got exams soon, I can't just bunk off.'

'Of course you do, darling. I hadn't forgotten, I just thought you could do with a break. We don't spend enough time together, I miss you, sweetheart, and silly old school will still be there next week—'

It's as if she still thinks I'm in kindergarten. *I nearly had sex with my boyfriend on his sofa this afternoon, Mum! Why don't you know to ask me about that?*

'You're not getting it, Mum,' I snap, going to the sink and running cold water over my scald. 'I don't want to go to bloody Brighton and see the sea. I'm not five years old, I'm seventeen and I've got to study!'

'All right, darling. No need to get quite so huffy. I just

thought it would be fun, I was only trying to help take your mind off—'

Suddenly I'm so angry I want to scream. Why can't she just be normal for once? Why does she always have to be like this?

'Look, if you really want to help, call Eithne and ask her about the artwork she promised us!' I yell. 'The auction's on Saturday and her name's in all the brochures and if she doesn't turn up I'm just going to die!'

She looks bewildered. 'I'm sure she'll—'

'Oh, never mind! I'm going over to Clem's!'

I grab my bag and storm back outside. Tears blur my vision. It's like I don't belong *anywhere* – not at school; not at home; not with Dan. I wish I could just do my own thing and not have to be responsible for anyone.

I take the short-cut to Clem's, ducking down an alley-way that runs past the railway station. My breath forms smoky plumes as I jog quickly along the path in the dark, imagining rapists and murderers lurking in every shadow. I wish I'd brought Cannelle. My heart's racing by the time I get to the car park and turn towards Clem's street, though it slows a bit when I spot a couple snogging in one of those disgusting 4x4s parked near the platform gate (Dad bought one last year; like doesn't he even *care* about the planet?). At least someone's around if I get jumped by the mad axeman. God, look at them, they're really going for it—

They suddenly separate, and the woman flings open her door, so the light comes on inside. I think I know her. She's got the kind of mad hair you don't forget, like rusty bedsprings – shit! She was the doctor who looked after Sam when he was little! I got dragged along to his annual check-ups every year until he was about five.

I recognized Dad instantly, of course.

'Christ,' Dan mutters. 'Are you *sure*?'

'Of course I'm sure. I've only lived with him, I don't know, *my whole life*.'

'You couldn't have made a mistake? Maybe he was just giving her a lift—'

'A lift? From where I was standing, she looked ecstatic.'

'There's probably an innocent—'

'Look, I didn't like get it wrong or imagine it or anything, all right?' I snap. 'Basically, my dad had his tongue down another woman's throat, and he wasn't giving her mouth-to-mouth, OK?'

'Are you going to tell your mum?'

I watch my mother stagger on stage with Eithne's stupid bronze statue. She usually hates this sort of thing, but she'd do anything for Eithne. It's bizarre, it's as if that hippy lezzie has some strange hold over her— Yeah. That'll be the day. My mum do anything blackmail-worth.

'Course I'm not telling her,' I retort. 'You want her to flip out again and try to slash her wrists with the loofah?'

'So what are you going to do?'

As if I know. It's so confusing. I mean, I should be mad at Dad, and I *am*; but at the same time, I can't really blame him. Basically, Mum's a complete basket case most of the time. And she's so *boring*. She never wants to do anything, she just sits around all the time crying or feeling sorry for herself. OK, sometimes she gets all manic and paints and stuff, like she has this last week or two, but then she never does anything with it. It never goes anywhere. Eithne says she could be this huge artist if she wanted to, but she just gets all depressed again and goes back to being helpless and pathetic. I know she's ill, but couldn't she make a bit of an *effort*?

She'll never cope on her own if he leaves. Which means I'll be the one stuck looking after her.

Up on stage, Mrs Buchanan points to the statue. 'An Eithne Brompton,' she says with this fake enthusiasm, 'surely we have some takers? At the back there? Come on, ladies and gentlemen, it's for a good cause! Now, who'll start me at a thousand pounds?'

'She'll be lucky to get a fiver,' Dan whispers.

'Whatever.' I scuff my boot on the grass. 'Stupid auction. I only came to get her off my back.'

Mrs Buchanan looks beaten. 'Five hundred, then.'

'Come on, Dan. This is so gay, I don't know why you wanted to come. Let's get out of here,' I plead.

'We can't. I promised your dad I'd give your mum a ride home.'

'Yeah, well, he'd know all about *rides*.'

'Come on, everyone,' Mum urges into the microphone. 'This is an Eithne Brompton. Do you know how much her artwork is worth on the open market? There's a waiting list two years long for commission pieces.'

Behind me, two girls from my class snigger.

'Great, Mum,' I mutter, closing my eyes. 'Just great. *Now* you decide to come out of your shell.'

'Cate—' Dan begins.

Which is when my mother strips off all her clothes and, in front of my entire class, my teachers and my boyfriend, runs naked across the playing fields waving her arms in the air.

Dan whips off his coat and chases after her. I don't bother to follow him. My eyes are dry and hard as I shoulder my way through the excited, buzzing crowd towards the exit.

I'm never going to forgive her for this. Never, never, *never*.

I'm so humiliated I want to die, except I'm not going to give her the satisfaction. How could she do this to me? I'll never be able to show my face at school again. Thank God it's the Easter holidays, and I can just shut myself in my room with Cannelle. I don't want to see anyone, even Dan. I hate her. She's ruined my entire life. The only good thing is that I've dropped six pounds, but since I'm going to spend the rest of my life hidden from the world, even that doesn't cheer me up.

For as long as I can remember, I've had to make allowances for Mum. *She's sick. She can't help it. She doesn't know what she's doing.* When she sits all day staring out of the window, or doesn't even bother to get dressed, 'It's the pills,' Dad says. 'It's not her fault.'

But he gets to escape to the office. He's not the one who has to come home and mop up the kitchen floor because she's left the tap running for eight hours. He didn't have to repaint my bedroom after Mum decided on the spur of the moment to paint it orange. He didn't save his pocket money for three months to buy a journalist's Billington bag, only to watch her give it all away to the Salvation Army when she was having one of her highs.

He wasn't the one to come home and find her That Day.

I wonder what she's like. His girlfriend. She always seemed OK, but that was before I knew she was shagging my dad. How can she be having an affair with him when she knows he's got kids? Doesn't she care?

What if he leaves us for her? He'll have a baby with her, a whole new family, and forget about us. Mum'll go to pieces. Or worse. If his girlfriend knew how much we need him, she'd have to leave him alone and find someone else. She's a *baby* doctor. She can't be that much of a bitch, surely?

Only one way to find out.

She's not hard to find. Still at the same hospital, though she's moved offices. Less than an hour from home, door to door. Handy for Dad.

She's got *cojones*, that's for sure. She doesn't even look surprised to see me when I turn up outside her office.

'It's Caitlin, isn't it?' she says.

'Cate.'

'Cate.' She nods. 'Well, you'd better come in.'

I follow Doctor Ella Slapper Stuart into a bright, cramped room that reminds me of Dad's new office, but without the amazing view. Her fancy glass desk is covered with heaps of forms and papers, weighted down with coffee mugs and books; two thin computer screens dovetail neatly in the centre of the desk, like a book that's been left propped open. The walls are filled with shelves of thick, boring-looking leather-bound books.

There are no photographs anywhere.

She waves me to a squishy grey chair on my side of the desk, but doesn't sit down herself, perching on the edge of her desk instead. 'What was it you wanted to talk to me about?'

'Dad,' I say.

She unclips her long red hair, scrapes it back more firmly from her face, then clips it up again. 'What exactly did you—'

'Don't pretend you don't know what I'm talking about. I saw the two of you last week in the station car park. You were *kissing*,' I accuse.

For a long moment, we just look at each other.

'You were about thirteen the last time I saw you,' she says finally. 'You were angry – I think you'd had to miss a concert or something to come up with your little brother—'

'Fourteen. Were you sleeping with my dad then?'

'Still angry,' she observes.

'Well? Were you?'

She fiddles with a row of books, straightening their spines. She looks thinner than I remembered, and kind of pale, as if she's been sick or something. I shake myself. God, I'll be feeling sorry for the cow in a minute.

'How did you get here?' she asks.

'Train. Tube. Then I walked. Finding the hospital wasn't exactly rocket science. I'm not a kid any more. You still haven't answered my question.'

'What exactly do you want me to say?'

I open my mouth: *I want you to say sorry, that you'll stop. I want you to promise you're not going to steal my dad away from me.* Instead, 'Do you love him?' I ask.

'I don't think that's any of your business,' she says softly.

'He's my dad. He's married to my mum. I think that makes it my business.'

'No. That just makes them your parents.'

'Aren't you at all sorry?' I demand hotly.

'For what?'

'You're having an affair with my dad! How can you just sit there and act as if it doesn't matter? You're basically a – a home wrecker!'

She leans back against her desk and folds her arms. She's wearing the coolest knee boots, kind of chocolate and orange and cinnamon paisley suede, with little kitten heels. 'I haven't wrecked your home. I would never do that.'

'How do you *know*? What if my mum finds out?'

'Are you going to tell her?'

Why does everyone keep asking me that? 'I won't need to, if you keep snogging Dad all over the place. You were practically doing it in our back garden! Anyone could've seen you!'

'I'm sorry about that,' she acknowledges. 'I shouldn't have gone down there. I'd had a bad— Never mind. It won't happen again.'

She twists a ring nervously on her left hand. It takes a moment for the gesture to register.

'You're married!' I exclaim. 'Does your husband know?'

She hesitates. 'He died.'

'Oh. I'm sorry. I didn't know.'

'Why should you?' She digs her fists deep in the pockets of her white coat. 'He died a month ago today. And no, he didn't know.'

'Was he really old?'

'No. Though he might seem it to you, I don't know. He was forty-one. Two,' she corrects herself. 'I keep forgetting it was his birthday.'

'Did he have an accident?'

'A virus attacked his heart. It was just one of those things. Chance in a million. No one could have known—'

'Do you have kids?'

She ducks her head. For a moment, she doesn't seem any older than me or Clem. 'No. He wanted them, but I didn't.'

'Bet you're glad now.'

'Not really.'

I don't know what else to say. This isn't going the way I thought it would. I had some hazy idea that she'd be so shocked and embarrassed when she saw me, she'd break down and promise never to go near Dad again. I suppose I thought she might put up a bit of a fight and argue, maybe even cry a little, but in the end she'd realize the game was up and go quietly.

Her husband's just died. Shit. And she's so normal, giving me proper answers and not treating me like a stupid kid. She seems almost – well, *nice*.

I ask her quickly, before I totally lose my bottle.

'So are you and Dad going to go off together?'

'Is that what you're worried about?' Her cheeks are flushed. 'I'm not going to run off with Will – with your dad. I'm not a home wrecker. I know how it seems, but I loved my husband. I never meant for anyone to get hurt—'

'Doesn't it worry you that he's cheating on my mum?' I ask curiously. 'I mean, he could be cheating on you, too. He might have loads of girlfriends.'

'You could say the same about me,' she says, with a strained smile.

God, she looks awful. Her hands are shaking. 'Are you . . . Dr Stuart, are you OK?'

She sucks in a breath. 'Could you pass me – some water . . .'

There's an unopened bottle of mineral water on the desk.

I unscrew the top and hand it to her. She's panting like she's been running: she's starting to freak me out.

'Dr Stuart? Ella? Would you like me to get someone?'

'Oh, Cate. I'm so sorry,' Ella manages.

She collapses like a rubber doll. I try to catch her, but it all happens too fast. There's a sickening thud as her head hits the corner of her glass desk.

'Ella! Ella! Are you OK?'

She doesn't move. I crouch down and gently turn her head towards me. Oh, God, there's so much blood! I can't see if she's actually poked out her eye – my stomach turns – or simply hit her head. I call her name again, but she doesn't respond. She's so pale. I can't even tell if she's breathing.

I open the door to the corridor and scream my head off.

5

Ella

I'm not scared of flying. Terrified of crashing, yes. 'In the event of an emergency, ladies must remove high-heeled shoes' – only a man would come up with that rule. What if I happened to be wearing my favourite pair of Manolos? Maybe they'd let me carry them; other women take their babies down the emergency chute, so why not—

An unexpected jolt of terror-laced adrenalin almost bounces me out of my seat.

I inhale deeply, and focus on the steward as he fastens his demonstration life-jacket. Of course I'm upset. My husband's just died. Pollyanna would be hard put to get in the holiday mood, given the circumstances.

The aircraft pulls away from the stand: the point of no return. A warm wash of sweat sweeps over me. I reach up and fiddle with the air vent, but it doesn't seem to make any difference.

'Miss?' The steward taps me on the shoulder. 'Excuse me, but we need to put that in the overhead locker for take-off.'

'It's OK, I'll hold it.'

'I'm sorry, miss. I'm afraid we have to—'

'It's Mrs.'

'Sorry?'

'It's not Miss, it's Mrs.'

'Yes, ma'am. If I could take that from you now . . .'

My chest tightens. A knot twists my stomach: nausea and fear. The passenger on my left shifts irritably in his seat. He's about five stone overweight; the armrest won't go down over his massive thigh. His flab spills into my seat, invading my space. I'm hemmed in, trapped. It's not fair – I bet *he* hasn't been charged £240 for excess baggage. It wasn't my fault, I couldn't decide what to pack; I spent a full twenty minutes this morning sobbing on the floor by my wardrobe, unable to choose between charcoal wool trousers or black. In the end, it was easier to pack everything.

Another wave of adrenalin surfs through me. My arms tingle with pins and needles. I start to feel really scared. Dear God, am I having a heart attack? Is this how Jackson felt?

The steward reaches across me. 'I really need to take that—'

'No! I'll hold it.'

'I'm afraid I can't let you do that, miss.'

'It's Mrs!' I shout. 'Mrs Garrett! *Mrs!*'

The steward backs nervously down the aisle. I can't breathe. I scrabble with my belt buckle as the aircraft gathers speed. I can't breathe, I have to get out of here, *I have to get off the plane—*

A cool, steady hand reaches across the aisle for mine.

'You're going to be fine,' a woman's voice says reassuringly. 'You're hyperventilating. You need to breathe slowly. In through the nose, out through the mouth. *Slowly*. In through the nose. Out through the mouth. In through the nose. Out through the mouth . . .'

Hyperventilating. Yes. I know what that is. A page from my med notes swims in front of my eyes: 'hyperventilation (or hyperpnoea) is the state of breathing faster or deeper (hyper) than necessary, and thereby reducing the carbon dioxide concentration of the blood below normal . . .'

Gradually the feeling of suffocation eases. For several moments, I can't speak.

'You had a panic attack, dear,' the woman says gently. 'I used to have them, after my mother died. It's very frightening, but they won't actually do you any harm.'

I yank my hand free. 'I don't have panic attacks.'

'Sometimes they come on out of the blue, if you're stressed or over-anxious. Anyone can get them. It's nothing to be ashamed of.'

'It's probably just the altitude. I feel fine now.'

She doesn't need to point out that we're barely off the ground.

The steward comes back down the aisle. '*Mrs* Garrett,' he emphasizes nastily, 'we really can't permit you to endanger yourself and other passengers like that again. You need to stow your belongings during—'

'It's my husband,' I say.

'I'm sorry?'

I shelter the wooden box in the curve of my arm. A sunlit memory flickers across my mind's eye: Jackson crouching by the side of a red dirt road in Paraguay, laughing as he barters with a young boy of no more than eight, knowing that whatever price he pays in the end, it'll be ten times what the cumbersome carved box is worth. 'But how on earth will we get it home?' I'd asked him, already planning, organizing. 'We'll find a way,' Jackson said carelessly. 'It'll be part of the fun.'

'It's my husband's ashes,' I tell the steward, taking bleak pleasure in the way his jaw drops. 'I'm taking him home.'

I've never met Jackson's brother, but I recognize him instantly. He has the same features: the Caribbean-blue eyes, the wide, full mouth, the square jaw. But whereas Jackson's beauty is so much more than the sum of his parts, Cooper's manages to be just that little bit less.

His expression is flinty and unwelcoming; the deep grooves between his brows and bracketing his mouth suggest it's habitual, rather than personal. He nods unsmilingly when I introduce myself, and leaves me to push my trolley after him as he turns on his heel and heads towards the airport exit. Clearly Jackson scooped the family charm lottery too, I think crossly.

I follow Cooper out to the car park. My heart sinks when he stops by a battered two-door Ford pick-up. It looks as if its last passengers were a pair of mud-wrestling hippos.

He climbs into the driver's seat without bothering to help me load my suitcase into the filthy truck bed, but reluctantly gets out again when he sees me struggling.

'Thank you,' I pant, as he tosses the case over the tailgate.

He ignores me and gets back into the pick-up. So much for the fabled Southern manners. I can't believe how different Jackson is from his brother—

Was. *Was.*

Cooper swings the truck on to the busy interstate, leaving his window open so that conversation is impossible over the rush of air. My hair whips around my face, getting into my mouth and eyes. Four lanes of huge American cars belch out clouds of grey fumes as they overtake us on both sides – the one thing Jackson really loved about England, apart from Maltesers and double-decker buses, was our small, neat little cars. I shiver as the air whistles round my shoulders. When I turn the car heater on, Cooper immediately reaches past me and turns it back off. No wonder Jackson's brother never married, if this is the way he goes about winning friends and influencing people.

Slumping against the hard bench seat, I pull my jacket close and shut my eyes. His driving is as aggressive as his attitude, but I'm just too damn tired and miserable to care. In the two weeks since Jackson died, I've deliberately pulled back-to-back double shifts at the hospital: work is the only thing that helps right now. Even on the days I haven't been on duty, I've found myself gravitating towards the warmth of the NICU anyway, spending hours hunched over baby Hope's incubator, willing her to keep on battling. For some reason, the tiny baby has touched the part of me I'd call my soul, if I still believed in God. It's as if, in saving her life, I have somehow made her a part of mine.

My stomach lurches. Sitting here next to Jackson's brother, I'm literally sick with guilt. William says I've got to stop blaming myself for Jackson's death, but how can I? I'm a doctor; if I'd been home, instead of with William, I might have realized how serious it was. If only—

If only *what*, Ella? He'd got to the hospital in time?

You'd got the chance to say goodbye? You hadn't spent the last eight years cheating on him?

'That him?' Cooper says suddenly, jerking his thumb at the box on my lap.

I start at the sound of his voice. His expression is sour. Can he tell just from looking at me what kind of woman his brother married?

I nod. Cooper's jaw sets, but he says nothing further.

After an hour of driving we turn off the interstate and on to a series of increasingly narrow and neglected roads, the last of which isn't even paved. The pick-up jolts over deep ruts and potholes, spraying me with a fine mist of dirt through the open window. Live oaks looped with grey skeins of Spanish moss arch across the track, plunging us into a deep, green gloom. The air is still, oppressive. The damp smell of mould and decay seeps into my bones. I'd often wondered why Jackson never found time to take me home. I'm beginning to understand.

Cooper swings the truck into an overgrown dirt drive running alongside a peeling post-and-rail fence. A horse snickers in the distance as he pulls up in front of a surprisingly large and well-kept antebellum mansion straight out of *Gone with the Wind*. I'd expected some grim, Gothic horror, but this is beautiful.

I lean out of the pick-up window, trying to picture Jackson growing up here – a six-year-old boy perched on the balustrade, a teenager kissing his first girl on the porch. An eleven-year-old wriggling uncomfortably in his stiff new mourning clothes, his hair wet and slicked against his head, trying to be brave like his big brother as he buries his parents.

Cooper grabs my suitcase from the truck bed and heads

into the house. I clamber out of the cab, clumsily cradling the awkward box.

A small black woman in her mid-seventies is waiting for me in the airy hall at the bottom of a sweeping curved staircase, hands folded against her crisp white apron. There's no sign of either Cooper or my suitcase.

'You must be Miss Ella,' she says warmly, her Southern accent painfully familiar. 'I'm Lolly. Y'all must be wore out now after your journey. Let me show you up to your room, so you can freshen up before dinner.'

'It's so good to meet you at last, Lolly. Jackson's told me so much about you—'

Her gaze rests on the box in my arms. 'Oh, Miss Ella. I can't believe he's gone.'

'Me neither,' I whisper.

'He was such a strong boy. Could run outside all day and still have plenty of fizz left in him when he got home. Always playing pranks – frogs and bugs and I don't know what-all in my bed. Once, he got this hognose snake in a burlap sack—' Her brown eyes fill with tears, and she dashes them away with the back of her hand. 'Listen to me, chattering on like a silly old woman, with you all but dead on your feet. You follow me, now. Cooper's put you in the Blue Room at the end of the hall. There's fresh towels laid out in the bathroom, but y'all must tell me if there's anything else you need.'

She shows me upstairs and into a bright, high-ceilinged room. On the far side, a pair of French windows leads on to a small balcony. In the centre of the room, an old brass bed is cloaked in a drift of white duvet and mosquito netting. The polished oak floor gleams gold with the patina of age.

I place Jackson's ashes carefully on the wooden dresser,

next to a pair of silver-backed hairbrushes and a hand-mirror monogrammed with initials too worn to read. Beside the bed is a simple rag rug in the same shade of pale blue as the papered walls. My suitcase stands on it at a dislocated angle, as if it had been thrown from the doorway. Knowing Cooper, it probably has.

Lolly watches as I kneel on the floor and yank the case flat to unzip it.

'You mustn't mind Cooper,' she says hesitantly. 'He can be a little ornery, but it's just his way. This has hit him hard. He loved Jackson like he was his own son.' Her eyes wander to the box on the dresser. 'After their parents died, he gave up everything to raise him. You know Cooper had won himself a place at Juilliard just a month before the fire? He came home so excited that day, I swear he was a foot off the ground. He was such a talented musician. Even now, when he sits down at the piano, it's like the world stands still.'

I sit back on my heels. 'Jackson never mentioned that.'

'Oh, he never knew. Cooper didn't want the boy feeling guilty. Never mentioned Juilliard again. Lord knows how much that cost him.'

'And he never married?'

'There was a girl, once.' She sighs. 'Jackson was still just a boy, and she didn't want to be stuck raising him. After that, I guess Cooper gave up on the idea of a family of his own. Jackson was all the family he needed.'

She tells me that dinner is at six-thirty, and leaves me to unpack. It doesn't take long; I leave most of my clothes in the suitcase, since I'm only going to be here a couple of days. Just long enough to scatter Jackson's ashes and say goodbye.

When I've finished, I glance longingly at the bed. I'd like nothing more than to slide under the crisp covers, but I know if I do that now, I'll be wide awake at three in the morning with jet-lag.

Instead, I splash water on my face and run my fingers through my hair, already kinking even tighter than usual after the plane journey. Maybe I'd feel better if I went for a walk. My muscles ache from being crammed into the cattle truck that passes for economy these days.

Downstairs, the sound of a piano drifts through the hall. I pause on the bottom step, arrested by the music, the world pouring through me like light. Cooper's grief and sorrow is given voice by the plaintive notes spilling from his fingers. My heart swells with pity. I loved Jackson as well as I knew how, but the ties of blood are different. I've seen enough bereaved parents to know that the loss of a child is visceral, akin to having your heart cut out. Cooper mourns his brother the same way. Listening to him play, I'm strangely embarrassed, as if I have stumbled on a private grief I have no right to witness.

Quietly, I open the front door and let myself into the garden.

'We're here?' I ask, as Cooper parks the truck.

He nods brusquely. After three hours together driving up into the Smoky Mountains, during which we've exchanged no more than five words, I didn't really expect actual conversation.

I open the pick-up door, and reach back for Jackson's ashes. Cooper makes no move to follow me. 'You're not coming?' I ask in surprise.

He stares ahead impassively.

Suddenly, unexpectedly, he reminds me of his brother. Something about the stubborn set of his mouth, the angry, defensive tilt of his chin. I realize that if Jackson hadn't had the path of his life smoothed by his protective elder brother, this is the kind of man he might have become: worn, cynical, closed off. I wonder what Cooper would look like if he smiled.

I leave him smouldering in the truck, and shield my eyes as I glance up the path I have to climb. Oh, Jackson. It had to be a four-hundred-foot vertical rock, didn't it?

'If I check out while I'm living on this godforsaken island,' he'd said cheerfully over breakfast one wet Sunday morning, shortly after we'd moved to London, 'don't y'all dare bury me in one of your gloomy English boneyards. I want you to take me back home and scatter my ashes from Chimney Rock.'

'Chimney what?'

He dipped his cereal spoon into my Ben & Jerry's, grinning when I slapped his hand away. 'Chimney Rock. It's a rock, and it's shaped like a chimney—'

'Carry on like this and I'll just flush your ashes down the loo.'

'I love the way you say that. "The loo." It's so British, like "bugger" and "*shed*ule". And red buses and Marmite and—'

'You sound like a bloody tourist.'

'I *am* a bloody tourist. Chimney Rock, you ignorant Brit, is on the edge of the Blue Ridge Smoky Mountains in North Carolina, the most beautiful spot on God's green earth. Y'all can see a couple hundred miles from the top on a good day. I'm surprised you never checked it out when you were at Duke.'

'Scared of heights,' I confessed. 'I've never liked going anywhere near mountains – all those narrow hairpin bends and sheer drops.'

I stare up at the wall of rock in front of me now, and feel sick. Fortunately, I don't have to don a climbing harness or equip myself with ropes; a winding staircase has been cut into the rock. But it's still nearly four hundred feet high, and I've barely reached the first landing when the vertigo hits.

Oh, Jesus. I'm not sure I can do this.

Focus. One foot in front of the other. Don't look up, and it'll be fine. If these stairs can stand the weight of the average American, they can stand you.

Clinging to the stair rail, I climb steadily for twenty minutes, and emerge panting at the top. It's quite sheltered here, and I begin to feel better. That wasn't so bad. And there's a nice stone wall at the edge, not some rickety parapet—

Shit. Shit shit *shit*. This isn't the top. I've got to go up more stairs and – Jesus. Across some kind of Indiana Jones plank bridge. You have *got* to be kidding me.

I sink on to a bench. Oh, Jackson. Aren't *you* having the last laugh.

William thought I was mad coming all this way to scatter his ashes. Heaven knows, I did little enough for my husband when he was alive; maybe it is pointless to go to all this trouble now. But (and at the risk of sounding like a talk-show victim) I need closure. If I do this one last thing, perhaps I can start to move on.

Wearily, I get up and climb the last set of stairs, stopping when I reach the bridge. It must be a thousand feet down to the valley.

There's only one thing to do. When the going gets tough, the tough shut their eyes.

As soon as I'm over the bridge, I collapse on to the rock. And stay there. Nothing is going to get me to stand at the flimsy guard rail by the edge. I'm on a narrow rock the size of my kitchen, four hundred feet up. It's not even flat. I could just topple over the side.

My throat closes. I grip the box tighter, my heart racing. A clammy sweat swamps me. I can't do this. I can't move. *I can't do this*.

An arm cradles my elbow, and propels me on to my feet.

Gently but firmly, Cooper leads me towards the guard rail. The Smoky Mountains are spread out before me, the blue haze that gives them their name softening and blurring the landscape. A silvery river twists its way towards the horizon. The air smells cleaner, more fresh, than anything I've ever experienced. Jackson was right; it is the most beautiful place on God's green earth.

Together, his brother and I open the box. A light wind lifts the ashes, scattering them like rainfall.

Cooper turns to me, his blue eyes navy with grief. I only realize I'm crying myself when the tears splash on to my shirt.

He holds out his hand, and leads me back over the bridge.

*

The evening is unseasonably warm for the first week of March. I open my French windows and step on to the balcony as a cool breeze rustles the live oaks, stirring the Spanish moss. The black night presses down on me, starless. Clouds scud across a nail-paring new moon. Out here there are no streetlights, no neon. Nothing but darkness and the beat of wings.

I lean on the balustrade and sip my bourbon nightcap, enjoying the balmy caress of the night air on my bare skin. In the morning, I'll leave and go back home to London, grey in every sense of the word, shutting this door for ever. For the first time in my life, I'll be truly alone.

It sounds ridiculous – he was my husband, after all – but I hadn't realized quite how much space Jackson took up in my life until he left it. His quiet, reassuring presence was the solid rock on which I built my house of cards. Without him, it's just a matter of time before it comes tumbling down.

I could fool myself that my heart is broken, but that would just pile lie upon betrayal. There are people whose deaths make you ache with misery. And there are people whose deaths are the end of everything, a biblical darkness descending on the land, deaths that send a scream through your head like the keening of lost souls. Hard as it is to admit, losing Jackson hasn't come close to this second kind of grief.

My eyes have adjusted to the dark. On the far side of the lawn is a small lake; as I watch, an owl swoops low over it.

I mourn my husband more than I would have thought possible, but it's fear that's uppermost now, not Cooper's raw kind of anguish. I've already lost Jackson; will I lose William too?

Our relationship worked because it was perfectly balanced. We each had as much to lose; we shared the power. But now, instead of being an equal partner, I've suddenly turned into a needy cliché: the Other Woman.

Whether William knows it or not, part of my attractiveness to him has always been my unavailability. I never needed to play hard to get, because with Jackson in the picture, I actually *was*. But that's changed now. William's probably shit-scared and ready to run for the hills. And to be perfectly honest, I can't blame him. If he ever left Beth, I'd be the same.

Lucy thinks I'm shameless (the unfortunate thing about best friends is that they tend to know you rather well), but that's not entirely true. An affair with William was one thing – if not with me, it would've been someone else, maybe a woman who'd want Beth's wedding ring on her finger and would stop at nothing to get it. That's never been me. I've always sworn I'd never steal another woman's husband.

Easy to do when you're not tempted. I can dress it up as altruism, but the simple truth is I was too much of a snivelling coward to leave Jackson.

Now that he's gone, the moral high ground looks decidedly less bucolic.

For a moment, I allow myself to imagine what it might be like to share a real life with William. Waking up together every morning, spending weekends lazing around with the papers, getting the Eurostar to Paris for the bank-holiday weekend on a whim. Now I'm a widow (I still can't get used to that word; it conjures Greek crones in black picking olives) I'm going to have to get used to doing so many things alone. Unless—

What is it you want, Ella? What do you *want*?

For the first time, I can't give myself an honest answer.

I'm startled by a noise in the room behind me. I spin round, dropping the empty bourbon glass and instinctively covering my nakedness with my hands.

Cooper is framed in the bedroom doorway, his expression unreadable. I recognize that I'm not surprised. The air between us has been charged since we left Chimney Rock two days ago.

When I walk into a room, he leaves. We don't speak, except the briefest banalities at dinner. But every time I look at him, I see Jackson. Every time he looks at me, it's like he can plumb my soul.

Something primitive and visceral in me takes over. I want this man in a way that has nothing to do with who he is, nothing to do with who I am; everything to do with lust and escape and anger and bourbon and the need to remind myself that I am living, breathing, beating flesh, not a box of grey ashes tipped over a mountainside.

I drop my hands and meet his gaze, allowing his eyes to travel over me. My nipples stiffen in the cool breeze from the window.

I don't know what it is I see in his eyes as he crosses the room, and I don't care. Stepping over the broken bourbon glass, I rip at his denim shirt; buttons rattle on the floor. He pushes me roughly back on to the bed, unbuckling his jeans, shucking them off.

In moments he's inside me; I'm already wet. I claw at his back, pulling him harder, deeper within me. He bites my shoulder, his callused hands rough on my breasts. Our

bodies are slick with sweat. The brass bed bangs rhythmic-
ally against the wall as Cooper pounds angrily into me, his
blond hair drenched with perspiration. We come together
in an explosion of grief and heat.

His body is heavy on mine. I ease myself free, spent and
strangely soothed.

Cooper stands up and pulls on his jeans; we haven't
spoken a word from start to finish. He walks towards the
door, then abruptly stops and turns, his eyes dark. For an
insane moment, I wonder if he's going to tell me he loves
me.

'I always wondered what kind of woman my brother
married,' he says coldly. 'Now I know.'

I've never been so humiliated and furious in my life. What
kind of fucked-up bastard sleeps with his brother's widow
just to prove he can? Jesus. I thought *I* was screwed up.

It's not the first time I've regretted having sex for the
wrong reasons, but I've never felt as dirty and ugly afterwards as I do now. Ashamed, as if I've been publicly
caught naked.

I'm so disturbed I forget to take any Xanax before
boarding the plane home. Eight hours later, tired, anxious
and depressed, the panic hits. I suddenly find myself standing in the middle of the concourse at Gatwick, clinging to
my suitcase and unable to move, terror blossoming inside
me like a mushroom cloud. A hot band tightens around my
chest. The airport is suddenly airless, suffocating. People
press all around me. I'm buffeted from every direction. I
drop my case and gasp for air, clawing at my chest, trying
to undo my buttons, desperate for breath.

Somehow, I contain the fear. Scrabbling through my bag, heedless of the coins and papers and keys I scatter on the floor, I grab my phone, and for the first time in eight years I call William at home.

His expression is stony when he meets me at his local railway station, where he's told me to come. Wordlessly, he picks up my suitcase and walks me out to his car. My relief at seeing him fades as a newer fear grips me.

I don't want to be alone.

'I'm sorry,' I say, as soon as we're in the car.

'You can't call me at home,' William says tightly. 'Please don't do it again.'

The seatbelt cuts into my shoulder as I twist towards him. 'Jesus, William. Thanks for the tea and sympathy.'

'Come on, Ella. You know the score.'

'One call in eight y—'

'My wife was next to me in the kitchen, Ella!' he exclaims.

I'm appalled by his lack of understanding. 'William, I've just flown halfway across the world and back to scatter my husband's ashes from a mountaintop, and in a moment of weakness, I just thought that seeing you would make me feel better! Clearly I was wrong!'

I gaze out of the window at the ill-lit station car park, so that he won't see the sudden tears filling my eyes. Damn it, what's *wrong* with me? Dragging him from his home in the middle of the evening for no reason. No wonder he's angry. I've got to get a grip. I don't want to drive him away with this nonsense. I'll end up in adjoining beds with his wife at the nuthouse.

'Ella—'

'I'm sorry. I shouldn't have called.'

'Ella, it's not that I don't care. You know I do. But things are so difficult at home right now.' He rubs the side of his face. 'Beth's in one of her manic phases, it's impossible to reason with her—'

A train pulls into the station behind us, briefly drowning out his voice.

'. . . some damn contractor was just about to bulldoze the garage as I pulled into the drive,' William is saying. 'God knows how much she's blown this time. I should have paid more attention to what she was up to, but things have been so insane at work with the takeover bid I lost track.'

'James Noble?' I say, grateful for the distraction.

'Bastard. I didn't build up my company from scratch so some eviscerating card sharp could march in and take it over when he felt like it.'

He's been fending off friendly and not-so-friendly feelers from Noble's company for more than a year. Six months ago, William was in a position to tell him where to get off, but Ashfield's has lost several key accounts in the past few months. The company is vulnerable to attack, and much as William tries to put a brave face on it, I know it's eating him up.

I unbuckle my seatbelt and slide towards him, brushing a clump of dried mud from his shirt without pausing to wonder how it got there, and inhaling his familiar woody, lemon scent. God, I've missed him. I need to remind him why he's missed me.

My hand slips between his legs. Briefly, I wish I'd had a chance to shower after the plane as he pulls my head to him and kisses me, mouth hard and insistent. Heat spreads through my body. Cooper was about meeting a physical need, but this is so much more—

I freeze. How *much* more, Ella? Jackson isn't here to safeguard you now. Are you sure you know what you're doing?

Without warning, the panic returns. The weight of the night presses in on me. Suddenly the car is stifling. I push William away from me, fumbling at the door handle. His hand catches my wrist, and I wrench it painfully away.

'Ella, what is it? Ella!'

The light comes on as I open the door. The chilly air revives me, and instantly I feel better. I sit half in and half out of the car, hands on my knees, breathing deeply the way the woman on the plane showed me. *In through the nose, out through the mouth.*

In the distance, a cat yowls. Someone runs quickly across the car park in the dark. A couple of teenagers kick a can across the station platform. Slowly, my heart rate returns to normal.

William looks distinctly fed up. Hardly surprising, given the way I'm blowing hot and cold. He gets enough tears and histrionics at home – the last thing he needs is more of the same from me. I need to get things back on track with him, and then perhaps I can figure out what my next move needs to be.

I don't want to be alone.

I slam the car door shut and pour every ounce of the old Ella into my smile. 'Let's go back to my place,' I say.

'Ella?'

I'm lying on my back, floating on the warm ocean. A gentle wave sends me drifting towards the white spun-sugar beach, then tugs me back out to sea again. I'm a frond of seaweed, a piece of driftwood, at the mercy of wind and tide. The salt water laps against my face, splashing in my eyes. The sun warms my skin. I can't remember the last time I felt this relaxed, and at peace.

'Ella? Can you hear me?'

The water splashes my face again, cold this time. Something tugs at me, pulling me down. I begin to choke. The sun is so hot, it's *burning*. God, it hurts, it *hurts*—

'Don't try to move,' a voice says in my ear.

It feels as if a giant is pushing his thumbs against my eyes. It takes a huge effort to force them open. 'Lucy? Have I been in an accident?'

'You fell, and hit your head against the corner of your desk. You've been out cold for about five minutes. Can you remember what happened?'

'What's going on?'

She peers into my eyes with her penlight. 'Nausea? Double vision?'

I flinch from the bright light. 'It feels like there's a road-drill in my head, but that's all. What happened?'

'What's the last thing you remember?'

'I remember the flight from North Carolina, and meeting William at the station – were we in a car crash?' I sit bolt upright, and the room spins wildly. 'Is William OK? Oh, God, please tell me he wasn't hurt—'

Lucy frowns. 'Ella, that was a week ago. There wasn't any crash, the accident happened here, at the hospital—'

'A *week*?'

'You don't remember anything about today? We did our rounds this morning, Ella – remember, Hope's doing so well, she's made amazing progress – and then you had a row with Richard Angel over closing the NICU beds.'

I shake my head, and instantly regret it as the room tilts again.

'Afterwards, you came down to your office to do some paperwork. Gina said there was someone waiting for you, a blonde girl. She was with you when it happened. Apparently the two of you were talking, and then you fainted mid-sentence. You hit your head on your desk as you went down. The girl screamed the bloody place down, it sounded like someone was being murdered.'

'Cate,' I breathe.

'You remember?'

A tape fast-forwards in my head: William's daughter, the panic attack, her question: *Do you have kids*? And my instinctive response – despite the fact that I've never wanted children – my first visceral, gut response: *If I'd given Jackson the baby he wanted, I wouldn't be alone now.*

I haven't told Lucy about the panic attacks, or the constant knot of anxiety lodged below my ribcage. For weeks, I haven't been able to eat: I'm too sick with nerves. I wake three, four, five times a night with adrenalin flooding my body, my heart pounding, feeling as if a suffocating weight is pressing on my chest. I'm so exhausted I can't see straight. I look in the mirror and I don't recognize myself.

I've always been in such control of my life. I've never been remotely nervous or anxious about anything. I sailed through my finals. How can this be happening to *me*?

'I remember now,' I say painfully. 'Not all of it, but at least the edited highlights.'

'The rest will come back. That cut's going to need a couple of stitches.' Lucy snaps on some gloves and opens a suture kit. 'You were lucky you didn't lose an eye. You need to start eating properly,' she adds crossly. 'Look at you: you must have lost fifteen pounds in the last couple of weeks. No wonder you fainted.'

I wince as she sterilizes my forehead. 'The girl was Cate,' I say, 'William's daughter – ow! Watch what you're doing, Lucy!'

'Sorry. What on earth was she doing here?'

'She found out about us. Came to warn me off, I think. Although . . .' I hesitate. Her hostility didn't seem quite real; almost as if I wasn't its focus. It must have taken a lot of courage to come and confront me. I wish she hadn't, but I can't help liking her for it. 'I'm not really sure what she wanted. I'm not sure she knew, either.'

'So what now?'

For the briefest moment, I think of Cooper, and the straightforward, if brutal, need that brought us together.

Since when did my free-and-easy relationship with William become so *complicated*?

'I have no idea,' I sigh.

'Are you going to tell him?'

He needs to know that his daughter has discovered us; but I promised her I wouldn't say anything, and, stupid as it may sound, I don't want to let her down. Oh, God, I'm so *tired* of all the lies.

Knowing he had a family was one thing; being confronted by his teenage daughter, seeing the pain and confusion in her eyes, is another. She may affect a tough front and take her daddy's side, but she loves her mother too, whether she acknowledges it or not. How can I let things go on, now that Cate knows?

How can I bear to lose William too?

'Look, Lucy. Thanks for putting me back together, but

I need to get going. I've got to finish this paperwork for Angel, or he'll shut down half the hospital.'

'Ella, forget work! You just knocked yourself unconscious! Don't even think about going back to your office. And you're getting a taxi home. I'm not having you wandering around the District & Circle Line in a daze asking people what your name is. Besides,' she adds, peeling off her gloves, 'Richard will understand. He's not as bad as people think.'

' "*Richard*"?'

'If you give him a chance, he's actually OK,' she mutters.

'I thought *I* was the one with concussion,' I say, narrowing my eyes.

She doesn't meet them. 'I'll call you a taxi.'

Today is taking on a surreal quality. First Cate turns up, and now Lucy's defending the Angel of Death. Maybe when I hit my head, I woke up in a strange parallel universe where all this actually makes sense.

I allow myself to be bundled into a cab, and give the driver William's address. Thirty minutes later, I let myself into his flat; he gave me a key years ago, though obviously I never turn up uninvited. The apartment's in darkness; he's clearly still at work. Thanks to my little medical drama, I'm an hour early.

I sink into the sofa without turning on the lights. My forehead throbs. This is not what I wanted from this evening. I meant to be fun and sexy for William, back to the old Ella, to wipe out the neurotic impression I've been giving over the past few weeks. The last thing I wanted was to sit here with my head swathed in gauze, looking like romantic roadkill—

Something is digging into my back. I reach beneath the sofa cushions and pull out the TV remote, but there's still something—

A boned slither of lace and silk falls into my lap. A very sexy, very expensive black basque, at least two sizes too small for me.

He could be cheating on you, too. He might have loads of girlfriends.

It doesn't belong to his wife.

October 24, 2000

Felden Street
Fulham
London SW6

Dear Cooper,

      You've no idea how good it was to get your letter, bro. I thought you were going to stay mad at me for ever. I wish we'd made up before I left the States; I hated not being able to say a real goodbye. But wild horses couldn't stop me coming home for Thanksgiving, so you'd better get Lolly started in on her baking! What I wouldn't give right now for a mouthful of her sweet potato pie!

   Look, I shouldn't have said the things I did, and I'm sorry. You know it was just the Jack talking. You've been the best brother a man could have, and I owe you a lot. But Ella is my wife, and I love her. It's killing me that the two people I love most in the world can't love each other.

   She keeps asking to meet you, and I'm fast running out of excuses. I wish you'd just give her half a chance. I don't know why you've taken against her so when you haven't even met her. She isn't what you think, Coop. She's a good wife. I know you've always held a woman ought to stay home and take care of her man like Mom did, but if you could just see the way she talks about her babies at that hospital, you'd think different. What she does is real important. I'll admit, sometimes I wish I got a bigger slice of her time, but those tiny ones need her as much as I do.

   It's not fair to blame her for us moving to London – that was my idea. Thing is, I reckon if she's in her home town, she'll feel differently about us starting a family of our own.

Tess Stimson

She always says she doesn't want children, but I know she can't mean it. She just needs to feel settled and secure, is all. After what happened to her mom, you can't blame her. She needs a lot of gentling, like a skittish mare. Remember how I got Star to trust me, how long that took? Man, but I took some hard falls from her before I was done! For a time there, seemed like Lolly was always rubbing liniment on one bruise or another!

Jackson Junior – how about that for a wild idea! Bet you never thought you'd see the day when your crazy-ass brother would be looking forward to changing a diaper!

I'm not saying it's been plain sailing. We got our troubles, same as everyone. She works too hard, for a start, and she's always pushing me to climb the greasy pole. But you know me, my job's never been the be-all, end-all. I don't deny, she gets me all fired up at times. She's not the easiest woman in the world to live with, but I can't do without her, Coop.

Why don't you come over and stay with us awhile, get to know her properly? This is an amazing city, for all it's so crowded a man can scarce breathe for tripping over his neighbor. And the cars! Man, I love their cute cars. Our townhouse is so small I can touch both sides of the kitchen without shifting, but it's in a real neat neighborhood and I've already met so many interesting folk. Ella says I gotta stop bringing home my 'strays', but how you ever going to make friends if you don't talk to people? No one has any time for each other any more. That's one thing I miss about home. You could spend all day just passing the time of day with your neighbors and no one's going to think badly of you for it.

I guess I'd better haul ass if I want this to reach you

114

*before Christmas. You gotta go find yourself a 'letterbox'
over here – they don't collect mail from home like they do in
the good old US of A. There's a lot of stuff here takes some
getting used to. Did you ever hear of something called
Marmite? Tastes like shit rolled in salt and looks like tar,
but these Brits are addicted to the stuff! Makes me feel queasy
just thinking about it. I'll take Lolly's biscuits and cranberry
sauce any day!*

   Give her a smacker for me, and tell her I'll be home soon.

   Jackson

6

William

Carolyn was definitely giving me the eye this morning. Christ, that skirt. Any shorter and I'd have seen her breakfast.

I ease the Land-Rover out of the station car park, drumming my fingers on the steering wheel as I hit rush-hour traffic. Carolyn's a nice girl, bright, but I don't shit on my own doorstep; not any more. She can't be much older than Cate, for heaven's sake. Twenty-four, max. Amazing body (you could lose yourself for a week in those tits), but the *ingénue* thing doesn't do it for me. I like a woman who knows what she's doing in bed, and tells you what she wants. Isn't afraid to get down and dirty. Carolyn's not the type to take it up the arse or let you come all over her face, far too proper.

God, I miss Ella. Apart from the obvious, I could use her company. No one makes me laugh like Ella. What with Beth painting like Tigger on speed, Ben demanding another two grand to clear his college bar bill (what's he drinking?

Bloody Moët?), Cate making bedroom eyes at that fucking hippy boyfriend of hers and James Noble breathing down my neck in the boardroom, I need some down-time. If Beth knew how close we are to the whole bloody house of cards collapsing—

I slam on the brakes as a cement mixer reverses out into the road. Where the hell is Ella when I need her? She's the only one who understands. Why she had to scatter the poor sod's ashes in person I don't know. Couldn't she have FedExed them or something?

OK, that was a bit harsh. I take it back. Anyway, she's home today, that's the main thing. With any luck, I'll see her next weekend.

I turn into our road. Got to be very careful I don't let things get out of hand. Be a bit too easy to start seeing Ella more often, now she doesn't have to answer to the husband, and tempting though it is, I don't want to rock the boat at home. Once a month is one thing. But Beth might ask questions if I had to 'take clients out' every week—

What the fuck?

I abandon the car, engine running, and race up the driveway, silk tie flapping over my shoulder. The bulldozer raises its claw, ready to smash down into the garage. I shout to attract the driver's attention, waving my arms and getting as close to the caterpillar treads as I dare.

My life flashes before me. I'm reminded, amongst other things, of the reason I don't return my mother's calls. A bloody great clod of mud falls from the bulldozer bucket on to my shoulder, and I close my eyes, bracing myself for the groan of metal, glass, brick and, quite possibly, flesh.

'You want to get out of the way, mate,' the driver calls. 'You could get hurt.'

'Beth!' I yell, as I slam into the kitchen five minutes later.

There's no sign of my wife. There is every sign, however, of her latest manic episode: tubes of paint and dirty paintbrushes fill the sink, milky jars of white spirit are ranged along the windowsill, and half a dozen squares of paint-smeared glass are spread over the Aga to dry. Of dinner, laundry, shopping or, in fact, I notice as I go to put it on, the coffee percolator, there is no sign.

'Beth!'

She bumps open the back door with her hip, her arms full of photographic equipment. 'All right, William. There's no need to shout.'

'Christ almighty. I'm putting in an eighty-hour week to put a roof over our heads. Is it really too much to expect for it to still be there when I get home?'

She beams. 'Oh, did you meet Murray?'

'If you mean the sadistic bastard intent on knocking down my house and demanding my first-born in payment, yes, I have,' I say darkly.

'Now you're being silly.' She puts down the equipment and pushes her hair back off her face in a gesture that reminds me of Cate. 'I need to expand my studio, and since you wouldn't let me move the conservatory last year – well, it's not as if we need the garage—'

'Need it?' I yelp. 'Where am I supposed to put the car?'

'For heaven's sake, I don't know. You can't expect me to take care of everything. Did you see Cate on your way up from the station? She should be back from school by now – she must've gone over to Dan's. I wanted to ask her about Brighton.'

She's making even less sense than usual. It's like stepping into a Dali painting.

My mobile rings. I pull it out, and nearly drop it into the nearest jar of turps when I see Ella's number come up. In eight years, she's never called me on it at home.

'Who is it?' Beth says brightly.

'Work.'

'Aren't you going to answer it?'

'It's a client. Confidential.'

She pulls a face. 'Oooh, all right. I can take a hint. I'll be in my studio if you need me.'

I wait till Beth's safely out of earshot.

'Ella? Are you there? What's wrong?'

'William, you have to come and get me. You have to come. William, William, can you come? Can you come and get me, now, please. Please, William—'

'It's OK,' I say, alarmed. 'Ella, it's OK. Just tell me where you are.'

When I find her sitting on her suitcase like Little Orphan Annie at the edge of the station platform, I almost don't recognize her. She's lost a huge amount of weight; her face is drawn, her eyes bruised by tiredness. But what really throws me is her air of uncertainty. She looks as if she's woken up in a country she doesn't recognize, and no matter how hard she keeps trying, she can't find her bearings. I've never seen Ella anything but brazenly confident before.

'I'm so sorry,' she says, as soon as we're in the car.

I start the engine, but don't put it in gear. I'm thoroughly unnerved, and anxiety makes my tone sharper than I intend. 'You can't call me at home. Please don't do it again.'

'Jesus, William. Thanks for the tea and sympathy.'

'Come on, Ella. You know the score.'

'One call in eight y—'

I expect this kind of neediness from Beth, but not Ella. Her unexpected vulnerability has thrown me more than I care to admit.

'My wife was next to me in the kitchen, Ella!'

'William, I've just flown halfway across the world and back to scatter my husband's ashes from a mountaintop, and in a moment of weakness, I just thought that seeing you would make me feel better! Clearly I was wrong!'

She turns her back on me. Shit. As if I don't have enough emotional, neurotic women at home.

I remind myself she's just lost her husband. How would I feel, if it were Beth?

'Ella—'

'I'm sorry,' she says tightly. 'I shouldn't have called.'

'Ella, it's not that I don't care. You know I do. But things are so difficult at home right now. Beth's in one of her manic phases, it's impossible to reason with her. She's up all hours of the day and night painting, and ordering thousands of pounds' worth of canvases and who knows what else on my credit cards, which are already maxed out from paying off Ben's student loans. We're up to our ears in debt – it's only the overdraft keeping Sam at school. Then today I find out she's spent a fortune on architect's fees to build a bloody new studio. Some damn contractor was just about to bulldoze the garage as I pulled into the drive.' Wearily, I rub my hand over my face. 'God knows how much she's blown this time. I should have paid more attention to what she was up to, but things have been so insane at work with the takeover bid I lost track.'

She looks up, alert. I wish Beth showed half as much interest. 'James Noble?'

'Bastard. I didn't build up my company from scratch so some eviscerating card sharp could march in and take it over when he felt like it.'

Ella unbuckles her seatbelt and moves into my lap, her hand reaching between my legs. I kiss her, hard. She smells sweaty and slightly stale from the plane; bizarrely, it turns me on. My palm slides up her calf. I want to fuck her, right here in the middle of the car park. Anyone could see. Eight years and it's still as exciting as the first—

Suddenly she goes rigid in my arms and pulls away, grabbing the door handle. I try to catch her, but she yanks her hand free.

'Ella, what is it?' *God damn it, what now?* 'Ella!'

A blast of cold air puts a brake on my ardour, and my dick shrivels to Squirrel Nutkin proportions. Ella sits on the edge of her seat and sticks her head between her knees, breathing in short little pants as if she's about to give birth. Her face looks green in the dim interior light. Fuck, I hope she isn't going to puke everywhere.

I wonder if I should get her out into the fresh air, or drive her somewhere for coffee. Maybe it's something she ate on the plane. Sometimes I wonder if having two women in my life doesn't just mean twice the bloody hormones.

Clearly a fuck is now out of the question!

'Let's go back to my place,' Ella breathes.

I don't need asking twice.

The workings of a woman's mind are mystery understood only by God. The working of her body, on the other hand . . .

'Shit, that was good,' I pant, two hot and sweaty hours later.

'You have *no* idea,' Ella agrees.

She swings her long legs out of bed. Beautiful arse. Great tits, too. No breastfeeding, of course.

'Sorry about earlier,' she says ruefully, twisting her wild Pre-Raphaelite hair into a knot and starting the shower. 'I guess this whole grief thing is a bit more complicated than I thought. Staying at his childhood home freaked me out.' She shivers. 'Too many ghosts.'

I'd noticed there are no photos of Jackson anywhere in the flat; no sign a man has ever even lived here, apart from the state-of-the-art sound system and forty-two-inch flat-panel plasma TV. No bike in the hall, no jacket on the banister. No tacky fishing trophies on the wall, or car magazines on the coffee table. It's as if he never existed. I wonder what she's done with it all.

In the morning, Ella's up before I am, brewing coffee in the kitchen. She hands me a mug with a smile; her old self again, I'm relieved to note. 'Got to run, William, sorry. Mother at twenty-six weeks with pre-eclampsia has just been admitted, and it looks like we're going to have to deliver the baby.' She grabs her keys from the fruit bowl. 'Just let the door slam behind you when you leave.'

'You free this weekend?'

'Sorry. Double shifts for the next week, payback for the time I took off. But I'm around next Friday, if that works for you.'

Bugger. I've already told Beth I have to be in London on Saturday. If I cancel now, she'll drag me along to that bloody school fête of Cate's.

'I don't suppose,' Carolyn says shyly to me later that morning, 'you're going to be in town this weekend? Only a friend of mine is in this band – they're doing rather well, actually – and he's thinking of going solo, but I thought he should talk to you first. He's coming down from Manchester on Saturday. I was wondering if you'd have time for a quick drink with us. If you're in London, of course. I wouldn't want you to come up specially.'

I don't look up. The latest quarterly accounts make worrying reading. Malinche Lyon, my star signing, and Equinox Hotels are the only accounts making any real money. That bastard Noble. He's poached two of my best rainmakers this past few months; no wonder the company's suffering.

'Which band?' I ask absently.

'WdLuv2Meet. I don't know if—'

Suddenly she's got my full attention. 'Who's your friend?'

'Davy Kirkland. We were at school together . . .'

You've got to be kidding me. Cate's bedroom wall is plastered with posters of the kid. Cross Robbie Williams with Brad Pitt, throw in a dash of the young Paul McCartney, and you've got Davy Kirkland. The group isn't bad, as boy bands go, but the other three lads are nothing special; they're holding Kirkland back. He's headed for the stratosphere once he breaks free.

Thank you, God.

I could kiss Carolyn. The little star has all but got Kirkland in the bag. I'll have to take her out somewhere really hot this time to celebrate.

Let's face it, I needed a bit of good news after the shitstorm that went down at the weekend. What *possessed* Beth to strip off and streak across the fucking playing fields, for God's sake?

Cate's been a bloody hermit ever since, holing up in her room; can't say I blame her. Obviously she's not speaking to her mother, who's treating the whole thing like some kind of joke. Thank God it's the Easter holidays. With any luck, the fuss will have died down by the time she goes back to school. Sometimes, I could bloody murder Beth.

I let myself into the apartment block, taking the stairs two at a time. I'm surprised to find my flat in darkness when I unlock the front door. Strange. Ella said she'd be here by seven-thirty, and it's gone eight—

'Christ Almighty, Ella! What are you doing sitting in the dark! Are you trying to give me a bloody heart attack?'

She winces. Shit. Not the best thing to say, in the circumstances.

'Sorry I'm late. Meeting ran over.' I throw my jacket over the back of a chair, and pour myself a Scotch. 'Let me jump in the shower, and I'll be right out—

I pause. Ella's sitting unnaturally upright on the sofa, hands in her lap, spiky lovat-green boots pressed neatly together as if she's having tea with the Queen. She hasn't taken off her jacket. I switch on the lamp, and suddenly see the gauze taped to her right temple. 'Ella! What in hell happened?'

She ducks away from me. For the first time, I register the chill in her expression.

'Ella, sweetheart, is everything OK?'

'I was rather hoping you'd tell me.'

'Sorry. I don't get it.'

'Prescient of you,' Ella says drily. She holds up a lacy black corset, and waits. I realize I'm supposed to say something, but I haven't a clue what.

Ella sighs with exaggerated patience. 'This isn't mine, William. I found it down the back of the sofa.'

'Whose is it?'

'Ah. Straight to the heart of the matter.'

'It's probably Beth's—'

'Come on, William. We both know it's not your wife's.'

'Well, it's not mine,' I say tersely. 'Who knows how long it's been there? Ben stayed here last month; one of his girlfriends probably left it behind. I still don't—'

'The thing is, William,' Ella says pleasantly, 'it's the lying I've always hated most. Having to lie to Jackson about where I was and who I was with. You lying to Beth every time you see me. Lying to my friends by omission – there's a whole side of my life most people know nothing about, and that makes me a fraud. But I've come to terms with all of that, because I always thought that at least we never had to lie to each other.'

The penny finally drops.

'Wait. Are you asking – Ella, do you think there's *someone else*?'

She smiles. 'I know. Ironic, isn't it?'

'No, it's bloody ridiculous!' I explode. 'Of course there isn't!'

'Why "of course"? We never said this was an exclusive arrangement.'

'Because I never thought it needed to be said! Do you think I've got some sort of revolving-door policy at this flat? A different girl every night of the week? What sort of man do you think I am?'

'The sort who cheats on his wife,' she says coolly.

I'm taken aback. Doesn't she know what this – what *she* – means to me? How can she think there'd be anyone else?

'Oh, don't look so shocked. I'm no better, am I?' she laughs. 'Come on, William. We're not Romeo and Juliet. We've always known what this is about, haven't we? If you've met someone else—'

'I bloody haven't, Ella!'

'Look, you're free to see who you please. I'd just—'

An unpleasant thought surfaces. 'Ella, are you trying to tell me something?'

She smiles sweetly. 'Such as what, William?'

'Are you – have you – is there . . .'

'Would you mind?'

Mind? Of course I'd bloody mind! I never much liked the thought of her in bed with Jackson, but I could hardly tell her not to grant her own husband his conjugals. The thought of her fucking someone else makes me want to reach down the bastard's throat and choke him on his own balls.

'As you said, we're free agents,' I say stiffly.

'Absolutely.'

'So *you* wouldn't be jealous if there were someone else, then?'

She meets my gaze head-on. 'Not at all.'

'Fine, then.'

'Yes, fine.'

I knock back my Scotch. 'So, just out of curiosity. Have you slept with someone else?'

'No one important.'

I nearly choke on my drink. I didn't bloody expect her to say yes!

I want to slam my fist into the wall. I force a casual smile. 'And are you still—'

'It was a one-off.'

I get up and pour myself another drink. My hand shakes with suppressed fury. I have no idea what to do with this information. Jealousy eats at me like acid. Now Jackson's gone, they'll be swarming like bees to a honeypot. Christ. Christ! And I just have to sit and take it. It's not like I can offer her anything permanent. I can't leave Beth. I wouldn't want to. Obviously.

The irony is that Ella's the only woman I've slept with in more than eight years. Unlike most adulterers, I really *don't* have sex with my wife.

She curls her feet under her on the sofa. 'So,' she says conversationally, 'whose underwear is this, then, William? I'm sure she'll want it back. It's so annoying when you lose half a matching set.'

'I've told you, I've no—'

Oh, shit.

'William?'

I pick up the ridiculous Spongebob backpack from behind the sofa. I'd recognize it anywhere. Somehow she's got a key to the flat and come up here behind my back and – with that fucking hippy bastard – prancing around in black underwear – I'll kill him, *I'll rip his fucking throat out*—

'Cate,' says Ella.

I hammer on my daughter's bedroom door. 'Cate! Phone!'

She doesn't respond. Hesitating briefly, I try the door-knob. Locked.

'Cate!' I thump the door again. 'It's Paris! Are you coming out to take it or shall I—'

The door opens.

'There's no need to shout,' Cate says primly.

She snatches the phone and waits. I get the hint. 'Send Fleur's parents my best.'

The door slams in my face. Charming. I pay twenty grand a year for these manners.

I stomp back downstairs, nearly tripping over the dog, and wonder what the hell my daughter's up to now. That friend of hers has always been trouble. She and Cate palled up when Fleur's father was posted to the French Embassy in London and she went to Cate's school for a couple of years. Cate was devastated when the family moved back to Paris last summer, though I'll admit I was rather relieved. A bad influence, Fleur. Too clever by half. And she has a disconcerting way of looking at you: altogether too knowing for a seventeen-year-old.

Reminds me of Ella, in a way. Must be the French influence.

I pull a couple of T-bones out of the fridge, setting them out of Cannelle's reach, and put a bottle of white in to chill. Beth's got her art class tonight, Ben's staying with his posh Oxford totty and Sam's on a school trip, so it's just Cate and me. Thank God she grew out of the vegan phase. There are only so many things you can think of to do with tofu that are strictly legal.

Maybe tonight would be a good time to have our father–daughter chat. I can't put it off any longer. It's already been a week, and I still haven't tackled her about the bloody corset – Beth said she'd deal with it, but Cate's my daughter too. I don't want things going on in her life I know nothing about. I want her to feel she can tell me anything.

Even if it's the last thing I want to hear.

The back door slams open and Beth whirls into the

kitchen on a gust of cold air. She looks pink and flushed, as if she's been running.

'Oh! William! You're home already. I'm not stopping, just needed to get a few bits, then I'm going back for the life class – I did tell you I'd be out tonight, didn't I?'

I nod briefly.

'You don't mind, do you, darling? I don't have to go, of course, but they don't like us to miss classes and I did promise—'

'Of course I don't mind,' I say irritably. 'I told you, I think it's good for you to get out a bit.' I stop tenderizing the steaks, throwing her a suspicious glance. She looks rather excited. 'You are taking your pills, aren't you, Beth? We don't want another repeat of—'

'Yes, yes, all right.'

I reach for the pepper. Beth hovers by the Aga, fiddling nervously with her charm bracelet. Changed her mind about going, no doubt. I can probably stretch the steaks to three.

'William,' she blurts suddenly, 'I invited your mother down for lunch on Sunday.'

My hand stills.

'It's Easter Sunday, William, and she's eighty on Tuesday. You can't let this silly row go on for ever. I mean, twenty *years*. I thought now was as good a time as any to let bygones be bygones, and since Ben and Sam will be home tomorrow too—'

'You – did – *what*?'

' – and I knew you'd just say no if I asked,' she gabbles. 'Come on, darling. I know you don't get on with her, but my mother isn't all sweetness and light either, and I manage to—'

'It's hardly the same thing!'

'Yes, but I understand how you—'

'Your mother didn't kill your father!'

Beth flinches, but stands her ground. 'Nor did yours, William.'

'You weren't there,' I grind out.

'She's your mother, William,' Beth says staunchly.

There are times when I actually hate my wife. 'Cancel.'

'I can't, it'd be too—'

'I said, *cancel.*'

'Please, William. If something happens to her and you still haven't—'

'Aren't you going to be late for your class?' I ask coldly.

She opens her mouth to say something, then thinks better of it. I turn my back, my hands gripping the Aga rail so hard my knuckles turn white, and moments later hear the soft click of the back door.

Twenty years, and I can still smell the metallic stench of fresh blood.

It happened just a few months before I met Beth. (No doubt the trick-cyclists would make something of that, but cod psychology didn't get her pregnant, I did.) Dad had been out of work for three years by then, one of the victims of Thatcher's victory over the miners' unions. He was a small-town Nottinghamshire solicitor who'd made a modest living from writing wills and settling minor local disputes; when the miners had nothing left to leave or fight over, the firm he'd built up over nearly forty years collapsed almost overnight.

It destroyed him. He aged about twenty years in the space of a week. As far as he was concerned, his life was over; without purpose or hope.

For three years, he sat in his favourite armchair and just

stared into the distance. I got used to having one-sided conversations; very useful, as it's turned out.

My mother (whose estate agency went from strength to strength as the buy-to-let market took off) taunted him daily with his failure, demeaning him at every opportunity. Useless. Hopeless. Worthless. Wish I'd never married you. Always knew you wouldn't amount to anything. He said she wouldn't let up. *She wouldn't bloody let up.*

I knew as soon as he called the morning of his sixty-fifth birthday that this was goodbye. I knew; and I couldn't do a bloody thing about it.

When he told me he loved me and put down the phone, I got in the car and drove like the hounds of hell were behind me. I only lived ten minutes away back then. I was nearly in time. I nearly made it.

I heard the gunshot as I pulled into the drive.

You have no idea how much blood and brains a human head contains until you see your father's splashed over the floor, and walls, and ceiling, and doors, and windows, of your family home.

'Dad? Are you going to cook those steaks or shall I give them to Cannelle?'

I jump and stare uneasily at the pulped and bloody flesh in my hands. 'Changed my mind. D'you fancy Chinese?'

Cate shrugs.

'Find me the takeaway menu, and I'll call them. You can give these to the dog, but don't tell your mother. What did Fleur want?'

'Nothing special.'

She lurks in the doorway, twisting the rope bracelet on her wrist, her mother's *doppelgänger*. 'Dad, can I talk to you about something without you flipping out?'

Dear God, she's pregnant.

'I'm not pregnant, Dad, if that's what you're thinking,' Cate snaps. 'This is serious.'

'Fine. I'm listening.'

'The thing is, Dad, I need to get my applications in for uni soon, and we still haven't had a chance to—'

'Have you decided what you fancy? I thought I'd go with the hot-and-sour soup, and then maybe a beef chow mein—'

She snatches the menu out of my hand. 'Dad, why do you always do this?' she cries. 'Every time I try to talk to you about it, you pretend it's not going to happen! I'm not twelve any more!'

'I know that,' I sigh.

'Look, Dad,' she pleads. 'I don't want to keep fighting you, but you're not giving me any choice. Sometimes it feels like I can't breathe around here. You've got to give me some space.'

I pull out a kitchen chair and sink heavily into it. 'OK, Cate. Let's talk.'

'I want to study journalism,' she says firmly.

'But you're so good at science! What happened to being a doctor?'

'I wanted to be a doctor when I was, like, seven, Dad.'

'OK. But a science degree would be so much more useful—'

'Dad, I want to be a journalist.'

I note the set of her jaw, the resolute squaring of her shoulders, and realize who she reminds me of. I had the same battle with my mother a few years before Dad died, when I refused to join her property business and insisted on a 'useless' history degree.

'Journalism it is,' I say brightly. 'I don't know which colleges are best for that, but we can easily find out—'

'Not Oxford, Dad. And not Cambridge, either,' she adds quickly.

'I see. Well, at least if you're in London we'll still see plenty of you—'

'I want to go to NYU.'

'NYU? But that's in New York.'

'No shit, Sherlock,' Cate mutters. 'Dad, it's the best in the world for journalism. I probably won't get in, but I really want to try. I've got quite a good portfolio from editing the school paper, and those local stories I wrote, and if I can get some serious work experience this summer, like at the *Mail* or something, I might—'

'New York! No, Cate. Out of the question, I'm afraid.'

'But you'd have let Ben!'

'That would've been different.'

'Why?'

'Ben can look after himself. It's girls who get attacked and raped, or murdered. It might not be fair, but that's the way it is. The answer's no, Cate.'

'I'll be eighteen soon, Dad! You can't stop me—'

'True. But since I'm the one paying for your education, I do still have some say in the matter. And I say no to New York. There are plenty of good universities in this country. You don't need to go halfway across the world—'

'Has it ever occurred to you I might *want* to go halfway across the world?' Cate cries. 'I hate it here! I'm fed up with looking after Mum! Every day I come home and wonder if she's going to be running naked round the garden cos she hasn't taken her pills! I'm too embarrassed to bring my friends home, I never go anywhere, and you're never here!

Everyone depends on me! I'm always the one left to handle everything, and I'm sick of it!'

'It's not your mother's fault—'

'It's not mine either!'

I sigh. 'I know, sweetheart. And I'm sorry. If I could do anything about it—'

'You could come home a bit more often! Why do you think she acts this way? It's not just the illness. She's lonely! You're never here for her!' She takes a breath. 'You think because you haven't actually left her, that's enough. Don't you get it, Dad? She *loves* you. She knows you don't love her back. No wonder she goes a little mad sometimes.'

'Cate, that's not true—'

'Does she know you're screwing Sam's doctor?'

I stare at her, ashen-faced.

'I saw you,' she accuses tearfully. 'A couple of weeks ago. In the car park by the station. You were kissing her—'

'Oh, Jesus.' I get up and go to her, but she shrugs me off. 'Cate, I am *so* sorry, I never meant for you—'

'Oh, forget it, Dad.' She knuckles her eyes, looking nearer seven than seventeen. 'I don't really blame you, I guess. I mean, Mum's not exactly easy to live with, is she? But you're the one who married her, not me. It's not fair if I've got to pick up the pieces when you leave.'

'I'm not going to leave, Cate. I promise.'

'You're not that good at keeping promises, Dad,' she sniffs.

I wince.

'Daddy, *please*. I really want to go to NYU. It's not just about getting away from all this. I'd come back every holidays, you know I would—'

'Is that your price, Caitlin?' I say sharply. 'I let you go to New York, or you'll tell your mother about Ella?'

She gasps, as if I've punched her in the stomach.

'Cate, look, I didn't mean—'

'I'm going to New York, Dad. I don't care if you support me or not. You can't stop me.' Her expression is suddenly hard. 'Just because you screwed up your life, doesn't mean I have to waste mine. You only married Mum so you could fix her and make up for what happened to Grandpa. Well, fine. Just don't expect me to hang around any more and share suicide watch with you!'

Her feet thunder up the stairs. Moments later, her bedroom door slams.

She knows about Ella. How in hell did that happen? After all this time. We've always been so careful.

She's still only a child. How can I possibly let her go off to New York? Who'd be there to look out for her if I wasn't?

Atoning for Dad? Is that what I've been doing all these years?

I'm still standing shell-shocked in the kitchen when Ben saunters in ten minutes later, munching a wedge of pizza. 'Just saw Cate storming off down the road,' my son mumbles through a mouthful of melted cheese. 'You two have a row?' He slings his backpack on the table. 'Leave her to it, Dad. She'll get over it.'

'She wants to go to New York next year,' I manage. 'To study journalism.'

'Oh, she finally told you?' Ben says. 'Good for her.'

'You knew?'

'Course. Don't sweat it, Dad. She'll be fine. She's tougher than you think.'

'Doesn't seem much I can do about it, either way. Looks like she's made up her mind.' I put the kettle on the hob. 'What are you doing home tonight, anyway? We weren't expecting you back till tomorrow.'

'Candida bailed. Her parents are taking her to Aspen. Figured I might as well come home. Not a problem, is it?'

'Frankly, Ben, I couldn't be happier to see you. I could do with a bit of testosterone round here. If you want, we could – shit, sorry. I really need to take that call.'

Ben raises a hand and ambles cheerfully towards the stairs as I flip open my mobile. If only Cate was as even-tempered as my oldest son. Mind you, that probably has more to do with the spiky plants at the end of the garden than any natural Pollyanna temperament.

'Hi, Andrew. What's up?'

My lawyer gets straight to the point. 'You lost Kirkland. Noble just signed him up; it's all over the wires.'

'Shit! I thought we had that one in the bag!' I close my eyes in despair. 'How the hell did Noble find out? Davy said he wasn't talking to anyone else; this was to be kept strictly under wraps till he told the rest of his band he was leaving.'

'Well, someone leaked. Noble's representing him for half his usual percentage. And it gets worse.'

'How much worse?'

'Looks like he's been putting out feelers to Equinox. I don't have to tell you how hard that'll hit your bottom line. God knows how he discovered their contract is up for renewal, but if I were you I'd get myself on a plane to New York ASAP and turn this around before it's too late.'

My gut spasms. If I lose the international hotel group, I might as well give up and go home.

'Listen, William,' Andrew says cautiously. 'I'm not making any wild accusations, but if I were you, I'd review your internal security. This is the fourth time in the last two months that sensitive information has reached Noble before it's become public knowledge. It's really beginning to hurt you.'

'Plain English, Andrew.'

'Someone very close to you is screwing you over.'

After he rings off, I go into my study and pour myself a neat Scotch. It's not Carolyn; apart from the fact that she was the one who brought Davy Kirkland to me in the first place, she didn't know anything about the Equinox contract. The only person other than me to work on that account is Harry Armitage, and he's been hiking in New Zealand for the last three weeks. He's out of the loop on Kirkland, which rules him out too.

I knock back my drink. There are only two people who knew about both those deals.

Beth. And Ella.

7

Beth

No more pills. No more pills!

Except I promised William.

I hate them. Oh God, how I *hate* taking them. I can't paint, I can't think, I can't feel. It's like a fog envelops my brain. I fumble for the right word, forget friends' faces, pick up a corkscrew and can't remember how to use it. Someone will tell me their mother's just died, and I'll stare at them in puzzlement, like an autistic child, not even knowing what my response should be. It's like I'm trapped in a glass bubble: nothing can get in, and I can't get out.

I unclench my fist. The pretty, brightly coloured drugs in my palm iron out the highs and lows and save me from the worst depression – but, oh, the price! No sadness, but no happiness either. No misery, and no joy. Who wants to experience a life without love, grief, fear, ecstasy? That's not living, it's existing.

I tip them into the sink and turn on the waste disposal.

In the end, I'll have to take them again, or I'll get so

manic they'll lock me up. But while I have this window where I am truly *me*, this brief interval between stupor and madness, I'm going to make the most of it.

Dress like *you*, Eithne said when I asked her what to wear today. They're coming to the gallery to look at your art, not your shoes.

How can I dress like me when I don't know who I am? I've never had a chance to find out. Clara's daughter, William's wife, the children's mother – all my life I've been defined in terms of my relationships to other people. What would Beth Ashfield, brilliant new about-to-be-discovered artist, wear to the most critical meeting of her life?

Not this shapeless turquoise suit, chosen by her mother for her sister's wedding, nor the shoes her husband picked out because he liked the high heels (never mind that they pinched her toes unmercifully). Certainly not the foul feathered hat. It looks like a pheasant died on my head. I snatch it off, and send it spinning across the unmade bed.

But the necklace? Yes. She'd wear the sea-glass and platinum necklace. She'd appreciate the irony: broken pieces of glass no one wanted, reclaimed from the sea, placed in an expensive setting and passed off as a work of art.

Well, never mind what Beth-the-Artist would choose, I think crossly as I shoulder my ugly old handbag and double lock the front door. It's this suit or my usual uniform of baggy T-shirt and supermarket jeans.

By the time I emerge from Green Park tube station ninety minutes later, I remember why I pensioned off the outfit after one wearing. The cheap skirt rides up over my flabby tummy, while the sloppy jacket constantly slides off one shoulder or the other. And it *itches*.

A splatter of rain hits my face. I glance up and another

fat raindrop slugs me in the eye. Oh, dear, that's all I need. I'm going to look like a bedraggled tropical parakeet by the time I get to—

Suddenly, I'm careening into the newspaper stand. Dozens of glossy magazines slide on to the wet pavement as I tumble across the plywood counter. Flushing scarlet, I apologize profusely to the startled vendor, wondering what on earth I tripped over.

Then I try to take a step, and realize: my heel has snapped.

No need to panic. I don't have to be at Cork Street for an hour – thank heavens I allowed myself plenty of time. Shoes. Shoes. Where to buy a new pair of—

William's flat! Bayswater is less than five minutes away by cab; I've left several pairs there from trips to the theatre and whatnot. Silly to buy new if I don't have to. The black courts will be perfect, and a lot more comfy too, which is what really matters. I've never understood the way some women get obsessed with what they put on their feet. Long as they get me from A to B with a minimum of blisters.

First, though, I call ahead on my mobile. I've learned the hard way: surprises aren't good for any marriage.

But the answer-machine picks up, which means William's at work; I leave a message, just in case, and jump into a taxi. The black flatties are exactly where I thought they'd be, and my feet thank me for them as I plonk on the sofa and slip them on.

I check my reflection in the mirror. A bit crumpled, but that just adds to the artist thing, doesn't it? Five-past three. My meeting with Eithne and the gallery owners isn't till three-thirty. It's only round the corner. Lots of time.

Goodness, I'm nervous. Eithne said they liked the canvases she took up to London, but liking isn't loving. Liking isn't agreeing to finance and organize a show. I know an artist has to be commercial these days. Marketable. I'm not a glamorous rebel like Eithne, all piercings and pink hair and headlining attitude. I'm just a fat, middle-aged house-wife, more suburban than urban rebel. If you ran me over in the street, you probably wouldn't notice.

Sighing, I pick up my keys, open the front door and let out a blood-curdling scream when I see Dan standing there.

'It's all right,' I tell the young lady who's very kindly (and rather bravely) run out from the flat next door to see who's being murdered, 'I know him. I didn't mean to cause a panic; he made me jump, that's all.'

'Someone was leaving the building as I arrived,' Dan apologizes. 'They let me in, so I didn't buzz up first.'

He saunters past me into the flat before I have a chance to gather my addled wits. I can understand what my daughter sees in him. He really *is* dishy: his eyes have that lovely blue David Essex twinkle, I remember I had *such* a crush on him when I was Cate's age – David Essex, obvi-ously, not Dan—

'Cate's not here,' I blurt.

'I know that,' Dan says. 'I came to see you.'

My heart beats faster. It's just the fright.

'How did you know where I was?'

'I – followed you,' he admits.

'You *followed* me?'

'I thought I was going to lose you when you hopped in that cab,' he adds unrepentantly. 'And I do mean hopped. What happened to your shoe?'

'Never mind my shoe! Why are you following me?'

'I've told you. I wanted to see you.'

'You can't.'

'And yet here I am.'

He folds his arms and watches me put on the kettle and hunt about for teabags and sugar (tea: first refuge of the discombobulated). He smells of smoke and trouble. I try not to think about how good his kiss tasted last Saturday: cool and sweet like home-made lemonade. I'm not manic at the moment; I'm very definitely in my right mind. There'll be no stripping off and streaking down Marble Arch this afternoon. Absolutely no kissing of daughters' boyfriends, no matter how close they stand or how delicious they smell, even if they run their fingers down my spine in a way that makes my insides turn to liquid and my heart beat faster than a – a – than a—

'Dan, stop,' I gasp.

It's so long since anyone just *touched* me. The children all think they're too old, even Sam, you know how they get once they go to school; and when William and I stopped having sex, the cuddles and hugs stopped too. I can't remember the last time he even held my hand.

Dan's lips feather the nape of my neck. 'Don't you like it?'

'No – yes – that's not the point!'

His erection presses the small of my back. An answering pulse beats unexpectedly between my legs. The long-forgotten sensation makes me giddy, and without really knowing what I'm doing, I'm spinning willingly in his arms, pulling him closer, fitting my body to his. His mouth meets mine, his kiss ripping along my nerve endings, jolting my body awake.

It takes every ounce of willpower to break away.

I clutch the sink. This is insane. It can't happen. We can't possibly do this. He's half my age. I'm married. He's my daughter's boyfriend—

'Oh, my God! Cate!'

'This has nothing to do with her. I'm very fond of her, of course, but it's always been about you, Beth, from the first moment at Eithne Brompton's show, I should never have—'

'No! Outside! It's Cate!'

'*What?*'

'Look! I'd know that silly backpack anywhere. She must be coming here! Oh, God, she mustn't find us together! Go, go!'

'I can't. She'll see me.'

'You'll have to hide! Quick, the bedroom!'

'Beth, this is ridiculous—'

'You followed me here, Dan! How do you plan to explain that? Or do you want to tell her we'd arranged a secret rendezvous?'

I fling open the bedroom wardrobe. It's crammed not just with clothes, but with boxes of files and papers, the work William brings home. I panic. Cate hasn't spoken to me all week (and now that the mania has passed, how can I blame her? If my mother had done that to me, I'd never forgive her either).

If she finds me here with her boyfriend, she'll never speak to me again, no matter how innocent the explanation. Although frankly I'm hard pushed even to think of one that doesn't sound very damning indeed.

'Under the bed!' I cry, shoving Dan's head down.

Still protesting, he nevertheless slides beneath the bed.

I thank God we have an old-fashioned brass bed in the Bayswater flat, rather than an expensive modern divan like we have at home. You couldn't hide a piece of paper under that, never mind a young man in a, well, rather *obvious* state of arousal.

Keys rattle in the front door. Dan sticks his head back out. 'Beth, I really don't—'

I throw myself flat on my stomach, wriggle under the bed and clamp my hand over his mouth.

Cate's voice echoes down the hall. 'Hi, it's only me.'

I feel sick. It's too late. She's seen us. Oh, how am I ever going to—

Dan shakes his head, and prises my fingers loose. 'Phone,' he mouths.

He's right. I squirm further under the bed, out of sight.

'Well, I did it, Fleur, I went to see her – no, for real, I swear—'

Dan smooths his hand along my hip, snaking beneath my blouse. At a time like this!

' – you'll never *believe* what happened,' Cate says. 'It was total drama! I'm in the middle of telling her – oh, really nice, actually, and she was wearing these really cute boots, all swirly orangey purply colours – anyway, so we're talking, and suddenly she goes all weird and—'

I hear her moving about the flat. What on earth is she doing here, anyway? I didn't even know she had a key to the apartment.

Dan nudges me. I twist round, and he dangles a lacy black basque an inch or two above my face with a grin.

'It's not mine!' I hiss indignantly.

He puts a finger to his lips, as Cate's chatter stills.

'Hang on,' she says, 'thought I heard something.'

I daren't breathe. Through the gap between the edge of the coverlet and the floor, I see her silver trainers return to the bedroom. Oh, God, if she finds us now – I shouldn't have panicked, after all, there is a perfectly innocent – well, not innocent exactly, but nothing *happened*—

'No, must have been next door. Look, I'd better get going. I only came here to nick some cash from Dad's desk, he'll never miss it. I'm supposed to meet Dan at the Tate in an hour—'

Dust is getting up my nose, and I suddenly feel the urge to sneeze. I cover my face with my hands, as Dan shakes with suppressed laughter. How can he find this funny? Doesn't he care about Cate at all?

In a sudden moment of clarity, I realize that whatever *Graduate*-style nonsense is going on between us, I'm no Mrs Robinson. No matter how much I'm attracted to Dan, even if I could bring myself to betray William, I could never hurt my daughter.

' – I haven't asked her yet. She'll only say no, like she always does. I hate her, Fleur. She's such a hypocrite. She bangs on about what's good for me, she's only thinking of me, blah blah blah, then she goes out and, like, ruins my entire life. I can't wait to get away from her—'

The front door slams. Dan prods me, but I don't move.

You don't expect gratitude from teenagers. They're supposed to hate you; if they don't, you're not doing your job.

How much easier it would be to be a bad parent and say yes. Yes, you can pierce your navel, have a cigarette, stay out till two a.m. on a school night, sleep with your boyfriend at fifteen. But you say no, and deal with the

Tess Stimson

tantrums and 'I hate you!' because you love them and want to protect them. You want to save them from the mistakes you made.

Of course I haven't always got it right. Children don't come with instructions. You muddle your way through in a mixture of trial and error. All right, lots of error, in my case. But I always thought, until now, I was doing all right. I made their packed lunches and ironed their school uniforms and read them stories and stayed up all night when they had earache. I took them to ballet and football, cooked nourishing meals and picked up wet towels. I've never been a jam-tarts-and-finger-painting kind of mother, but I've always been there when they got home from school, and I never missed a sports day or school play, even when I wanted to curl up in a ball under the duvet and never come out.

The irony is, before I actually had babies, I wanted to be a mother *so* much. No one ever tells you how dull and repetitive it is (although to be fair to Clara, she did try. I just thought she meant mothering *me*). But I did everything I was supposed to. I did the best I could.

To learn from my own daughter that I've comprehensively failed in the most important job of my life is almost too painful to bear.

'Come on, Beth. She's gone.'

I crawl out from under the bed, brushing dust from my clothes. Dan looks shame-facedly pleased with himself, a little boy nearly caught scrumping. I'm horribly ashamed of the whole farcical episode.

'So,' he smiles, twirling the corset around one finger, 'want to tell me about this?'

'I told you, it's not mine—'

We both suddenly realize what that means. I snatch it away from him and shove it out of sight down the side of the sofa.

Set against the conversation I've just overheard, the fact that I have cast-iron proof of my husband's affair seems almost irrelevant.

'I'm sorry, Eithne,' I say, 'please don't shout at me any more. I didn't mean to let you down. I wanted to be there. I did *try*. I know you went to a lot of trouble to arrange it for me, and it was terribly sweet of you, but I think we both know I'm not really cut out to be an artist. I never have been. I've got a little bit of a knack with a paintbrush sometimes, but that's all it is. Clara's right, I was getting above myself, thinking I could have a show and actually sell my paintings. I'm just a housewife, at the end of the day. This isn't one of those lovely Cinderella films where the dull little mouse suddenly turns out to be an amazingly talented genius and gets discovered. This is real life, and the truth is, I'm not a star, and never will be. It was silly to think I could be anything else. I *am* sorry, Eithne. Now can we please forget all about shows and paintings and just be friends?'

There's nothing very unusual about William not coming home all night. He often stays in London when he has to entertain clients in the evening, and I know he's very keen to get that young lad from the boy band signed to Ashfield PR.

But this time, it's different. This time, I know he's not

with his lawyer, or some teen pop star, but the owner of that very glamorous black corset.

I stare at the ceiling. It's one thing to suppose, in theory, that your husband may have had the odd fling here and there. After all, eight years is a long time to expect a normal red-blooded man to go without sex. There must have been – perhaps on trips abroad – and of course there was that upsetting business in Cyprus, though I never had any actual *proof*—

There was that pretty English teacher, who seemed strangely keen to discuss Ben's progress at school in her own time. And I've always wondered about that striking Titian-haired doctor who helped look after Sam when he was little. William talked about her endlessly, and then very suddenly never mentioned her again. There were others before that: secretaries, PAs, assistants who came and went over the years. All rather lovely girls, who looked at William adoringly and blushed whenever he walked past and then, after a while, abruptly left without working their notice. Little Carolyn worships the ground he walks on. It'd be impossible not to suspect that there must have been, at times, something with one or two of them.

But knowing is very different from suspecting. Knowing keeps you up all night, and leaves you no place to hide.

'You've only yourself to blame,' Clara says sharply, when she turns up (uninvited) for breakfast the next morning and prises it out of me. 'You've driven him to it with your selfishness and moods. Why the poor man stays with you I have no idea. The fellow's a saint.'

I put the kettle on the hotplate.

'Of course, he'd never have married you in the first place if you hadn't got yourself caught. You're lucky he's not a bolter. Not like your father. When I think of what I put up with from that man, and look how he repaid me.'

'Toast?'

'You're just like him, you know. Weak. I could tell as soon as you were born. You were a difficult, fretful baby. The doctors said it was just colic, but I knew.'

'There's some home-made marmalade from the tea shop in town,' I say brightly, 'so much better than the supermarket stuff. Lovely big pieces of peel.'

'I hope you're taking your pills, Beth. Poor Cate. She'll never forgive you, you know.'

Carefully, I put down the breadknife.

Then I go outside, walk quietly to the orchard at the end of the garden, and smash flowerpots against the low stone wall until I no longer want to murder my mother.

When I've finished, I sweep up the broken shards and spilled potting soil, wrap them in old newspaper and put them neatly in the dustbin. I don't need my mother to remind me how lucky I am to have William. Infidelity is no reason to end a marriage. Sex isn't love.

As long as he doesn't actually *leave*. I couldn't let that happen.

I'm not quite the pushover everyone thinks. I can fight for what I want, in my own way. I got William, didn't I? Any niggling doubt I might have felt about that was wiped out the instant Ben was placed in his arms and I saw the love light up his face. I knew then I'd been right: we were meant to be a family.

I'm not so proud of what I did when he was in Cyprus. But I had no choice. I thought he was going to run out on me – silly, really. Still. It all worked out in the end.

The thing is, I know William better than anyone. I know he needs me just as much as I need him.

When he finally comes home a little before six in the evening, I can tell immediately from the careful way he shuts the front door that he's in a towering rage. No one knows his moods like I do.

He storms into the kitchen and flings something on the table.

'You know what this is?' he demands.

Fortunately, he doesn't wait for me to answer. 'D'you want to know where I found it?'

I suck air.

'Down the side of the sofa in London!'

He waits, clearly expecting something more than gawping astonishment from me. But until ten seconds ago, I thought the undergarment in question belonged to his mistress. If *he's* asking *me*—

'Whose is it?' I gasp.

He looks at me as if I'm an imbecile. 'Cate's, obviously!'

Cate's? Cate's! Oh, why didn't I think of that?

'You know what this means?' he rants. 'Our daughter is running off up to London and having sex with that bloody gypsy in my bed!'

Cate's!

Cate and Dan.

I'm not jealous. Just concerned, as any mother would be.

'*Our* bed, surely, William?' I ask mildly. 'And they all have rather long hair these days, dear, it doesn't necessarily make him a gypsy—'

'Our daughter's been sneaking off behind our backs, dressing up like a hooker to indulge that hippy's perverted fantasies, and all you can talk about is his *hair*?'

I wonder curiously if he'll actually froth at the mouth.

'She's seventeen, Beth. Seventeen!'

'Yes, darling, I know, I was there the night she was born—'

'Who knows what else he's dragging her into – drink, drugs – she'll end up with a criminal record! That'll put paid to Oxford – she'd have made a wonderful doctor – before we know it, she'll be pregnant, stuck on her own in some appalling council flat with kids leaving syringes on the stairs and dealing drugs – that boy's not going to stay around, you can see it in his eyes, shifty, I've thought that from the moment I first—'

'William,' I say firmly, 'please stop pacing. I'll speak to her. Well,' I amend, 'once she starts talking to me again, obviously.'

William growls and retreats to his den. I lift the saucepan off the hotplate, add a knob of butter and mash potatoes for the shepherd's pie.

As a mother, I expected to feel many things when I discovered my daughter had started having sex; but relief wasn't one of them.

'Of course it's not mine,' Cate snaps, when I finally dredge up courage and corner her a few days later.

'Are you quite sure, darling?'

'Get real. Like I'd wear anything that sad.'

'So you haven't been to the Bayswater flat recently?'

Her eyes slide away. 'I told you, not for months.'

Now I know she's lying.

'Cate,' I venture, 'you and Dan, you will be careful, won't you? I'd hate to see you—'

'What? Trapped like you were?'

She doesn't mean it. She's a teenager. She doesn't realize how much it hurts.

'Miss out on chances you could have had,' I say calmly.

Her pretty face twists. 'I'm so sorry to have been such an inconvenience, *Mother*. If I'd known I was depriving the world of the next Picasso, I'd have taken care not to have been born.'

'Cate—'

'Give it up, Mum. We all know how much you wish you'd never had us. Well, don't worry, there's only me left at home now, you've managed to get rid of Sam and Ben. I'll be out of your way soon. Then you'll have Dad all to yourself, just like you've always wanted.'

'That's not—'

'You know, if that corset isn't mine and it's not yours, whose can it be, I wonder?'

I realize with shock that she *wants* me to think it belongs to another woman. She's enjoying this. Does she really hate me that much?

'Caitlin, I've never wished I hadn't had you for a second,' I say with sudden passion. I grip her fiercely by the shoulders. 'I *love* you and your brothers. You've brought more happiness into my life than you can possibly know. Motherhood is much harder than you expect, but I wouldn't undo a second of it. I just wish I'd had a bit more time to find out who *I* was before I took on responsibility for someone else, that's all.'

Cate trembles. With anger, misery or impatience, I don't know.

I let her go, and she immediately puts the width of the

kitchen between us. Much as I want to, I resist the urge to chase after her and hug her like I used to when she was small.

'Cate, you've got your whole life ahead of you,' I say. 'The world's your oyster. Don't be in such a rush. Do all the things I never had time to do,' I add, trying not to sound bitter. 'Follow your dreams. Be a journalist if you want to. Win that Pulitzer – oh, Cate, I'm not blind. I know how much it means to you to go to NYU. If that's what you really want, I'll support you. It's your father you have to convince, not me. But don't think I won't worry about you and miss you every second you're away, because I will.'

Confusion and yearning chase across her pale features. For a second, I almost think I've reached her.

Then the phone rings, and the moment is broken.

'Cate, darling, wait, please wait—'

The door slams. I want to go after her, but realize I'll only chase her further away. She has to come to me.

Miserably, I pick up the phone.

'Beth, it's Anne.'

Oh, Lord. The last person I want to talk to now is William's mother. I never know what to say to her. Her son's refused to speak to her for twenty years; against his wishes, I've maintained sporadic contact, mainly for the sake of the children, but also for Anne, as one mother to another. I just have to think how I'd feel if Ben or Sam were to cut me out of their lives.

Or Cate, of course.

I try to sound welcoming. 'Anne, how are you?'

'Not that good, actually, Beth,' she says briskly. 'I've just come from the doctor.'

'Oh dear, poor you. Is everything OK?'

'Actually,' she says, 'that's what I wanted to talk to you about.'

Fortunately, given the appalling way I let her down last week, Eithne doesn't stay angry with me for long – 'It's lucky I love you,' she sighs, 'or I wouldn't tell you about the three red SOLD stickers currently adorning your paintings; oh, calm down, Beth, I *told* you they were good' – and it's she who gets me to see the funny side of the fiasco with Dan.

'Why *wouldn't* he fancy you?' she demands, tilting her head (green this week, in honour of St Patrick's Day) to one side in that way she has. 'You're the experienced, exciting older woman Cate will grow into one day. No wonder he's smitten. And before you ask, he's the spitting image of William twenty years ago, which explains *your* damp knickers.'

She makes it sound so safe; so *normal*. I cheer up immensely. Every foolish, ever-so-slightly-lovestruck middle-aged woman should have a friend like Eithne.

So when Dan rings my mobile and begs me to model for our life class this evening – 'Please, Beth, it's for my teaching credits, my usual girl ran away with a trapeze artist, no, don't laugh, please, it's *true*' – well, how can I refuse? Frankly, after that depressing conversation with William's mother, I could do with letting my hair down. And if there's a little guilty *frisson*, well, where's the harm? It's not like I'd ever *do* anything.

I go home to change. Well, not quite change – after all,

it's not like I'm going to be wearing clothes – but *tidy up*. Exactly.

I burst into the kitchen feeling rather giddy and light-headed.

'Oh! William! You're home already.' I blush to the roots of my hair. 'I'm not stopping, just needed to get a few bits, then I'm going back for the life class – I did tell you I'd be out tonight, didn't I?'

He gives his steak a grumpy bash with the hammer.

'You don't mind, do you, darling?' I venture. 'I don't have to go, of course, but they don't like us to miss classes and I did promise—'

'Of course I don't mind. I told you, I think it's good for you to get out a bit.' He shoots me a suspicious look. 'You are taking your pills, aren't you, Beth? We don't want another repeat of—'

'Yes, yes, all right,' I say crossly.

I fidget, screwing up my courage to tell him about Anne. Got to tell him, got to, got to. Can't leave it any longer. Maybe, I think in burst of wild optimism, he'll even be pleased, once he's got over the surprise.

The words come out in a rush. 'William, I invited your mother down for lunch on Sunday.'

The blood drains from his face.

Oh, God. Oh, God, this is going to be even worse than I thought.

I gabble nervously. 'It's Easter Sunday, William, and she's eighty on Tuesday. You can't let this silly row go on for ever. I mean, twenty *years*. I thought now was as good a time as any to let bygones be bygones, and since Ben and Sam will be home tomorrow too—'

'You – did – *what*?'

' – and I knew you'd just say no if I asked. Come on, darling. I know you don't get on with her, but my mother isn't all sweetness and light either, and I manage to—'

He looks like he wants to brain me with the tenderizer. 'It's hardly the same thing!'

'Yes, but I understand how you—'

'Your mother didn't kill your father!'

Why is he so pig-headed? I appreciate that he needs to blame someone, but the only person responsible for his father's suicide is his father. No one drives another person to suicide. They choose it despite – to spite – you. I know that better than anyone.

'Nor did yours, William.'

'You weren't there.'

He wasn't there either: a child never knows the reality of its parents' marriage. But of course I can't say that to him. I wouldn't dare.

'She's your mother, William,' I say faintly.

'Cancel.'

There are times I almost hate my husband. 'I can't, it'd be too—'

'I said, *cancel*.'

'Please, William. If something happens to her and you still haven't—'

'Aren't you going to be late for your class?' he snaps.

She has leukaemia! I want to cry. She won't reach her eighty-first birthday and if you don't make it up with her, you'll feel even worse about her than you do about your father!

But I know this isn't a battle I'm going to win. I hoist

my bag on to my shoulder, and quietly let myself back into the night.

'Is it warm enough in here?' Dan asks.

I nod nervously, still strung out by my row with William.

The six students sitting in a semicircle around me are suddenly very busy with their paper and pencils.

Dan hands me a long red silk robe. 'You might want to put this on for now. Easier to slip it off when you're ready.'

I shut myself in the tiny bathroom to change. Oh, Lord. *Why* did I agree to this?

Get a grip, Beth. This is ridiculous. You stripped off happily in front of a thousand people the other weekend. Bit late to come over all shy.

Quickly, before I lose all confidence, I whip off my clothes and fold them into a small, neat pile on the loo, tucking my greying granny knickers out of sight beneath my jeans. Maybe if I pose carefully I can hide the floppiest bits of my tummy. Sort of lose them beneath the chenille throw on the chaise longue. I could squinch my bosoms together with my arms so they don't splay sideways like two fried eggs. And if I tilt my head back, that'll get rid of the double chin—

Oh, for heaven's sake. I'm forty-one, and the mother of three children. Short of turning out all the lights and blindfolding the students, I can't hide it.

I put on the silk robe and mentally gird my (rather cellulity) loins. I don't care what Dan thinks. It's not like he hasn't seen it all before.

I settle myself on the chaise longue in the centre of the

room. At least we're in Dan's private studio, not the huge one at the school. Though I do wish it wasn't *quite* so bright and revealing in here—

'Are you ready, Beth? Can I get you anything?'

I gulp and shake my head.

'OK. Whenever you're ready.'

I untie the belt of my robe, and let it fall from my shoulders. There are no indrawn gasps of horror. No one runs screaming from the room. Six pencils scratch at six easels, and I slowly start to relax. This isn't going to be so bad. It's only one class. I can do this.

'Feel free to chat, everyone,' Dan says, moving between the students. He puts on some music; I recognize it as Davy Kirkland from Cate's endless playing. 'Let's keep this nice and relaxed. Beth, how's your painting coming along? Finished that triptych yet?'

'Last panel's almost done,' I say, pathetically grateful for the distraction.

'Can't wait to see it. Did you try out that ochre pigment I told you about?'

We discuss light, and fresco techniques, and then the conversation moves on to more general topics: books we've read, films we've seen, the new logo he's designed for William's firm. Before I know it, the hour's flown past and Dan's telling the students to put their pencils down. 'You can get dressed, Beth,' he says absently, leaning over a student's shoulder to study his work. 'Make yourself a cup of tea next door if you want. I won't be long.'

I get up and knot my robe, wincing at the pins and needles in my legs. I could do with something hot to drink, actually. I'm rather chilled from sitting still so long without moving.

As I let myself into his flat, my silk belt catches on the door. Twisting round, I try to free it, but succeed only in tangling it further.

'You'll have to step out of it,' Dan calls, 'the fabric's hooked on the hinge.'

Flushing, I shrug out of the robe. Dan frees the snagged belt, then holds it up for me to slip on. His hands linger a fraction too long on my shoulders. My nipples harden automatically. It would be so easy to turn and fold myself in his arms, to give myself up to this – so easy—

But wrong.

I pull away, wrapping the dressing-gown tightly around my body. 'Dan, what are you doing?'

'Yes, Dan,' says my daughter from the doorway, 'what *are* you doing?'

8

Cate

'Mum? I'm going to sleep with Dan tonight – well, lose my virginity actually – and I was wondering if we could talk about it? Like, if you've got any advice or anything? Only I'm a bit nervous, so . . .'

Yeah, right. Not the kind of thing you can say to your mother, is it?

Not that mine's the type you can say anything to; at least, not if you want a clued-up response. We hardly have this great mother–daughter thing going on.

Clem's always complaining that her parents interfere in her life, but at least they *care*. At least they're involved. I'm not sure mine notice I'm there half the time. And when they do, they act like I'm still six years old. Well, Dad does. He thinks he's so on top of things, with his stupid 'Bed at ten on a week night, young lady,' but he's got no idea what's really going on in my life.

At least Mum sort of gets it. Yesterday was cool, actually. I think it's the first time she's ever taken my side against Dad. Maybe, if she talks to him about going to New York, he might come round.

Mind you, that whole thing with the corset. Like, what was *that* about?

Weird. Fleur reckons Mum's having this secret lesbian fling with Eithne, and asking me about the corset was a major double-bluff to throw Dad off the scent. That girl has *way* too much time on her hands.

Fleur did It the first time when she was fifteen. She's been telling me to get on with it for ages, and she's right, there's not really much point waiting any longer. I mean, Dan and I have been together ages; God, it's nearly four months now. OK, I don't love him, we're not talking marriage and babies, but he's fun and everything. At least I'll finally understand what everyone's talking about—

Suddenly there's a hammering at the door. 'Cate! Phone!'

I ignore him. It's probably Clem, she's been freaking out about the Chaucer essay—

'Cate! It's Paris! Are you coming out to take it or shall I—'

I quickly flip the duvet over the shiny Debenhams bag on my bed, and open the door. 'There's no need to shout.'

I wait for Dad to go away. I'm not discussing my sex life in front of him, if that's what he's thinking.

He sighs. 'Send Fleur's parents my best.'

Whatever. I kick the door shut and curl up on my bed with the phone. Must remember to paint my toenails, can't have sex for the first time with them all chipped, Dan'd think I'm a total slut. Clem's got this really cool purple from Hard Candy. I'm sure she'll let me borrow it.

Oh, God. This time tomorrow, I will no longer be *virgo intacta*.

'*Enfin!*' Fleur exclaims in my ear. 'I got your email! What are you going to wear? Where will you do it? Did you buy condoms?'

'Fleur!'

'What? You 'ave to think of these things. He's a man. It's not his problem.'

I jam the phone between shoulder and ear and take off my old toenail polish. 'Well, to be fair, I haven't actually told him yet. I thought I'd, like, go round after his stupid art class and surprise him—'

'*C'est parfait*! You 'ave to wear a trenchcoat, like Ingrid Bergman in *Casablanca*. But nothing underneath. Just sexy underwear.'

'Fleur, I can't go wandering around town in my knickers. I'll get arrested.'

'No one will see. It will be perfect! Very *film noir*! You arrive at his 'ouse. He will be surprised to see you. You will say nothing. You smile, and look mysterious. Then you undo the belt, you slide the coat from your shoulders – *merde*, it will be so sexy, just like a movie!'

I giggle. 'I don't have a trenchcoat.'

'Your mother must 'ave one. Did you get stockings?'

'Yes,' I say, putting down the nail-polish remover and pulling the bag out from beneath my duvet. A tremor of nervous excitement ripples through me. 'I went shopping this afternoon after school. And I got this really gorgeous body lotion too, it smells like chocolate oranges.' I hesitate, stroking the silky French knickers on my knee. It took me ages to decide what colour to buy; black seemed too obvious, red too tacky. In the end I went for a delicate coffee-coloured silk edged with antique cream lace. 'Fleur,' I say uncertainly. 'You know all those stories you hear, about the first time. The – the blood and everything. Does it really hurt a lot?'

'A little,' Fleur admits. 'But not for long. Don't worry, *chérie*. You just have to relax, and it will be fine.'

Relax. Yes. I can do that.

As if.

I push open the gate to Dan's semi, then hesitate. No going back after this.

I check my watch. I'm way earlier than I'd planned, thanks to that screaming match with Dad. Dan will still be teaching. But I couldn't stay at home another minute. Dad'll have me in a chastity belt next. Honestly, he treats me like a stupid kid sometimes. I'm nearly eighteen. When's he going to *get* it?

An old guy walking his dog throws me a dirty look as he goes past. Nervously, I retie Mum's black trenchcoat a bit tighter. (I can't believe all the cool stuff she has at the back of her wardrobe. It's, like, totally vintage. Sometimes I forget she went to art college.) It's OK for Fleur, going on about Ingrid Thingy and *Casablanca*. Now I'm actually here, I feel a bit gay. These stockings are really uncomfortable, for a start. I can totally see why they invented tights. Why do men find all this stuff sexy? I don't get it—

Shit, I hope he *does* find it sexy. Supposing he laughs?

No, Fleur knows what she's talking about. She's French. Everyone knows they're the chicest, coolest women in the world.

After a quick check to make sure no one's watching,

I slip down the side alley. I'll just let myself in through the back – he never locks the kitchen door – and wait in the sitting-room for him to finish teaching. I can sit on the sofa with my legs crossed, and kind of dangle my heel like they do in the movies. I wish I smoked. It's disgusting and makes me feel really sick, but it looks *so* cool.

It takes me a moment or two to understand what I'm seeing.

My boyfriend has his arms wrapped round my mother, and he's helping her take off this slutty red dressing-gown, and underneath she's naked, and his hands are all over her, and she's enjoying it, I can see it in her face, she's pink and sort of sighing and he's panting and I hate her, I hate her, how *could* they—

'Dan,' my mother moans, 'what are you doing?'

I bite down on my lip until I taste blood, and my legs stop shaking.

'Yes, Dan,' I say coolly, 'what *are* you doing?'

The look on their faces: it'd be funny if it wasn't so sad.

'Cate!' my mother cries, clutching at her robe. 'This isn't – I was modelling – Dan's life class—'

'I bet this looks really weird,' Dan says, giving me his best cute smile. 'I can imagine what you must be thinking—'

' – the class just finished – I was getting dressed—'

'Your mum did a great job, Cate. Everyone really enjoyed working with her. You should come through and see what they—'

'Get off me!' I scream. 'Don't you dare touch me!'

He backs away, hands raised. 'C'mon, Cate. You can't seriously—'

'How could you! With her! She's so – so *old*! It's disgusting!' I whirl round to my mother. 'And what about Dad? How could you do that to him? How could you do it to *me*?'

'I didn't – Cate, nothing happened! I promise!'

'He's my boyfriend! He's young enough to be your son! How *could* you?'

She starts to cry. Watching her, my own throat aches with misery.

'Why do you have to ruin everything for me? Why can't you just let me be happy?' I yell. 'I trusted you! All that stuff yesterday about not wasting my chances and helping me to go to New York! You don't really want me to have a life! You want me to end up as sad and lonely and pathetic as you are!'

'Of course I don't! I love you, Cate, you know that—'

I shake her off. She collapses on to the sofa, rubbing the back of her hand across her runny nose like a child. Her face is red and blotchy. She looks ugly. Old.

'You don't,' I say bitterly. 'You never have. You spoil *every*thing.'

'Cate,' Dan says, 'why don't we all just calm down and—'

'You're just a mean, wicked, jealous old woman. I wish you *had* died when Dad was in Cyprus. I wish I'd never come back and found you.'

She blanches. 'You don't mean that.'

'You *are* dead, as far as I'm concerned. I never want to speak to you again!'

Then I turn to Dan, and slap him as hard and furiously as I can.

Outside, I run, stumbling and tripping in the dumb heels. I take my shoes off, tearing through the empty streets in my stockinged feet, not caring how much it hurts. My chest heaves painfully, but I don't stop running. Everything feels strange and unreal, as if I'm moving under water. My whole life is disintegrating. It's all a lie. Nothing is real. Everyone is busy lying and cheating and no one cares what happens to me. No one would even notice if I was gone.

I want things to go back to the way they were. I want not to know all this grown-up stuff. I'm sick of protecting them. I want them to protect *me*.

Slamming into the kitchen, I catch sight of the corset, still lying on the kitchen table where Mum left it after our fight last night. My head explodes with rage. I pick it up and hurl it across the room, where it slaps against the dresser so hard the cups rattle.

I jump as my brother wanders in from the den, munching from a handful of tortilla chips cupped in his palm.

'Cool,' Ben says, picking up the corset, 'Candida was wondering where she'd left that. I thought it was at Dad's flat.'

I gape disbelievingly at him, and laugh. Suddenly, I can't stop.

'By the way,' Ben adds, spraying a fine mist of chips across his T-shirt, 'like the get-up, sis. You look like Ingrid Bergman in *Casablanca*. Way to go.'

I stay in the shower, tears mingling with the water, till it runs cold and I can't cry any more. Cleansing off the remains of my ruined make-up, I pull on a pair of cosy pink-flannel PJs, and scrape my wet hair back into a ponytail. The stockings and underwear, even the trenchcoat, I shove into the bin.

Downstairs, I knock on Dad's study. 'You busy?'

'Nothing that won't wait,' he sighs. 'Come on in, Cate. I could do with the distraction.'

Cannelle follows me into the room. I kneel and bury my face in his gold coat, as he closes his eyes and rumbles with pleasure. I'll miss him more than anyone. 'He's more like a cat than a dog,' I say. 'Listen to him. He's almost purring.'

Dad snaps his laptop shut. 'Is everything all right, Cate? I thought you were going over to Dan's this evening?'

'Didn't feel like it.'

'You're not still upset about the New York business, are you? I'm sorry, Cate, but—'

'Forget it, Dad.'

'Worried about your exams?'

'Bit.'

I pick up the bronze Buddha on the bookshelf, absently rubbing his fat tummy for luck. Dad brought him back from Tibet when I was four; over the years, I've worn a little shiny spot on his stomach. 'What were you and Mum arguing about last night?'

He doesn't answer for a moment, busying himself with the files and papers on his desk. He looks really tired: there are huge black bags under his eyes, and he's lost tons of weight. It's as if Superman suddenly turned mortal. It's kind of scary to see him like this. Who's going to take care of things, if he can't?

He summons a smile. 'Nothing that need worry you, Kit-Cat.'

'Dad—'

'It wasn't what you think. We were discussing Granny Anne.'

I chew my thumb. 'You and Mum – are you . . .'

'We're fine. Everything's fine. Now, Cate, if there's nothing else, I really need to get on.'

'I was wondering,' I blurt, 'if I could go to Fleur's? Just for a week or so. I wouldn't need to miss school. We're on study leave soon, and—'

He stops sorting papers. 'Out of the question.'

'But Dad—'

'Cate, be reasonable. You can't just skip school in the middle of term. Your exams are coming up soon, and you said it yourself, you need to get started on sorting out your university applications.'

'What's the point?' I mutter. 'You won't let me apply where I want to go.'

'There are plenty of excellent places here, we've been through this. First New York, now Paris: I really don't understand this sudden obsession with fleeing the country.' He checks his BlackBerry. 'Unless there's something wrong, Cate?'

I want to tell him. I really do. But I don't know where to start.

'You can trust me, darling,' he says, scrolling through his emails. 'I'm always here for you.'

'I thought you were going to New York on Friday?'

'Well, yes. But I'm here now. Come on, darling.' He finally puts his BlackBerry down and holds out his arms. 'What's on your mind?'

After a brief hesitation, I snuggle on to his lap. I'm safe here; suddenly none of that other stuff matters. It's like I'm four again, and Daddy can make everything better. I want it to stay this way. Why can't it stay this way?

'Hey, Kit-Cat. Are these real tears?' He tucks my head

under his chin, and rubs my back. 'Sweetheart, come on. Tell me. What is it?'

I can't stay here any more. Not with *her*.

'Take me with you to New York, Daddy,' I sniffle. 'Please?'

'You know I can't do that,' he says irritably. 'Cate, what's this about?'

If I tell him, he'll leave Mum. He'll leave, but I'll have to stay. I've got to tell him, or I'm going to burst. All these secrets are doing my head in.

I can't. I want to, but I *can't*.

'Come on, darling. Tell your old daddy.'

Maybe I should just spit it out. It would be such a relief. He'll know what to do. He'll sort it all out.

'Cate? You're starting to worry me. I'm sure it's nothing we can't – oh, shit. Oh, darling, I've got to take this call. I'm sorry, but it's really important.'

'It's OK.' I climb off his knee. 'Never mind. It didn't matter anyway.'

Fleur throws open her arms and envelops me in a gorgeous waft of jasmine and apples. '*Chérie!* It's so good to see you! But you've lost weight? A little from the chest, *merde*, but from the face, it's good. Very chic. Come, we take a taxi. Where's your luggage?'

'I only brought this.'

'One bag? We must go shopping. *Immédiatement!*' She tucks my arm through hers. 'Well, perhaps not immediately. But as soon as you are rested. Cigarette?'

I shake my head. Fleur lights up, heedless of the

DEFENSE DE FUMER signs posted around the Gare du Nord. She looks so wonderfully French.

I struggle to keep up as she skitters across the busy station concourse, marvelling at the speed she can move at in three-inch heels. Suddenly I feel a bit scruffy in my combats and silver Pumas. She looks so glam. Like, how does she get her long black hair that shiny? If I wore that shirt and pencil skirt, I'd totally look ridiculous, but she looks amazing, miles older than seventeen. And what is it about the French and scarves? She's twisted two through her belt loops, giving her classic outfit this brilliant funky edge. I'd look like a homeless squatter if I tried it.

'I love your combats,' she sighs, as we join the taxi queue. 'You look so cool.'

'Swap you,' I grimace.

She giggles. 'Why not? You give me London style, and I will teach you French chic. Fair, no?'

It's ages since I've been to Paris. Last time was about five years ago, when Dad took us all to EuroDisney for a special treat. I stick my head out of the open car window, not caring if I look like a hick from the sticks. I'd forgotten how different abroad is. All the signs are in French, for a start. PHARMACIE. BOULANGERIE. TABAC. It's so cool. The buildings are tall and elegant with their shutters and everything. It even smells different from London. And everyone looks so amazing, like they've stepped out of a magazine; even the men, with their leather satchels and purple shirts, not boring old white ones. You can tell straight away who the tourists are: the fat ones in T-shirts and trainers.

The taxi drops us off in a smart-looking part of town. Fleur drags me up some white stone steps and an actual maid opens the shiny black door when she rings, in a smart black-and-white uniform and everything.

'Papa!' Fleur yells, throwing her bag and keys on to the hall table. They slide straight on to the marble floor, but Fleur doesn't even notice. '*Cate est arrivée!*'

The maid picks up Fleur's things and holds her hand out for my giant rucksack. I feel a bit guilty, till I clock her expression. She's got the same arsey look on her face as one of those assistants in a posh shop. Skinny cow.

I trail Fleur into a huge high-ceilinged sitting room filled with museumy furniture, all spindly gold legs and teeny chair-backs. I'm scared to sit on anything in case I break it and it used to be Marie Antoinette's and is worth, like, a million pounds or something. The walls are this deep womb-red, though it's hard to see them properly because of all the gilt mirrors and paintings. It's like being on a movie set.

Her dad comes in and my stomach boomerangs all over the place. Fleur's dad is totally gorgeous: killer good looks mixed with this amazing French rumpled sexiness, all three-day-old stubble and dishevelled dark hair. He must be at least forty, but I've had the hugest crush on him for *years*.

'Cate, welcome,' he says, kissing me on both cheeks. 'Did you have a good journey?'

I nod, blushing furiously. Damn! That is *so* not cool.

'How are your parents? Would you like to telephone and let them know you arrived safely?'

'Dad flew to New York on Friday, Monsieur Lavoie,' I say quickly, hoping he doesn't ask about Mum. 'He knows where I am, though.'

Well, that's more or less true. I haven't *really* run away.

Dad'll figure out where I've gone straight away once Mum discovers I'm missing and tells him. He'll be really mad, but he's not going to interrupt his precious trip to New York just to come and get me. And Mum will be glad to see the back of me. She and Dan can have the place to themselves.

Like she's *really* gone to stay with Eithne.

Fleur's dad smiles deep into my eyes, and my palms are suddenly sweaty. 'Call me Hugo, please,' he murmurs. '"Monsieur Lavoie" makes me feel so old.'

'Hugo,' I mutter, crimson to the tips of my ears.

Fleur watches me with interest. 'You like 'im!' she giggles, once we tumble through the doorway to her bedroom.

'I do not!'

She shrugs. 'He has a mistress at the moment, so you are quite safe.' She picks up a scarlet lipstick from her vanity and holds it consideringly against my face. '*Mais non*. Too orange. She is very beautiful, his girlfriend. Very clever. My mother 'ates her, but she has a boyfriend 'erself, so she lives with it. *C'est la vie.*'

I throw myself stomach-down on the bed. 'Fleur, don't you *mind*?'

'It's better than divorce. Ah, I think this colour is better for you. I don't want to spend my time going from one 'ouse to the other. This way, they are both happy.' She laughs. 'Just not with each other.'

They certainly *seem* happy, I think, as they chat pleasantly to each other – in English, as a courtesy to me – from opposite ends of a shiny mahogany table bigger than our whole dining-room at home. I'm seated on Hugo's left, which basically means I can't eat anything; opposite me is Michel, Fleur's younger brother. He looks just like his father; in a few years he'll be totally hot, but right now he's only sixteen, still a kid.

'You don't like quails' eggs?' Hugo asks me. 'They're a little difficult to shell; let me help you.'

He reaches across and picks up one of the tiny eggs, his hand brushing mine. I jump as if I've been burned.

Fleur digs me in the ribs. 'I think she's lost her appetite,' she teases.

'You must be so tired after your journey,' says Mme Lavoie. She pins me with a glacial stare. 'Le Chunnel is an experience *terrible.*'

She's really beautiful, but her eyes are so cold. Even though she's smiling at me, I can tell she doesn't want me here. She's like the ice queen, with her white hair (very Cruella) and pale, pale skin – 'Forget St Tropez, no true Frenchwoman really likes the sun,' Fleur told me once, 'so bad for the skin, so *ageing.*'

I nod and duck my head so Mme Lavoie can't see my expression. I bet the old witch can read minds.

The maid clears our plates, then returns with the main course, a huge fish on an enormous silver plate that's almost as big as she is. It's still got the head on. It's staring at me. Oh, God, it's got *teeth*—

Don't look at it. It's just a big fish finger. With teeth and eyes.

I'm fiddling with the knives and forks on either side of my plate, wondering how to flee the table without seeming rude, when the maid comes back and whispers in Hugo's ear.

'Cate, your father is on the telephone,' he says pleasantly. 'Amélie will show you to the study, so you may take it in private.'

Shit. I didn't think he'd be this hot on my tail.

'What the hell do you think you're playing at?' my father yells as soon as I pick up the receiver.

'Dad, if you'll just let me explain—'

'For God's sake, Cate! Sneaking off to Paris without a word to anyone, not even a bloody note, your poor mother was worried sick' – frankly, I doubt that – 'on the verge of calling the police! I can't believe you'd do something this irresponsible! You can just get yourself on the next train back home, young lady, or you're going to find yourself in a world of trouble!'

'Please, Daddy, I only want to stay a few days. I promise I'll practise my French—'

'Screw your French! I want you home now!'

'Dad, I need a break!' I cry. 'I'm fed up with you and Mum arguing all the time! I can't cope with her any more!'

'You think *you've* got problems? I've got your mother on the phone in hysterics saying you've been kidnapped or murdered, while I'm in New York trying to save my company from going belly-up and throwing us all out on the streets! And you go and pull a stupid stunt like this!'

'You knew where I was,' I say sulkily.

'Luckily for you, the Lavoies are good people, but you can't just turn up unannounced on their doorstep, Caitlin! Grow up! This isn't just about you!'

'It never is, is it?'

'Don't be so damn childish! And I'd like to know where you got the money in the first – oh, Jesus.'

'What?'

'Keep still. Don't move.' His voice sounds distant, as if he's dropped the phone and is talking to someone else. 'Stay there, I'll get someone. Hold on.'

There's a scrabble as he picks up the phone again. 'Cate, I've got to go. Get yourself home. We'll talk when I get back at the end of the week.'

I'm left listening to the dial tone. I stare at the receiver in astonishment. Fuck knows what's going on his end, but whatever it is, I think it's just bought me some time.

'Cate? You didn't go out with Fleur?'

'Didn't really feel like dancing. Thought I'd get an early night.'

Hugo shuts the door of the tiny study – the only room in the house, other than the loo, that's less than a thousand miles across – and perches on the arm of the polished-conker leather sofa in front of the fire. He's wearing this thin black silk polo-neck and black jeans, and he looks *totally* fit.

'A beautiful young girl who doesn't want to go dancing? Either she is ill, or she is very sad. Which is it, *chérie*?'

He called me beautiful! 'I'm fine, honestly—'

'Cate. For three days, you don't leave the house. This is Paris! No woman comes to Paris to hide away and read books!'

'I can't really afford to go shopping—'

'Since when has that stopped a woman?' His voice softens. '*Chérie*, I don't know why you are here – *bien sûr*, perhaps you are just visiting your very dear friend Fleur, as you say?' He shrugs elegantly. 'Or perhaps there is trouble at home, something that is making you unhappy?'

I pull a cushion into my lap and pick fretfully at the fringe.

'I don't wish to poke, Cate. Your business is your business. You are welcome to stay with us as long as you like. Three days, or three months, you must stay until you feel ready to go home.'

Tears prick the back of my eyes.

Hugo sighs. '*Ma petite*, your mother telephones every day, and you don't want to speak to her. Your father doesn't call, and I think you do want to speak to him.' He leans forward and squeezes my hand. 'Sometimes, it's better to talk to someone, a friend, instead of keeping everything inside. Whatever it is, your secret will be safe with me.'

The logs in the grate snap, and I startle. Hugo unfolds gracefully and jabs them with the poker, adding more wood. It's April, but this big old house is cold, and I'm grateful for the warmth as it flares.

He opens a small drinks cabinet and pours two drinks, then hands one to me. '*Tiens*. To warm you inside, too.'

It smells disgusting, but I knock it back in one go.

'*Doucement*, Cate! Easy! That's Armagnac, not water!'

I cough and splutter for a good five minutes after it's burned its way down my throat. Hugo laughs, and once I finally catch my breath, I laugh too; for the first time in what seems like years.

'Here,' he says, pouring me another drink. 'Slowly, this time. Armagnac should be savoured, never rushed. Like good food. Or,' he smiles, 'a good woman.'

The two of us sit peaceably, staring into the fire. There's something very soothing about watching the flames leap and dance. The knot in my stomach slowly loosens.

I sip the drink carefully.

'Dad's having an affair,' I blurt suddenly.

Hugo nods, but says nothing.

'And I found Mum with my boyfriend – she wasn't wearing anything – they said nothing happened but I could *see* – I want to go to New York but no one will listen to me—'

'I am,' Hugo says.

For the next forty minutes, he doesn't say a word. When I start bawling, he hands me his gorgeous green silk handkerchief and lets me snivel into it. He tops up my drink, throws another log on the fire, and really seems to care how I feel. I wish Dad could be more like this. I used to think he was too busy with work, but he wasn't too busy to find time for Ella, was he?

When I finally run out of words, Hugo gives me a warm hug. I bury my head in his chest. God, he smells yummy, kind of like toffee apples—

All of a sudden, I stop feeling cosy and comforted, and begin to feel something very different. A tingle spreads to my fingers and toes. He really *is* sexy. His hand brushes the nape of my neck as he strokes my hair, and my body goes into meltdown. My heart's pounding, my hands are clammy, and there's a little fish of excitement leaping hotly in my knickers.

I tilt back my head, and kiss him.

For a moment, he kisses me back. Then he breaks away, holding me at arm's length. 'Cate, no.'

'Why not?'

'*Chérie*, this isn't the answer. You're looking for something else, not this. It would be wrong of me to take such advantage – much as I might want to,' he adds ruefully.

'Don't you like me?'

'But of course. You're a beautiful girl. Charming.' He stands and rubs his jaw, eyeing me regretfully. 'If you were a little older, a little more experienced—'

'I'm experienced enough.' I fling my arms round his neck, stumbling slightly. 'Fleur said you liked girls like me.'

He fends me off. 'Fleur has a vivid imagination. Cate, you're very tired. And perhaps the Armagnac wasn't such a good idea. I think it's time for bed—'

'That's a very good idea,' I slur.

'*Alone*, Cate.'

My eyes fill with tears. Hugo doesn't want me. Dan didn't want me. He preferred my own mother. There must be something wrong with me.

I hate myself. I hate my life. I wish I was dead.

I run out of the room, my chest heaving. I'm crying so hard, I can't see where I'm going, and run full-tilt into Fleur's brother as he comes out of the sitting-room, spilling his cup of coffee over both of us.

He puts out a hand to steady me.

And doesn't let go.

9

Ella

Hope's mother carefully lifts her tiny daughter from the incubator on to her lap, delicately mindful of the tubes and wires snaking into the fragile body. In an automatic, instinctive gesture, she drops her face into her daughter's dark hair, breathing in the scent of her child.

The baby yawns and shoots out a tiny pink fist. Anna strokes it, and the miniature fingers unfurl like sea fronds, and then curl back around Anna's finger. She glances up at me, and smiles radiantly.

I want that.

The thought – visceral and unexpected – knocks me off balance. I busy myself with the disinfectant dispenser. Hormones, that's all. I don't want children. I never have.

'Ella,' Anna says, concern shadowing her voice. 'Can you come here a minute?'

I examine the baby with my eyes. Anna's instinct is right. Something is wrong, I can sense it. Nothing obvious, but—

'Gina,' I call to the nurse on duty. 'How's she been feeding?'

'Actually, not so well today.'

'Stools?'

'Only one, early this morning.'

Gently, I palpate the baby's tummy. Abdominal distension and redness. Slightly elevated temperature. Alarm bells ring. She shouldn't have it; NEC typically occurs within the first two weeks of life, usually after we withdraw the feeding tube and milk feedings have begun, but—

'I want a CBC, full panel, CHEM-7 and X-ray of her abdomen,' I say briskly. 'Monitor for hematochezia.'

The nurse nods and takes Hope from her mother, placing her carefully back into the incubator.

'What's wrong?' Anna asks nervously.

'It may be nothing—'

'Ella, please, what is it?'

'You remember we talked about some of the challenges that face babies as little as Hope?' I say carefully. 'One of those challenges is a gastrointestinal disease called necrotizing enterocolitis, or NEC—'

Her eyes widen. 'The flesh-eating bug? Oh, God, she's going to die, isn't she? That's what you're telling me—'

'Anna, calm down. That's *not* what I'm telling you. You're thinking of something called necrotizing fasciitis, which is quite different. Forget what you read in the newspapers. NEC involves infection and inflammation of the bowel, and although it's serious, it's also quite common with babies this small.'

'Will she be all right?'

'We don't even know if she has it yet, but if she does,

it's extremely treatable. The majority of infants recover fully and have no further problems—'

'But if she doesn't . . .'

I rub Anna's cold hands between mine. 'She's only five weeks and one day old, darling,' I say softly. 'If you were still carrying her, you'd only be twenty-eight weeks pregnant by now. You know there are no guarantees. But we'll do our very best for her, and there's absolutely no reason to panic. I'm sure she's going to be just fine.'

I study the X-rays a couple of hours later. I had hoped I'd be proved wrong, but the diagnosis of NEC is confirmed by the presence of an abnormal gas pattern in the walls of the intestine and air in the abdominal cavity. It's a serious setback, but there's no reason to think Hope will make anything other than a full recovery. We'll start her on intravenous fluids, antibiotics and nasogastric drainage. Her condition should start to improve dramatically.

But it doesn't. The antibiotics slow the rate of her deterioration, but there's no doubt she's still getting worse. I don't go home for forty-eight hours, cat-napping on the sofa in my office when I can. By the third day, Hope's abdomen is so swollen that it interferes with her breathing, and we have no choice but to put her on a ventilator, something I've done my best to avoid up to now.

'Can't you do something to help her?' Anna begs tearfully.

'We're doing everything we can—'

Dean grabs my arm. 'You're not feeding her! She'll starve to death if this goes on much longer!'

'She won't starve, Dean,' I say, gently freeing myself. 'She's getting all the nutrients she needs through the IV.

Her tummy needs to rest so it can heal. I know it's frightening not to see her being fed, especially when she's so small to begin with. But it's for her own good, I promise.'

'What if she doesn't heal?' he demands. 'What if she doesn't start to get better?'

'If she doesn't improve soon, we may have no choice but to operate,' I say quietly.

I'm caught between a rock and a hard place. I don't want Hope on the IV longer than absolutely necessary because of the risk of nosocomial infections or other complications. Neither do I want to operate on an infant this vulnerable unless I've got no option. There's a very real chance she won't survive the trauma of anaesthetic and surgery.

But if we do nothing and her bowel *does* perforate, allowing faecal matter to leak into her abdomen, the infection will spread very quickly to all her major organs and she will certainly die.

'How long do we wait?' Dean asks.

'Please, Dean. Let me worry about that,' I say, with more confidence than I feel.

I go back to my vigil, filled with foreboding. Somehow, even in the most high-pressure, life-or-death situations, I've always known instinctively what to do. When to intervene, and when to pull back. When to medicate, and when to let nature take its course. When to resuscitate; and, hardest of all, when to let go. I haven't always been right, of course, but I've been able to weigh up the pros and cons in a moment and somehow know exactly which course has the best possible chance of a good outcome.

But suddenly, I'm floundering. I know I'm over-thinking

this case. I'm too close to my patient. I just have to pray that, should it come to it, instinct will take over and something will tell me what to do.

I spend another sleepless night at the hospital, monitoring Hope every half-hour. By six the next morning, her condition has finally stabilized, but she still shows no positive sign of improvement.

I watch her chest rise and fall with the ventilator. At least she's no longer getting any worse. Perhaps the tide is slowly turning. She was extremely premature, after all. No point putting her through the trauma of surgery if the antibiotics are able to do their stuff.

But if her bowel has been weakened by days of infection – if it perforates now—

A cold wash of panic engulfs me.

Dear God, not now.

I struggle to hold the monster at bay. I know its signs: the surge of adrenalin, the painful prickling along my arms and legs, the tightening around my chest, the shortness of breath. I'm woken by it every night, sometimes two or three times, my heart pounding, drenched in sweat. It's got so that I dread going to bed; I stay in the armchair in the sitting-room, watching mindless television, until exhaustion finally takes over and I fall into a restless sleep.

Sometimes I can control it, push it back into its box by sheer force of will; but other times it overwhelms me, and I give in to the panic, gasping and choking and witless with terror, until, eventually, it passes, leaving me limp with exhaustion.

I've started to avoid anything that might trigger an attack. I can't cope any more with the tube, or an underground car park. I'm afraid of bridges, crowds, the dark, going to a movie. I'm beginning to understand how people become trapped in their own homes for years.

But I've always been safe working. Until now.

Fear wreaths my chest like smoke as I watch Hope struggle to breathe. *I don't know what to do for the best.* For the first time in my life, my legendary certainty has deserted me.

The night-duty nurse checks the baby's vital signs. 'What do you think?' she asks.

I don't know.

'She's certainly a fighter, this one. Reckon she's turned the corner?'

I don't know.

'Let's just wait and see,' I prevaricate.

Maybe Hope will get better and I won't need to do anything. Maybe (God forbid) she'll get worse, and I'll have no choice but to send her for surgery.

Maybe I'll wake up tomorrow and know what to do.

For the rest of the day, we watch and wait. And then at quarter to midnight, three and a half days after my unofficial vigil started, Hope's temperature begins to climb. And climb.

I don't need the surgeon to insert a needle into her abdominal cavity to withdraw fluid so that we can determine whether there's a hole in her intestines. I know immediately her bowel has perforated. We need to remove the diseased section as soon as possible, before it infects her entire abdomen and causes sepsis. Depending on the location and extent of the bowel removed, she may need a colostomy, or repeated surgical procedures; she may have problems with blockages or malabsorption in the future. But if her entire intestine is involved, we won't be able to do anything. Which will mean—

I'm hopelessly involved with my patient. It's unprofessional and counter-productive. It's utterly unlike me.

But as Hope is wheeled to the operating room, I feel as if my heart has gone with her.

William's phone call the next morning comes as I'm writing up Hope's case notes.

'New York?' I repeat. 'Tomorrow?'

'Please, Ella. It's make-or-break time for the company. I really need you there.'

I put down my pen. It's seven years since we went away together. To risk reopening that very dangerous can of worms, William must be truly desperate.

We'd been seeing each other for just over a year when he took on a new client, a prestigious multinational Arab bank based in Cyprus. William's business trip coincided with Thanksgiving in the US; Jackson was flying home, as he did every year, to spend the holiday week with his brother. Since Cooper hadn't seen fit to include me in the invitation, as usual, I'd been left kicking my kitten heels alone in London until William suggested I join him in Cyprus.

Aware that we were taking our casual affair to a new – and hazardous – level, whilst pretending I knew no such thing, I told Jackson I was going to Oxford for a girls' week with Lucy, and switched my mobile to international roam.

During the day, I lounged by a glittering pool while

William went hunter-gathering in the corporate jungle. In the evenings, we ate by candlelight on a terrace beneath the stars, or got a taxi out to the beach and walked hand-in-hand along the moonlit sand. It was like a slushy montage from a Hollywood rom-com – we even rented a sit-up-and-beg bicycle, and I sat on the handlebars as William cycled along the shore – but we revelled in the cliché of it all. It never occurred to us, as we ironically pastiched falling in love, that it might actually *happen*.

On the last day, William decided we should go windsurfing. As we skinned up in wetsuits, my zip jammed. I tried to free myself, and instead caught my breast in the plastic teeth. Blood welled, and I gasped in pain.

William reached over and caught the drop of blood on his fingertip. I glanced up, and saw it in his eyes. I knew, from the confusion chasing across his features, that in the same moment, he'd seen it in mine.

Outwardly, it was a very prosaic moment. No drumroll, no explosion of fireworks. A fraction of time: in which everything changed.

If he'd asked me, then, to leave Jackson, I would have gone.

He didn't. And when we got back to the hotel, the message from Beth's friend Eithne was waiting.

After that, there was no question of love coming into it. If there had ever been a tiny part of me that had once hoped for that Hollywood ending, a sliver of me unregulated by my sensible, realistic, self-preserving instincts, Cyprus had extinguished it. The original, pragmatic terms of our agreement still stood. But there would be no going beyond its boundaries. What we had now was all we would ever have.

I realized I was trapped in a paradox of my own making. If I wanted to keep William in my life, I had to excise every shred of love I felt for him.

I succeeded. But that sort of radical emotional surgery is indiscriminate. It wasn't just my feelings for William that ran up against a brick wall whenever they tried to get a purchase. Slowly, what I felt for Jackson dimmed too. Somewhere along the line, I lost touch with the best part of myself.

'Ella?' William's voice prompts now.

My instinct is to say no. Getting over what happened in Cyprus took reserves of strength I don't have any more. And just thinking about getting on a plane is enough to set my heart pounding with fear. Plus I've had so much time off recently. Richard Angel's baying for my blood; if I take any more unscheduled leave, I could hand him the ammunition he needs to get me fired.

My case notes swim in front of me. After everything that's happened in the last six weeks, losing my job doesn't seem to matter much any more in the grand scheme of things. And William *needs* me.

I close the file on my desk. 'Of course I'll come.'

I can't stop thinking about Hope. Or, despite everything, wishing she'd been mine.

William wakes me from my pharmacological coma when we land at JFK. We take a yellow New York taxi to a small boutique hotel serendipitously close to Fifth Avenue and my personal shopping nirvana, while I try to shake off my Xanax hangover.

A skinny Hispanic girl with disfiguring acne shows us

to a large wood-panelled room with red-oak floors and a vast white-linen four-poster bed. Fresh flowers scent the room; in the bathroom is an old-fashioned claw-foot tub, surrounded by unlit scented candles, and a heap of marshmallow towels. In the heart of Manhattan: I can only imagine how much this must cost.

'I like your style,' I comment, biting into a ripe peach from a bowl on the antique credenza. 'Going down in a blaze of glory.'

'All guns firing,' William agrees. 'And talking of going down . . .'

Laughing, I evade his amorous advance. Peach juice dribbles down my chin. 'Let me shower first, then we'll see.'

'Story of my life.' He pulls off his tie, and checks his BlackBerry. 'OK, I've got to make a couple of calls, so I'll see you downstairs. Italian work for you this evening?'

'Depends. Can he breathe through his ears?'

William snorts. I blow him a kiss, go into the bathroom and lock the door. For a moment, I simply lean back against it, too drained to move. Now that I'm alone, I don't need to keep up the pretence.

I lever myself forward and start the bath running; I haven't got the energy to shower. As the room fills with steam, I slide to the tiled floor and rest my forehead against the edge of the bath. William needs me to be bright and cool and distracting; the careless, carefree Ella he's always known. His whole life is on the line: the next few days will decide if his company, his baby, survives, or is swallowed whole by Noble. I have to send him out refreshed, energized and ready to do battle. I may want to curl into a ball and cry my eyes out, but this isn't about me.

I allow myself the blessed relief of a therapeutic five-minute pity bawl in the bath, then get out and pull my emotional corset back on. Carefully, I apply make-up to hide any trace of tiredness or tears, and slither into an iridescent pink, turquoise and black Pucci swirl of a dress.

Perching on the edge of the bed, I open my new Gina shoebox with the reverence that is its due, and slip on the sparkling silver sandals.

'Blaze of glory,' I tell my reflection.

William whistles as I walk into the hotel reception. If we'd run off together in Cyprus, he wouldn't be whistling like that, would he? We'd have grown complacent by now, taking each other for granted, in and out of the bedroom. Far better this way.

Later, after dinner, we go back to our room, and William eases the delicate spaghetti straps over my bare shoulders; my dress ripples down my body and pools at my feet. He kisses my neck, my collarbone, my navel, his stubble grazing my skin as he unhooks my strapless bra and eases my panties down my thighs and over my feet. I step clear, naked but for my silver shoes and the aquamarine pendant we bought together in London. I've never dared wear it before, in case Jackson asked where it came from.

William unpins my hair, running his fingers through it as it spirals on to my shoulders.

'You are so goddamn beautiful,' he sighs.

I help him undress, enjoying his tensile strength as he pushes me back on to the linen sheets and hovers over me like a panther. His body is hard and brown, the body of a man who keeps himself fit not out of vanity, but practicality.

He kisses me: I taste zabaglione on his lips.

Tess Stimson

My body stirs, anticipating his touch. His hands skim
my skin – I feel the calluses from years of tennis on his
palms – and a wetness spreads between my legs. I arch
towards him, but he smiles and holds my wrists over my
head with one hand, dipping his head to my breasts. My
nipples tighten beneath his tongue. He smells of sweat and
city dirt and lemons. I lose any sense of time and place as
pleasure ripples through my body. Hooking one leg around
his waist, I draw him towards me, aching to have him
inside me, but he pulls away and slithers down the bed.

Gripping my buttocks, he tugs me to the edge of the bed
and drops to his knees, drinking from my pussy as if it
were a flute of champagne.

I twist my fingers in his thick hair, keeping him there.
He kneads my breasts with a firmer touch now, and I groan
at the sensory overload. In a rush, my orgasm sweeps over
me, and I jerk against his mouth, driven higher and further
by the rasp of his stubble against my clitoris.

William flips me expertly on to my stomach and slides
his fingers into me, his cock thrusting against my pussy.
The motion skates my nipples back and forth against the
cool linen, and I come once more, wetly, against his hand.

I turn in his arms, kissing him and tasting myself on his
lips. His cock brushes against my stomach as he licks the
sweat in the hollow of my throat. I pull him towards me,
the delicious ache rising in me again. Parting my thighs, I
guide him into me with my hips. He thrusts inside me and
I rock with him, our eyes locked as firmly as our hands
above our heads.

In that moment, something cracks and breaks inside me.
Without warning, I'm open to him, heart and soul, and

even though I know it's the worst thing that could happen, *the absolute worst thing I could do*, a part of me wants this surrender more than I ever thought possible.

Afterwards, he curls against my back, spooning: the classic position of lovers down the centuries. I clasp my hands over his, dizzy with self-knowledge. While I could tell myself that it was just an affair, I was safe. He had his life to go back to, and I had mine. But I can't fool myself any longer. I love him. Without Jackson to hide behind, sooner or later, I'm going to want more. I'm going to want all of him, and that can't happen. I can't destroy his marriage, and his family, and attempt to build my happiness on another woman's misery. That's what having William for myself would cost.

I love him.

I have no choice but to let him go.

I love him.

'Crazy badger,' William whispers in my ear.

I want to ask him what he means, but he's already asleep.

When all else fails, a girl still has shopping.

With every swipe of my credit card, I'm a little more in control. Purchasing power is better than no power at all. First the élite department stores: Henri Bendel, Bergdorf's, Neiman Marcus; and then the funky vintage shops: Alice Underground, Screaming Mimi's. I buy a stunning coral necklace from Anthropologie, a striking bottle-green ankle-length velvet coat from Anna Sui. I can't afford it, any of it, but I don't stop until I am so laden I literally can't carry anything else. There's nothing quite as effective as a glossy, rope-handled bag to help mend a broken heart, and mine is in a million tiny pieces.

I bump into William in the hotel lobby – literally, as a cascade of bags slither off my shoulders at his feet. There is one upside to being single: I don't have to apologize for my extravagance. *No, darling, I haven't had it ages, and I didn't get it half-price in the sale.*

'How did the meeting go?' I ask.

He peers into a bag from La Petite Coquette. 'It went. Is that for me?'

'Only if you're very bad. What did they say?'

'They're going to think about it over the weekend,' he says tightly. 'We'll meet again on Monday. One of the three directors is a lost cause, but I think the other two are genuinely undecided. I pointed out to them that if Noble uses these kinds of practices to win their business, they can't expect him to play by the Queensberry Rules once they've signed with him.'

'How did that go down?'

'Christ knows. I think it struck a chord, but he's offering them a hell of a deal. I can't compete financially. I just have to hope my track record speaks for me.'

'D'you want me to go and give them all Chinese burns?'

'It may yet come to that. So,' he says, shrugging off his dejection with a visible effort, and pulling me close, 'looks like we're stuck in New York with nothing to do tomorrow. How *will* we fill the time?'

The contents of the La Petite Coquette bag help. Late on Sunday morning, we finally stumble out of bed and emerge into a brilliant spring day, the kind that lifts the spirits and soothes the soul. A cool breeze sweeps gently through the Manhattan streets, freshening the workaday city. We take our papers to an outdoor café, and William tucks into a fluffy mushroom omelette – morels, shiitakes and oysters; simple but delicious – while I enjoy a fresh berry fruit salad and hot, crispy *pain au chocolat*. There's a dull, pleasurable ache between my legs. Every so often, William looks up from his newspaper and smiles, and the thought of saying goodbye to him for ever is almost more than I can bear.

At a nearby table, a young couple struggle to contain their shrieking children, twin girls aged about four and a boy of about eighteen months. All three have streaming colds and freely wipe their snotty noses on anything that comes to hand – their sleeves, each other, their mother's skirt. Then the toddler picks up his mother's coffee and pours it over his nearest sister's head. She retaliates by upending the table, spilling pastries, milk and more coffee.

As the wailing reaches a crescendo, the parents wearily get to their feet and gather children, pushchairs, hats, jackets, bags, toys.

William snaps his *New York Times*. 'Thank God mine are past that stage.'

I watch them leave. I'd be a dreadful mother. A newbie shrink could point out the keloids on my psyche. Abandonment by a philandering father, a passive mother who abdicated responsibility to her nine-year-old daughter: who knows what damage I'd inflict in my turn on an innocent infant? It'd be like opening a fridge and throwing random ingredients into a bowl blindfold, stirring them for twenty years, and waiting to see what resulted.

A good-looking man in his mid-thirties takes the young

family's table, and gives me an openly appraising glance as he sits down. He clearly likes what he sees; he smiles and tilts his coffee in salutation.

Beside me, William stiffens.

It was a calculated risk, telling him about Cooper. Whether William realized it or not, Jackson's death must have changed the way he saw me; my availability was bound to make me seem needy, demanding, even pitiable. At a stroke, the knowledge that I'd slept with someone else dispelled that notion; he hasn't been this attentive since our first year together.

But jealousy is a dangerous game. I hit where it hurt most: his pride. I've made my point; no need to overplay my hand.

I turn carefully towards William, not even glancing in the stranger's direction.

Later, he takes my hand and we stroll through Central Park, walking off our brunch, just another ordinary couple on just another ordinary Sunday.

The mild weather has brought the blossom out early; the air smells sweet and clean. I lean on the parapet of Bow Bridge, enjoying the feel of smooth warm stone beneath my palms. William wraps his arms around me, his chin resting gently on the top of my head.

'Damn it!' I say suddenly. 'I left my book in the café.'

'Forget it. It'll be long gone by now. Buy it again at the hotel bookshop.'

'You don't understand. It was one of a special set, Lucy gave it to me for my thirtieth birthday. I have to go back, I have to find it.'

'Ella, sweetheart—'

'I can't lose it,' I panic, 'we have to go back. You know

how much I hate losing one of a pair, I need to find it, we—'

'Ella,' William says, tucking me against him and stroking my back as if I were a child. 'Forget the book. It's time to tell me about Hope.'

Even after the surgeons discovered her bowel had perforated, as we'd feared, I didn't lose hope; I was so sure they'd save her.

So sure; but in the end the sepsis was too widespread, there was nothing they could do. She didn't even make it out of the OR. Her brave little heart gave out there, on the operating table, and she died surrounded by monitors and machines and medics who didn't even know her name. Alone, without anyone to hold her and tell her they loved her, that even having known her for just five weeks and six days, they'd miss her.

I broke the news to her parents myself. Dean toppled like Saddam's statue, collapsing forward into a chair, smashed by grief. Anna slapped my face.

When I tell William, dry-eyed, that it was my indecision that killed Hope, he doesn't say it's not my fault, it couldn't be helped. He doesn't serve up the usual platitudes, or tell me I shouldn't feel responsible. He knows there's nothing he can say that will take the grief and guilt away. He simply holds me tight against him, and somehow, for the moment, it's enough.

William slams into the hotel room the next afternoon, his expression grim. I pause in my packing, my heart sinking.

The meeting went against him, then. He's lost the Equinox contract. Lost his company.

'I could bloody strangle her!' he cries. 'What the hell does she think she's playing at? As if I haven't got enough on my plate!'

I rock back on my heels, a shoebox in each hand.

'Cate!' he explodes, finally noticing my mystified expression.

'I don't understand. What does she have to do with Equinox?'

'What? Oh, the meeting with Equinox went fine. They'll let me know tomorrow, but I think I swung it. It's Cate who's giving me the bloody headache! Running off to Paris! What on earth does she think she's playing at!'

He slumps on to the end of the bed and loosens his tie. 'Beth rang an hour ago in hysterics. Cate's run away, no note, but she's taken her bloody silver trainers and that damn backpack, so she's clearly gone of her own free will. Beth was on the verge of calling the police before I talked her out of it.' I hand him a bourbon from the mini-bar and he knocks it back in one gulp. 'I know where she is. She was on at me before I left to let her go and stay with her best friend in Paris. Bloody Fleur. I knew the two of them were up to something.'

'What are you going to do?'

'Cancel her credit card, for a start! I should never have given in to Beth and let her have one. I'm paying for this bloody nonsense!'

I picture the determined white face of his daughter in my office, as she tried to make sense of the mess a bunch of adults who should know better have made of her life.

'Don't do that. You don't want her stranded in a foreign country with no money. Have you tried calling her mobile?'

'Switched off. I tried ringing Fleur's parents, but the bloody French maid answered the phone, either doesn't understand English or doesn't want to—'

'Give me the number.'

I speak briefly to the maid in French, and then hand the phone to William. 'She's there. Amélie has just gone to get her.'

I tune him out as he yells at his daughter. I've got a headache already, and to be honest, I'm not feeling too brilliant. Hot and dizzy. My shoulder is aching as if I've been playing tennis for a month. And I've felt nauseous since I got up this morning. Probably the thought of having to get on the plane again, although the panic attacks have abated these last few days. Perhaps I just needed something real to worry about—

I'm knocked sideways by the worst pain I've ever known.

It's like my insides are being twisted by a giant fist. For a moment, it's so intense, I can't breathe. I cling to the back of a chair, my knuckles whitening. Too vicious for food poisoning. It must be appendicitis – only I had mine out when I was twelve—

William is still shouting at his daughter. If I can just get to the bathroom—

A film of sweat sheens my face. I'm going to be violently sick.

I try to make it to the lavatory, but my legs refuse to work, and I crumple to the floor. William turns and drops the phone.

I vomit uncontrollably where I lie, in too much agony even to feel embarrassed.

'Oh, Jesus.' William yanks the coverlet from the bed, and tucks it around me, then wipes my face with his shirt. 'Keep still. Don't move.'

I shiver convulsively, and the room begins to spin. I didn't think it was possible to be in this much pain and stay conscious.

'Stay there, I'll get someone. Hold on.'

Dimly, I hear him sign off with Cate and tell someone to call an ambulance. Then he's scooping my head into his lap, and stroking my damp hair back from my face.

'They'll be here soon. Whatever it is, we'll get you sorted out. The best care money can buy. Don't worry, darling. I'm here. It's probably something you ate. Nothing to worry about.'

You're wrong! I scream silently. *It is something to worry about!*

William wouldn't be nearly so solicitous, wouldn't be tenderly wiping the vomit from my lips with his linen shirt, if he realized what was really wrong with me.

November 25, 2001

Felden Street
London SW6
England

Dear Cooper,

> *This is the hardest letter I ever sat down to write. But you got to know the truth, and tough as this is, saying the words out loud would be a hundred times harder, else I'd pick up the phone. Just read it through, Coop. Once I'm done, I don't ever want to talk about this again.*

She's made a fool out of me. How could you see what kind of woman she was, Coop, when you never even laid eyes on her? How could I live with her, eat with her – Jesus, <u>sleep</u> with her – for four years and never realize?

I wouldn't believe it still, if I hadn't seen her with my own two eyes. Lolly would say it's all part of the Lord's plan, that I was meant to fly back two days early to bring her home to you for Thanksgiving, and find her right there, in the airport, kissing the face off some bastard in a fancy suit. All I can say is, the Lord has a fine sense of humor. I just spent the last week telling you how wonderful my lovely wife is, and begging you to give her a chance. Turns out you were right about her all along.

God's will or not, if I'd had my twelve-gauge with me I'd have put a slug straight between the asshole's eyes.

But instead I hid so she wouldn't see me; she never even knew I was there. Daddy would have turned the gun on himself before he let a carpetbagger treat him that way. I'm shamed, Coop, and the worst of it is, I don't give a damn. If I could turn back the clock and go back to not knowing, I would.

How could she do this to me? I've given her everything she ever wanted. Hell, I'm not perfect, I know that, but I thought I made her happy. How could I not <u>know</u>?

It's killing me. Every time I look at her, I see her in bed, spreading her legs for another man. It's been three days, and I still can't face her. I can't bear to say her name, I can't stand to touch her. I'm sick to my stomach every time she smiles at me. It's got so I can't stand to be in the same room. She's so lost in her own world, I don't think she's even noticed. What kind of marriage do we have, that we can have such secrets from each other?

My head's buzzing with so many questions, I can't think straight. Did she take him home, did they do it in our bed? How long has it been going on? Is he better in bed than me? Smarter, richer, funnier? Is he married, too? Does he love her?

Does she love him?

I'm so scared, big brother. Right now I'm numb, like after Mom and Dad died. But I know what comes next. It's like having your arm cut off and looking at the bloody stump and knowing it's going to hurt more than you can imagine, but you can't feel it yet. I'm not sure what I'll do when the pain hits. I don't know if I can go through it again.

You know the worst thing, the very worst of it? Even more than picturing the two of them in bed, even more than the shame and humiliation and anger?

God help me, I still love her.

How is it possible to love someone who gives you so much pain? She's not the kind of wife I ever planned on; she lies and cheats, she blows hot and cold, she won't even have my babies. I should kick her to the curb. If I stay, she'll cause me nothing but more grief. Maybe I'll wind up hating her. It'd almost be a relief. This kind of love, it's more than I can bear.

I don't want your pity, Coop. I know what you'll say: same as any right-minded person would. But a part of me wants her so bad I'd settle for just a piece of her, if it means I don't lose her. And another part of me knows it'll kill me in the end. She'll break my heart.

You're the only one who's never let me down. I know I don't tell you this as often as I should, but I love you, bro.

Jackson

10

William

I'm screwed. My company is about to go to hell in a hand-basket, and there's bugger-all I can do to stop it.

'Wonderful news!' I exclaim, leaping up from behind my desk.

Malinche blushes. 'Isn't it? Although the girls think it's terribly embarrassing, proof positive their parents are having sex – well, Sophie does, she goes absolutely *scarlet* whenever anyone mentions the baby. Evie is another kettle of fish entirely, as you can imagine: she keeps answering the phone and saying Mummy and Daddy are too busy making a baby to speak to anyone, Nicholas' poor mother was rather shocked when she called the other day—'

'He must be thrilled,' I say, when I can get word in.

'Oh, he *is*, especially when the scan said it was a boy, at *last* – although of course they said that last time, and then along came darling Metheny.'

She settles herself into the inhospitable black leather chair opposite me and beams radiantly. Despite the financial bombshell she's just lobbed my way, I beam back. Malinche Lyon is one of the few clients on my books I actually like.

Her career as a celebrity chef is undergoing a surprising renaissance at the moment. Fifteen years ago, Mal was a hot property, with a shelf-full of best-selling cookbooks and a cable-TV deal, but then she married a rather dull divorce lawyer, moved to the country and more or less vanished off the radar overnight. She and Nicholas hit a bit of a rocky patch a year ago, but it blew over, and next thing I know, she's opening a shit-hot gourmet restaurant down in Salisbury. Off the back of it, she's got a new cookbook at number one, another in the pipeline, and a hit BBC show that's put her right back at the top.

Naturally, her success has been good for my agency (a lifesaver, actually); but, hand on heart, I can think of few people I'd rather see good things happen to.

'I know it messes things up for the new series,' she says apologetically, 'but I really don't think I can juggle the three girls and a tiny baby and work, even with the new nanny – Nicholas was so sweet about that, he absolutely wouldn't take no for an answer, positively in*si*sted we hire her—'

I grasp at straws. 'Could they shoot round you?'

'They could, they've been terribly sweet about the whole thing, but actually, William,' she says, dimpling, 'I do rather want to take a bit of time off – after all, I am thirty-nine, this is a bit of last-chance baby – and I want to enjoy every minute without worrying about film schedules and recipes and things. I realize it leaves everyone in rather a muddle – ' understatement *du jour*, ' – but I *prom*ise it'll only be for a year. Of course, if you really need me to—'

'Mal, please don't worry. I'm delighted for you both,

couldn't be happier. I'll issue a press release tomorrow to take the heat off you, and I'm sure the BBC will be more than happy to take you back whenever you're ready. You just concentrate on looking after yourself, and leave the rest to me.'

She levers herself awkwardly out of the chair. 'You are a poppet, William.'

I'm not sure the taxman will see it quite like that when I can't pay my next bill.

'By the way,' she adds, shouldering a huge black bag and absently spilling half its contents on the floor, 'who was that rather beautiful blond young man chatting up your secretary just now? He looks *terri*bly familiar, but I can't quite place him.'

I help her pick up keys, mints, tampons (clearly it's been a while since she used this bag) and assorted fluffy toys. 'That would be my daughter's boyfriend.' I scowl. 'She sweet-talked me into letting him design the new company logo. I hate to admit it, but the bastard's actually bloody good.'

'Oh, dear. Fathers and daughters. I've got all this to come with the girls. Nicholas is already muttering about shotguns and convents—'

'There's a good one in Romania. I can give him the number if he likes.'

Malinche peals with laughter as she kisses me goodbye.

I tell Carolyn to hold my calls and stare broodingly out over the glittering Canary Wharf skyline. Losing Mal, even temporarily, is a body blow. We still have a decent bedrock of bread-and-butter clients, but I have forty-two staff to pay, and crippling overheads. These new offices are a good investment, but it's going to take time to reap the rewards.

For the past six months, we've been haemorrhaging cash; thanks to Noble's poaching, we're barely keeping our heads above water. Tomorrow's trip to New York is more vital than ever. Thank God Ella agreed to come. I need the kind of moral support only she can give me.

Without Malinche, the grim reality is that if I can't persuade Equinox to stay loyal, we're not even going to make it to next Christmas.

While Ella sleeps on the plane, I review the notes I've pulled together on the three key players at Equinox. I'm fairly sure John Torres, the chairman and CEO, is in our corner: we've worked well together over the years, and he's already intimated over the phone that he wants to stay with Ashfield PR. But he's barely a year from retirement; his vote counts for less than it used to. And his finance director, Drew Merman, is pushing hard for fresh blood. Charming and slippery, he's cast from the same mould as Noble himself. I wouldn't be surprised if they've already done some sort of back-room deal.

The new V-P, Mina Gerhardt, is the real unknown quantity. She's only been with Equinox eight months, so we haven't had the chance to build up much of a working relationship, and she has a reputation for ruthless unsentimentality. Who knows which way she's going to jump?

Damn it, who the hell is selling me out to Noble? *Who?* I can't believe it's Ella. What possible reason would she have? Unless he's her mystery one-night stand—

Ridiculous. Beth, then? If she's found out about Ella, she might want revenge. But if she sinks us, she'll be cutting off her nose to spite her face. The house is mortgaged to the hilt; if the firm goes down, we'll be left with nothing. No juicy divorce settlement. She wouldn't want that, surely?

I rub my hand across my face. I'm nearly forty-nine. Too old to start again. If the firm goes under, where will that leave me?

Ashfield PR has been my life for twenty years. The kids have their own lives; they'll be gone soon, even Sam. Christ knows what'll happen when it's just Beth and me rattling round that huge house on our own. If we didn't have Cate to referee, we'd be at each other's throats already.

I won't have Ella for ever, either. Not now Jackson's gone. She'll find someone else, someone free; she's young and beautiful, she won't be a widow for long.

I reach over and tuck the thin airline blanket more securely around her shoulders. Funny that she's scared of flying; she's usually so sensible. Rather endearing, in a way. I've always found her confidence exciting, but it can be a little disconcerting at times. I know she hates showing any sign of weakness, but actually, far from putting me off, it just makes me love her more—

In the ordinary way you love those close to you, of course. Ella wouldn't stand for any of that soulmate, can't-live-without-you stuff. She's not the sort to get swept away by feelings. If I was so pathetic as to declare myself madly in love with her, she'd run a bloody mile.

I unscrew my miniature Scotch and top up my glass. There was a moment, years ago, when I *did* wonder, though. The trip to Cyprus: something happened that week. I don't know if it was the sun or the booze or all that romantic walking along the beach (enough to give anyone daft ideas; I even hired a bicycle and did the whole *Butch*

Cassidy and the Sundance Kid thing, cycling through fields with Ella perched on the handlebars. Thinking about it still brings a smile to my face). It was the first time we'd spent more than a night together, and it must have gone to my head, because I found myself wondering what it'd be like if this was real, if I could fall asleep every night with Ella beside me, knowing that I had a lifetime of waking up to her the next morning.

I took her wind-surfing the last day we were there, and she managed to catch the bloody zip of her wetsuit on her skin. Daft thing to do, and not in the least romantic; but when I saw her wince, saw the blood, it twisted my guts in the kind of primitive, knee-jerk way it does when one of the kids gets hurt. And even though I was married, with three young children – Sam was barely a year old at the time – in that moment, none of it mattered. If she'd crooked her finger, given me the merest hint, I'd have left Beth in an instant.

On the way back to the hotel afterwards, the question rattled around my brain; I couldn't think of anything else. *Would she leave Jackson if I asked?*

Then, as we walked up the hotel steps, the concierge came running out to meet us. Cate had been the one to find her mother, Eithne told us over the phone. She'd forgotten something she needed for school, and had come back to get it. She'd found Beth in the kitchen, barely conscious in a pool of blood. My wife had slit her wrists.

Cate was just ten years old, but she'd bandaged her mother's arms with a couple of tea-towels and called 999, and sat there staunching the flow with her small hands until the paramedics arrived. What must it have done to her, to find her mother like that? I'd been in my twenties when my father killed himself, and I still regularly wake screaming from the nightmares.

'I didn't mean for her to find me,' Beth had said sullenly from her hospital bed. 'Eithne was coming over, I thought Cate would be safely at school—'

'But *why*, Beth?' I demanded. 'You've been doing so well since Sam was born. Why now?'

She turned her head into the thin pillow. 'I thought you were going to leave me. I couldn't bear that. I didn't want to live without you.'

'Of course I'm not going to leave you—'

'I wouldn't blame you. You must hate me.'

I sighed. 'I don't hate you, Beth.'

I sank on to the edge of her narrow bed and took one of her bandaged wrists in mine. Clearly this wasn't just a cry for help: if she'd simply wanted attention, it would have been much easier, and safer, to have taken an overdose; she certainly had access to enough pills. No one slits their wrists, and takes the trouble to do it lengthwise, along the vein, unless they're serious.

The room suddenly seemed smaller and darker. 'I'm not going to leave you,' I said.

Beside me, Ella stirs restlessly in her plane seat. On our way back from Cyprus, she asked me if I wanted to end things, without a trace of self-pity. Calm and collected, she was sanity itself. She made everything so easy. Of course I couldn't let her go. Not then; not now. She's the only one keeping me sane.

After we land at JFK and check in at the hotel, I leave Ella to take a shower and go down to the lobby to make my duty call to Beth. Cate answers the phone; to my surprise, she tells me Beth's staying in London with Eithne for a couple of days. Beth never mentioned that. I'm not sure I like the idea of Cate being left alone in the house right now. She sounds tense and unhappy. It could just be the pressure of exams, of course, but I get the feeling it's something more. When I mention Dan, she quickly changes the subject. I want the bastard out of the picture more than anyone, but if he's used and dropped her like a snotty tissue, I'll string the fucker up by his balls.

Damn it. I knew something was up when she came to my study the other night. I should've made time to listen to her, but this thing with Equinox – I *had* to take that call from John Torres – it'll be different once this contract is sorted . . .

I tell Cate to call if she needs me, and spend the next twenty minutes setting up the Equinox meeting. Christ. Power breakfasts on a Saturday morning. Welcome to America, Land of the Workaholic.

I nearly drop the phone altogether when Ella walks into the lobby. She's pulled out all the stops this evening: a clinging silky multi-coloured dress that skims her thighs and barely covers her nipples, and sky-high silver fuck-me shoes. I'm tempted to forget dinner and take her straight back upstairs.

We eat at a laid-back restaurant in Little Italy which serves the best zabaglione I've ever tasted. Ella is at her sparkling, witty best; if you didn't know her, you'd miss the giveaway signs of tension hidden beneath cleverly applied make-up. Sometimes she's so self-controlled it's fucking scary.

By the time we get back to our hotel room, you could run the Stars and Stripes up my erection. I unclip Ella's hair, fanning it out across her shoulders. She looks like an erotic Renaissance painting. 'You are so goddamn beautiful,' I mutter thickly.

I push her back on the vast bed, holding her down lightly as she arches impatiently towards me. Not yet, Ella. Not yet.

Taking my sweet time, I mouth my way down her body, her sweat salt on my tongue. I stroke her heavy tits as they splay either side of her ribcage, pink nipples darkening to mulberry beneath my touch. Dipping my tongue into her navel, I trace delicate whorls down her pale belly, then spread her legs and pull her to the edge of the bed, burying my face enthusiastically in her wet pussy. She tastes sweet and clean, and as she comes in shivering waves, I lap noisily, relishing the uninhibited way she gushes into my face.

Before she's even spent, I flip her on to her stomach, lifting her arse so that I can drive my thumb deep inside her, the way I know she likes. I love her big arse. Can't stand skinny bitches. A man needs something to get hold of.

Ella claws at the bed, her body going rigid as she comes again. I can't wait any longer. She spins slickly in my arms and I thrust my cock inside her, pinning her hands above her head with mine as we move together. Technically, she's not the best I've ever had – Christ, there was a Spanish girl my third year at Oxford, she had a cunt that could crack walnuts – but no one has ever made me feel like Ella. She's under my skin and inside my head; there are moments when I have no idea where she ends and I begin.

Afterwards, I pull her into my arms, stroking her glorious hair. Something was different tonight. I'm inexplicably sad, as if Ella's grief has leached into me.

'Crazy 'bout you,' I whisper before falling into a dreamless sleep.

When Beth's number is displayed on my mobile for the fourth time in ten minutes, I realize I've got no choice but to interrupt the most crucial meeting of my life and call her back.

I push my chair back from the table. 'Sorry, got to take this.'

John Torres stands with me. 'Go right ahead. I think we could all do with a ten-minute break. Mina, how about you call down for some fresh coffee? Tell them to go out to Café Dora, none of that machine piss.'

'Thanks, John,' I mutter, as he shows me to an empty conference room. 'Sorry about this—'

'Forget it. Take your time, you shouldn't be interrupted here. And quit worrying about the contract, William. It's a done deal. Let me tell you, Mina was very impressed by your presentation Saturday. She's with us. Drew may kick up some, but in the end, he'll come round.'

Relief engulfs me. 'You won't regret it, John.'

'I know that.' He claps me on the shoulder. 'Go make your call, buddy.'

For a minute or two after the door closes, I stare dazedly out of the window at the rainy New York streets forty-one floors below. I hadn't realized until the axe was lifted just how fucking terrified I was. We came *this* close to disaster . . .

I hit the speed-dial. 'Beth? What's up?'

'Oh, William, thank God! I've been going out of my mind, I've been calling and calling you – I know we have to ring the police but I wanted to talk to you first. You have to come home—'

Don't tell me she's pranged the bloody car again.

'Beth, calm down! What the hell is going on?'

'Cate's gone – I just got back from Eithne's and she's not home, oh, God, William, what are we going to do—'

'What makes you think she's not at Dan's, or out with friends?'

'She's not at Dan's, they broke up – oh, William! Supposing she's been abducted, she could be lying in a ditch somewhere—'

'Beth, get a grip, for God's sake. She's probably just gone shopping with Clem, and forgotten to leave you a note.'

'But she hasn't been home for two days!'

'How do you know?'

'She left Cannelle with the Franks across the road on Saturday—'

'Well, she can't have been kidnapped then, can she!' I exclaim, exasperated. 'For heaven's sake, Beth! If she left the dog with the neighbours, she's obviously gone off some- where. Has she taken anything with her?'

'Like what?'

'I don't know! Her silver trainers, for a start, they're practically welded to her feet. And that bloody yellow back- pack.'

I tap my fingers in an impatient tattoo on the conference table while I wait for Beth to come back on the line. Bugger Cate, for putting her mother through all this unnecessary upset. And bugger Beth, for overreacting as usual.

'She's taken them,' Beth pants a moment later. 'And her make-up bag and the Diesel jeans I bought her for her birthday—'

'I don't need a bloody inventory,' I snap. 'All right, we know she's run off. And I can guess where she's gone. She was nagging me before I left to go and see Fleur.'

'But Fleur's in Paris!'

'I'm aware of that. Give me the number, and I'll ring and put a bloody rocket up her arse. She'll be on the next train home, believe me.'

I punch in the number as soon as I hang up with Beth. I could swing for Cate. As if I haven't got enough on my plate with the Equinox deal, and poor Ella, breaking her heart over that baby—

'Allo?'

'Bonjour. May I speak to Cate Ashfield, *s'il vous plaît?'*

'Je ne comprends pas.'

The bitch! She just hung up on me!

I redial. 'Cate Ashfield, please—'

'Parlez français.'

'Je veux parler à Cate Ashfield,' I say again, through gritted teeth.

'Je ne comprends pas.'

'No, don't hang—'

I have steam coming out of my ears by the time I get back to the hotel. Bloody maid! Bloody Cate! Bloody women!

'I could bloody strangle her!' I yell, as I burst into our room. 'What the hell does she think she's playing at? As if I haven't got enough on my plate!'

Ella looks up from her packing in bewilderment.

'Cate!' I shout.

'I don't understand. What does she have to do with Equinox?'

'What? Oh, the meeting with Equinox went fine. They'll let me know tomorrow, but I think I swung it. It's Cate who's giving me the bloody headache! Running off to Paris! What on earth does she think she's playing at!

'Beth rang an hour ago in hysterics,' I say, a little more calmly. 'Cate's run away, no note, but she's taken her bloody silver trainers and that damn backpack, so she's clearly gone of her own free will. Beth was on the verge of calling the police before I talked her out of it.' Ella hands me a bourbon from the mini-bar, and I knock it back. 'I know where she is. She was on at me before I left to let her go and stay with her best friend in Paris. Bloody Fleur. I knew the two of them were up to something.'

'What are you going to do?'

'Cancel her credit card, for a start! I should never have given in to Beth and let her have one. I'm paying for this bloody nonsense!'

'Don't do that,' Ella says quickly. 'You don't want her stranded in a foreign country with no money. Have you tried calling her mobile?'

'Switched off. I tried ringing Fleur's parents, but the bloody French maid answered the phone, either doesn't understand English or doesn't want to—'

'Give me the number.'

I'd forgotten Ella speaks fluent French. She rattles off a few rapid-fire sentences, then hands the phone to me. 'She's there. Amélie has just gone to get her.'

She's safe. Thank God.

She's safe, while we've all been running around like headless chickens—

As soon as Cate comes to the phone, I give her both barrels. I don't care if she saw Ella and me writhing naked by the light of the silvery moon! It doesn't excuse her putting her mother and me through such grief. Nor am I mollified when she starts on about improving her French. Improving her French my arse!

'You knew where I was,' Cate mutters sulkily.

I want to reach down the phone and throttle her. 'Luckily for you, the Lavoies are good people, but you can't just turn up unannounced on their doorstep, Caitlin! Grow up! This isn't just about you!'

'It never is, is it?'

'Don't be so damn childish!' I shout. 'And I'd like to know where you got the money in the first—'

There's a sound behind me. I turn just in time to see Ella crumple to the floor.

I gape in shock.

'Oh, Jesus,' I whisper, as she vomits uncontrollably on the carpet. Suddenly I'm galvanized into action. Yanking a blanket from the bed, I tuck it round her and wipe the puke from her face with the tail of my shirt. 'Keep still. Don't move. Stay there, I'll get someone. Hold on.'

I hang up with Cate, dial zero and yell at the hotel receptionist to call an ambulance. Ella's doubled up with pain, her lips white and bloodless. Fear sluices through me as I cradle her head in my lap. I can't stop thinking about Jackson. Supposing the virus *was* contagious? Supposing Ella has it too? I can't lose her. She means the world to me.

Who am I trying to kid? She *is* my world.

This woman. This one woman: of course, of course. I love her. Not in a controlled, organized, tidy fashion. Not once a month, when she can be fitted into the spaces of my tidy, comfortable life. I love her because I can't help myself, because it comes as naturally to me as breathing, because she's the only woman I've ever met who knows more about jazz than I do.

I can't believe I've fooled myself for so long. Of course I love her; there's never been a moment when I didn't.

'They'll be here soon,' I tell her, stroking her damp hair back from her face. She's barely conscious. 'Whatever it is, we'll get you sorted out. The best care money can buy. Don't worry, darling. I'm here. It's probably something you ate. Nothing to worry about.'

My voice sounds hollow even to me. I've never seen anyone collapse like this, as if the life's been sucked out of them. I cling to Ella's hand as paramedics arrive and load her into an ambulance. We rocket around the streets of New York, and I feel strangely detached, as if I'm watching an episode of *ER* on television. This can't be happening. None of it seems real.

When we reach the emergency room, Ella is whisked out of sight by the paramedics. I try to follow her, but a security guard bars my way. I'm shunted, protesting, towards a glassed-in counter near the door.

'Insurance card,' the receptionist barks.

'What? I don't – I'm not sure—'

'Credit card?'

Dazedly, I hand it to her. She shoves a clipboard with a dozen multi-coloured forms towards me, and waves me to one side. 'Next.'

'Where have they taken—'

'Someone will be with you shortly. Next!'

A passing nurse takes pity and hands me a ball-point

pen. There's nowhere free to sit down, so I lean against the peeling wall and fill in the forms, ad-libbing when I don't know the answer. It's not like we've ever discussed whether she's had her tonsils out. I don't even know her full address.

When it comes to next of kin, I hesitate a moment, then put down my name.

Four hours later, I still have no idea what's happening. I've drunk a dozen cups of ersatz coffee from the machine, accosted anyone and everyone in a white coat, including the vending-machine filler, and been escorted firmly back to the waiting area twice by the menacing security guard, who's clearly of the thump-first-ask-questions-later school. No one seems able to tell me anything. I only know Ella's alive because I haven't yet been taken to the sinister windowless room off the long hallway.

The stroppy receptionist won't even speak to me. Actually, she threatened to call the cops if I went near her again. Even the wild-eyed methadone junkies are giving me a wide berth.

My phone rings, and I quickly take it outside. 'Christ, Beth, I'm so sorry. Cate's with Fleur, I meant to call you back—'

'For God's sake, William! I've been beside myself! I had to call the Lavoies myself in the end and get them out of bed! What on earth have you—'

'Look, I said I'm sorry,' I snap irritably. 'Something came up.'

'Something more important than your *daughter*?'

'Look, she's OK, that's the main thing. She'll be home in a day or two—'

'A day or two? When? What's she doing? Are you sure she's all right?'

'Mr Ashfield?'

I swing round. A doctor roughly the same age as my eldest son motions me to follow him inside.

'Look, Beth. I have to go. I'll talk to you tomorrow.'

I snap shut my phone and hasten into the hospital.

'Your wife is doing much better,' the doctor smiles, flashing orthodontic braces. 'She's in recovery. It was dicey for a bit, but she's gonna be fine. You can see her now.'

I don't bother to correct his assumption: *my wife*. If only.

Ella is several shades whiter than her hospital sheets, but produces a wan smile when I burst into the recovery room. 'I wouldn't recommend the fish,' she says thinly.

'I'll bear that in mind.' I perch gingerly on the edge of the bed, painfully aware of the last time I visited a woman in hospital. 'You gave me quite a scare back there.'

'I gave myself one,' she grimaces. 'I'm so sorry, William. You've got enough on your plate without—'

'Don't be bloody ridiculous! Christ, Ella. I thought I'd lost you!'

'Sorry. You'll have to try a bit harder next time.'

'Not funny, Ella. I had no idea if you were even dead or alive. No one would tell me anything. What in hell happened? '

She shifts, wincing, against the pillows. 'Let's just say, if your appendix ever puts in a formal complaint, listen to it.'

'Talk about "Physician, heal thyself." '

I hesitate. Ordinarily, Ella would slap me down if I so much as hinted the L-word, but she's changed since Jackson died. There's a softness to her, a vulnerability, that wasn't there before. It gives me the balls to tell her the truth. 'Ella, you've no idea what it did to me, seeing you like that,' I say carefully. 'I realized this afternoon how much you mean to me, how much I—'

'William, I'm sorry, but could you ask the nurse for some more codeine?'

I summon a candy-striper, who bustles in with some pills. Ella sips slowly from a paper cup, her features etched with pain. I notice for the first time how much weight she's lost recently. She's got cheekbones like Katharine Hepburn.

'Ella—'

She covers my mouth. 'Don't say it.'

'I've spent the last eight years not saying it! It's time we—'

'All this drama,' Ella says lightly. 'It's enough to make anyone get carried away and say things they might regret later.'

'But I—'

'William,' she cries fiercely. 'You're *married*. It doesn't matter what either of us feel, or think we feel. We agreed at the beginning that this wasn't going to go anywhere. Beth needs you. Your children need you. Talking like this just makes everything worse.'

'I can't keep on pretending I don't care, Ella! It'll make things a total farce!'

Her eyes are bright. Fear swirls around me like fog.

'William. I think we both know it's over—'

'Of course it's not over! Look, I'll leave Beth. If that's what you want. I'll leave her, she'll be fine, she'll still have the children—'

'No! That's not what I meant!' She struggles to sit

upright. 'We should never have let it get this far. We should have ended it after Cyprus; *I* should have ended it. Think what Beth might do if—'

'I'm to spend the rest of my life held to ransom?'

'She's your *wife*. Please, William. Don't make this more difficult than it has to be.'

I stand up. 'Look, you've just had surgery. God knows what drugs are still in your system. You're probably still in shock. Hormones all over the place. We'll talk about this sensibly when you've calmed down.'

'I am calm!' Ella yells.

'Of course you are. I'll be back tomorrow morning. Sleep well, darling.'

A pillow thumps against the door behind me.

She doesn't mean it. It's just post-traumatic stress, or whatever the bloody hell they call it these days. Emergency surgery, on top of the last few weeks she's just had. It's guilt and grief talking. She probably doesn't know whether she's coming or going. She doesn't mean it. She can't.

The teenage doctor stops me as I'm about to leave. 'I wanted to say how sorry I am, Mr Ashfield. It's a real shame.'

'Well, yes. But she's on the mend now, that's the main thing.'

'Sure. Good. You got a great attitude, sir. You keep saying that sort of thing to her. She needs to know she's just as much of a woman to you now as she always was. It can be a terrible blow if—'

'Excuse me,' I say, 'but what the hell are you talking about?'

He looks horrified. 'She didn't tell you?'

'What didn't she tell me?'

'I think maybe you should speak to—'

'Look, doctor. I've had enough of this. I don't mean to be rude, but if you don't tell me what the fuck is going on, I won't be responsible for my actions. Do you follow me?'

He swallows.

I open the door to the sinister death room. 'After you.'

'I really shouldn't—'

I take a step forward.

'Mr Ashfield, as you know, your wife had an ectopic pregnancy,' he says quickly, shutting the door behind us. 'That's when the embryo implants in the fallopian tubes, rather than the womb. Unfortunately, we only found out about it when the tube burst. Ordinarily, that wouldn't be the end of the world, as she'd still have had the other tube. It'd make pregnancy more difficult, certainly, but not impossible.'

Pregnant? *Ella*?

'The problem,' he adds nervously, 'is that in your wife's case, there was already considerable scarring on her other tube. She must have gotten an infection at some point, probably years ago. She might not even have known about it. It means she'll never conceive naturally. I'm so sorry.'

I sink into a chair. Clearly it can't be mine; we took care of that the week after Beth discovered she was pregnant with Sam. Jackson died, what, six weeks ago? Christ. A posthumous baby.

Why didn't she *tell* me? Why pretend she had appendicitis? Did she think it'd make any difference to the way I feel about her?

'There's always IVF,' the young doctor says encouragingly. 'She still has plenty of eggs for a woman her age, which is good news. You could—'

'We've never wanted children,' I say faintly.

'Well. Look. I need to get back to my patients . . .'

'You go. I'll be fine. I just need to take a minute.'

The door shuts softly behind him. I bury my head in my hands, trying to get my mind around what he's just told me.

Jackson's baby. Dear God. And now she's lost even that.

I wait for Ella to tell me. For three days, we discuss the weather, the news, the origins of man and the latest series of *American Idol*, but we studiously avoid any mention of the future, and Ella doesn't tell me she's lost Jackson's child and will never have any man's baby again.

When I arrive at the hospital to collect her and sign her discharge papers, I wonder if this is finally it. I should never have tried to tell her I love her. She hates that kind of clinginess. I've driven her away.

I just thought – I had a feeling – she seemed more *open*, somehow.

If we can just go back to the way things were, I'll take it. Whatever her terms.

My mobile rings as I pay off the taxi. It's an international number; I head towards the parking lot to take the call.

'Beth! Where are you?'

'Paris. Cate didn't come home, so I came to get her.'

'I hope you gave her hell,' I exclaim. 'She needs to grow up and think of other people for a change. I can't believe she's been so irresponsible—'

'Shut up, William! Would you just shut up!'

I'm taken aback. It's not like Beth to get angry. Sad is

what Beth does. Sad, defeated, depressed. 'There's no need—'

'Cate's not here!' Beth cries.

'Of course she's there. I spoke to her on Monday.'

'She left this morning. No one knows where she's gone!'

I jam the phone against my other ear. 'She's probably on her way back to you. I bet you crossed each other in the Chunnel.'

'She hasn't gone home, William! She could be anywhere. She's only seventeen.' Beth's voice cracks. 'Anything could happen to her. We have to find her!'

'I'm sure she'll—'

'William! Would you just *listen* instead of talking! Your daughter is missing, and no one has any idea where she is! I don't care what you're doing or how important you think it is. For once in your life, you need to put Cate first. I expect you to get a plane to Paris the moment you arrive in London, and I'll pick you up at the airport, do you understand?'

She hangs up with a sharp click. I'm speechless. I can't remember Beth ever talking to me like that in her life. Who knew she had *that* in her?

Ella is waiting for me at the hospital reception. 'Don't wait till tomorrow,' she urges, when I tell her about Cate. 'There's bound to be a flight to Paris this afternoon. You could be there by tomorrow morning.'

For the first time, the reality of the situation sinks in. I picture my daughter, alone in a foreign country, too scared to come home. Seventeen is so young. She thinks she knows it all, but she's not one of those street-wise teenagers you see hanging around shopping malls or falling out of nightclubs. I suppose I'm to blame for that, protecting her too much. Wrapping her up in cotton wool.

I'm torn. 'But you've just come out of hospital—'

'William, don't fuss. I'll be fine. I *am* a doctor,' she says. 'You need to put your family first. Call me when you find Cate.'

The next flight to Paris via Philadelphia leaves in four hours. I book myself on it, and drop Ella at the hotel. She kisses me goodbye. I ask when I'll see her again, but she doesn't answer: a reply in itself.

Maybe she's right, I think bleakly. Maybe it *is* over. We've driven Cate to this, Ella and I. If anything happens to my daughter, I'll never forgive myself.

I'm exhausted by the time I arrive in Paris the next morning. Beth is waiting for me at Charles de Gaulle, as arranged. She waves when she sees me, and I push my trolley towards her, then freeze with shock.

I haven't seen her in twenty years, but she looks exactly the same.

Standing behind Beth is my mother.

11

Beth

Cate wasn't supposed to be the one to find me. It should have been Eithne, I knew she was coming round that morning for coffee (laced, as always, with vodka, even at 10 a.m.); it wouldn't have been pleasant for her, of course, but she owed it to me. One-all, as it were.

Eithne would've known I didn't mean it. She'd have understood I had to do *some*thing to get William's attention.

It was all Clara's fault, of course. She knew how much I hated leaving the house on my own, but William was in Cyprus and the baby needed milk and nappies and Clara simply refused to go shopping, so I had no choice but to drive to the supermarket myself. Naturally the car park was terribly crowded, I couldn't find a space, and of course I got into one of my panics. I only hit a wall, nothing serious. But I needed to find the insurance papers, and when I got home I realized I had no idea where they were.

I'd never have dreamed of going through William's desk, so I had to phone him at his hotel, even though I knew how much he hated being disturbed by domestic trivia when he was away on business.

The receptionist couldn't find his reservation at first. 'No Mr Ashton,' she said in thick English—

'It's Ash*field*,' I corrected in relief. 'William Ashfield.'

'Εδώ είναι! Here is, Mr and Mrs Ashfield, room two-oh-one. But they gone out, I call them the taxi myself. You want take message me?'

I put down the telephone and sat quietly thinking for a very long time. The girl could have made a mistake – her English was quite atrocious – but somehow I knew she hadn't. Mr and Mrs Ashfield. This wasn't just a fling with some floozie William had picked up in a Cypriot bar; a one-night stand. This was planned. She was staying with him, he'd booked her into the hotel with him, which meant this was something altogether more serious.

I knew what I had to do. I was fighting for my marriage the only way I knew how. I didn't have much else to offer William. As Clara often reminded me.

Guilt can be more powerful than love, sometimes.

An overdose would have been the easiest way, but that's so unpredictable, and too easy to dismiss as a cry for help. William had to believe I *meant* it. I had to choose a way that left no room for doubt – whilst making sure, of course, that there was plenty of room for doubt after all.

I was very careful. I knew where to cut, and how deep. (It didn't hurt. I expected it to, but it didn't. There was something rather soothing about watching the blood flow out of my wrists, though when I saw the sticky red mess, so *much* blood, I felt a moment of absolute terror. If Eithne didn't come—)

What I didn't know was that Cate would forget her

school project that morning, the one she'd spent weeks and weeks working on with William, that she'd catch the bus back home and burst into the kitchen to find me on the floor (where Eithne would be sure to see me, through the kitchen window, when I didn't answer the door). I didn't know she'd be the one to rip up tea-towels to bind my wrists, and call 999, and explain to the doctors and policemen – and later, no doubt, to a therapist – that her mother had tried to kill herself when she was ten years old, and she'd been the one to find her.

'You were *ill*,' Eithne groans now, for the umpteenth time. 'You couldn't help it.'

'She was only ten,' I fret, pacing the length of her studio. 'How could I do that to her? I'm her mother! I'm supposed to *protect* her!'

Eithne stretches out on the filthy, paint-smeared sofa, hands behind her head. Sunshine streams through the grimy windowpanes, blocking the studio floor with faded gold diamonds. The room shakes as a train rattles along the Northern Line beneath us. It may not be quiet here, but I envy her all this space. I should never have had children.

'Why do you keep worrying at it?' she demands. 'You're like a dog with a bone. Yes, you fucked up, but haven't we all? It was seven *years* ago, Beth. Let it go.'

I chew at my nails. 'Cate can't. I see it in her eyes, every time she looks at me. She doesn't trust me. She never has. Even before—' I hesitate.

'Your little *flagrante*?'

'It wasn't—'

She flaps her hand laconically. 'Yes, yes, I know. Look, she'll come round. Give it a few days—'

'She won't, Eithne. You know she won't. She hasn't

227

spoken to me since it happened. I thought, if I stayed with you for a few days and gave her time – but she's not even picking up the phone when I call. How can I explain what happened if she won't speak to me?'

'You have to let her work it out in her own time, Beth. You and William have over-compensated with that child. It won't do her any harm to grow up a little.'

I open my mouth to object.

'Look.' Eithne swings herself upright. 'Shit happens, Beth. You did something stupid, but you were ill, and Cate knows that. She's seventeen now, not ten. Old enough to see beyond the myth that Daddy's a conquering hero and you're a nutty old bat who should be locked up in an attic.' She gets up and pours herself an inch of neat vodka. 'William, Cate, Clara – none of them takes you seriously. They all treat you somewhere between an old lady in her dotage and the village idiot. And you just *let* them.'

'Eithne, stop. This isn't helping.'

'I give up. You're so damn *passive*, Beth! You're taking a back-row seat in your own life. When are you going to step up to the plate and take some responsibility?'

I take a pace backwards. 'I've tried—'

'Don't you dare hide behind your illness!'

'You were the one who just said I couldn't help it!'

'You can't help being ill, but you can help what you do about it,' Eithne says sharply. 'Plenty of people have manic depression and achieve all sorts of things. Winston Churchill had it, and saved the bloody country!' She gesticulates wildly, spilling her drink. 'Some of the greatest artists and writers and scientists have been bipolar – Mozart, William Blake, Isaac Newton, Mark Twain – it didn't keep them from using their talents and living their lives to the full, did it?'

'They were all men,' I mutter. 'It's different for women. I have three children, don't forget—'

'Beth, sometimes I want to slap you! You could do so much! You could *be* so much! And you won't even *try!*'

'It's the drugs!' I shout suddenly. 'It's easy for you to say! You don't understand! They take everything! Mozart and Churchill didn't have to spend their lives feeling dead and numb, just so they could function! They didn't have to drug themselves into oblivion just to give the semblance of being a normal wife and mother—'

Eithne puts down her glass, cups my face with her hands, and kisses me with such force my teeth graze my lips. All the passion and anger and frustration I see in her art, she pours into that kiss.

I'm too shocked to kiss her back, but it doesn't seem to matter. My arms stiffen. Something unexpected stirs inside me: neither revulsion, nor the kind of desire that drenches me when I think of Dan; it takes me a moment to identify it as curiosity. I've never kissed a woman before. I close my eyes, but it's still – different. *Other*. Eithne is taller than I am, as tall as any man, and broad-shouldered from years of heaving stone and iron sculptures; flat-chested and crop-haired and rangy, she could pass for a man from a distance. And yet she is more womanly than any woman I've ever met, and her kiss so clearly feminine in a way I can't begin to explain.

She steps back, her expression defiant, and waits.

'Oh,' I squeak.

'Is that all you have to say?'

'I'm a little surprised, I suppose—'

She snorts.

'Well. It's just – the thing is, Eithne. First Dan, and now you. It's not as if I – I'm hardly – it's never happened quite so – I mean, *why*?'

Eithne takes me by the shoulders and propels me towards the florid rococo mirror taking up two-thirds of a wall on the far side of her studio. 'What do you see, Beth?' she demands.

'Oh, you know,' I mumble, ducking my head. 'Just me.'

'You really have no idea, do you?' She leans over my shoulder, lifting my chin and meeting my eyes in the mirror. 'You're too used to seeing yourself through the eyes of your bloody mother, or that bratty daughter of yours, or the man who's been sharing your bed and taking you for granted for twenty years.' She gives me a gentle shake. 'Look at you! You're beautiful. And you don't even know it! That's what's so amazing about you! You don't even realize how lovely you are!'

For a moment, I almost see it. Sometimes, years ago, I'd see a photo of myself, taken in an unguarded moment, and think, *Goodness, I nearly look pretty . . .*

But that was a long time ago.

'You love me,' I say wonderingly.

'Well, of course I do,' she retorts crossly.

I turn from the mirror, looking into her angular, intelligent face. Eithne Brompton has been my dearest friend for two decades; we've weathered loss and grief, enjoyed happiness, survived children and marriage, disaster and success, our lives as opposite as it's possible for two women's to be, and yet she's closer to me than anyone; William included. There's nothing we haven't shared. How could I not have known this about her?

I knew it.

'I love you, too,' I say, 'but not like that—'

'It's all right,' she says. 'I didn't expect you to.'

'I know,' I say.

And then I kiss her back.

I don't love her *like that*, but I love her enough. And she loves me. Love, even from the wrong person in the wrong circumstances, has a rightness all its own. Not to receive it with gratitude seems like arrogance of the worst kind.

I've never been a very bohemian sort of artist. More the Tupperware kind, if truth be known. Just once, I'd like to see myself the way Eithne sees me. To be the person she seems to think I am.

And – and it wouldn't really *count*, would it? With a woman. Not like it would, oh, God, with Dan.

So I lead her towards the low Japanese bed in the corner of the vast, dusty studio, her fingers running up and down my spine like a nun counting rosary beads. I untie the belt of my neat shirt-waister, and help her with her own buttons when her hands shake too much to undo them herself. My hands flutter over her bare bony shoulders as she unfastens my bra and cups my heavy breasts. It's impossible to be touched by someone with such love and not feel anything. Impossible to remain *un*touched.

But when she pushes me back on the bed and slides down between my legs and touches and tongues and strokes me to the first orgasm I've had since before Cate was born, my gratitude is no longer theoretical.

I kiss her and taste myself on her lips, and wonder if I can love her like that after all.

'I'm sorry,' I say, leaning up on one elbow. 'I wish I was a lesbian. I'd really *like* to be.'

Eithne nearly chokes with laughter. 'Oh, Beth. This isn't netball. It's not like picking whether you want to be reds or yellows.'

'It was very nice, and everything—'

'Next you'll be thanking me for having you.'

'It's just – well. I don't think it's exactly *me*.'

She sits up, bare-breasted, and stubs out her cigarette. Despite everything we did last night – my cheeks flame – I primly avert my gaze from her nakedness.

'Look, Beth. I'm not under any illusions here. I know you're not what William would no doubt term a rug-muncher. I wish it were otherwise,' she smiles ruefully, 'but you don't have to apologize for being the way you are. I've loved you since the moment you picked me back up off the floor after Kit, but I've always known I hadn't got a cat in hell's chance. Don't start blaming yourself. You've never given me false hope. Last night was unexpected, the most wonderful gift, a dream come true, but I realize that's all it was.'

She gathers the sheet around herself, and perches on the edge of the platform bed next to me. 'Nothing's changed, Beth,' she says softly, linking her fingers with mine. 'We're still OK, aren't we?'

I look at our entwined hands, and nod.

'Separate beds in Italy next month, though,' she adds wryly. 'I'm not that much of a saint. This was just a one-off, Mrs Suburban-wife-and-two-point-four. Nothing to get your sensible knickers in a twist about, OK? No going home and immersing yourself in yet more guilt and self-doubt.'

'I'm not sure William would see it quite that way—'

'William would just sulk because we didn't let him watch.'

I can't help but laugh.

'You're a much happier person when he isn't around,' she sighs. 'I'd never ask you to leave him for me, Beth, but I wish you'd consider leaving him for *you*. He's made you so helpless. He's just taken over control of your life from where Clara left off. I'm sure he thinks he's doing you a favour, but—'

'No,' I say firmly.

There are places even Eithne isn't allowed to go.

She stands up, still wrapped awkwardly in the damp sheet, and hugs me. 'It'll be fine, Beth. Go home. And talk to Cate. Even if she doesn't talk to you.'

Eithne is right, I think, as I let myself into the house later that afternoon. I can't expect Cate to make the first move. I have to go to her, even if she spits on my olive branch. Surely, if I give her enough time, prove that I'm here for her . . .

The hallway is cold and dark. I feel a moment of concern, before remembering that it's Monday, and Cate will still be on her way home from school.

I'm expecting the usual pile of dirty plates in the kitchen sink and butter-smeared knives left on the counter – why are teenagers physically incapable of reaching that extra ten inches to the dishwasher? – but the kitchen is as neat and tidy as when I left it on Saturday morning. I smile in surprise. Perhaps this is Cate's way of saying she's sorry, too.

Someone knocks at the back door as I go to put the kettle on the hob. A moment later, Cannelle bounds into the kitchen, buffeting me with enthusiasm and rank doggy breath. 'Hey! Where have you been?' I say, ruffling his glossy coat. 'Did you miss me, boy? Did Cate take good care of you?'

'Sorry to pounce the moment you get back,' my neighbour, Jean, apologizes, 'only I've got to take my mother to the dentist at five, and I saw your car pull up—'

'You've been looking after Cannelle? That's very kind, Jean, but Cate didn't need to ask you. He's all right on his own for a couple of hours. She knew I'd be back this afternoon—'

Jean looks confused. 'But she left him with me on Saturday. She said she had to go away for a few days. I thought you knew. She said you'd be back to pick him up sometime today.'

I feel the first stirrings of alarm. 'Did she say where she was going?'

'No. I assumed she was going to stay with you— Oh, dear. Beth, is there a problem?'

'No, no,' I say, mustering a smile. 'Thanks so much, Jean. I'm sure it's just a few crossed wires, that's all.'

I run upstairs, and check Cate's room. The bed hasn't been slept in: the pile of clean laundry I left on her duvet on Saturday morning is still there.

The panic escalates. She's been gone nearly three days; anything could have happened. She could have been kidnapped, murdered – even now, she could be lying in a ditch somewhere. We might never know what happened to her. That poor estate-agent girl, it's been twenty years and she's never been found, what her mother must have gone through—

'For heaven's sake, Beth!' William exclaims five minutes later. 'If she left the dog with the neighbours, she's obviously gone off somewhere. Has she taken anything with her?'

'Like what?'

'I don't know! Her silver trainers, for a start, they're practically welded to her feet. And that bloody yellow back-pack.'

I run upstairs with the phone, and fling open her wardrobe. Relief engulfs me. William's right: half Cate's favourite clothes are missing.

'She's taken them,' I confirm, almost giddy at the reprieve. 'And her make-up bag and the Diesel jeans I bought her for her birthday—'

'I don't need a bloody inventory. All right, we know she's run off. And I can guess where she's gone. She was nagging me before I left to go and see Fleur.'

'But Fleur's in Paris!'

'I'm aware of that. Give me the number, and I'll ring and put a bloody rocket up her arse. She'll be on the next train home, believe me.'

I sink on to the edge of Cate's bed, cradling the phone between my knees. Thank God William's so sensible, thank God, thank God. He's right. Of course he's right. A kidnapper wouldn't have let her take the dog over to the Franks! She's just bunking off. Gone to see Fleur in Paris. William will bawl her out, and she'll be on the next train home.

He'll call me back in a minute and tell me she's safe with Fleur.

Twenty minutes later, when he still hasn't rung, I start to worry again. I get up and put away Cate's clean laundry, willing myself not to get carried away again. It could be as simple as the Lavoies' phone being engaged.

I twitch her duvet into place, then go downstairs, feed Cannelle and water the plants. It's nearly an hour since I spoke to William. If she definitely wasn't with Fleur, he'd have called me back by now. He must still be trying to get hold of the Lavoies. No news is good news. Perhaps they've taken Cate out to dinner or something. No need to read anything sinister into it.

Another hour passes. I leave an anxious message on William's mobile, and wander distractedly around the dark house, straightening pictures and book spines. This is all my fault. If I'd stayed home this weekend, got her to see reason over Dan—

I leap on the phone, but it's only Eithne. I promise to call her back in the morning, and then hang up, in case William's trying to get through.

By eleven, I'm frantic. Why hasn't he phoned? What can he be doing all this time?

It's only midnight in Paris, I tell myself as I dial the Lavoies' number. *I have to know she's safe.* Everyone knows they go to bed later in Europe.

Five minutes later, fear has been replaced by fury.

'Christ, Beth, I'm so sorry,' William says, when he finally answers his mobile. 'Cate's with Fleur. I meant to call you back—'

'For God's sake, William! I've been beside myself! I had to call the Lavoies myself in the end and get them out of bed! What on earth have you—'

'Look, I said I'm sorry. Something came up.'

My outrage is so consuming, it takes me a moment to recover my voice. 'Something more important than your *daughter*?'

'Look, she's OK, that's the main thing. She'll be home in a day or two—'

'A day or two?' I cry. 'When? What's she doing? Are you sure she's all right?'

'Look, Beth. I have to go. I'll talk to you tomorrow.'

He hangs up. I stare at the phone in disbelief. Our daughter's run away to France! What kind of father is he? Doesn't he *care*?

But then he isn't the one riven with guilt.

I jump at the sound of the back door opening. Cannelle immediately leaps up, barking madly. Standing in the kitchen is the last person I expected to see.

'Beth, please, let me speak before you throw me out,' Dan says urgently. 'There's something very important I have to tell you.'

I clench my fist around the pills. A handful of poison. God knows I don't want to take them. I know what that will mean.

But I also know what it will mean if I don't.

Cate needs me in my right mind. It's been three days since William spoke to her, and she still isn't home. I have to go to Paris and find her. For once, I have to be the mother Cate needs and deserves.

I'm not just swinging from one extreme to the next now; I'm living all kinds of extreme at the same time. Despair and mania and a spinning, tilting reality. Water-sprites in the bathroom; Jesus's face in a hunk of Stilton. I can't control it any more.

I take a large gulp of water and knock them back.

My throat closes. I can't swallow. I hold the pills and water in my mouth, my cheeks bulging. I can't bear it. To surrender to the fog, to lose touch with everything that makes life worth living. Especially now, after Dan—

Maybe I'm a fool for believing him. It could just be another lie. At the very least, I should tell William. Warn him.

Swallow!

Coughing and choking, I lean over the kitchen sink and spit out the pills. Failure heaves itself into my mouth, more bitter than the medication.

I push my hair back from my face with my wrist, and run the tap, watching the last of my pills spiral down the drain. That's it, then. No going back.

When I look up, William's mother is standing in the doorway.

'Of course I'll come with you,' Anne says.

'Are you sure you're well enough?'

'For the moment,' she says, taking the kettle from my hand, 'and frankly, my dear, as things stand, I don't have a lot to lose.'

I drift towards a chair while Anne bustles about the unfamiliar kitchen as if it's her home, not mine. I watch helplessly. 'I don't know how long we'll be gone—'

'Don't worry, dear.' She nods towards the small blue

BOAC bag by the door. 'I've got everything I need in there, and I'm not above rinsing my smalls in the basin if needs be.'

She sets two clean mugs on the table and briskly warms the pot, trim and neat in her pressed cream blouse and calf-length tweed skirt. I know she's already been through two gruelling rounds of chemotherapy, but her silver hair is still perfectly coiffed, her discreet make-up flawless. Her only concession to illness is an antique silver-topped ebony cane. I'm certain that when we reach Paris, everything will emerge pristine from her holdall, her slacks creaseless and newly dry-cleaned, crisp shirts sporting the full complement of buttons, polished shoes stuffed with newspaper and carefully packed in their own cloth shoe bags so there's no chance of the immaculate heels marking any of her clothes. Even before I had children I never went anywhere without at least two bulging and battered suitcases, and no matter how carefully I pack, everything always emerges looking like crumpled Oxfam rags.

I'm perfectly capable of getting myself to Paris (my teenage daughter managed it, for heaven's sake) but Anne smoothly takes over, booking our train tickets, organizing my packing – 'Now, dear, it may be springtime in Paris, but I think *two* sweaters, don't you?' – and arranging for Cannelle to spend his second holiday in a week with the neighbours.

Despite her well-meaning kindness, I feel helpless and diminished. There's a rebuke to her efficiency, an *If you want a job doing well* ... This is exactly what William does, I realize suddenly. He takes control, suffocating me with his capability.

I want to tell Anne to leave me alone, let me run my own life, but of course I don't.

I never do.

Sabine Lavoie shrugs her elegant shoulders. 'If you had telephoned first, it would have saved you a wasted journey.'

'I didn't want to frighten Cate away,' I say.

'Instead, she has already left.'

Next to me, Anne's eyes are as Arctic as the French-woman's. 'Perhaps we could come in, rather than discuss this in the street.'

Mme Lavoie hesitates, then nods curtly and turns. We follow her into an overdone, rococo drawing-room crammed with gilt chairs and ornate furniture. It might seem impressive, were the pieces of the same period, or even from the same country. A Louis XVI tri-fold mirror is hugger-mugger with a Spanish baroque tabernacle and two Italian Renaissance armchairs. A pair of mid-nineteenth-century majolica bottleneck vases sit atop a sixteenth-century Florentine credenza. The effect is a cross between an Arab souk and a country-house car-boot sale.

'Coffee would be perfect,' says Anne, as though Mme Lavoie had spoken. 'Thank you so much.'

Mme Lavoie signals to the maid, who scuttles out of the room, eyes wide with delight. I suspect her mistress isn't discomforted in her own home too often. If I weren't so concerned for my daughter, I might enjoy this clash of the titans too.

'Where is she?' I burst out. 'She was here last night, wasn't she?'

Another Gallic shrug. 'I had an engagement. She was here when I left at five.'

'Your daughter must know,' Anne says firmly. 'We need to talk to her.'

'My daughter was also out last night, I believe.'

'Your husband, then.'

'*Désolée*. He is working. Perhaps, if you come back after six—'

'Madame Lavoie,' Anne says, rapping her cane sharply against the marble floor. 'I don't think you understand. My granddaughter is missing. She is only seventeen years old. The last time anyone saw her was here, at your house. We appreciate your hospitality, but things are more serious now. Naturally, we're reluctant to involve the police in a private matter, but we must find her as soon as possible. I'm sorry if that causes you embarrassment, but—'

Sabine Lavoie stands. 'I'll see if I can reach my husband.'

'I'm going to talk to that maid,' Anne says, *sotto voce*. 'Servants always know what's really going on.'

'I need to call William,' I say. 'My mobile doesn't work here—'

'There's a phone in the hall. Don't let him off the hook,' Anne warns. 'That boy needs to be brought to heel. Stand up to him, Beth. It's the only way to earn his respect. Men don't love where they don't esteem, remember that.'

I can quite see why, after growing up with a mother like Anne, William felt the need to marry a woman like me. And why he's been regretting it ever since.

'Beth!' William exclaims. 'Where are you?'

'Paris. Cate didn't come home, so I came to get her.'

'I hope you gave her hell. She needs to grow up and

think of other people for a change. I can't believe she's been so irresponsible—'

Irresponsible? I want to scream. Who's the one living it up in New York doing who-knows-what with who-knows-whom, while his daughter is missing? Who couldn't even be bothered to call me back to say he'd found her because *something came up*? Where did she learn *irresponsible* from, if not from you?

Suddenly, my simmering anger reaches boiling point.

'Shut up, William! Would you just shut up!'

He sounds as startled as I am at my tone. 'There's no need—'

'Cate's not here!' I yell.

'Of course she's there. I spoke to her on Monday.'

'She left this morning. No one knows where she's gone!'

'She's probably on her way back to you. I bet you crossed each other in the Chunnel.'

'She hasn't gone home, William!' I say impatiently. 'She could be anywhere. She's only seventeen. Anything could happen to her. We have to find her!'

'I'm sure she'll—'

'William!' I shout. 'Would you just *listen* instead of talking! Your daughter is missing, and no one has any idea where she is! I don't care what you're doing or how important you think it is. For once in your life, you need to put Cate first. I expect you to get a plane to Paris the moment you arrive in London, and I'll pick you up at the airport, do you understand?'

I slam the phone into its cradle. 'About time,' Anne says behind me.

'Did you speak to the maid?'

'We had a very interesting conversation. Apparently, Medusa in there *did* see Cate after last night: they had a screaming row this morning, which ended with Cate slamming out of the house just after eight.'

'The bitch,' I breathe.

I start towards the *salon*, then turn.

'Anne,' I say, 'I don't want to be rude, but I need to talk to Fleur's mother by myself, if you don't mind.'

She forces a smile. 'Of course.'

Mme Lavoie is on her mobile when I find her. I shut the *salon* door behind me, and she looks up, then mutters something unintelligible in French and snaps her phone shut.

I fold my arms and channel Clara into my expression.

'Now,' I say grimly. 'How about you tell me what *really* happened this morning between you and my daughter?'

'What the fuck is *she* doing here?' William snarls.

Anne stiffens, but her smile doesn't slip. 'Hello, dear,' she says calmly.

He starts to push his suitcase trolley past us, but I block his way. 'She came to help me find our daughter,' I say sharply. 'Since *you* weren't available. And right now, I don't give a damn whether Anne beat the soles of your feet with bamboo canes or force-fed you slugs in castor oil when you were a baby. Cate is our priority, and until she's found, she's the only one I care about.'

Astonishment, fury and confusion chase each other across William's features.

'Same goes for you, Anne,' I add, more gently. 'Whatever you need to say to William, it waits until Cate's back.'

'May I ask where we're going?' my husband enquires icily as I lead the way to the taxi rank. 'Or would you like a group hug and a quick round of "Kumbaya" first?'

'Sabine Lavoie thinks Cate may have gone to Marseille,' I reply. 'Fleur was showing her pictures of their holiday home the other night, apparently. I suggest we go back to the hotel Anne and I stayed at last night, and work out what we're going to do from there.'

No need to mention that Mme Lavoie threw Cate out of her house, or why. William has had enough shocks for one day.

'Sounds like a wild goose chase, if you ask me—'

'No one did, William. Unless you have a better idea?'

'Fine,' he snaps.

He climbs into the taxi, his anger evident in the rigid set of his shoulders. I don't care. For the first time in as long as I can remember, pleasing William isn't top of my concerns.

'Go and check in,' I tell him, when the taxi drops us off at the hotel, a short walk from the Lavoies'. 'I'm going for a walk, to clear my head. I won't be long.'

He stalks up the steps. My heart shivers, watching him. Whatever our differences, there's nothing I wouldn't do for this man.

I've always known he doesn't feel the same about me. Over the years, I've grown to accept his tepid, damning-with-faint-praise affection; to see it as my due.

Maybe it's because I haven't taken my pills for a few weeks; perhaps Cate's disappearance has stripped every-thing down to the bone. But suddenly affection isn't enough. I don't want to settle for the same careless fond-ness he bestows on the dog. I'm his *wife*! I want him to long for me the way I ache for him; to race home at the end of the day eager to see me. If I can't have that, I don't want second-best.

I cross the Seine, heading towards the Jardin des Tuileries. The air smells of traffic fumes and cut grass and springtime. William and I should be strolling along the Left Bank hand-in-hand, enjoying a second honeymoon. Instead, thanks to my reckless stupidity, we're here to search for our missing teenage daughter. Dear Lord, how did it come to this?

I should have stood up to William long ago. Eithne was right. I've let him treat me like an incapable, pitiable fool. And in the end, that's what I've become.

I sink on to a bench beneath a block of linden trees. What if Cate's not in Marseille? *What if we never find her?*

A teenage girl is huddled on a bench near me, knees drawn up under her chin, cheek resting on them. She looks dishevelled and unkempt, as if she's slept in her clothes. It could be Cate, I think despairingly. She's about the same age. Still not much more than a child—

The girl wearily unfolds herself, and picks up the bag at her feet.

Silver feet.

She hoists her filthy yellow back-pack on to her shoulder, glancing listlessly in my direction. I get up as if in a dream. For a moment her gaze drifts past me; and then suddenly her eyes widen with recognition and shock.

'Cate, please,' I cry.

She hesitates. I reach out my hand, too terrified to move. And watch her run.

12

Cate

No one ever tells you how, like, *clumsy* sex is. The first time I kissed a boy – Patrick Corcoran, when I was thirteen and a half, at the bus stop by the cemetery – I didn't even know which way to tilt my head so we didn't bump noses. How do people find out this stuff? Is there some rule, like driving on the right? Or is it in your genes, like being left-handed?

Mum and I had the birds-and-the-bees conversation, of course, and we all sniggered over the drawings of long-haired hippies getting it on in Biology (you'd think they could update the pictures once in a while). But I don't remember anyone saying Prince Charming would stick his finger in your eye trying to get your bra off, or you'd knee him in the balls when he got on top of you, or that when he'd finally stopped swearing, your sweaty bodies wouldn't just fit together neatly like two pieces of a jigsaw puzzle, but that you'd have to shuffle up-a-bit, down-a-bit, going *Excuse me* and *Oops sorry* till you got it right. Or that his thing would bang blindly around down there like a disorientated mole trying to find the right burrow. I'm sorry, but God is definitely a man. No woman would come up with such a dumb idea. I mean, how much thought's really gone into it? Fleur always says if their stuff tasted of chocolate milkshake instead of yukky and salty, men would get a lot more blow-jobs.

I don't care what it tastes of. No way am I *ever* putting a man's willy in my mouth. I mean, they don't even wash their *hands*.

In the end, I reach down and sort of help Michel before he ends up in the wrong hole. He doesn't seem to know what he's doing any more than I do, but I've got to give him props for enthusiasm. I guess there's a lot to be said for instinct, after all.

I flinch as he pushes into me and meets resistance. He smells a bit of BO. 'It's OK?' he asks anxiously.

I nod, bracing myself.

He thrusts again, and there's a kind of sharp, searing pain, like putting a tampon in when you're dry, only a hundred times worse; and then suddenly he's moving inside me. I wait for some kind of lightning-bolt moment, but it just *hurts*. A lot. It's like having someone stick their finger up your nose. We rock together, banging hipbones and chins, totally out of time. It's as if I'm dancing with someone who's got zero sense of rhythm and two left feet. In the end I keep still, and let him bang away by himself. My head thumps the padded headboard with each thrust; every time I try to wriggle down the bed, he jolts me back up. It's not really painful any more, but I can't say I'm exactly hooked, either. It isn't even as nice as kissing, to be honest. There's none of the fizzy, tingly anticipation. In fact, now it's stopped hurting, it's a bit, well. Boring, actually.

Is this *it*? Is this what all the flirting and butterflies and snogging come down to? This damp, kind of lame in-and-out, in-and-out?

He starts to move faster, and I squirm uncomfortably. His elbow is on my hair. I hope he hurries up and finishes soon. I thought teenage boys were supposed to come as soon as they unzipped their trousers.

Suddenly he goes rigid and yelps, sounding just like Cannelle when you accidentally step on his tail. *Finally*.

He flops heavily on to the bed beside me. *'Merde.'*

Stuff trickles stickily between my legs. I'm cold and sore; I swear I've got third-degree friction burns. I can't believe how *crap* that was. Fleur says it gets better after the first time, but frankly I'm not sure how it could get worse. If this is sex, I'm sorry, I really can't see what all the fuss is about.

Michel lights two cigarettes, and hands one to me. I'm about to tell him I don't smoke, but I don't run away from home or get pissed on Armagnac or lose my virginity as a rule either.

'Good, *oui*?'

I exhale, coughing. 'I guess.'

'Next time, it will be better,' he says confidently.

The cigarette makes me feel sick. The room starts to whirl, and suddenly I know I'm going to throw up. I leap out of bed and run to the *en suite* bathroom, semen running down the inside of my thighs.

The Armagnac burns even more coming up than it did going down. I retch until I'm just dry-heaving, then flush the toilet and flip the lid down, resting my head against it. Oh God, what have I just done?

It seemed like a good idea an hour ago, when I ran into

him and spilled coffee all over us. I could tell from the hot way he was looking at me that he fancied me; I knew exactly what he really meant when he asked if I wanted to come to his room to fix my shirt. I just wanted someone to *want* me for a while.

My thighs are smeared with blood. I turn on the shower. The water's freezing, but it sobers me up in an instant. I never thought my first time would be like this. I imagined . . . I don't know what I imagined. Soft music and candles and kisses that made me melt. Romance and fireworks and a feeling like you've just won the lottery.

I wash carefully, my skin goosefleshing with cold. No point getting all girly and hysterical about it. This isn't a Mills & Boon novel.

When I return, Michel flips back the covers and pats the damp bed. 'Come.'

'I should go back to my room—'

'Later,' he says, with a surprising grin that tells me he's going to be just as irresistible as his father before long. '*Maintenant*, is your turn.'

The first thing I notice when I wake is the ache between my legs. I smile. He really *was* a fast learner. The next go round was much better, and the third—

The third. *Wow.*

The second thing I notice is the time.

I double-check the bedside clock. Seven-fifteen! *Shit!* I must've fallen asleep after that last sesh. Hardly surprising, but—

Michel is lying on my coffee-stained shirt and jeans. I kneel up, trying to yank them out from under him without waking him up. There's no doubt it was fun in the end last night, but I don't think I'm ever going to be a morning-sex kind of person. Oh, come on, *come on*.

There's a light tap at the door. I freeze.

'*Michel? Es-tu prêt?*'

Oh, fuck. Fuck, fuck and double fuck.

'*C'est sept heures et quart, Michel. Tu seras en retard pour l'école.*'

'Michel!' I hiss. 'Michel, wake up!'

He grunts and rolls on to his side, snoring loudly. Quickly, I grab my clothes as he moves off them. I'll have to hide in the bathroom until she's gone and sneak back to my room later—

His mother knocks again. 'Michel?'

I'm halfway to the loo when I spot my pink bra lying brazenly in the middle of the floor for the world to see. I run back in a Neanderthal crouch and scoop it up.

The doorknob turns.

I am *so* dead.

I don't know exactly what '*putain*' means, but I don't think it's very nice.

I stand on the doorstep, wondering what the hell to do now. I've only got about twenty euros in cash – that won't even get me a taxi to the station. I've still got Dad's credit card, of course, but I've no idea where the nearest ATM is. I don't know where *anything* is; this is the first time I've been outside the house since I got here. If only Fleur hadn't already left for school, I bet her mother wouldn't have dared throw me out.

God, what a bitch. It's not like I was the only one

involved. Michel was there too. She didn't say a bloody
word to him. I can't believe she's just chucked me on the
streets like this.

Shit. I can't go home, and I can't stay here. Maybe if I
go south to Provence, I can get a job or something while
I figure out what to do. Picking grapes, maybe. Are grapes
ripe in April?

The front door opens again and I dart down the steps
before Cruella flays me alive.

'Cate, *attend!*' Michel pads after me barefoot, wearing
nothing but a pair of jeans.

I wait. God, he *is* hot. Next to him, Dan's got all the sex
appeal of Mr Bean.

'*Ma mère,*' he shrugs. 'She is a beetch. I'm sorry she do
this.'

'Yeah, sure. Whatever.'

'Please, Cate. I worry for you. We 'ave a villa in Marseille. I write for you *l'adresse.*' He shoves an envelope into
my hand. 'I 'ave telephone Lauren, the 'ousekeeper, and
tell 'er is OK.'

In the envelope is a thick wad of euros. 'I can't take
this—'

'You give me back after, OK? I tell Fleur what 'appen
when she come 'ome. She come see you at *le weekend.* I'm
sorry, Cate. I like you *beaucoup.*'

'I like you *beaucoup,* too, Michel,' I smile.

He runs back up the steps and, with a brief wave,
disappears inside.

I shove the money and address into my backpack, pick
up my holdall and trudge towards the nearest main road.
OK. I can do this. I'll hail a taxi, go to the station, and get a
sleeper to Marseille. If I use cash to pay for my ticket, Dad

won't be able to track me through his credit card. I'm not staying away for ever; I just need to get my head together before I'm ready to go home and face the music.

As I turn a corner, three teenage boys are lounging against a wall. When they see me, they step forward, not quite blocking my path, but crowding me all the same.

I keep my head down, trying to shrink into myself. I hate it when guys do this. They think it's just a bit of fun, but actually, it's really scary. They cat-call in French, laughing and jeering, but not actually touching me. Then, just as I get past them and think the worst is over, a fourth boy steps out from the shadows of a doorway, right in front of me.

Without stopping to look, I run across the road. Cars swerve round me, blaring their horns. I keep running, until I'm sure they haven't followed me.

Finally I stop to catch my breath, hands on my knees. A second later, I scream when someone taps me on the shoulder.

'Hey, are you OK?'

A girl not much older than me, with sun-bleached cropped hair and a huge, travel-stained rucksack on her back, peers into my face. 'You been crying?'

'I'm fine.'

'Sorry, didn't mean to scare ya.' She grins and sticks out a tanned hand. 'Jodi Crane. Originally from Oz, as you can prob'ly tell. I was doing Europe with some mates, but we kinda fell out a while back. I'm making my way down to Damascus to hook up with my sister. What's your name?'

'Cate Ashfield. I was staying with some friends, but we – we fell out too.'

'Fancy a coffee? You look like you could use a bit of cheering up.'

I hesitate. I don't even know this girl—

I sound just like my mother.

'I'd love one,' I say firmly.

Jodi leads the way to a small pavement café near the river. Over coffee and croissants, we exchange notes – 'Your mother sounds like a right nutter, but at least she didn't drag you to church eight times a week like mine' – and swap tips: 'Never trust a bloke who says "Trust me,"' Jodi says, 'especially if it has anything to do with contraception.' She's forthright, funny, and outrageous. It's impossible not to warm to her. By the time we order a second round of espressos, it's as if I've known her for years.

'Look,' she says suddenly, 'if you ain't got any plans, why doncha come to Damascus with me? It's much safer travelling with a mate, and we'll have a great time. Whaddya say?'

I'm taken aback. Syria is a *really* long way away. Don't you need visas, or something? I won't be able to just jump on a train and go home when I've had enough. What about my exams? They start in a couple of weeks. I never meant to be gone that long.

But what's the point of doing exams if Dad won't let me go to NYU? I want to be a journalist. Who says I have to have a piece of paper to do that? I could get some real-life experience and work my way up instead. I might even be able to sell a few travel pieces to the *Mail* on the way. I'm never going to get anywhere if I don't learn to take a few risks. Woodward and Bernstein didn't get Pulitzers sitting at home playing Scrabble. I don't want to end up like Mum, scared to travel to the end of the road.

It's about time I took charge of my own life.

'OK. Why not?'

Jodi breaks into a huge smile. 'Neat! This is going to be so cool! We should get going straight away, head south. We can get you a visa at the British Embassy in Rome. Ever done any bar work?'

'Not yet.'

'It's real easy, and looking the way you do,' she winks, 'your tips are gonna be great.'

Her enthusiasm's contagious. This could be the best thing that's ever happened to me! Mum and Dad have babied me for too long. An adventure like this will prove to them I *can* cope on my own.

I push back my chair. 'Just need to use the bathroom—'

'In the back, towards the kitchen. Only don't use the john on the left, I was in there earlier and it sucked big-time, if you know what I mean.'

I leave Jodi minding my bags, and thread my way between the crowded tables to the back of the restaurant. Damascus! It sounds so biblical and exotic. It's not like I'm taking that much of a risk. Jodi's been around, she clearly knows what she's doing. It'll be fun travelling with her. And it's not like Mum and Dad are going to miss me.

The loo isn't exactly clean, but I tell myself I'd better get used to roughing it for a bit. I don't know much about Syria, but I've a feeling sanitation isn't high on their list of priorities.

I emerge into the sunshine, and realize I've come out the wrong side of the café. Jodi must be on the other side.

It takes ten minutes before I acknowledge the truth.

She's disappeared. So too have my backpack and holdall, along with all my money, my credit card, my passport and my mobile phone.

She didn't even pay for the coffee.

I collapse on to a chair. I can't believe I was so stupid. How could I trust a girl I'd known for half an hour with all my stuff? And I was going to run off to Syria with her! Maybe Dad's right. If I can't last five minutes on my own in Paris, how could I survive alone in New York?

The waitress tucks the bill beneath my saucer. I drop the last of my euros into it, and drift aimlessly through the park, fighting a rising tide of panic. What am I going to do? I don't even have a jacket: it was in my holdall, along with the rest of my clothes. I'll have to wait until it gets late, then go back to Fleur's. I'm sure she'll lend me enough money to get down to Marseille. After that – well, I don't know what I'll do after that. But I'll think of something.

Except that when I go back to the Lavoies', after spending all day wandering around the Tuileries, the house is in darkness. When the maid finally answers the door, she takes great pleasure in telling me the family has gone to Geneva for the weekend, before slamming it in my face.

I traipse back to the park, not knowing what else to do. It's starting to get dark. Fear ices my veins at the thought of staying out all night.

I climb over a low wall and hide in some thick bushes. I'd rather risk being disturbed by foxes in here than get attacked by a rapist or worse out in the open.

I trip over something soft, and nearly scream. Then I see a glimpse of yellow fur.

Near by, I find my holdall too. A sound, half laugh, half sob, escapes me. Jodi must have thrown my bags here when she'd taken what she wanted. The money and my phone and credit card have gone, but she's left my passport and clothes. At least I'm not going to freeze tonight.

I pull on my Gap sweatshirt, and try to sleep, but it's impossible. Every sound sets my heart racing. I shuffle over to a tree and sit with my back against it, so that no one can sneak up behind me. Oh, God, I'm so scared. Part of me wants to call it quits and go home, but Mum and Dad will be so mad, I just can't face them. Maybe I can get hold of Ben in the morning. He might be able to find a way to get some money to me without grassing me up. And then—

There is no 'and then'.

The night is full of terrifying sounds and snuffles. Every distant footstep is a mad axeman coming to get me. Each cracked twig is a killer on the prowl. My eyes ache with the strain of peering into the darkness. I can't stop shivering, from fear as much as the cold. Eventually, I fall into a fitful, exhausted sleep just before dawn.

I'm woken by bright sunshine slanting through the trees. I scramble to my feet, and brush the leaves and mulch from my clothes. Jodi's left my washbag; I squirt some toothpaste on my finger and rub it around my teeth, then feel stupid for bothering.

I'm bone-achingly tired, cold, stiff, and sick from lack of food. The only meal I've had in the last thirty-six hours was that croissant with Jodi. I've got to eat. Maybe if I look on the pavement near the café, I can find enough dropped coins to get a sandwich and ring Ben.

It takes me three hours to collect enough loose change for a small cheese baguette. I wolf it down, then curl up miserably on a park bench. It's hopeless. I can't do this. I'm not even sure why I ran away now.

Mum was telling the truth about Dan. Of course she was. She wouldn't do that to me. She loves me. I know that. She can't help that she's got an illness that makes her do strange things sometimes.

What the hell am I doing here?

She must be worried sick about me. I remember how she used to freak out if the school bus dropped me off late, thinking there'd been an accident. She'd sit outside ballet class and Brownies rather than leave me on my own, even for an hour. She was always lecturing me about accepting sweets from strangers, and going on about not taking the alleyway to the station after dark. OK, she screwed up big-time too. But she was *sick*. She couldn't help it. I've told myself this a thousand times before, but for the first time I actually believe it.

How could I ever have thought she didn't care?

If I can find a phone – call her – I bet she'll – I bet she'll—

I grab my bag and stand up, tears running down my face. *I want my mum.*

And suddenly she's there.

It's like a mirage. She's really here.

She reaches out her hand. 'Cate, please—'

For a moment, I can't even move. And then I'm running into her arms, sobbing into her shoulder, saying her name over and over again.

'I'm so sorry, Mum,' I mumble, when I finally stop howling.

'Don't cry any more, darling. Please. I can't bear to see you so unhappy.'

'But after everything I did! Aren't you mad?'

'Of course not!' She hugs me tighter. 'How could I be angry now? I've been half out of my mind with worry.'

'But why? I've been such a bitch—'

'Because you're safe,' she says simply.

I duck my head, thoroughly ashamed. What have I put my mother through? Her eyes are puffy and red from crying, and she looks, like, ten pounds thinner. She can't have slept for days.

Mum picks up my rucksack. 'You must be famished. Why don't we go and get something to eat, before we go back and face the music?'

'Have you – have you spoken to Dad?' I ask.

'Of course. He got the first plane from New York when I told him you weren't with Fleur. I just picked him up from the airport.'

'Dad *came*?'

Mum dumps my bag on the café table and waves a waitress over. 'Oh, we're mob-handed on this one,' she says drily. 'I've got Granny Anne in tow as well. I'm sure she and Daddy are having a lovely heart-to-heart right now.'

'Mum! You didn't!'

'Things are going to be a bit different from now on, darling.'

The waitress takes our order, and returns a few minutes later with two coffees and a *croque monsieur*. I grab the toasted sandwich, scalding my mouth on the hot cheese and ham.

'Cate,' Mum says, 'I owe you an apology.'

'Mum, of course you don't! I was the one who—'

'Please, darling. Just hear me out.'

She picks up a packet of sugar, tapping it nervously against the side of her cup.

'I don't blame you for thinking the worst about me and Dan,' she says. 'I've never given you any reason to trust me, have I? Nothing happened with him, but why should you believe that?'

'I do, Mum,' I say quickly. 'I was just being a stupid cow—'

'I would never intentionally do anything to hurt you, Cate. But I know I haven't been fair to you, and I can't just blame the illness,' she adds, swallowing hard. 'You've suffered more than either of the boys, and I can't forgive myself for that. I treated you the way my mother treated me, the way I always swore I'd never treat a child of mine: like some kind of second-class citizen. I didn't mean to, Cate, I promise. I've always loved you just as much as Ben and Sam. It's just—'

She puts down the sugar and twists her fingers together. I hold my breath; I can't remember my mother ever having a real conversation like this with me.

'I was jealous of you,' she whispers. 'Such an appalling thing to admit, being jealous of your own daughter. Oh, not because you're young and pretty, though you are, of course. But I was young and pretty too, once, hard as that is to believe now. I was jealous because you have energy and optimism and such a huge capacity for happiness. You're so determined to enjoy your life. You showed me what I *could* have been, if only I hadn't been born with this – this—'

'Mum, you're a brilliant artist,' I say helplessly. 'I haven't got half your talent.'

'But I've never done anything with it, have I?' she cries in frustration.

For the first time, I look and really *see* her. She's only

forty-one; just five years older than Ella. And still lovely, beneath the layers of worry and disappointment, her tropical blue eyes warm, her skin clear and unlined. Suddenly she's not just my mother, the boring, middle-aged housewife who's scrubbed and cooked and kept for me all my life, but a beautiful, still-young woman with her own dreams and fears. This can't have been the way she expected her life to turn out when she was seventeen. We both know Dad doesn't take much notice of her – she might as well be part of the furniture for all the attention he pays her. And part of that's my fault, I realize suddenly. I wanted to be the most important girl in his life. I elbowed Mum out of the way.

I remember when she planned for the two of us to go camping at the end of the garden as a birthday surprise; I can't have been more than six or seven. She'd bought a little tent for us, and sleeping bags and even a tiny camping stove. She must have been so excited about it; she'd been arranging it for weeks.

When I opened my presents and saw the tent, I was thrilled. 'But I want to go camping with Daddy,' I said, running over and climbing on to his lap.

I watched her face fall, and knew how much I'd hurt her. She never said a word, though. She packed our sandwiches and rolled up our sleeping bags and waved us off cheerily on our Big Adventure.

What a brat.

'Mum, it's not too late,' I urge. 'You could still do something with your painting. Eithne said you could do a show, didn't she? You could—'

'Cate, darling, we both know it's not going to happen.' She squeezes my hand. 'I need to start taking my pills again. Sooner or later I'm going to go off the rails if I don't. Sooner, probably. Once I go back on them, I won't be able to paint. I'll let everybody down.'

'Have you,' I ask, 'ever *really* tried?'

She picks up her coffee, then puts it back down untouched. An elderly couple at the next table crumble some bread and throw it on the ground. Birds peck at their feet, just inches away.

Mum's eyes fill with tears. 'Cate, I'm sorry. Sorry for so many things. I put far too much responsibility on your shoulders – what I did to you when your father was in Cyprus—'

I feel sick. I always try not to think about That Day. All the blood. I was so scared – oh, God, *so* scared. I had to shut down and pretend it wasn't real, I was watching a video, I could just press STOP any time and it'd all go away. It was the only way I could save her. I ripped up some tea-towels – *Granny Clara gave Mummy these for Christmas, she's going to be so mad* – and wrapped them round her wrists like they do on TV, and it all seemed so weird, like it was happening to someone else. When the ambulance men arrived, I almost expected Mum to get up and laugh, say it had all been a silly joke, it wasn't real, she hadn't actually tried to kill herself rather than be my mum any more.

Afterwards, I was so *angry*. And frightened. Even when the doctors said they'd given her medicine so she'd get better, and Dad brought her home, the knot of fear in my stomach didn't go away. She could do it again. Any time, she could do it again, and I might not be there to save her.

I had to keep watch. I didn't dare let down my guard, even for a moment. I hid all the sharp knives in the cupboard under the stairs. I emptied the bottles of aspirin and paracetamol. I threw out the weedkiller and bleach, though of course she just kept buying more. When Dad was home, at weekends or in the evening, it was OK, I knew she wouldn't try anything then, but when she was on her own – when it was just the two of us—

I never knew what I might find when I came home from school. I'd drag my feet as I walked up the path, dreading opening the back door.

'I was so scared, Mum!' I cry, unable to keep it in any longer. 'I didn't dare love you, I couldn't take the risk! It wasn't that I didn't want to – it wasn't that I didn't care—'

Mum stares at me, white-faced.

'I *had* to hate you. Don't you see? I had to make myself believe it wouldn't matter if you – if you weren't there. I didn't mean it,' I plead, tears streaming down my cheeks. 'I thought it was my fault you did it. I didn't know how to stop you doing it again. I was so terrified I'd lose you, I had to stop loving you – I had to protect myself—'

She throws herself out of her chair and pulls me into her arms. 'Cate, oh, Cate. It wasn't because of you, it had *nothing* to do with you,' she whispers fiercely into my hair. She disentangles herself, and cradles my damp face between her palms. 'Cate, listen to me. I didn't mean it. I never meant to kill myself. I would never have left you, do you understand that? I love you and the boys more than anything. I was sick. I didn't really know what I was doing.'

'But supposing – supposing you get sick again?'

'No matter how sick I am, I would never do that again. I didn't understand then what I was doing to you. I thought it was all about Daddy and me, and I was wrong.'

'I love you, Mum,' I sob. 'I'm sorry I ran away.'

'I love you too, Cate,' she says. 'I told you, it's going to be different from now on. No more being scared, darling. Not for either of us. I promise.'

I don't know what Mum says to Dad when we get back to the hotel, but when he comes to see me, he doesn't scream or yell or do any of the things I'd expected, but hugs me tightly like I've been gone for years.

I go to bed and sleep for eighteen hours straight, and when I wake up, I experience a flood of relief, like you do when you open your eyes after a terrible nightmare and discover none of it was real. It's like a huge weight has been lifted from my shoulders. I'm no longer filled with dread. It's going to be OK, I realize. I throw back the covers, giddy with happiness. *It's going to be OK.*

When I shower, I spot a series of tiny bruises, like fingermarks, on the inside of my thighs. I put what happened with Michel firmly to the back of my mind. What's done is done.

Over breakfast, I notice something different about Mum and Dad. I don't know what it is, but they're both being really weird. She insists we all go home together on the Chunnel train, and won't let Dad stay on in Paris for some business meeting, but what's really amazing is, he never says a word. He went out and bought her this beautiful pale blue Hermès scarf when we were shopping with Granny Anne; it's exactly the same colour as her eyes. He *never* buys her presents like that.

At first I think it's just because of the *Days of Our Lives* drama of the last few weeks and the whole running-away-to-Paris thing, but even after we get home and go back to normal (or what passes for it in our house), it doesn't wear off. He's coming home every evening before seven, and he doesn't stay up in London once. Mum's more chilled, too; she's taking her happy pills again, of course, but it's not just that. She's not exactly full of the joys, skipping around and crocheting friendship bangles; she's more like someone who's been in a terrible car crash and thought they were maimed for life, and then checked and realized they weren't that badly hurt after all. But it's a start.

It's all kind of freaky, but in a good way. I can go to school and have panic attacks over my exams like normal people. I don't know how long the peace-in-our-time routine will last, but I finally feel like I can breathe.

Three weeks after we come back from Paris, I take my last exam, go to bed and sleep for, like, a week.

When I finally get up around lunchtime, I mooch downstairs in a pair of Ben's boxers and an old T-shirt. Mum's been painting in her studio for days, so I'm not surprised when I don't find anyone in the kitchen. I've made myself some toast and Marmite, and I'm sitting at the kitchen table, flicking through the *Mail* and waiting for the kettle to boil, when Mum and Dad come in together and sit down opposite me like some kind of interview board.

I look from one to the other. 'What's going on?'

'I thought you didn't like Marmite,' Mum says nervously.

'I don't usually, I just fancied some today. Mum, why's Dad home from work? Is something wrong?'

'Nothing's wrong,' Dad sighs. He looks grey and tired. 'We've got something important to tell you, we've just been waiting for you to finish your exams—'

'I knew it. You're getting divorced, aren't you? That's what all this is—'

'This is about you, Cate. We want to talk about university.'

I look away. 'What's the point?'

'Hear your father out,' Mum says sharply.

Sometimes, I'm not totally sure this New Mum is a good thing.

'Your mother and I have discussed it at length. We realized – *I* realized – that this is your decision. We don't have the right to stop you doing what you want to do. But,' he adds quickly, 'we want you to be safe. Cate, you're still so young. Moving to New York is such a huge step. It's not like nipping over to Paris. You'll be so far from home if anything goes wrong.'

'So you've said,' I say, trying not to sound bitter. 'Why the big song and dance now?'

'Ben finishes at Oxford in two years,' Mum puts in. 'He wants to do a postgraduate course at Columbia, and his tutors think he'll have no trouble getting in.'

I shrug. 'So? What's that got to do with me?'

'Columbia's in New York—'

'She knows that, Beth. Look, Cate,' Dad says, 'what we're trying to say is that if you really want to go to NYU, we'll give you our full support if you'll wait a year and go with Ben. You don't have to live there together – I know you'll be doing your own thing, and so will he – but your mother and I would feel so much better just knowing he was near by.'

'You mean, take a gap year after my A levels?'

'Lots of students do it. And I could use a keen pair of

hands and eyes at the agency. How do you fancy coming to work for me?'

'Are you *serious*?'

'I might even be able to get you some work with one or two of the papers, too, if I pull a few strings—'

I throw myself at him. 'Daddy, that's fantastic! I don't mind waiting – it'll give me time to build up my portfolio – I can't believe it! Oh, thank you! I promise I'll take care.' I hug my mother. 'I know you talked him into it, Mum. I'll be really careful. Oh, God, this is so amazing—'

'Look, I'd better get going,' Dad says, standing up. 'I've got a meeting.'

He kisses Mum on the cheek as he leaves; something else he wouldn't have done a month ago. He smiles at me, but it doesn't quite reach his eyes. He looks defeated, somehow. For the first time, I wonder what this family harmony has cost him.

I'm not a baby. I don't want my parents to stay together for my sake. I just want them both to be *happy*, so I can get on with my own life without worrying about them.

Mum gets up to make some tea. 'Sometimes it's easy to forget how hard your dad works,' she says, watching him through the kitchen window. 'He's been under so much strain recently. James Noble has had it in for him since Dad turned down his takeover bid last summer. He's not finished yet, either. Several of Dad's key accounts have—'

'James Noble?' I interrupt.

'Sorry, darling. He's the man causing all the trouble.' She takes the lid off the kettle and peers inside. 'Wretched thing's boiled dry. I wish your father would just let me get a plug-in.'

Nausea pushes its way into my throat. 'Mum,' I say urgently.

'Cate? Darling, are you all right? You look like you've seen a ghost—'

I shove back my chair. It slams against the dresser, toppling plates, but I don't even notice.

'James Noble,' I gasp. 'I know him. He's Dan's stepdad.'

13

Ella

'They're *suing* me?'

'I'm so sorry, darling,' Lucy says helplessly. 'I know how hard you tried to save her. They're just looking for someone to blame, and you're the easiest target. I'm sure it's not personal—'

'They think I killed their baby! How can that not be personal?'

I push my chair back and pace towards the window, struggling to take it in. A lawsuit! How can Anna and Dean think it's my fault Hope died? I did everything I could to save her! I didn't leave the hospital for a single second after their daughter became ill. If she'd been my own child, I couldn't have tried harder.

Except I couldn't save my own child either, could I?

'*Is* it my fault?' I cry, scrabbling through the folders on my desk for Hope's file. 'You were there. Was there something I missed, something I should have done—'

'Stop second-guessing yourself, Ella. You shouldn't even

be back at work yet, never mind poring over paperwork. Go home and get some rest.' She takes Hope's folder out of my hands. 'The Shores may not even go through with it. They're in shock at the moment. And so are you,' she adds gently. 'It's only been two weeks since you lost your own baby, Ella. Look at you, working all hours of the day and night, running yourself ragged. You need to give yourself time to grieve.'

She thinks the baby was Jackson's, of course. There was a brief moment, as I lay on the floor of the hotel room in New York and realized what was happening to me, when I'd thought that too; and then I'd had a sudden, clear memory of standing in William's bathroom the morning I got the news that Jackson had died, hunting through my bag for an emergency tampon, annoyed that my period had started early, unaware that in a few minutes my mobile would ring and everything in my life would change.

Even as pain had snatched the air from my lungs, my mind raced. *William's, then*?

Vasectomies weren't 100 per cent reliable. It wasn't impossible. I shouldn't be pregnant at all; I wasn't some foolish teenager, taking chances. I hadn't missed a single pill, and yet here I was. Who was to say that William—

And then I'd remembered.

That night when Cooper had come to my bedroom, and we'd fucked each other in every sense of the word.

It hadn't been Jackson's baby I'd lost, but his brother's.

Lucy jumps as my office door opens. 'I think you should see this, Dr Stuart,' the duty nurse says, picking up the remote on my desk and pointing it at the flat-screen TV on the wall. 'Sky has been running it for the last half-hour.'

I clutch the edge of my desk. 'Oh God,' I breathe.

Anna Shore looks directly into the camera, as if she can see me watching. 'We placed our trust in what we were told would be the best hands at the Princess Eugenie,' she says, her voice breaking. 'We trusted them with our daughter. We were promised she'd get the very best care. But she was left to die by doctors who didn't think she was worth saving. She was just a number to them, an expense they could do without.'

My fingernails dig into my palms. She doesn't think – she *can't* think—

On screen, Dean steps forward and hugs his wife as she turns and sobs into his shoulder. He reads awkwardly from a piece of paper in his hand.

'We hope the General Medical Council will apportion the appropriate discipline in answer to the levels of negligence of the staff involved, and that hospital procedures are enforced to ensure such devastating failures never happen again,' he says stiffly. 'The mark of a civilized society is the way it cares for its most vulnerable members, the very young, the very old, and the disabled. No other parents should have to go through what we've been through in the past few weeks.'

A reporter picks up the story as Richard Angel walks out of the hospital towards a cluster of microphones. 'The Princess Eugenie Trust offered an apology to the Shore family, and promised an investigation was under way into the affair.'

'I wish immediately to apologize for any distress to Mr and Mrs Shore,' Angel says smoothly. 'We have not yet received a formal complaint, but an internal investigation was launched as soon as their case was brought to my attention, and we will of course keep you updated.'

'That's *it*?' I exclaim, as Angel swivels on his heel, fingers snapping. 'That's all he has to say? No vote of confidence in his own staff?'

'It's just a formal statement,' Lucy says uncomfortably. 'I'm sure he'll make certain you have every legal—'

'You're right,' I interrupt coldly. 'I should go home and get some rest.'

'Ella—'

My throat closes as I slam the door furiously behind me. For the first time, it dawns on me that this lawsuit will put not just my job and career on the line, but my dearest friendship as well. Not once has Lucy said she believes in me. Does she think I'm to blame, too? That I brought my personal life into work, and made a mistake that cost my tiny patient her life?

I need her to believe in me, because I can't.

The following Saturday, I get up early, throw on an old pair of jeans and a T-shirt and pull down the trap-door to the attic. I hesitate for a moment, my hand on the tread of the ladder, gazing up into the stuffy darkness. I wish I'd swallowed my pride and asked Lucy to come round and help me.

Don't bottle out now.

Carefully, I climb the ladder, my healing stitches pulling painfully with the unaccustomed exertion, and play my torch across the rafters.

The cramped, airless space is filled with cardboard boxes and black bin bags, thrown haphazardly on top of one another. Jumbled inside them are Jackson's clothes and books, his collection of antique hunting knives and a treasured ivory chess set, framed photographs of our wedding day, CDs, fishing rods, clay-pigeon trophies, tennis racquets, ski boots, defunct computer parts, DVDs, tapes, dog-eared outdoor-equipment magazines, the American flag folded neatly in a triangular display case, stars uppermost, a four-foot carved wooden fish – all the detritus of his forty-one – no, forty-two – years on this planet.

I haul down each bag and box, one by one, and lug them, panting, into the bedroom. After Jackson died, I couldn't bear to see anything that reminded me of him. But I have to deal with it if I'm to move on. I can't put it off any longer.

I start to sort slowly through it all. My cheeks are soon wet with memories. Even sadder are the keepsakes that mean nothing to me: a spray of pressed flowers that still carry a faint trace of jasmine, a pair of worn cream evening gloves I've never seen before, a small Tiffany box containing a silver baby's rattle. What did these things mean to Jackson? What are their stories?

I throw open the battered leather steamer trunk at the end of the bed – inherited from his parents, it's one of the few things Jackson shipped over when we moved here – and toss aside the spare blankets stored inside. Carefully, I fill it with the things I can't bear to give or throw away: the wedding pictures, his notebooks and knives. I add a worn pale blue cotton shirt that I used to love him in, and the college sweatshirt he wore every day when he went running. The rest of his clothes I'll give to the One World charity shop on the King's Road, along with most of his books and CDs.

On impulse, I place the pressed flowers, the gloves and the Tiffany rattle in the trunk. Perhaps I'll send them to

Cooper. If they meant enough to Jackson for him to bring to London, they're too important to throw away.

By the end of the day, I'm physically exhausted and emotionally drained. Summoning my last reserves of energy, I load Jackson's eco-friendly Toyota hybrid with cardboard boxes, and slide into the driving seat, adjusting it so that I can reach the pedals. We used to joke that Jackson's legs were so long, he could have reached the pedals from the back seat. When I turn on the engine – to my astonishment, after two months sitting in the garage, it starts first time – his favourite CD, Rascal Flatts' *Feels Like Today*, automatically begins to play. I eject it, slip it into its cover and add it to the nearest box on the front seat.

I double-park on the pavement outside the charity shop. A middle-aged woman in a hideous pansy-print dress and blue rinse comes out to help me unload.

'Thank you, dear,' she says, in ringing Home Counties tones, as I dump the last of the boxes near the shop counter. 'D'you mind holding the fort a moment while I take some of these things out to the back?'

She disappears before I have a chance to say no. I hover near the window so I can keep an eye on the car and make sure I don't get clamped. You can tell this is Chelsea, I think drily, glancing round the shop: all the donated bags are Louis Vuitton and the suits last season's Chanel.

A beautiful white linen layette is displayed in the window. I lean forward, marvelling at the tiny clothes and exquisite stitching. It's so beautiful. Utterly impractical, but beautiful. I hardly ever see babies in anything but miniature hospital gowns or the ubiquitous babygro.

A little pair of pale pink leather shoes embossed with

minute gold suns sits on a shelf near my shoulder. I pick them up and balance them in the palm of my hand.

The grief bursts over me like a tsunami, whipping in out of nowhere. I stand there in the shop window, huge, wrenching sobs convulsing my body as I howl like a child, in ugly, gasping wails, hiccupping and struggling for breath. I cry for Jackson, and my poor barely-there lost baby, and all the children I'll never be able to have. Snot and tears mingle on my cheeks. I cling on to the nearest shop rail and give myself up to it because I simply can't do anything else, the enormity of my loss is so utterly over-whelming.

I'm barely aware of the saleswoman taking me in her arms and leading me towards the rear of the shop, where she pulls me to her capacious floral bosom and pats my back as if I'm an infant.

'Get it all out, dear,' she soothes. 'It helps. That's it. Go on, you have a good cry.'

I bawl against her shoulder until I have no tears left. Two months ago, I'd have been appalled and embarrassed at breaking down like this in public. I've always prided myself on my self-control. But grief has transported me to a new world, where self-discipline and professional success count for nothing. I've always been the one dispensing hope and saving lives. Now I'm dependent on the kindness of strangers just to get from one day to the next.

Moments ago, I pitied this woman in her sitcom blue rinse and suburban smock. Now I'm clinging to her as if she's all that stands between me and the end of the world.

I've always seen vulnerability as some kind of weakness. How could I have been so *arrogant*?

'I lost my son three years ago,' the woman says unexpectedly, as the storm of grief finally blows itself out and I sink, exhausted, on to a wooden stool near the storeroom. 'He was blown up in a roadside bomb in Iraq. I coped well the first few months, it was like he was still away on duty. It was when I went to get the Christmas decorations down it hit me. He was the only one tall enough to reach the top shelf of the cupboard.'

I blow my nose loudly on a tissue. 'My husband died two months ago,' I say. 'He caught a virus and died, there was no warning. I never even got a chance to say goodbye.' I take a deep breath, and look her straight in the eye. 'I wasn't in love with him. He was my best friend but I didn't love him the way I should, the way a wife should love her husband.'

'Oh, my dear,' she says softly. 'I'm so sorry.'

She doesn't mean she's sorry he died. She's sorry for me, because I didn't know how to love him first.

I wrap my arms tighter around my knees in the darkness, drawing my feet up under me on the sofa. It's two in the morning, but I can't sleep. Of all the things to set me off. Baby clothes. I'm a walking cliché.

In my work at the hospital, I've met dozens of women who've spent years desperately chasing the dream of a child of their own: IVF babies are more likely than those conceived naturally to be premature, especially since so many are multiple births. For mothers like Anna Shore, the wizened infant in the Perspex butter dish represents the culmination of years of tests, injections, failures and disappointments; often, this treasured, fragile baby is their last hope. They've told me stories of falling apart in the babycare aisle of the supermarket; of crossing the road to avoid walking past BabyGap; of flinching at the cry of a child on an aircraft, and fantasizing about seizing the baby left unattended in his pushchair for a few brief moments. I've listened sympathetically, and then wondered how empty their lives must be that they need a child to complete them.

Baby hunger. I never understood the term until now. This visceral gnawing at your insides, an agonizing emptiness that nothing can fill.

I smile bitterly into the dark. I've spent most of my adult life working with babies, and never felt a single maternal pang. I wrecked my marriage by refusing, amongst other things, to give my husband a child. Now I'm a barren widow, my hormones have finally woken up and leaped into action. If there is a God up there, She has a sick sense of humour.

I get up and pour myself a large glass of white wine from the fridge. I thought I had my life all worked out. A high-flying career, child-free independence, a charming husband I was very fond of, and – the icing on the cake – a passionate, worldly older lover when I needed a quick thrill. I thought I could have it all; I thought I could keep all the plates spinning at once without dropping any of them. The word 'hubris' could have been invented for me.

Jackson had a theory: the Karma Credit Plan. He believed you built up karmic points, good and bad, depending on how you lived your life. Sooner or later, you'd be called to account.

It's all slipping away from me. Husband, lover, career, children – all gone.

I knock back the wine and pour another glass. I was so

terrified of ending up like my mother, or like Lucy, or any of the other thousands of women who get kicked in the teeth by men on the lookout for someone younger, prettier, perkier. I thought I'd ring-fenced myself from hurt by marrying a man I didn't really love. All I did was shut out everything that makes life worthwhile.

I must have fallen asleep, because I'm startled into wakefulness by the sound of the phone. I sit up, my heart racing. It's not even light yet. I glance at the set-top box on the television – 05:35. My chest tightens with panic, and I struggle for control. *It's just the phone.*

The answer-machine kicks in, and I listen to myself tell callers to leave a message.

'Ella? Are you there?'

Despite myself, I experience a miserable thrill of pleasure at the sound of his voice. It's two weeks since we last spoke, when he told me Beth had found Cate sleeping rough in Paris. I know I'm taking the coward's way out by dodging his calls, but I haven't trusted myself not to give in if I speak to him.

'Look, I know it's the middle of the night, and I'm sorry if I've woken you. I can't sleep. I don't know if you're busy, or if you just don't want to talk to me, but you can't leave it like this, Ella. If you're there, please pick up the phone.'

His voice echoes round the flat. I back quietly away from the answer-machine, as if he can hear me.

'Ella, we have to talk. There's something important I have to tell you. If it's really over, I can accept that, but I need to know what happened first. You owe me that, at least.'

Oh, God. This is so hard. *Why* did I have to fall in love with the one man I can't have?

'Ella, I know about Jackson's baby,' William says quietly.

The room tilts.

'I know how hard this must be for you. Actually, I don't, but I can imagine.' He sighs. 'It doesn't affect how I feel about you, Ella. Nothing could. You may not want to hear it, but I love you. You don't have to do anything with that information; I'm not even sure if I want you to. I just had to say it, that's all.'

There's such a long silence I think William's hung up.

I jump when he speaks again. 'We always said we'd stay friends. I never thought of you as a deal breaker, Ella.'

It took me eight years to admit I was in love with this man. Now I have to give him up, because I've finally understood that doing the right thing – at last – is the only way I can put my life back together.

He's right. I owe him an explanation, if nothing else.

I pick up the phone. 'I'm not,' I say.

'God, you look like hell,' William says.

'Thank you. I feel so much better now.'

He grins and pulls out a chair. I'm glad he chose somewhere public and upbeat like the Chelsea Brasserie for lunch. It makes this easier.

No it doesn't. Nothing could make this anything other than sheer desperate agony.

I edge my chair into the shade. The English weather is up to its usual tricks, seducing us with blistering August sunshine in late April, which no doubt will become freezing November fog by May. It's taken me thirty-six summers, but I've finally learned the hard way that, as a redhead, I *never* tan.

'Flip-flops?' William snorts, eyeing my footwear.

'Gold leather flip-flops. Metallics are very in this summer,' I say defensively.

'You hate sandals. I hadn't realized things were so serious. If I'd known you were reduced to sackcloth and flip-flops, I'd have acted sooner.'

William has already ordered wine, an expensive Montrachet. He pours me a cool glass and I sip it, fiddling uncomfortably with the stem. Neither of us seems willing, or able, to start a real conversation.

We order lunch – spatchcocked partridge for William, and the salade quercynoise with a confit of duck gizzards for me – and watch the foot traffic around Sloane Square. A crocodile of children from nearby Hill House School file past in their trademark cinnamon knickerbockers and beige shirts, giggling and jostling. A little girl of about five with thick red plaits and a splatter of freckles catches my eye. She looks just like I did at her age.

If I'd had a daughter, I wonder if she'd have looked like that.

I snap a breadstick, and line the pieces up neatly on the table. 'How's Cate doing?'

'Good,' he says, his tone surprised. 'I've no idea what went on in Paris – I'm not sure I want to know. But she's been much happier since we got back. Of course, Beth is levelling out again, so that helps.'

'She didn't miss any exams?'

'Got back just in time. Her last one's tomorrow. You know how focused she is, you never get much out of her at the best of times. But she's given the bloody boyfriend the elbow, which is the best news I've had in a long time.' He hesitates. 'She knows about us, Ella. She saw us that night in the station car park.'

I busy myself with my napkin, playing for time.

'You knew,' William accuses suddenly.

'She came to see me,' I admit. 'A few weeks ago. She asked me not to say anything.'

He pours us both another glass of wine, then stares into the bottom of his as if the answers to everything are written there.

'Is that what's behind all this?' he says finally. 'What's happening with you and me?'

'Partly.' I sigh. 'It's *everything*, William. When we started, no one was supposed to get hurt. It was supposed to be fun.' I push my salad away untouched, suddenly sickened by the thought of food. 'I thought this was just about the two of us, but it isn't, is it? There's a whole chain of people affected by our affair. Beth, of course, and Jackson – he didn't even know about you, but it still poisoned everything between us. And now Cate. We're the reason she ran away. She could have been raped or murdered because of us. We can't pretend it doesn't matter.'

'Of course it matters, Ella. But Cate understands. She knows her mother and I—'

'She's seventeen, William. She's still a child.'

'She's lived with Beth all her life,' he says soberly. 'She understands.'

'It's not just Cate. There's Ben, and Sam—'

'Ben's away at university, he has his own life. He'll be going to Columbia as soon as he finishes Oxford. He doesn't need his parents any more. And Sam is at boarding school. He'll always have a home to come back to, whatever happens, but his day-to-day life is bound up in his school, not us.' He frowns. 'Ella, my children aren't the issue. You've known about them for eight years. What's really going on inside your head?'

'You're married, William. Suddenly, that matters. I can't explain it.'

'I told you. I'll leave her.'

'William, you know that's not—'

'I've already discussed it with her.'

I knock over my glass, spilling wine across the table.

'Well, in a manner of speaking,' he amends. Suddenly he won't quite meet my eye. 'Cate running away brought everything to a head, in a funny kind of way. Beth doesn't actually know about you, but I think she's guessed there's someone. She asked me not to leave until Cate finishes her exams next summer.' He reaches for my hand, but I pull away. 'Ella, please. Wait for me. It won't be much longer. We've waited eight years, surely you can—'

'William, I never asked for this!' I exclaim, aghast. 'You can't leave because of me!'

'What do you think all this has been about?'

'I never wanted to break up your marriage—'

'For Christ's sake, Ella! Take some damn responsibility!' he cries with sudden fury, slamming his fist on the table. 'You can't sleep with me for eight years and let me fall in love with you and then back away with your hands up and say it's got nothing to do with you! The moment you kissed me in the park, it became something to do with you! Why else would I leave, if not for you?'

I stare at him, appalled. *I did this.* I set all this in motion. I started a chain reaction that's wrecking the lives of everyone connected to me.

William pulls himself together with a visible effort, and produces a wary smile. 'Ella, can we put this behind us, please? Let's think about the future, not the past.'

I have to put things right.

'Ella? In a couple of weeks, Beth's going off on a painting holiday in Italy with Eithne, it's been arranged for months. We could—'

'I don't love you, William,' I say clearly.

He recoils, as if I've punched him.

'I'm sorry,' I say, my gaze unflinching. 'I'm very fond of you, of course. We've had a great time. But I don't love you. I don't want you to leave your wife for me. There's no point.'

'I don't believe you,' he says hoarsely.

My hands are shaking. I hide them beneath the table.

'We always said that if either of us wanted to end this, we'd walk away, no questions asked. It's just not working any more, William. I need someone with less baggage—'

'You don't think I'll leave her, do you? That's it, isn't it? I can't blame you, it sounds like the oldest line in the book.' He leans forward eagerly. 'I mean it, Ella. Just give me a chance, and I'll come through. I know you love me—'

'It wasn't Jackson's baby.'

He stares at me, stunned.

'You haven't been the only one, William, you know that. After all, we're not married to each other, are we?'

I watch the light in his eyes die. The pain and disillusion

that replace it are almost more than I can bear. Instinctively, I reach out to him, and he looks at my hand on his arm as if my touch is poison.

'You bitch,' he breathes.

He stands up so abruptly his chair topples backwards, and plucks half a dozen notes from his wallet, flinging them on the table. 'This should just about cover your fee.'

'William—'

He looks at me with disgust. 'Jackson was the lucky one,' he says stonily, and walks away without a backward glance.

'You idiot,' Lucy sighs, when I turn up on her doorstep and fling myself, sobbing incoherently, into her arms, 'you can't just hand him back to his wife like he's a toy you've got tired of, it doesn't work that way. I know you're trying to do the right thing, Ella, but it's gone too far for that. Sometimes staying and living a lie is more dishonest than having the guts to leave. I should know. I thought when Lawrence walked out, it was the worst thing that had happened to me, but once the shock wore off I realized he was right to go. We'd been faking our marriage for years. By leaving, he gave me the chance to have an honest relationship with someone else. You and William love each other, Ella. I don't want to come over all Mills & Boon, but love is so precious. You don't have the *right* to throw it away.'

'Oh, God,' I cry despairingly. 'What have I done?'

*

He doesn't return my calls. After ten days, I stop making them. I wanted to make the break irreversible. How marvellous that I've succeeded.

I go to work because I don't know what else to do, but it's no longer an escape. I'm terrified of making another mistake. It's like I've suddenly forgotten how to walk; what once came to me instinctively, I now ridiculously over-analyse, hobbling myself with my own fear. I'm painstakingly thorough, checking and double-checking the most basic procedures. Hope isn't the first baby I've lost by making the wrong call; every doctor lives with the stark reality that their errors and misjudgements *will* kill a patient at some point. Her death didn't cause my loss of confidence; my self-doubt is what led to her death. How can I trust my judgement at work when it's so clearly lacking in every other area of my life?

I volunteer to work the May Day bank holiday because I can't bear to be at home. I'm sitting in my office, staring at Hope's autopsy report without reading it – I don't need to: I know every word by heart – when Richard Angel walks in without knocking.

'Dr Stuart. May I have a word?'

I shrug.

He jerks the leather chair on the other side of my desk further away from me, as if my proximity is toxic, and sits down. Given my recent run of luck, perhaps he's wise.

'I'm here at Dr Nicholson's request,' Angel opens sharply. Naturally: he doesn't want me to mistake his presence for anything approaching professional solidarity. 'Lucy has prevailed upon me – against my better judgement, I might add – to ask the Trust to convene a meeting to discuss the Shore case in advance of our official inquiry.'

He grimaces as if he's sucked a lemon. 'This will be your opportunity – your *only* opportunity – to put your case before we decide what level of support the hospital will be able to offer you. I don't need to tell you that your future depends on its outcome.'

'You're not settling with the Shores?' I ask in surprise.

'They have already gone public with their complaint, which, I am sure you are aware, is extremely serious,' he says unpleasantly. 'This is most unfortunate. Clearly a swift and discreet resolution of the matter is now impossible.' What he means is that the hospital trust can't just pay up to minimize the negative press coverage, thereby throwing me to the wolves by effectively admitting liability.

I'm not fooled by his promises of an impartial inquiry. If he has his way, I'll be left to sink or swim on my own, at the mercy of the red-top newspapers, which love nothing better than a tragic dead-baby story to boost circulation.

'You don't like me, do you?' I say conversationally.

He stiffens. 'My personal preferences don't come into it.'

'Oh, come on, Richard,' I jeer. 'You've made your "personal preferences" very clear. You've been waiting for an opportunity like this ever since you took over.'

'If you're referring to my dislike of your intuitive approach to your work, then yes, I have indeed feared just such a development as we now have,' he snaps. 'You are emotional, instinctive in your approach to client diagnoses, and wilfully empathetic—'

'Wilfully empathetic?'

'This is not a charity, Dr Stuart. This is a business. Our clients expect the very best—'

'Our *patients* expect to be treated as human beings, not

battery-farmed chickens on some sort of medical conveyor belt!' I exclaim. 'Three-quarters of the time an accurate patient history will give you a correct diagnosis before you even put on your stethoscope. To do that you have to know who your patients are and what's brought them to you. Of course you have to be empathetic—'

He stands up. 'This is pointless. I can see we have a fundamental divergence in our approach to client care. Regardless of the outcome of the inquiry, you may wish to consider, Dr Stuart, if your philosophy is entirely compatible with that of this hospital.' He pauses at the door. 'The board will convene on the twenty-third of this month. I cannot emphasize enough how crucial it is for your sake that you are there.'

My paperweight hits the door as it shuts behind him, shattering. Bastard. *Bastard*! What the hell is Lucy doing with him?

I know the answer to that question, of course. Richard Angel is everything Lawrence Nicholson was not: predictable, organized, morally upright – in his own way; he would never break a promise, or a rule – and disconcertingly honest. He truly believes that his way of running the hospital is in the best interests of his 'clients'. If he were a forensic pathologist, I'd find his dedication and attention to detail admirable. It's just unfortunate, given his dismal bedside manner, that our patients still have a pulse.

By the time I get home, my anger has given way to despair. If the hospital doesn't support me, my chances of winning a lawsuit are slim. And if I lose that . . .

All doctors are covered in theory by NHS indemnity for mishaps whilst working, but in practice it's not worth the paper it's written on. Like most medics working in a high-risk specialty, I've got extra insurance, which I pay for myself. Or at least I had. What with everything that's happened over the past three months, I've rather lost track of the paperwork.

I fumble for my door keys. I could lose my licence to practise medicine, my job, everything.

Just twelve weeks ago, I'd have been in a frenzy of terror. Now, it doesn't matter. My career seems almost unimportant next to everything I've already lost.

A figure steps out of the shadows. His face catches the light, and I scream.

Jackson.

'I didn't mean to scare you,' he says.

'What do you expect when you hide in the shadows and leap out at me! What the hell are you doing here?'

'I've been waiting on you to get home.'

'You'd better come in before someone calls the police.'

I'm shivering with shock. I drop my bag in the hallway, and am about to go into the kitchen to put on some coffee, but turn towards the drink cabinet in the sitting-room instead. I need alcohol.

I pour us both a generous double measure of Scotch, and hand him a glass without bothering to ask if he wants one. 'You scared me half to death. Why didn't you tell me you were coming?'

'You'd have set the dogs on me.'

He has a point.

I drain my drink, and pour another. 'Look, Cooper. It's late, and I'm really tired. I've had a miserable day at work, and I need to sleep. I don't know what it is you want from me, but I can't deal with it tonight. If you need a place to stay, there's a spare room—'

'I came to give you these.'

He thrusts a bundle of papers awkwardly towards me. I put down my glass, but make no move to reach for them.

'Take them,' Cooper says, almost angrily.

I stare at him, this fierce, bitter, beautiful man who is so much like my dead husband to look at, so like William in his absolute, arrogant certainty, and yet utterly different from both of them. I barely know him; I certainly don't like him. And yet I'm drawn to him in a way I can't explain. He has a brooding intensity that sucks you in, a dark, danger-ous charisma that's almost hypnotic. An unexpected pulse beats between my legs.

I take the bundle of envelopes, my hand trembling: from fear, or desire, I can no longer tell. There are about thirty; judging by the postmarks, they date back more than ten years. All are addressed to Cooper in Jackson's familiar, flamboyant script.

'I don't understand. Why are you giving me these?'

He ignores my question. 'Keep them. I don't want them back.'

'Why are you really here, Cooper?' I ask tiredly. 'You could have sent these. You didn't need to bring them yourself. Is there something you want? I've given most of Jackson's things to his charity, but I kept a few bits and pieces in case you wanted them.'

He doesn't reply.

I touch his arm. 'Cooper?'

'If I'd posted them,' he says, his cobalt eyes blazing, 'I couldn't have done this.'

His kiss is hard, hot, passionate, searing. My breasts

crush painfully against his chest, and there's a slippery rush of wetness between my legs.

'I've hated you since the moment I saw you,' Cooper murmurs into my hair. 'Oh God, how I hate you.'

Gently, I kiss his angry mouth. 'I hate you too,' I whisper back.

February 14, 2008

Felden Street
London SW6

Dear Cooper,

*Happy Valentine's Day, bro! And thanks for
the b-day card. Ella forgot again; like this is news. Guess I'm
buying my own present this year. Time this letter reaches
you, I should be the proud owner of a 1972 250cc Indian
Cub! Gonna cost, but not as much as it should, thanks to
eBay. I reckon I can talk Ella round if I play the guilt card!*

*She doesn't know it yet, but I'm giving her a fair trade.
Something she's wanted for years, too. I'm coming home,
Coop. For good.*

*Hope you and Lolly could use the company because I'm
going to need somewhere to lay my head for a bit. Sorry to
spring it on you like this, but I didn't want to say anything
till I'd gotten things sorted my end. Turns out One World
have a new office opening a short ways out of Charlotte, so
I'm transferring there soon as I hire a replacement for my old
job. They even threw in a raise, but it's still going to take a
while to put away enough cash for a place of my own. I don't
want anything from Ella. This house in London has never
felt like my home anyways. I'll bring the Indian and my
books and Grandpa's chest, but I'm leaving the rest. I don't
need any reminders.*

*Seven years is a long time for a man to wait for a woman
to love him. I don't just mean me; I'm talking about William
Ashfield too. There was a time I wanted to string him up,
but I can't find it in me to be angry any more. A part of me
almost feels sorry for him, poor bastard. Must be going soft*

in my old age. I went to his house once, did I tell you that? Years ago. Stood outside in the rain and watched him flipping pancakes with his little girl in the kitchen.

Ella's not mine. She never was. You knew it, didn't you, bro? Tried to warn me, but I wouldn't listen. All this time I've been fooling myself I had enough love for the both of us. I never should have married her. I knew I wasn't the one for her, same ways as I knew she was the only one for me. Love works like that sometimes, doesn't it? We all like to think we got a soulmate out there, just waiting to be found. No one says they gotta love you back, though.

Remember when I was a kid, I found that stray, the one with the broken leg? Man, I loved that mongrel. Stayed up night after night nursing him. I couldn't have been more than seven. Spent all my allowance buying him treats and whatnot, even skipped school till Mom caught me out in the old barn, playing ball with him. But soon as he was healed, he wanted to be off. He'd pull at his leash, whining fit to bust. He didn't belong with me, I just didn't want to see it.

Mom said then that if you loved something, you should let it free; if it came back to you, it was yours. And if it didn't, then it never was.

Well, I'm setting Ella free. I should have done it years ago.

Guess I've only clung on so long because I wasn't ready to say goodbye. I knew she'd never leave me, she's got too much stubbornness in her. She's like you, Coop. Reckon you'd have been better for her than me, come to think of it. I rolled over too easy, gave her what she wanted. A woman doesn't respect you if she always has the upper hand. Hindsight's 20/20, right?

I should have stood my ground when I first found out

*about William, and told her to choose. Maybe back then she'd
even have chosen me, but I guess I'll never know now. I've
been weak, bro. All I can say is, love makes fools of us all.
You never know what you'll do for it until the time comes.*

*Figure you're wondering, why now? I'm not sure I know
the answer to that one. Daddy would say I'm finally growing
some balls, and maybe he's right, but it's not just that. Sure,
I got dreams. I want to know what it's like for a woman to
love you, really* love *you, like you're her reason for
breathing. I want to see that in my woman's eyes. I want
babies, I want to take all that love and see what we make of it
between us. Ella's never going to give me any of that. All the
time I'm loving her, there's no room for me to love anyone
else. What I feel, it's like a creeper, strangling everything else
before it has a chance to take root. I don't know if I can
change that, yet it seems I've gotta try, before it's too late.*

*But the simple truth is, I love Ella too much to stay. She's
not happy with me, not the way a woman should be happy.
I've tried my damnedest but I can't give her what she needs.
I've got to step aside, and give her a chance to be with
someone who can.*

*If I can see her happy, I reckon that'll be the first step to
being happy myself. You know what I'm talking about, Coop.
It's no more than you did for me.*

*You've been the best brother a man could have. If I
screwed up, it's not because of anything you did. I hope
I haven't disappointed you too much.*

*I'll be telling Ella at the weekend. Soon as I work out
when I'm coming home, I'll let you know. Reckon it won't be
more than a few weeks. I can't tell you how much I'm looking
forward to leaving the British weather behind me! You
wouldn't think the world had this many shades of gray.*

Seems I most always have a cold these days. Couple weeks of Lolly fattening me up with her home cooking, and I'll be a new man!

Fire up the grill, bro. I'll soon be home.

Jackson

14

William

Christ! This is all I fucking need!

I storm into the hotel room. My daughter's missing, my girlfriend's just lost her dead husband's baby, I'm fighting to save my company from going tits-up, and my wife has picked this moment, of all moments, to come off her drugs and start rapid-cycling her moods. Now, to top it off, my bitch of a mother has just crawled out from whatever rock she's been hiding under for the past twenty years.

Any more liquid ordure coming my way?

My mother tips the porter and shuts the door carefully behind him.

'So,' I say tightly, 'to what do I owe this honour?'

'I'm dying, William.'

As opening gambits go, it's a showstopper.

I crack open the mini-bar. 'Here's to you, Mother,' I say, downing a miniature of Bell's in a single gulp and unscrewing another.

She takes it away and pours it down the bar sink. 'Get a

grip, William. I didn't come all this way to watch you fall apart. If I can deal with it, so can you. No wonder your daughter ran off, if *this* is the kind of thing that's been going on at home.'

'Don't worry, Mother. You haven't driven me to drink. This is the first good news I've had in a week.'

'Sit down, William.'

I'd forgotten how much taller I am. In memory, she still towers over me—

'I said, sit *down*!'

I fling myself into an armchair. 'Fine. Keep your bloody wig on.'

'How observant of you. I could have gone for something a little younger, of course, but one doesn't want to draw attention. Chemotherapy, William,' she adds acidly, as I gawp. 'Pay attention, I don't wish to go through this twice. I have acute myeloid leukaemia. It's terminal.' She smooths her skirt over her lap, picking off an imaginary piece of lint. 'I was diagnosed eleven months ago; I've already had two courses of chemotherapy and radiation, but the cancer has come back. If I were younger, I'd be a candidate for a bone-marrow transplant – oh, don't worry, William, I'm far too old. You won't be called upon to make a display of filial devotion and donate.' Her thin lips twist. 'That would have been an interesting moral dilemma for you, though, wouldn't it?'

I hate the bitch, but she's got balls. We could be discussing the weather.

'The prognosis is bleak – well, from my point of view.' Another tart smile. 'The doctors are talking now in terms of weeks. Curious, isn't it, how we measure the start and end of our lives in weeks, not years, every day precious.'

Tess Stimson

I find my voice. 'So what's this about, Mother? Looking for a deathbed reconciliation?'

'Oh, I didn't come for me, dear. Well, not as far as you're concerned. I wanted to see my grandchildren again, I must admit; I have a particular fondness for Caitlin. Girl's got more balls than all the men in our family put together.'

I grimace at the ironic echo of my own thoughts.

'No, I came, William, because there are things that need to be said.'

'Sorry to disappoint, but I don't give a damn what you need to get off your miserable chest before you check out,' I say coldly, getting to my feet. 'My daughter is *missing*. Right now, salving your conscience is the last thing on my mind. Whatever self-serving crap you came to dish up, save it. As far as I'm concerned, the next time I see you, you'll be in a wooden box.'

She doesn't flinch. 'I'm not here to salve my conscience, dear. You're the one in trouble.'

I fold my arms contemptuously, waiting.

'I'm quite aware what you think of me, William. You've made that very clear. I've watched you turn your father into a saint, while you pushed me firmly in the other direction. I've sat by and said nothing while you made a complete mess of your life, because you wouldn't have listened anyway.' She waves her hand dismissively. 'Oh, I'm not talking about Ashfield PR – you've made exactly the same mistake I did, and poured all your energies into your company: of course it's a success. I'm talking about your marriage. You're more like me than you realize.'

My hackles rise. 'I've spent the last seven years trying to *stop* my wife committing suicide. You *drove* Dad *to* it!'

'You'd like to believe that, William. And perhaps there's

296

even a grain of truth in it. But your real problem is that deep down, it's not me you blame, but yourself.'

I feel the air rush from my lungs. Punctured, I deflate on to the edge of the bed.

'It's much easier to tell yourself I harangued your father into his grave, isn't it? You've certainly done your best to convince yourself that's how it happened. Trouble is, it won't wash. You still believe it's *your* fault. It's why you married Beth.'

'Oh, please. Don't give me the fucking cod psychology,' I snap, but my voice lacks conviction. 'You haven't got a clue—'

'You weren't to blame for what your father did, William.'

'I bloody know that! *You* pushed him over the edge, not me! Telling him he was a failure, going on about how useless and pathetic he was—'

'When?'

'When *what*?'

'When did you hear me tell him that?'

'Christ, what does it matter now?' I slump forward, my head in my hands. 'Whatever he needed to hear, I didn't give it to him, he blew his brains all over the shagpile, end of story. And spare me the California psychobabble, Ma. I got a woman pregnant and married her. Forget the redemptive bullshit. She was up the duff, I did the honourable thing. I had no idea I was a bloody suicide magnet till it was too late.'

'I've never heard anything so ridiculous. Suicide magnet indeed. It's part of the illness, you know that—'

'What illness? What are you talking about?'

'Your father was manic depressive, William.'

My head jerks up. 'No. I'd have – he can't – I *know* about manic depression!'

'Then you should understand. I thought you realized. It ran in his family, though I didn't know that till after he died, of course. I found an old family photograph in the attic when I was sorting out his things, a boy in the back row who didn't look quite right; and there was an aunt who was locked up and died young.' She gives a self-mocking smile. 'I thought I could save him. We're not so different, you see.'

I'd have known. Surely.

I can't have got it so wrong.

I attempt to rally. 'You expect me to believe this shit?'

'I'm many things, William, but a liar isn't one of them.'

I revisit my childhood, observing it through the lens of my life with Beth. Dad's extraordinary bursts of energy; the endless unfinished DIY projects. The dark, inexplicable moods: 'Your dad's having a bad day. Let him sleep.' Twice, when I was still very young, he disappeared altogether for several months; probably to a clinic, I realize now.

Dear Christ. If my mother endured half of what I've had to put up with from Beth . . .

The silence between us stretches.

'Your father wasn't a fool. He knew I didn't mean some of the things I said; he understood I was angry at the illness, not him. But I still shouldn't have said them. In that sense, perhaps his death *was* partly my fault. But it certainly wasn't yours. He stopped taking his medicine when he lost his job. You've lived with Beth long enough to know what that means. Nothing you could have said or done would have made any difference.'

Medicine?

It wasn't my fault?

It wasn't my fault.

'William, I spent more than thirty years trying to fix something that couldn't be mended,' my mother says urgently, grasping my sleeve. 'It turned me into someone I didn't recognize, eaten up with anger and bitterness. In the end, I lashed out at him not because I hated him, but because I hated what his illness had made *me*. I don't want you to make the same mistake, son. I don't want you to become bitter and resentful. I know you have the children to consider, but don't do what I did. Don't become someone they despise.'

I shake her off, but without venom. Dear God, a bloody shrink would have a field day with this. I thought it was women who married men like their fathers.

She's right, of course; but what she doesn't realize is that she's too late. I hate myself already. I'm a one-woman man; I believe in faithfulness and loyalty and love. And I've been cheating on my wife for most of our marriage.

My mother struggles to her feet, leaning heavily on a silver-topped cane. I'm struck suddenly by how frail she's become.

'Beth's a good woman,' she says firmly, 'but she's not good for you.'

I laugh disbelievingly. 'You really are a viper, aren't you? She's played fair with you all these years, let you see the kids, brought you to Paris, and now you're telling me to leave her!'

'I'm just warning you what will happen if you don't.'

I lock eyes with the woman who gave birth to me, who gave me her chin and colouring and ruthless ambition, and feel nothing. Which is progress, of a sort, given my feelings towards her for the past twenty years.

So much left unsaid.

'This doesn't change anything,' I manage. 'You can't just waltz in and say your piece and expect everything to be OK between us overnight.'

'Certainly not,' she says crisply. 'You're my son. A tough negotiator. I wouldn't expect anything less.'

'She's my daughter too, Beth! I want to see her!'

'She's not ready to see you,' my wife says, with infuriating calmness. 'She needs to sort herself out first. Not to mention shower; the state of her, quite extraordinary, she'll need sandpaper, not soap. Anyway,' she adds, 'we need to talk before you go rushing off like a bull in a china shop and scare her away again.'

I've had just about enough of women and their cosy little chats for one day.

'I didn't fly halfway round the world to twiddle my thumbs in another bloody hotel room!' I snap, pushing past her towards the door. 'There's nothing we need to discuss that can't wait.'

'What about your affair, William?'

Ah. Except that.

'Well. Affairs, plural, I should say,' my wife amends, 'I'm sure there's been more than one. After all, we haven't had sex for eight years. You'd have to be made of stone not to want it from someone, and trawling King's Cross isn't really your style.' She pulls back the curtain and looks down at the Paris streets, her back ramrod straight. 'Cate ran away because we let her down. A lot of that's my fault,

I know. I've damaged her, and that's something I have to live with. But a lot of it has to do with *us*. You and me. She's still a child, William. She still needs us.'

'Beth,' I say carefully, 'I never meant to hurt you—'

'I'm not blaming you, William. That's not what this is about.'

I pinch the bridge of my nose. 'It's been a hell of a day. Do we have to talk about this now?'

'Cate's afraid everything's going to fall apart,' she continues, as if I haven't spoken. 'She's running away so she doesn't have to see it happen. You're too wrapped up in your – work. I'm too wrapped up in my own problems. We've both failed her.'

Screw these miniatures. What I wouldn't do for a bloody stiff drink.

'What is it you want from me, Beth?' I say wearily to my wife's back.

'We've got two choices. We can paper over the cracks, pretend everything's OK, and watch our daughter lurch from one crisis to another and wreck her life. Or we try to do something about it.'

'Fine. I'll cut back at work—'

'I'm not talking about work.' Finally, she turns from the window to face me. '*We're* the problem, William. I told you. This pathetic apology of a marriage isn't doing anyone any good, least of all Cate. We've got to start being honest. Either we try to fix it, or we give up and call it a day.'

The words hang in the air. She's pale, but in control. No tears. No histrionics.

I can't quite believe it's *Beth* who's finally daring to acknowledge the elephant in the room.

'Are you talking *divorce*?'

'If that's what you want, yes. I won't stop you,' she adds. 'I won't fight it or – do anything silly. Ben's left home, Sam's at boarding school; it'll be tough on them, but they'll survive.'

'This – this is what you want?'

'No! Of course it's not what I want! William, I love you more now than the day you offered to help straighten my picture at the exhibition,' she cries fiercely. 'But even I can see this isn't working the way it is. Sooner or later you'll meet someone who won't put up with sharing you. If you don't want to be with me, I'd rather end things now, while we can still be friends.' She takes a deep breath. 'I just want one thing.'

Here it comes. The house? Half the company?

'A year.'

She rushes on. 'Do it for Cate, if not for me. She'll be going to university next year and getting on with her own life. If we can just see her through her A levels. Give our marriage one last, final chance. If we both give it our best shot and you still feel the same in a year, if you still want to leave, I won't stand in your way.'

She's offering me freedom. A way out without guilt or recrimination. The promise of a new start with Ella, without having to worry if my wife's going to slit her wrists again or jump off a cliff.

I can't leave her—

It's not my fault my father killed himself.

She's giving me a choice. Marriage as penance short-changes us both.

Ella will wait twelve months for me, surely.

'A year?'

'No more lying,' Beth says quickly. 'If we're going to do this, we have to mean it. You have to honestly try, William. You have to *notice* me.'

'And you'll take your pills?'

She hesitates.

'It won't work if you don't, Beth. You know that. You know what you get like.'

'Yes. I'll take my pills.'

'A year,' I say.

It doesn't even occur to me I might want to stay longer.

'There's one other thing,' Beth says, moving towards me.

Slowly, nervously, she unbuttons her neat blouse. She unfastens her plaid skirt, and lets it fall to the floor. She's wearing underwear I haven't seen before: lacy, pink and cream. Her whole body is trembling.

Her blonde hair swings forward, hiding her face, as she reaches behind and unhooks her bra. I'm suddenly reminded of the first time she undressed for me, more than twenty years ago. Her hands shook so hard she dropped her watch, then knocked over a full wineglass when she bent to retrieve it.

My cock springs to life. *She's beautiful.* I'm ashamed how much that surprises me.

Her breasts sway lushly as she bends to peel off her knickers. Gravity and three children have taken their toll, but they've given her curves she didn't have before, a voluptuousness I don't remember. It suits her. There's something else different about her, too. It takes me a moment, and then with a shock I realize: she's shivering not from nerves, but desire. She *wants* this.

She sinks to her knees and reaches for my flies. She reeks of sex, I think suddenly. Where the hell has *that* come from?

Her lips close around my cock.

I can't – she's rapid-cycling – it would be taking advantage – she's manic, it's not her – I can't – oh, God, that feels—

'Beth – are you sure . . . ?'

She looks up. 'No more papering over the cracks, William. If we're going to do this,' she adds, returning to the task in hand, 'we're going to do it *properly*.'

For once, I don't mind letting let my wife have the last word.

'For God's sake, Ella, pick up,' I mutter, drumming my fingers on my desk.

I glance apprehensively at the closed study door. It's five-thirty in the morning; if Beth wakes up, she's bound to wonder why I'm not in bed beside her.

Come on, pick up! It's been two weeks since I got back from Paris, and I still haven't had a chance to tell her the news. My initial excitement has been gradually leached away by worry. She can't mean what she said in New York, surely? If I can just tell her what's happened. I realize she's avoiding me, but I'm starting to get desperate. I've already called the hospital; she's not working today. She has to be home. Where else would she be at this time of night?

I swear under my breath as her answer-machine kicks in. 'Look, I know it's the middle of the night, and I'm sorry if I've woken you. I can't sleep. I don't know if you're busy, or if you just don't want to talk to me, but you can't leave it like this, Ella. If you're there, please pick up the phone.'

Nothing but the crackle of static.

'Ella, we have to talk,' I say urgently. 'There's something important I have to tell you. If it's really over, I can accept that, but I need to know what happened first. You owe me that, at least.'

The floorboards above my head creak. *Shit.*

'Ella, I know about Jackson's baby. I know how hard this must be for you.' I correct myself. 'Actually, I don't, but I can imagine. It doesn't affect how I feel about you, Ella. Nothing could. You may not want to hear it, but I love you. You don't have to do anything with that information; I'm not even sure if I want you to. I just had to say it, that's all.'

I picture her hunched up in bed, refusing to pick up the phone.

I can't leave it like this. I have to know she's at least OK.

Playing my final card, I take aim at her pride. 'We always said we'd stay friends. I never thought of you as a deal breaker, Ella.'

'I'm not.'

'Ella! Thank God! I've been going frantic—'

'Sorry. I've been – busy . . .'

Her voice sounds thick, disused.

'Is everything all right? Are you OK?'

'Not really. What is it you need to tell me?'

'Not over the phone.'

A sigh. Then, 'Where?'

'How about the Chelsea Brasserie? Thursday, say seven-thirty—'

'Thursday's OK. But not dinner. Lunch.'

'But—'

'Lunch, William.'

She's not going to make this easy. But I can win her round. As soon as she hears the news, she'll change her mind.

I'm counting on it.

Ella looks at me in horror. 'William, I never asked for this! You can't leave because of me!'

A waiter tops up our wineglasses. I wait impatiently for him to go.

'What do you think all this has been about?' I hiss through gritted teeth.

'I never wanted to break up your marriage—'

Bitter disappointment swamps me. *This isn't how she was supposed to react.*

'For Christ's sake, Ella! Take some damn responsibility!' I slam my fist on the table; an elderly couple walking past the pavement café leap as if they've been shot. 'You can't sleep with me for eight years and let me fall in love with you and then back away with your hands up and say it's got nothing to do with you! The moment you kissed me in the park, it became something to do with you! Why else would I leave, if not for you?'

She recoils as if I've slapped her. In the harsh April sunshine, the fine lines sketched around her eyes and mouth are clearly visible. Her eyes are bruised, her expression hunted. I tell myself it's only been a couple of months since her husband died; less than four weeks since she lost his baby. No wonder she looks like death.

Ironically, Beth's blooming. She's never looked better, in fact.

With a supreme effort, I settle back in my chair and summon a smile. 'Ella, can we put this behind us, please? Let's think about the future, not the past.'

Her gaze drifts. I suppress a resurgent beat of anger. Doesn't she understand? *I'm going to leave my wife for her.* 'Ella? In a couple of weeks, Beth's going off on a painting holiday in Italy with Eithne, it's been arranged for months. We could—'

'I don't love you, William.'

My stomach goes into freefall.

'I'm sorry. I'm very fond of you, of course. We've had a great time. But I don't love you. I don't want you to leave your wife for me. There's no point.'

Is this some sort of *joke*?

I laugh uncertainly. 'I don't believe you.'

She folds her hands in her lap and regards me coolly. 'We always said that if either of us wanted to end this, we'd walk away, no questions asked. It's just not working any more, William. I need someone with less baggage—'

'You don't think I'll leave her, do you? That's it, isn't it?' Silly girl; why didn't she just *say*? 'I can't blame you, it sounds like the oldest line in the book. I mean it, Ella. Just give me a chance, and I'll come through. I know you love me—'

'It wasn't Jackson's baby.'

I search her eyes for some sign she's kidding.

'You haven't been the only one, William, you know that.' She shrugs carelessly. 'After all, we're not married to each other, are we?'

She's fucking serious.

I want to be violently sick. Bad enough that she screwed someone else, but that she got pregnant by him – *pregnant*—

Jesus Christ almighty. I held her hand in the ambulance, I was the one pacing up and down all night at the fucking hospital!

Anger courses through me like a molten river. I want to kill someone. The conniving, cheating, deceitful whore! I should have bloody seen this coming. She opened her legs eagerly enough for me. I was an idiot to think I was the only one.

'You bitch,' I spit, shaking her hand off my arm and standing up so sharply my chair falls backwards. I throw a fistful of twenties on the table. 'This should just about cover your fee.'

'William—'

'Jackson was the lucky one,' I snarl.

I walk blindly without a fucking clue where I'm going. I can't believe I've been so comprehensively *had*. I got it all wrong. No wonder my company is going under. My judgement's shot to shit.

She's played me for a fool. It was all fine and dandy while she could invoke the sainted Jackson, but now she's on her own she hasn't got anywhere to hide. She never really wanted me. She just wanted to get her kicks, taste a bit of forbidden fruit. Of course she didn't want me to leave Beth. I was just her bit on the side. She's probably got another married sucker on the line already.

How could I have been so fucking *blind*?

*

I sleepwalk through the next few weeks. It's my turn to ignore Ella's calls; I delete her number from my phone and put a block on my email. If only I could block out the pain as easily.

I cling on to my anger as long as I can, but in the end grief forces its way to the surface. It's like having my heart fed through a shredder. The fact that she's made a patsy of me into the bargain rubs salt in a mortal wound.

The irony is that if this had happened any time in the past eight years, it wouldn't have killed me. Until three months ago, our relationship was a two-dimensional, compartmentalized fling. Outside of our nights together once a month, it didn't really exist. I made sure I knew nothing about her life, or what went on in her head, and she never asked about mine.

Jackson's death changed everything. For the first time I met the real Ella, the vulnerable, fallible woman behind the perfectly controlled façade. I fell in love with her in a way I never could have done with the confident old Ella. I fell in love with her fear of flying, her ridiculous shoes, her hatred of losing half a pair of anything – gloves, books, earrings – the way her nose ran when she cried, her mercurial and unpredictable moods.

Except I hadn't met the real Ella at all, had I? It was all an act.

I pick up the red leather box on my desk and put it in my pocket. A gold love bangle from Cartier; my fashionista daughter will appreciate its cachet, even if Beth doesn't. I've had it inscribed with my wife's name.

She's really trying. The sex isn't ground-breaking, but it's regular, and she even makes the first move sometimes.

She's gone shopping for new clothes with Cate, and changed her hairstyle for the first time in twenty years; the *gamine* crop suits her. It's not just the way she looks, either. In her own quiet way, she's made it clear she's not taking any shit from anyone. She overruled me on the new Hummer and insisted on a bloody hybrid, for God's sake (I see Cate's hand in that). It's all taking a bit of getting used to, but I have to admit I rather like the bolshy new attitude. I hadn't realized how tired I've been, carrying this marriage on my own. It's the first time in all these years I've felt as if we're in things together.

Beth was the one who came up with the compromise on New York. I'd still rather Cate didn't go at all, but at least if she's with Ben, it'll go some way towards putting my mind at rest.

When Beth asked me to wait a year, all I saw was a way out. Maybe, just maybe, it's actually a way forward.

I'm half out the office when the phone goes. I look for Carolyn, but she's already left.

'William? It's Malinche Lyon. William, it's been bothering me for days, but it finally came to me – in the supermarket, of all places, they've got the most extraordinary range of spices these days, I remember when I had to get Kit to bring me sumac from Dubai, it was the only way to get it fresh – anyway, I was dithering over the cumin, whether to go for whole or ground, and then I remembered where I'd seen that lovely boy in your office: Cate's boyfriend, I mean. I *thought* he looked familiar. I know it probably doesn't matter, but Nicholas said he'd heard something on the grapevine, you'd been having some problems with a hostile takeover bid, and the name rang a bell—'

'Mal,' I say patiently, 'what *are* you talking about?'

She giggles. 'Oh, dear, baby brain again, Nicholas says I'd forget my name if it wasn't sewn into my knickers. Dan, of course. He came to my restaurant just before Easter with his real father, I've known Simon for years. Dan is James Noble's stepson, William. I just thought you ought to know.'

'Dan's not the mole,' Beth says.

'What are you talking about? Of course he bloody well is!' I storm across the kitchen, nearly tripping over the dog. 'And I bloody *employed* him, for fuck's sake! I gave him a job at my office!'

Beth puts another dirty plate in the dishwasher. 'It's not Dan,' she repeats stubbornly.

'Haven't you been listening? It must've been a set-up from the beginning. Look at the way he turned up here out of the blue! Obviously Cate had no idea he was using her to get to me, but—'

'William, would you shut up for *one minute*!'

There are times when I'm not entirely sure about this new assertiveness.

She slams the dishwasher shut and turns to face me. 'It isn't Dan! You can't go charging off to his house in the middle of the night accusing him of industrial espionage! What do you plan to do, drag him out of bed and lynch him from the nearest apple tree?'

'Don't be so bloody melodramatic.' I stop pacing, my eyes narrowing. 'Why are you so sure it's not him?'

'It's not me either, if that's what you're thinking,' Beth snaps.

I'm aware of Cate watching TV in the next room. I lower my voice.

'Look, Beth. It all makes sense. For the last six months, James Noble has been one step ahead of the game, poaching my best members of staff and stealing clients out from under me. He has to have someone on the inside, someone privy to more than the usual office information. Some of the stuff he's got hold of was just too damn sensitive. And Dan mysteriously appeared on the scene just before Christmas. You do the maths. No one else fits the bill.'

Beth busies herself with wiping down the kitchen counter. For a long moment, neither of us speaks.

'There is one person,' Beth says.

I sit in my car in the darkness, staring at her house. The lights are on downstairs; through the wooden shutters, I see her shadow move around the sitting room. I have no idea how long I wait, or why I'm even here. A gentle wind stirs the branches of a tree overhead; May blossom falls like confetti on the bonnet of my car.

God defend me from my friends; from my enemies, I can defend myself.

In the distance, a church bell chimes eleven. A cat yowls; moments later, a dustbin lid clatters to the ground.

Unexpectedly, Ella's front door opens. I duck down in the car, but she can't see me. She's wearing a pale silk dressing-gown; the breeze sculpts the flimsy fabric to her form, silhouetting her against the light spilling from the doorway. She looks like a goddess: beautiful, and treacherous.

A second figure appears behind her, tall and broad-shouldered. As he steps into the pool of light, I curse beneath my breath. He looks so like Jackson, there's only one person he can be.

Ella turns. Her face lifts to his, and he kisses her. I feel the passion, the intensity, in that kiss, even from here.

I start the car, angrily forcing it into gear. It's time to stop fooling myself. Ella and I were never real. A hothouse romance, unable to survive in the real world. She gave me passion and excitement and challenged me in ways I can't begin to explain, but those aren't the proper foundations of a marriage. She was the perfect mistress. And that's all she was.

Beth loves me. It's not perfect, but she's my wife. We've got three children and twenty years between us. She's right: it's worth fighting for.

It's past midnight by the time I let myself quietly into the house. I toss the car keys on to the hall table. Cannelle whimpers softly, and I fondle his golden head as he slumbers in his basket in the warm kitchen.

Pouring myself two fingers of single malt, I shut myself in my study. Time to grow up, Will, old son. Be grateful you didn't make a bloody arse of yourself and dump the wife for a cheap bit of totty.

She cheated on Jackson with me, and now cuckolds me with his brother. It's fitting: almost biblical.

It also hurts like fuck, but I'll get over it. I'm not a callow youth in the flush of first love. I've been around the block enough times to know that, much as you might want it to at times, a broken heart doesn't kill you. I still have Beth. She adores me. We're still good together. There's a lot to be said for the companionship and security that come with two decades of shared experiences. She still laughs at my jokes, no matter how many times she's heard them.

I knock back my drink, and turn out the light. It's about time I tried a bit harder with Beth. She's been pulling out all the stops for the last month, but if I'm honest, my contribution has been a bit half-hearted. Apart from the sex, of course. I don't think she could fault me there.

To my surprise, Beth's sitting up in bed, reading. When she sees me, she lays the book aside and puts her glasses on the bedside table.

'You didn't have to wait up, darling. I told you I'd be late.' I yank off my tie, and perch on the edge of the bed to unlace my shoes. 'Something wrong?'

'Yes, William, I'm sorry.'

I look up. 'Sorry for what?'

'My mind's made up, I'm afraid,' Beth says clearly. 'I'm leaving you.'

15

Beth

Seeing Jesus in the cornflakes is a warning sign by anybody's standards.

I've been given a second chance with my daughter. I won't get a third.

I always knew I'd have to start taking the pills again, sooner or later. I wouldn't have brought them to Paris with me, tucked into the lining of my handbag where I could pretend I'd forgotten all about them, if I hadn't known time was running out. This morning I spent €900 on exquisite Meerschaum pipes for William in the hotel shop. He doesn't even smoke.

I can't afford another manic episode. I took the drugs. Now I just have to make sure it's worth the price.

My husband tries to push past me to the door. I screw up the courage to take the biggest gamble of my life, knowing I could lose everything.

'What about your affair, William?'

The blood drains from his face. Guilty as charged. I realize how much I'd still hoped it wasn't true.

I turn to the window, so he can't see my face. 'Well. Affairs, plural, I should say,' I add lightly. 'I'm sure there's been more than one. After all, we haven't had sex for eight years. You'd have to be made of stone not to want it from someone, and trawling King's Cross isn't really your style.' I'm surprised how normal my voice sounds. 'Cate ran away because we let her down. A lot of that's my fault, I know. I've damaged her, and that's something I have to live with. But a lot of it has to do with *us*. You and me. She's still a child, William. She still needs us.'

I sense William wondering how to handle this, how to handle me. He hates scenes.

'Beth, I never meant to hurt you—'

'I'm not blaming you, William. That's not what this is about.'

When I tell him what I want, I'm ready for him to affect surprise; to protest at the idea of leaving me, even. Perhaps, at some level, he might actually mean it: William is a man, after all. Used to his creature comforts, the familiar routine of home. He won't want to leave unless he has somewhere – some*one* – to go to. Most men don't.

I'm not ready for the raw, desperate hunger in his eyes.

I watch him weigh my future in his mind. I know he isn't seriously considering my offer – at least, not in the sense I want him to. If he agrees, it won't be because he wants to give our marriage a chance to work, but because he's looking for a guilt-free, no-strings way out.

But a lot can happen in a year.

'A year,' William repeats slowly.

Now or never, I tell myself. Dan wanted me. Eithne

wanted me. If I'm to hold on to my husband, I must make him want me too. Somewhere out there is a faceless woman who knows how to sigh and flatter and please my husband, who has stolen him away from me with her long legs and come-to-bed eyes and pliant body. I have to win him back. I have to make him want me again.

Whether *I* want *him* is irrelevant.

'There's one other thing,' I say.

I don't take my eyes off him as I undress. My mouth is dry; I can't seem to stop my hands trembling. He hasn't seen me, really *seen* me, for a long time. I'm forty-one. (How old is *she*?) My breasts sag; my stomach is pleated and covered in stretch marks. (Does *she* have children?) Will he be repulsed at the thought of making love to me? Will he *laugh*?

I can't meet his eye. I drop my gaze as I unhook my bra, but find myself staring straight at his crotch. There's no mistaking the bulge.

You're beautiful. That's what's so amazing about you! You don't even realize how lovely you are! If I'm beautiful to Eithne, I can be beautiful to William, too.

I strip off my knickers and close in on William, reaching for his flies. His penis springs into my hand, bucking beneath my touch. What do all those sexpots in shiny beach novels usually do next? Something the old Beth would never try. I fall to my knees and take him in my mouth. It doesn't taste *too* bad. He shudders violently, gripping my shoulders so hard it almost hurts. I've never been very good at this, but I do my best, licking his penis like it's an ice-lolly melting in the sun. He groans, so I'm obviously doing something right.

'Beth – are you sure . . . ?'

'No more papering over the cracks, William,' I say firmly. 'If we're going to do this, we're going to do it *properly*.'

I open my jaw wide, praying I don't gag. Experimentally, I stroke his testicles. His response is to pull me to my feet, scoop me up and almost throw me on the bed.

For the first time, I actually start to feel aroused myself. William parts my thighs, and puts his head between them. I sit up, about to protest – *I haven't washed! I'm not ready!* – and then remember the sexpots. Perhaps, when men talk about wanting dirty sex, they mean it literally.

I've never been very adventurous in bed. Having one's bottom whacked with a wooden spoon sounds so unhygienic. And I've never really seen the point of handcuffs.

But in the last few months, I've been propositioned by a boy young enough to be my son, and fallen into bed with my oldest girlfriend. I think a little cunnilingus is allowed.

'A bit faster, please,' I say firmly.

He's not as silver-tongued as Eithne, I think absently; and then, quite suddenly, I find I'm pleasantly unable to think at all.

'He's not really *trying*, of course,' I say, 'apart from in the bedroom, naturally.'

Eithne slugs back another shot of vodka from her silver hip-flask. 'I wouldn't call *that* trying at all,' she says waspishly.

'You're very sweet, darling, but we both know I'm not Cirque du Soleil material in the boudoir, and never will be. No, William's been very conscientious in that department, but it's quite clear his mind's not on the job.'

'I wish I could say the same,' Eithne sighs.

I turn back to the carrots. 'He was fine for the first week or two after we came back from Paris – rather *too* fine, actually,' I say painfully, 'like a child waiting for Christmas. And then last week he came home in a foul mood, and he's been in a complete funk ever since. I've no idea what's the matter with him, he won't tell me. He just sits brooding in his study for hours. To be honest, Eithne, I'm beginning to think the business is about to collapse and he's scared to come clean. And to make things even worse, he keeps buying ridiculously expensive presents to make up for being so miserable, then forgetting what he's bought, and giving me the same thing again.' I stop peeling to move tonight's roast further out of Cannelle's reach. 'I've had to take back two Cartier bangles already, much to Cate's disapproval. She was all for selling them on eBay and buying herself a car.'

'Smart girl. She's rather gone up in my estimation, I must say.'

'Not necessarily a good thing,' I observe.

'She's not pining over the boyfriend, then?'

'Dan?' I'm suddenly very busy with my root vegetables.

'Yes, *Dan*,' Eithne mocks. 'You really are a terrible liar, Beth.'

'I didn't say anything—'

'You didn't need to.'

I finish the carrots, and reach for a string bag of sprouts. 'He keeps calling me,' I confess. 'He's left dozens of messages on my mobile since we got back from France. Obviously I haven't returned any of them—'

'Why "obviously"?'

'Why?' I splutter. 'Eithne, it's – well, it's obvious!'

'Oh, absolutely. I can quite see why you'd prefer to abase yourself for your worthless husband rather than entertain the idea of a gorgeous young man who's completely infatuated with you and would no doubt happily go down on you for *hours*. It makes perfect sense. Honestly, Beth. Haven't I taught you anything? You should be biting his bloody hand off in gratitude – and I say this as one who has a vested interest,' she adds grumpily.

'He's not infatuated—'

'Adultery *really* isn't your forte,' Eithne says, 'you're the colour of a tomato.'

'Pass me that saucepan,' I say crossly.

She hands it to me, and lights a cigarette. 'Is it because of Cate?'

'No! Well, yes, of course. She may be over him, but she'd hardly be terribly pleased if her mother – if he— Anyway, that's not the point!'

'I'm sorry. What *is*?'

'Eithne,' I say, exasperated, 'I'm *married*. That still means something to me, even if it doesn't to anyone else these days. And even if I wasn't, Dan is half my age! What do we have in common? I was studying light and colour at St Martin's when he was still trying to stack plastic bricks!' I drop the carrots in the water and put the saucepan on the Aga. 'He was barely out of nappies himself when I had my first baby! You know it'd never work. And it's bound to be me who'll end up heart-broken,' I add realistically, 'you know I never do anything by halves.'

'You're making too much of this. It's just *sex*,' she says. 'Isn't it?'

I hesitate. Eithne is never without a metaphoric bucket

of very chill water to hand. I know Dan is just flattering me, to get what he wants, but he seemed genuine—

Suddenly, I feel very foolish. I *need* a moral drenching. I've let that young man lead me up the garden path. In the cold light of day, it all seems very different. I should've told William as soon as Dan confessed. If he loses his company now, it'll be my fault.

'There's something very important I have to tell you,' Dan had said, when he turned up at the house the afternoon Cate went missing. 'Actually, two things. Please, will you just hear me out?'

I'd assumed he was talking about Cate, of course.

I'd watched Dan pick up a pot of thyme on the windowsill, put it down, then take a paring knife from the rack and test it against his thumb before laying it back on the butcher's block. He was so clearly cat-on-hot-bricks, I'd actually smiled. Cannelle lifted his head from his paws, panting. Dan knelt down and gave him a couple of the doggy treats he always kept in the pocket of his cargos.

The dog trusts him, I remember thinking, *he can't be all bad*.

'Dan, please, I don't have much time—'

He'd stood up and fixed me with those amazing green eyes.

'I think I'm in love with you,' he said simply. 'I've tried very hard *not* to be. No offence, but this isn't exactly a result for me. A married woman twice my age, with grown-up kids and everything—'

'Yes. I can see that,' I said faintly.

'Cate wasn't a game,' he added quickly. 'I never meant to hurt her. It's just, she's so *like* you. I thought I could find in her what I felt about you, but—'

I couldn't really take it in. All I'd cared about was finding my daughter. At the time.

'What's – what's the other thing, Dan?'

'You have to believe me,' he'd pleaded, 'I didn't know what James was doing. It was nothing to do with me, I had no part in it, I swear—'

'And *do* you believe him?' Eithne asks now, when I've finished telling her everything.

'I should never have trusted him,' I say bitterly. 'I let him persuade me he had nothing to do with James Noble because I wanted to think he'd meant the rest of what he said. I've just been fooling myself. Of course he doesn't love me! It sounds ridiculous, even to me—'

'Is it really so ridiculous that someone might fall in love with you?'

'He's just trying to buy time, so I don't go running to William. He's using me, like he used Cate.'

Eithne looks at me strangely. 'And if he *wasn't* James Noble's stepson?'

I start to protest, but Eithne's right: I'm a terrible liar. I've been drawn to Dan from the first moment we met at the art gallery. I just haven't acknowledged it before.

I'm not going to rip my family apart for a fling with a young boy who'll swiftly tire of his Mrs Robinson moment and move on. I'm not *that* much of a fool. But his attention has meant more to me than I care to admit. He made me believe in myself, if only for a moment. It hurts to know it was just another lie.

I shrug, my eyes glittering with tears.

'Dan does love you,' Eithne says flatly.

'No. It's time I stopped—'

'It's not Dan who's been spying for James Noble,' Eithne says, 'it's me.'

'I always told you that girl was trouble,' Clara snipes. 'All those piercings and tattoos.'

'She doesn't have tattoos, Mother. And actually, you never said—'

'I don't take any pleasure in being proved right, Beth. You know me. Live and let live, that's my motto.'

I yank a weed out of the flowerbed with more force than is strictly necessary.

'I'm not surprised William's hardly talking to you – that's not a weed, dear, you'll have no flowers left if you carry on like this – the poor man's been working all the hours God sends, and all the time you've been undermining him, harbouring a viper in your bosom.'

Haven't I just, I think grimly, shooting her a glare. I count to ten and pray for patience.

'You can't blame him for being upset. It shows such lack of judgement on your part, Beth. You take after your father, of course. He's always been a *dreadful* judge of character—'

I rock back on my heels and brush dirt from my forehead with the heel of my gloved hand. 'Aren't the roses doing well this year, Mother? Dad sent you roses every week for a year when you were courting, didn't he? He was absolutely mad about you in those days. Quite head over heels,' I add meaningfully.

My mother sucks lemons. *One to me.*

'I do wish you hadn't cut your hair,' she says pettishly. 'I'll never get used to it.'

'I was thinking of getting a tattoo next. A dolphin, on my right shoulder—'

'Really, Beth. I'm surprised you're in a mood to joke.' She tucks a stray tendril of pink clematis neatly beneath the kitchen windowsill. I immediately free it again. 'I assume the girl was being paid? Eithne, I mean. Thirty pieces of silver, or whatever the going rate for betraying your friends is these days.'

'Actually, I think in a funny way she was just trying to help,' I sigh.

'I don't know how you can possibly defend her,' Clara snaps. 'She's practically put you out on the streets.'

'It's complicated. Look, Mother, I really do need to get on—'

'At least you won't still be going ahead with this ridiculous Italian nonsense,' she sniffs, 'not now that woman's shown herself in her true colours. Absurd idea in the first place. Jetting off to the Continent to mess about "discovering art" at your age. Lord knows what would have happened to your poor family when you were gadding about Europe.'

I contain my simmering temper.

'They'd have been fine. Cate's perfectly capable—'

'Perfectly capable! She's a delinquent! You should've taken a much firmer hand with her when she was young. I'm sorry to be the one to say I told you so, but—'

I pick up my trug, and get to my feet. 'Cate is *not* a delinquent. She's beautiful, and funny, and bright, and I'm so proud of her it hurts to breathe!' Suddenly, I can't contain my anger. 'My daughter has determination and talent and ambition, and she's already twice the woman you or I could ever hope to be! I will not have you coming to my house and pouring your poison on my family! You've made my life a misery since the day I was born. I won't have you turning your venom on my daughter!'

I'm trembling. I've never spoken to my mother like that in my life. I half expect her to stand me in a corner, or wash my mouth out with soap.

'Well! It's no wonder she's run off the rails if this is the example she gets at home!' Clara snatches the edges of her quilted jacket together. 'I won't be treated this way by my own flesh and blood! *When* you're ready to apologize, you know where I am!'

I sink on to the stone steps by the rose garden as she storms away, a half-laugh-half-sob dying in my throat. It's taken me forty-one years to find the courage to stand up to Clara, and I know already I've wasted my breath. I'll just have to apologize to her now, and she'll make me crawl over hot stones before she'll accept it.

Oh, Eithne. What *possessed* you?

She's never approved of William, I know that, but I had no idea she'd go this far to sabotage us. Did she really think that wrecking his company would force me to stand on my own two feet – 'If he wasn't there to prop you up all the time, Beth, you could do so much more, *be* so much more; please, you must believe me, I would never do anything to hurt you, I was only trying to *help*' – or was it simply revenge?

The awful irony is: in some ways Eithne was actually *right*. As William's struggled to keep his company afloat, his confidence has gradually leached away. For the first time in all these years of marriage, I don't feel overwhelmed by him.

I look up at the sound of footsteps.

'Mum? Are you OK?'

I give my daughter a lopsided smile. 'I'm not quite sure.'

Cate plonks herself on the step next to me. She looks a bit pale; I think she stayed up too late last night when she slept at Clem's. 'Is it true?' she asks. 'Is Eithne really the mole?'

I nod.

'But why? I thought she was your friend?'

'She's never really forgiven me for marrying Daddy,' I sigh. 'She thinks it's his fault I stopped painting.'

'Well, it is, a bit,' Cate says.

I stare at her in astonishment.

'Come on, Mum. You've got to admit he's a bit of a control freak. You always let him have his own way, same as you do with Granny Clara.'

'He's always been very encouraging about my painting—'

'Yeah, as a *hobby*. Can you imagine what he'd have said if you'd wanted to, like, do it as a career or something? He'd have gone ape.' She picks a fragile white climbing rose and smells it. 'Gorgeous. They're amazing this year—'

'Cate, it's not your father's fault,' I interrupt. Suddenly it's important she understands. 'I *let* him take over. I blamed him, and I blamed the illness, but the truth is it's *my* fault I stopped painting.'

It's the first time I've admitted it even to myself.

'I was afraid to fail,' I confess. 'It was easier not to try.'

Cate picks up the secateurs, and cuts a dozen white blooms, filling the trug. Their scent, sweet and strong, drifts towards me.

'Are you still going to Italy on Saturday?'

'No. I was in two minds about leaving you anyway. I suppose Eithne and I will get over this eventually, but it's going to take time. She had no business interfering the way she did, whatever her motives. I trusted her, Cate. She's the one always telling me not to be such a doormat and let people walk all over me.' I smile sadly. 'She's got a lot of grovelling to do before we can be friends again. I sort of understand why she did what she did, but I don't think we'll ever be quite the same.'

'You don't need her, Mum.'

I ruffle her hair. 'Not when I've got you.'

Cate shrugs me off. 'Mum! I meant, to go to Italy. You should go on your own.'

'Darling, I couldn't.'

'Why not? It's only for three weeks. Mrs Ghedini can come in and clean and stuff. Dad and me can manage.'

I open my mouth to tell her not to be so silly, and then pause. I'd been looking forward to Rome *so* much. The 'Pietà' – the Sistine Chapel – the catacombs of St Callistus – hours and hours to walk and look and think and maybe even paint. Eithne would've been great company, of course, but she can be very – well, *demanding*. I've never had a holiday by myself; not even a weekend away. And the children *would* be fine—

'What about your father? I couldn't leave him, it wouldn't be fair.'

'Mum, it's time to think about *you* for a change,' Cate says.

I look into her silvery-blue eyes, the colour of the sea just after a storm has passed, and suddenly realize she's not just talking about three weeks in Italy.

'You don't have to stay for me,' she says softly. 'I'll be

gone soon. If you don't leave now, you may never bring yourself to do it. I want you to be happy, Mum. I don't want to worry about you any more. When we did the *Titanic* at school,' she adds, looking down and fiddling with the secateurs, 'Mrs Buchanan said some of the people who drowned might have survived if they'd stopped clinging to each other. Sometimes you – you just have to let go.'

I'm washed by a wave of love for this brilliant, difficult, unique child of mine.

'Since when did you get to be so wise?' I gasp.

'Mum, it's OK,' Cate says. 'Go. I'll be fine. Dad'll be fine. We'll all be OK.'

'I do love your father, Cate. Very much.'

She nods, her eyes suspiciously bright. 'Not always enough, though, is it, Mum?'

'No.' I pull her into my arms, grieved that she's had to learn this lesson so young. 'No, it isn't.'

What was the turning point? I wonder. That brief, unguarded moment in Paris when his eyes told me, clearer than lipstick on his collar ever could have done, that he was having an affair? Seeing his longing for *her* written on his face when I offered him a chance of escape? Was it when he stood over me while I took my pills, a jailer, not a lover?

Virginia Woolf lies unread on my lap. Perhaps it was Cate bringing home our failure as parents when she ran away to France. Or when I begged William not to send Sam to boarding school, and he sent him anyway.

Maybe it was when he took the children skiing, but left me home because he said I played up to their fears.

Or perhaps it came the day he laughed at the idea of me opening a little art shop. Or when he ordered for me at a Vietnamese restaurant because he assumed I couldn't cope with the menu.

Did I finally start to get angry when I went to bed with Eithne, and saw myself, just for a moment, through her eyes instead of his? Or when Dan told me he loved me, and I realized how much William has denied me?

No. It goes back beyond that. Back to Cyprus, when William booked another woman into a hotel with my name.

Back further: to that dreadful place where they held me down, strapped me to a table with leather buckles and glued electrodes to my head.

Back to the beginning: when I built a marriage on a lie, the biggest lie of all.

It's not William I'm really angry with.

The pages of *Mrs Dalloway* blur. For years I've accepted a second-rate, second-hand love because I was too scared to demand better. I've cheated both of us. I used a lie to trap William, and I've used pity and guilt to bind him to me. All I've done is make us both miserable. Cate's right. I need to set us free now, before it's too late.

William's tyres crunch on the gravel drive. I glance at the digital clock on the bedside table. Nearly midnight. Where on earth has he been?

I check myself. What does it matter now?

It's another twenty minutes before he comes upstairs, smelling of bitterness and whisky. I take off my reading glasses and put my book aside.

'You didn't have to wait up, darling,' he says wearily. 'I told you I'd be late.'

Yanking off his tie, he tosses it on to the floor for me to pick up and put away tomorrow, and slumps on the end of the bed to unlace his shoes. 'Something wrong?'

'Yes, William, I'm sorry.'

'Sorry for what?'

Suddenly, it doesn't seem hard at all.

'My mind's made up, I'm afraid. I'm leaving you.'

For a moment, he doesn't react. Then he laughs.

He laughs.

I'm engulfed by a fury so incendiary I'm surprised the bedclothes don't burst into flames. I spring out of bed, planting myself right in front of him where he can't ignore me, or pat me on the head and send me away.

'Do you think my life is so wonderful with you I couldn't dream of leaving? Do you think I *enjoy* it when you look at me like shit on the sole of your shoe?'

He looks taken aback. 'That's not what—'

I'm shaking with indignation. 'You've treated me like a charity case for twenty years, as if I should be grateful to have you, and, fool that I am, I've let you! You, Clara, even the children – you all act as if I'm the village idiot, incapable of independent thought or feelings of my own! For forty years, I didn't even dare to change the way I did my hair! Did it ever occur to you how difficult *you* are to live with?'

He pushes past me into the bathroom and throws cold water on his face. 'What's this really about, Beth? Is it your pills? Because it's been one hell of a day, and I really don't need to come home to a fucking harpy who wants to use my balls for target practice.'

'This is not about the *pills*, or your affairs, or the hours you spend nursing your bloody company instead of being where you should be, with your family. It's about *me*.'

'Did it ever occur to you that *you're* the reason I don't want to be with my family?'

'Did it ever occur to you that that's bullshit?'

We glare at each other. A pulse beats in his forehead; my chest heaves. We haven't felt this passionately about each other for twenty years.

Suddenly my anger evaporates. 'William, we've both used my illness as an excuse for far too long,' I say tiredly, sinking on to the edge of the bath. 'Let's be honest with each other for once. If I hadn't been pregnant with Ben, you'd never have married me. You never loved me, and I knew it. *That's* the truth at the heart of this marriage. My illness gave you the excuse you needed to opt out of it, and it gave me a reason to stop trying. It's time to stop kidding ourselves. This marriage was over before it even began.'

'And whose fault's that?'

'Mine.' I swallow, hard. 'Ben wasn't an accident, William.'

He stares at me for a long moment, then swivels on his heel and leaves.

I follow him downstairs into his study, and shut the door quietly behind me. No need for Cate to hear any of this.

Neither of us speaks.

'Aren't you – aren't you angry?' I venture.

'Would it help if I were?'

'I did a terrible thing to us, William,' I whisper.

He pours slugs of whisky into two crystal tumblers, and hands me one without looking at me. The alcohol burns my throat without melting the block of ice in the pit of my stomach.

William slumps forward in his chair, cradling the glass

between his palms, defeat written in every line of his body. He looks utterly exhausted, as if he can't even find the energy to argue. Only the certainty that I'm doing the right thing prevents me from throwing my arms around him and begging for forgiveness.

'Are you sure about this?' he asks, without looking up. 'We could try again – *make* it work—'

'I think we both know we've passed that point, don't you?'

'What happened to waiting a year, for Cate?'

'Cate needs me to be happy more than she needs me to be here,' I say quietly.

William nods, once. When he speaks again, his tone is resigned. 'What do you want me to do?'

'Answer me honestly. Do you love me, William?'

He closes his eyes, and tilts his head back against the chair. Outside, an owl hoots. The grandfather clock in the hall ticks in time with my own heart. 'No. Not the way you deserve.'

'Thank you for that,' I say softly.

'So. What do we do now?'

I sink on to the window seat, leaning my head against the cool glass. The moon is full, bathing the garden in an eerie white light. A fox runs on to the lawn, scents the air, and disappears into the darkness.

'I'll go to Italy on Saturday,' I say. 'It'll give us both the time and space we need to sort out where we go from here. When I get back, we can discuss all the details, the practicalities. I don't want much, William—'

'You should keep the house. The flat in London is enough for me. What do you want to tell the children?'

'Sam doesn't need to know anything just yet. We can wait until I come back from Italy, and break it to him together in the summer holidays. Ben and Cate are old enough to know the truth now.'

He turns tired eyes towards me. 'And what is that?'

'That their parents love them, and always will. That they are the best of us, that they make us proud, that we'll always be there for them.'

'I didn't just marry you because of Ben,' William says. 'I'd have done it anyway.'

'I hope she makes you happy, William. Whoever she is.'

'There's no one,' he says bleakly. 'No one at all.'

A week later, I'm floating in a sea of pink, almost drunk on the scent of azaleas covering every inch of the Spanish Steps behind me. I had no idea the Romans did this every May. The carpet of flowers stretches all the way up the stone steps to the French church at the top, the Trinità dei Monti, where, in the eighteenth century, the most beautiful women and men of Italy gathered, waiting to be chosen as an artist's model. I remember my own foray into modelling, and think briefly of Dan.

Pushing my new sunglasses on top of my head, I thread my way between the couples sitting below me on the steps, and join the throng of tourists in the Piazza di Spagna taking pictures and throwing coins for luck into the boat-shaped fountain at the heart of the square.

A couple in their late forties catch my eye. The crisp creases of new clothes fresh from the cellophane tell me this is probably their first time away together in years, perhaps decades. I imagine children newly flown from the nest, a second honeymoon. When they stroll away, they're holding hands.

I miss William dreadfully; there hasn't been a moment in the last four days when I haven't ached for him. Every morning I wake wondering if I've done the right thing.

It's just as well I put some distance between us. I don't know how strong my resolve would have proved if I'd stayed.

I push William from my mind. Dodging the mopeds whizzing like mosquitoes along the narrow streets, I head down the Via Bocca di Leone towards the tiny cheap flat I've rented on the fifth floor of a crumbling old apartment building. I'm sharing a cramped, spider-filled bathroom with five other apartments, there is no lift, and the building smells of other people's cooking; but the light in my tiny bedroom is extraordinary. I've already filled three canvases; I have to climb over them to reach my bed.

I know I'll never have a career as a painter. The day before I left England, Eithne returned my paintings; only four had sold, probably to Eithne herself, though she'd die before she'd admit it. This isn't a Hollywood movie; I'll never be 'discovered'.

But it doesn't matter. My mania has ebbed; the depression is rolling in again, like a fog from the sea. Its first wisps already wreath and twist around my ankles. Soon I won't be able to see my hand in front of my face. When I paint, I'm able to believe it will lift again, if I can just be patient.

I reach my building and push open the small post door cut into the vast great double doors, towering twenty feet tall. The steps up to my apartment have been worn into hollows by countless pairs of feet over the centuries. Behind closed apartment doors, children screech, couples argue. I had thought I might feel lonely, travelling by myself, but it turns out I love my own company. I'm at peace, for the first time in my life.

My apartment is unlocked; there's nothing to steal. Panting slightly from the climb, I push open the door, and cross straight to the open window. I can still see the mass of pink flowers on the steps, if I lean out over the balcony.

I reach back into the room for my camera, and jump, startled.

Life's full of surprises.

16

Cate

Jelly shots *suck.*

I crawl into the bathroom and clasp the toilet bowl. This is all Clem's fault. She said she hadn't made them too strong. I don't think I've ever been so drunk in my life as I was last night. I even smoked half a pack of cigarettes – my mouth tastes like an ashtray, and I've burned my oesophagus practically down to my stomach.

Oh, God. Surely I can't be sick *again*?

I puke into the loo, and wipe my mouth with a wet flannel. There's nothing left to barf up. I am never, *ever* going near vodka or strawberry jelly again.

Actually, I feel a bit better now. Maybe I've finally got it all out of my system.

I throw on some old clothes, and scrape my hair into a ponytail. Where's a bit of parental discipline when you need it? Dad should never have let me go round to Clem's when her parents are away. Has the man no sense of responsibility?

I hear the sound of raised voices outside, and peer out of my bedroom window.

Poor old Mum is bent over her weeding, while Granny Clara waves her arms and chases her along the flowerbeds like Lady Macbeth. Bitching about the whole Eithne drama, I bet. She couldn't wait to come and say 'I told you so.' Bloody ambulance chaser.

Dad, like, totally freaked last night when he found out what Eithne had been up to. He and Mum had a huge row. They've barely spoken since. I guess whatever deal they cooked up in Paris is off now. It was never going to work, anyway. OK, he's bought her all this fabulous stuff and came home early for a few weeks, but he looks like someone's cut out his heart. We did *Doctor Faustus* at school last term. You'd think Mephistopheles had just paid Dad a call.

I open the window for some fresh air. Granny Clara's voice drifts towards me like sulphur.

' . . . Absurd idea in the first place. Jetting off to the Continent to mess about "discovering art" at your age. Lord knows what would have happened to your poor family when you were gadding about Europe.'

'They'd have been fine,' Mum says. She sounds really tired. 'Cate's perfectly capable—'

'Perfectly capable! She's a delinquent! You should've taken a much firmer hand with her when she was young. I'm sorry to be the one to say I told you so, but—'

'Cate is *not* a delinquent,' Mum yells unexpectedly. 'She's beautiful, and funny, and bright, and I'm so proud of her it hurts to breathe! My daughter has determination and talent and ambition, and she's already twice the woman you or I could ever hope to be! I will not have you coming to my house and pouring your poison on my family! You've made my life a misery since the day I was born. I won't have you turning your venom on my daughter!'

My cheeks redden, even though no one can see me. I don't think I've *ever* heard Mum talk back to Granny Clara, never mind stick up for me like that.

It's strange. I know Mum really loves Dad, but it's like she's Superman and he's some kind of romantic kryptonite. Usually, he takes charge of things and she just fades into the background. But with him all weird and zoned out like he's been this last few weeks, she's been getting stronger and stronger. Without him telling her what to do all the time, she's even started to boss *him* about a bit. She stopped him getting that disgusting Hummer (does he want his grandchildren to be living on a charred rock?) and she put her foot down over going on holiday to Italy, though I s'pose that's off now because of Eithne.

Her new hair's really cool. And she let me take her shopping somewhere other than M&S – she bought this gorgeous red wrap dress online from Boden, and some bootcut jeans; like, *finally*. It's really nice to see her standing up for herself for a change.

Everything blurs. I want Mum to be happy. Dad, too. I bet Ella's got something to do with his miserable mood. They've probably split up or something. I don't want Mum and Dad to stay together just because of me. I'll be gone soon, anyway. I don't want that kind of responsibility.

I get up and go downstairs. Granny storms furiously into the kitchen. 'Your mother has taken leave of her senses!' she cries. 'Like mother, like daughter!' she adds, as I ignore her and go outside.

Mum is sitting on the garden steps, looking like she doesn't know whether to laugh or cry.

'Mum? Are you OK?'

She throws me a watery smile. 'I'm not quite sure.'

'Is it true? Is Eithne really the mole?'

She nods miserably, and I perch on the steps next to her.

'But why? I thought she was your friend?'

Mum bites her lip. 'She's never really forgiven me for marrying Daddy. She thinks it's his fault I stopped painting.'

'Well, it is, a bit.' I smile. 'Come on, Mum. You've got to admit he's a bit of a control freak. You always let him have his own way, same as you do with Granny Clara.'

'He's always been very encouraging about my painting—'

'Yeah, as a *hobby*. Can you imagine what he'd have said if you'd wanted to, like, do it as a career or something? He'd have gone ape.' I reach past her and pick one of her roses. 'Gorgeous. They're amazing this year—'

She puts a detaining hand on my arm. 'Cate, it's not your father's fault. I *let* him take over. I blamed him, and I blamed the illness, but the truth is it's *my* fault I stopped painting.' She hesitates. 'I was afraid to fail,' she admits quietly. 'It was easier not to try.'

'Are you still going to Italy on Saturday?'

'No.'

She starts making excuses for the old lezzie, but I'm not really listening. I cut a few more roses and drop them in her basket, trying to work up my courage to tell her how I feel. Of course I don't want my parents to split up, but I need her to know she doesn't have to worry about me any more. If it has to happen, I can deal with it. I'd rather have them both happy and doing their own thing than have to live this fake happy-families routine any more. I'm fed up with the lies and pretending. I just want things to be *real*.

'. . . but I don't think we'll ever be quite the same.'

'You don't need her, Mum.'

'Not when I've got you.'

I duck as she ruffles my hair. 'Mum! I meant, to go to Italy. You should go on your own.'

'Darling, I couldn't.'

'Why not? It's only for three weeks. Mrs Ghedini can come in and clean and stuff. Dad and me can manage.'

I know she's tempted. She's never been away on her own before; I bet she'd have a brilliant time. I've half a mind to go with her.

'What about your father? I couldn't leave him, it wouldn't be fair.'

'Mum,' I say carefully, 'it's time to think about *you* for a change.'

She looks at me sharply. 'You don't have to stay for me,' I say, feeling my way. 'I'll be gone soon. If you don't leave now, you may never bring yourself to do it. I want you to be happy, Mum. I don't want to worry about you any more.' I drop my gaze, not wanting her to see me cry. 'When we did the *Titanic* at school, Mrs Buchanan said some of the people who drowned might have survived if they'd stopped clinging to each other. Sometimes you – you just have to let go.'

For a long moment, she doesn't say anything. Oh, fuck. I shouldn't have interfered, should I, it's none of my business—

Except the pair of them have *made* it my business, haven't they?

She makes a little 'oh' sound, and covers her mouth with her hand. 'Since when did you get to be so wise?'

'Mum, it's OK. Go. I'll be fine. Dad'll be fine. We'll all be OK.'

'I do love your father, Cate. Very much.'

I swallow. 'Not always enough, though, is it, Mum?'

'No.' She hugs me so tight I can hardly breathe. 'No, it isn't.'

She releases me with a kiss, and I run upstairs to my bedroom. An unexpected idea has occurred to me, but I need to get myself together first. I can't go anywhere looking like this.

It takes a hot shower, half a can of hair gel and a ton of MAC, but an hour later I look recognizably human again. You'd never guess this was a girl with seven vodka jelly shots in her extremely recent past.

I turn side-on to the mirror. I'm not sure about this empire-line top, though. I bought it when I went shopping with Mum on Saturday, and it's totally cool with all this embroidery and beads and stuff, but it makes me look pregnant—

I grab my bag. Who cares what I look like? This isn't about *me*.

As soon as I see him, I wish I'd changed into the pink Fat Face T-shirt after all. I don't want him to think I've totally let myself go.

'Cate!'

I push past him before I lose my bottle. 'Can I come in?'

'Would it make a difference if I said no?'

I smile sheepishly. Dan smiles warily back.

For a moment we both stand in the centre of the living-room, not quite sure what to do next. I try not to think about the last time I was here.

'D'you want a coffee or something?'

I hate coffee. 'Sure.'

I follow him into the tiny kitchen. It's full of dirty plates and pizza boxes, and there's a line of jars filled with murky turps and paintbrushes on the windowsill like Mum's.

Dan messes with the coffee machine. Grounds scatter all over the grimy Formica; when he opens the cupboard beneath the sink to throw away the old filter, I notice the bin is overflowing with beer cans and mouldy teabags.

'So,' he says, his back towards me, 'how did the exams go?'

'Fine, thanks. French was a bit tough, but I think I did OK.'

'Well, you should. You've had a bit of practice.'

'You heard about that?'

He turns and grins. 'Village jungle drums, you know how it is.'

'I – I met someone,' I say, my cheeks flaming, 'in Paris. He's going to be spending the summer in Bath on a student exchange. We might meet up.'

'Great. That's great.'

I fiddle nervously with the fringe on my top. 'Look, I'm sorry about—'

'I'm sorry you had to—'

We both laugh nervously. I nod to indicate he should go first. 'Cate, what happened that day, I should've come to find you and explained. Nothing happened, I swear—'

'I believe you.'

'You do?'

The coffee machine hisses and burbles on the counter. A steady stream of water leaks from a crack in its side and drips on to the stained floor.

'Mum's going to Italy on Saturday for three weeks. On her own,' I add.

Dan nods, but says nothing.

'She and Dad – well. I think they're splitting up. He'll probably go up to London when she gets back, and stay in the flat he's got there. Mum's been doing a lot of painting recently. She seems to be really into it. I think she'll be OK about Dad leaving. In the end, anyway.'

'What about you?'

'I'll be fine. I'm not a kid any more,' I say, realizing it's true. 'Look, Dan. I just came to say sorry and to – to give you something.'

I hand him a scrap of paper.

'It's Mum's address in Rome. She's renting an apartment from a friend of Eithne's. It can get a bit lonely on your own. Sometimes it's wonderful when friends drop by unexpectedly.' I smile. 'I just thought you might like to know.'

It's not the jelly shots. Or nerves about Mum leaving.

I wrap my arms around my waist, rocking to and fro as I perch on the edge of the bath. I'm so scared I'm shivering.

It was just one time! I can't be pregnant! *I can't be!*

I've been sick every morning for a week, but that could be tension, or something I've eaten. My jeans won't do up, but I've been pigging out on doughnuts and chocolate. I'm really tired all the time, but my parents have just split up, my Mum's in Italy, and I'm not sleeping well. My breasts are sore, but that could just be hormones, couldn't it, it happens a lot when I get my period—

I can't even remember when I last had my period.

We only did it once – well, three times, but it was just one night! People try for *years* to get pregnant. What are the chances I managed it first time?

Fleur says every time you have sex, you have a fifty–fifty chance. Either you get pregnant, or you don't.

I wish I could call her, but I don't want Michel to know. I don't want anyone to know.

It must be five minutes by now.

I glance at my watch. Only two.

Why didn't I think about contraception? I know I was a bit drunk – OK, a lot drunk – but I've carried condoms in my bag, just in case, since I was fourteen! How could I have been so *stupid*?

I can't keep it. I don't want a baby. I want to finish my exams, go to NYU, become a journalist, there's no room in my life for a baby.

I pick up the little stick.

Oh, God. *Oh God oh God oh God*.

Everyone's very nice at the clinic. They don't treat me like a stupid little schoolgirl who's made a total screw-up of her life. The counsellor fills in all the paperwork and writes down the date of my last period (the 19th of March! And it's already the end of May! How could I not have *noticed*?) and doesn't even bat an eyelid when I tell her I had a one-night stand on holiday in France, and fib and say I don't know the name of the father.

I give her the urine sample they told me to bring to the consultation, and she tests it. I didn't quite believe I was really pregnant until she confirms it. Secretly, I'd still hoped all those stick things had been wrong.

She explains nicely that I'm eight weeks pregnant (it's only the size of a walnut, but I know from Biology it's already got arms and legs and tiny hands and feet) and asks me if I'm sure I want to end my pregnancy. She makes it sound so straightforward, like I'm terminating a lease. Which, in a way, I am.

It's way too late for a morning-after pill, of course (it's got eyes, too, and tiny nails, maybe it's even sucking its thumb), so she outlines the different options.

Vacuum. Aspiration. Dilatation and evacuation.

My head starts to swim. It all sounds so gruesome and medieval. I picture Sam when he was a baby inside Mum, being sucked into a vacuum cleaner, his arms and legs ripped off, his tiny body broken.

'Are you sure this is really what you want, Cate?' the counsellor asks.

'I can't have a baby,' I gasp.

'A termination isn't your only option. Have you considered adoption? And if you did decide to keep the baby, there are lots of support groups and—'

'No,' I choke out. 'I can't.'

'Cate,' the counsellor says, 'I know it sounds terrifying, but these procedures are much less painful than you think—'

'For me? Or the baby?'

'The foetus,' she corrects gently, 'won't feel anything. Cate, I really think you should go home and talk this

Tess Stimson

through with Mum. Lots of parents are upset at first, but once they've got used to the idea, they nearly always come round. Many actually look forward to being grandparents.'

I can't tell Mum. She'd be so disappointed. She'd come rushing back from Italy, it'd ruin everything for her. She'd think it was all her fault. I got myself into this. It's up to me to sort it out.

'Can't – can't I just take a pill, or something?' I ask desperately.

She sighs. 'An abortion isn't like getting rid of a headache. First we need to be sure you really understand what you're doing, and can live with the consequences. This is a big decision, Cate. You'll have to live with it for the rest of your life.'

I nod, trying not to cry. She'll never give it to me if I cry.

'If you do decide to go ahead, you can have EMA – an early medical abortion – up to nine weeks' gestation. You'd take medication to cause an early miscarriage. It doesn't involve any surgery, and you won't need an anaesthetic.'

'I'll do that,' I say, dizzy with relief. 'Can I take it now?'

She smiles. 'It's not quite that simple, I'm afraid. If you're really sure this is what you want to do, I'll arrange for you to see a doctor now. She'll complete the legal paperwork with you, and she'll probably want to confirm gestation with an ultrasound since you're near the nine-week limit. After that, she'll need to take a blood test, and discuss any possible risks and complications—'

'Risks? What sort of risks?'

'She'll explain those to you. An EMA is a very safe procedure, Cate. Most girls experience no more than some nausea, vomiting, that kind of thing.'

'How long do I have to wait?'

'You can see her right now.' She hesitates. 'I take it you haven't seen your own GP yet? If you want to have the procedure on the NHS, you'll need him to refer you to us. Otherwise, we'll have to treat you as a private patient.'

'I have to pay?'

'It'd be quicker that way. We could make your appointment for early next week, which would keep you within the time limit for an EMA. Otherwise, if we wait for your NHS referral—'

'I'll pay,' I say quickly.

'You can bring a friend or relative with you if you'd like.'

'No. I don't want anyone to know.' I shake my head violently. 'No one can know.'

The night before my appointment, I can't sleep. I toss and turn in bed, haunted by images of chopped-up babies and big blue eyes gazing up at me pitifully from black plastic bags. *It's just a bunch of cells*, I tell myself. *It's not a real baby*.

Two years ago, a couple from one of those anti-abortion groups came to our school and showed us photographs of babies in the womb, sucking their thumbs and running on the spot like tiny hamsters on wheels, and even hiccuping. They were a bit odd-looking, with their huge heads and everything, but they already seemed like real little babies, even the tiny ones: you could tell which ones would have big noses or need braces on their teeth.

They played a video of the unborn babies listening to Vivaldi; you could see them waving their tiny arms just like they were keeping time. Heavy metal got them bouncing around and kicking all over the place.

Then they showed us babies after they'd been vacuumed

out of their safe, warm hiding places. Some of them had had poison injected into their hearts. Others were born alive, and left in cold metal bowls to die.

I get out of bed and curl on the window seat, my hand instinctively fluttering to my stomach. It's still so flat; how can there be a baby in there?

After I saw the counsellor, the doctor put this probe thing inside me and I saw my baby on the screen. I heard its heartbeat.

Taking a pill's different, isn't it? It's not like chopping the baby up or anything. I read the leaflet. It says the drugs work by blocking the essential hormones that make the lining of the uterus hold on to the pregnancy. It just lets go. That's the same as having a period, right?

My cheeks are wet with tears. I can't have a baby. I'm only seventeen. I've got no money, no job. How can I look after a baby when I can't even look after myself?

In the morning, I dress in black, to suit my mood, and carefully pull back my hair into a neat French plait. I put on just enough make-up to hide the dark circles beneath my eyes. Dad's been going all-out to take proper care of me since Mum left for Italy; even though his head's all over the place these days, I don't want to take any chances. He stayed home from work last week when I said I had a headache; the last thing I need is him deciding we need to spend some quality father–daughter time together today.

I can't eat any breakfast. As soon as Dad turns his back, I give my bacon and eggs to Cannelle. He's going to have trouble fitting in his basket soon.

'No school today?' Dad asks.

At least I don't have to make up a lie about that. I shake my head. 'Half-term.'

'You could come up to London with me, if you like,' Dad offers. 'Do a bit of shopping, and then meet me for lunch—'

'I promised Clem I'd go round to hers,' I say, 'sorry.'

Dad looks genuinely disappointed. He must be lonely, I realize, with Mum gone and everything.

'Another time?'

I nod. Dad drops a kiss on the top of my head, and leaves for work.

I flit around the house, unable to settle to anything, trying to kill time until it's late enough to leave. I never thought I'd ever have to make this decision; I've always been sort of anti-abortion. But it's different when it happens to you. I can't give a child the kind of life I'd want to give it. I'm not ready to put my life on hold because I made a mistake; *one* mistake. With other mistakes you get the chance to go back and fix them. Why not this?

I'm doing the right thing.

The counsellor I saw the first time isn't there when I arrive. The admissions staff are perfectly nice, but brisk. I sit in the waiting room, surrounded by other girls not much older than me, none of us able to look each other in the eye.

Someone calls my name. I let them take my blood pressure and check my details, and it's like it's happening to someone else. They hand me a small tablet and a glass of water, and I sit there on the edge of the examination table with the pill in the palm of my hand.

'You'll need to come back in three days for the second dose,' the doctor tells me. 'You may experience some bleeding and cramping before then, but that's perfectly normal.'

This baby's already part of me. It has my genes; my blood is keeping it alive. I can't feel it yet, but it's had a profound effect on my body already. Does it know its mother is about to kill it?

I'm not ready to be a mother.

I swallow the pill.

I'll never even know if it was a girl or a boy.

I'm on the platform at Waterloo waiting for my train when the cramps begin. Within minutes, I'm doubled up with pain. I stagger towards the toilets and throw up before I can even make it to the loo. No one asks how I am or offers to help me.

Somehow I manage to make it outside and fall into a taxi. I tell the driver to take me back to the clinic, and collapse back against the seat.

I deserve this. *I've killed my baby, and now it's killing me.*

An allergic reaction, the doctor says. My body has rejected the pill, and because I vomited so much it hasn't been absorbed properly. After all that, I'm still pregnant.

I can't take another pill, so now I have no choice but to suck my baby out in bits.

You'd think after what had happened I'd keep it, wouldn't you? You'd think I'd decide it was clinging to life with all its might and deserved a chance to live, but if anything this has just made me more determined. I'm not fit to be a mother. I can't even do this right.

So three days later I go back to the clinic, where two nurses help me change into one of those hideous gowns that shows your bottom at the back, and they take me to an examination room, where I lie down on a table with my feet in some kind of rubber bands that are up in the air. They help me scoot to the edge of the table, and gently hold my legs apart. Their hands are so cold. The doctor comes in and chats to the nurses about the weather as she puts her fingers inside my vagina to check the position of my uterus, and then she shows me a speculum and tells me she's going to put it in and it might hurt a little. I feel the cold metal sliding inside me and opening me out, and it feels so horrid, so *invasive*, I wonder for a moment if my baby is just going to fall out on its own. Then she takes a long, scary-looking needle and inserts it into my open vagina and up into my cervix; it stings a little, but it's not too bad. She shows me something she calls the dilators and explains she's going to put them into my cervix to help it open wider and she reaches between my legs—

'Stop!' I yell.

'Is it hurting? We can give you some more meds—'

'I've changed my mind,' I gasp, struggling to sit up.

'Cate, we've just paralysed your cervix,' the doctor says, frowning. 'If we stop now, you'll miscarry anyway, because your cervix will open on its own.'

'I don't care,' I sob. 'I can't do this. I'm sorry, I'll pay you and everything, but I can't do this.'

The doctor nods to one of the nurses, and snaps off her gloves. They help me out of the stirrups, and one of them sits beside me on the examination table and rubs my back as I weep uncontrollably.

'Is there anyone you'd like us to call?' she asks gently.

I start to shake my head, then catch her arm. 'Wait. There is someone.'

*

'You're all dressed up,' I say. 'Are you sure I'm not interrupting something important?'

'Cate, it's fine.' She turns to the nurse. 'She's OK to leave?'

'You'll be staying with her, Dr Stuart?'

Ella nods. 'I'll keep her with me overnight. Has she had any meds?'

'Just codeine for the cramps. I'm afraid she waited rather too long before changing her mind,' she adds quietly; 'her cervix will probably dilate on its own now. After she miscarries, she'll need to return for a D&C to ensure there's no material left inside the uterus. The biggest danger now is an infection—'

'I understand,' Ella says coolly.

She turns and hugs me hard. 'I'm so sorry,' I sob into her shoulder. 'I've been so stupid, I've ruined everything. I didn't know who to call, I can't tell Dad, he'll be so disappointed, he'll blame Mum and she'll have to come back from her holiday—'

'Sssh. Cate, it's OK. I'm here now. It's going to be fine, we'll get through this.' She releases me and picks up my bag. 'Do you think you can walk a little way to the car?'

I nod. 'Ella, you won't tell Dad, will you?'

'I'm a doctor, remember? We're like priests, we can't tell anyone anything.'

'I'm going to lose the baby now, aren't I?'

'Yes, darling,' Ella says gently. She helps me down the front steps, and slips her arm through mine for support as we walk slowly towards the underground car park. My legs are rubbery, and now that the internal anaesthetic is starting to wear off, it feels like someone's shoved a red-hot poker up inside me.

'Will I still be able to have another one?'

A shadow crosses her face. She shivers, as if someone's walked over her grave.

Then she seems to collect herself, turning to me with a reassuring smile. 'There's no reason why you shouldn't, especially if we make sure you don't get an infection. But we need to think about contraception after this, Cate. Your parents don't have to know, but you can't take these sorts of risks with your health.'

A police siren screams a few streets away. Ella glances briefly at her watch, and hitches my bag on her shoulder.

'Can I ask you a personal question?' I ask after a moment.

'I think we know each other well enough now, don't you?'

'Why didn't you ever have children?'

'Oh, Cate. You don't pull your punches.'

'I'm sorry.' I bite my lip. 'You don't have to tell me if you don't want to.'

She sighs. 'No, I don't mind. This seems to be a day for exchanging secrets. OK, we have to cross here.' She presses the button, and we wait for the lights to change. 'I never wanted children with my husband. I could probably spend a solid year in therapy and never get to the bottom of why, but I think it's partly to do with my own parents, how they never seemed quite ready for me, and partly to do with me, my career, my need to prove something to myself; and partly to do with me and Jackson. I always knew I didn't love him the way I should. It seemed wrong to bring a baby into the world like that, almost under false pretences.'

The light flashes green for us to cross. Neither of us moves.

'What about Dad? Do you love him that way?'

She swallows. 'It's too late for us, Cate. I got in the way of your mum and dad, and I shouldn't have done. They've got a chance to—'

'Mum's left him,' I say baldly.

Ella jerks as if I've slapped her. 'She found out about me?'

'No.' I shake my head. 'In the end, it had nothing to do with anyone else.'

We've missed the lights. Ella presses the button again.

'Will you and Dad get back together now?'

'I can't have children. I got some kind of infection when I was younger,' Ella muses, as if she hasn't even heard me. 'It's why we have to take such care with you. I don't want you ever to have to stand in my shoes.' She smiles sadly. 'Ironic, isn't it? I mean, there's never been a time in my life when I've been less prepared for a child, and I've never wanted one more.'

'I'd have given you mine,' I say impulsively. 'If I hadn't . . .'

'Oh, Cate—'

The traffic signal beeps, telling us to cross. It's almost drowned by the police sirens a street or two away. I'm about to step on to the crossing when a souped-up car on elevated wheels jumps the red light and races past, music blaring from its open windows. Someone lobs a beer can from the car, and it bounces across the road, coming to a stop by my foot.

'That was close,' I laugh, as Ella's eyes widen. 'Do you think we could—'

I never get the chance to finish my sentence.

17

Ella

It's rained in the last half-hour. The night air smells of wet grass and acrid city streets: the scent of London. In the distance, a clock chimes eleven. A light breeze shivers the May tree outside the front gate, spattering me with wet blossom, and I wrap my kimono more tightly around me. Somewhere down the street, a car guns its engine and roars off into the darkness.

Cooper pulls me into his arms and kisses me goodbye. It occurs to me I've never met a man able to say so much with so few words.

'Sure you don't want me to call you a cab?' I ask softly.

He shakes his head, shouldering his battered rucksack. The wind slaps the hem of my kimono against my legs.

'Will you – will you at least let me know you're OK?'

'I'm OK,' he says simply.

I watch him until he turns the corner. He doesn't look back. *What did you expect, Ella? Flowers and a declaration of undying love?*

Later, after I've showered and thrown on a pair of old pyjamas, I pour myself a glass of Scotch and curl up on the sofa. Jackson's letters are heaped in my lap. It's three days since Cooper arrived and gave them to me, but I still haven't read them. Partly because of Cooper, of course; but mainly because I'm cravenly afraid of what I might discover, and what I might feel.

I turn the packet over in my hands. Cooper didn't give them to me to hurt me, I know that now. This is something I need to do if I'm ever to get my life back.

Pulling off the elastic bands holding the letters together, I riffle through the envelopes. There must be at least thirty of them. I had no idea Jackson wrote proper letters; emails and texts were more his style. But of course Cooper doesn't have a computer. I smile wryly. He was born a hundred years too late for the age that would've suited him best.

The first letter is postmarked March 1997 – the month we met. The last is dated the 14th of February this year.

I shiver. He wrote it the day he died.

I take a fortifying sip of Scotch, and pull the first letter from its envelope.

My first reaction is a shame so profound, I can hardly bear to wear my own skin. Jackson knew all along. *Seven years.* Every time I looked him in the eye and told him another lie, every night I said I was working late, he knew, and never said a word.

My deceit was a thousand times worse than I ever realized.

I put the letters down and stand up, my limbs aching as the blood rushes to them. It's not quite light; across the road, the newsagent's shutters rattle as he opens up to take delivery of today's papers. I thought I had Jackson all figured out. I knew he loved me, but I thought it was a child's love: needy, careless and demanding. I thought I deserved more.

The truth is, he loved me far more than I merited. How could he have kept silent all those years? How could he not have hated me?

I make myself a coffee, and prop myself at the kitchen table. My head swims with conflicting emotions. Dying confers a strange inviolability on its disciples: 'Don't speak ill of the dead.' For the past three months, I've heaped coals of fire on myself, unwilling to allow a whisper of criticism about Jackson even to cross my mind. I was the adulteress who betrayed a good and loving husband. I was to blame. I didn't deserve happiness with William, or anyone else. I didn't deserve a child. I put my career before my marriage; it was only just and fitting that I should end up with neither.

But Jackson's right. He *should* have called me on William.

For the first time since he died, I feel a flicker of anger at my husband. He knew I was only staying with him out of stubbornness and guilt, and he used that knowledge to keep me prisoner. Why couldn't he have had the balls to confront me? He trapped us both in a dead marriage. So much grief and pain on both sides, and for what?

Of course I shouldn't have had an affair, nothing excuses that; but by keeping quiet for so long, Jackson let himself become part of it.

I was right not to have a child with him.

A baby doesn't glue a relationship together. It would have been the worst thing, the most selfish thing, we could have done; Jackson knew that as well as I did. And yet he used my refusal to give him a child as a weapon against me for years.

Coffee splashes on to my hand; I find I'm shaking with anger. *Damn it, Jackson! Look what you did to us!*

We never should have married. Jackson knew that even better than I did. We both fooled ourselves I could learn to love him. We both knew, deep down, it would end in disaster.

Why didn't he say something?

I glance at the brightening sky. I should get ready for work; the last thing I need is to give Richard Angel any more ammunition in advance of the board meeting.

I dress on automatic pilot. *We both screwed up.* Jackson knew that. And he forgave me for my part in it.

He wanted me to be happy.

The realization is so startling, I drop the bottle of foundation I'm holding; the glass shatters on the tiled floor.

Jackson proved he loved me, not by staying with me all those years, but by finally having the courage to let go.

I clean up the spilled make-up. Cooper gave me the letters so that Jackson could finish what he'd set out to do: to set me free. No more guilt. No more regret. It's time to get on with my life.

I owe it to my husband.

Lucy chooses my clothes for the board hearing. She spends half an hour sorting through my wardrobe before deeming it all wildly inappropriate – 'For heaven's sake, Ella, don't you have anything that's not purple, slashed to the waist, fringed, beaded, or all four? If you didn't wear a white coat at work, you'd have been fired years ago' – and dragging me out to the one circle of hell Dante forgot to mention: the upmarket department store.

'It's not *supposed* to look sexy, that's the whole point,' she sighs, when I reject the latest in a line of identical neat, knee-length black suits in synthetic, sweaty fabrics.

'I'm sorry. But suppose I get knocked down by a bus? People might think I *meant* to dress like that.'

In the end, we compromise on a charcoal-silk trouser suit from Emporio Armani. The nipped-in waist is still too figure-hugging for Lucy, but at least it's black (well, nearly) and depressingly conservative. I'll team it with my vintage grey alligator boots. That should take the sensible edge off it.

She hauls me to an upmarket hair salon – 'Just do your best,' she sighs – and two hours later I emerge feeling like I've been mugged: my wallet is empty, and I'm strangely light-headed. But I have to admit it suits me. Cut short, my curls hang in becoming ringlets round my face instead of spiralling crazily in all directions like rusty bedsprings.

'Do you think any of this is really going to help?' I ask Lucy when we get home.

'You're a good doctor,' Lucy says. 'Everyone knows that. You did your best.'

'You didn't answer my question.'

She hands me my new lipstick, a thrilling shade of nude. 'Despite what you believe, Ella, Richard thinks you're a good doctor too. One of the best, in fact. Just turn up on time, play the game his way, and it'll be fine.'

My eyes suddenly fill with tears. I don't bother to hide them.

'I still miss him, Lucy,' I whisper.

She squeezes my hand. 'Of course you do,' she says, knowing better than to ask who I mean.

The night before the hearing, I can't sleep. I pace my bedroom, replaying the events in my mind. I shouldn't have to justify myself to a roomful of hostile pen-pushers. I *am* a good doctor. I did my best for baby Hope. We're doctors, after all, not miracle workers. Some things are just meant to be.

I glance thoughtfully at the huge vase of lilies on the coffee table. The whole room breathes with their scent. Cooper sent them to me this morning, to wish me luck for the hearing tomorrow. I don't know if Jackson told him they're my favourite flowers, or if it was just blind luck.

I'm ready long before I need to leave. Zipping up my boots, I check my reflection in the mirror. Even with the benefit of make-up, I still look like I haven't slept in a week. Maybe that'll play in my favour: Angel will know I've been up all night worrying. Showing due respect to his kangaroo court.

The phone rings as I'm double-locking the front door. I check my watch. I have time.

The answer-machine has already kicked in before I can pick up; a tinny voice echoes round the living room. 'This is Linda Biss at the Pregnancy & Planned Parenthood Advisory Centre. I'm calling on behalf of Ms Caitlin Ash-field—'

I switch off the machine. 'Hello?'

'Dr Stuart?'

'Sorry, I was halfway out the door. Who did you say you were?'

'I'm calling from the PPPA Centre in central London, Dr Stuart. We have a patient—'

I straighten my collar. 'I'm sorry, I think you've got the wrong number. I'm a paediatric consultant—'

Wait. Did she say *Cate*? Cate *pregnant*?

'Put her through,' I say sharply.

'Ella, I'm so sorry, I thought I could do it but I can't, and you're the only person I could think of to call—'

In my bag, my mobile beeps twice. It's Lucy, checking up on me. In less than one hour I have to be at the most important meeting of my life; my entire career hangs in the balance. Richard Angel isn't one to give second chances. There's no way I can make it into central London, collect Cate and then get to the hospital in time for the hearing.

She isn't my daughter; she's not even my stepdaughter, but the child of my ex-lover. She has two perfectly good parents of her own. I'm not her friend; in fact, she has every reason to hate me.

She's killing a baby I'd kill to have.

As Cate herself would say: it's a no-brainer.

'Give me your address,' I say.

'Ella, you won't tell Dad, will you?'

She looks so *young*. I smile, and give her a quick hug. 'I'm a doctor, remember? We're like priests, we can't tell anyone anything.'

'I'm going to lose the baby now, aren't I?'

'Yes, darling,' I say gently.

361

I pick up her silly yellow backpack and help her down the front steps. Cate always struck me as so *sensible*. How did she let this happen?

I check myself. At her age, I was leading a much wilder life. Who knows where I picked up the infection that wrecked my own chance of motherhood?

'Will I still be able to have another one?' Cate asks, eerily echoing my thoughts.

With an effort, I push the grief away. This isn't about me.

'There's no reason why you shouldn't, especially if we make sure you don't get an infection,' I reassure her. 'But we need to think about contraception after this, Cate. Your parents don't have to know, but you can't take these sorts of risks with your health.'

'Can I ask you a personal question?' Cate says.

'I think we know each other well enough now, don't you?'

'Why didn't you ever have children?'

'Oh, Cate. You don't pull your punches.'

'I'm sorry. You don't have to tell me if you don't want to.'

'No, I don't mind,' I sigh, as we reach the pedestrian crossing. 'This seems to be a day for exchanging secrets. OK, we have to cross here.'

She pushes her hair out of her eyes. I've always thought she looked so like Beth, but in this moment, it's William I see in her expression.

I try to find the right words to explain. 'I never wanted children with my husband. I could probably spend a solid year in therapy and never get to the bottom of why, but I think it's partly to do with my own parents, how they never seemed quite ready for me, and partly to do with me, my career, my need to prove something to myself; and partly to do with me and Jackson.'

Talking about it doesn't hurt as much as I thought it would. I realize I've finally started to reach some sort of acceptance; and that Jackson's letters have played a part in that. I offer him a silent prayer of thanks.

'I always knew I didn't love him the way I should,' I admit. 'It seemed wrong to bring a baby into the world like that, almost under false pretences.'

The pedestrian light flashes green, telling us to cross. I can't move.

'What about Dad? Do you love him that way?'

'It's too late for us, Cate,' I say painfully. 'I got in the way of your mum and dad, and I shouldn't have done. They've got a chance to—'

'Mum's left him.'

'She found out about me?' I whisper, appalled.

'No. In the end, it had nothing to do with anyone else.'

My mind whirls. William's free? Beth left *him*?

Except – it's too late. I've put a gulf between us nothing can bridge.

No point feeling sorry for myself. I can't change the past. I set this chain of events in motion the first time I kissed William. The game has played itself out; the cards I'm left holding are the ones I deserve. I hit the pedestrian button again.

'I can't have children. I got some kind of infection when I was younger,' I say. 'It's why we have to take such care with you. I don't want you ever to have to stand in my shoes. Ironic, isn't it? I mean, there's never been a time in my life when I've been less prepared for a child, and I've never wanted one more.'

'I'd have given you mine. If I hadn't . . .'

My heart twists. 'Oh, Cate—'

A boy racer jumps the lights, speeding past us in his souped-up Ford. Cate says something, but it's drowned out by the police sirens screaming towards us. She's laughing as she steps on to the pedestrian crossing.

She doesn't see the police car racing along the street in hot pursuit of the speeding Ford. She doesn't realize the young man at the wheel lost control as he hit a sharp turn in the road, trying to keep up with the car ahead of him. She is still laughing as he mounts the pavement, desperately trying to wrest back control of his vehicle, panic in his eyes.

She never even sees it coming.

Lilies.

For a moment, I think I'm still at home, half asleep on the sofa.

I try to open my eyes, but my lids refuse to work. Panicked, I try again. This time I succeed, and am rewarded with dazzling white brightness. I flinch; the movement sends a searing pain shooting through my neck and down my spine. I wait for it to pass, battling to stay calm. I can't seem to think properly. Disjointed words and pictures drift across my mind. *Focus.* I'm flat on my back; the pain and the grim ceiling tiles tell me I'm in a hospital bed. A bank of flowers surround me: clearly not A&E, then. I must have been here at least a day.

An IV pole on my left side tethers me to the bed. My right arm is heavily bandaged; my right foot is cradled in a sling a foot above the covers. I've broken my ankle. I move my left leg a little; the bedclothes wrinkle. I'm not paralysed, and I don't seem to have lost any limbs.

The fog starts to descend again. I try to fight it. There's something else – something I'm forgetting . . . something important . . .

I sleep.

'How are you feeling?'

I open my eyes. This time, it's easy.

Lucy strokes my hair back from my forehead. Her hand is cool.

'Would you like some water?'

She feeds me water from a sippy cup, like a baby. I want to speak, but my throat is too raw. I've been intubated, I realize.

'You were in an accident,' Lucy says gently. 'A car hit you. Do you remember?'

A jumble of shredded images blur in my head. The little green man telling us to cross. A beer can skittering down the street. Music, loud and distorted. *If it be love indeed, tell me how much.* Police sirens – the bite of a heavy bag on my shoulder – *There's beggary in the love that can be reckoned* – Cate laughing—

'Cate,' I whisper.

She doesn't hear me.

'Get some sleep,' she says, straightening my covers. 'I'll be back later.'

'*Cate,*' I scream; but the sound echoes only in my head.

Once more, I sleep.

*

The next time I wake, my mind is clear. I hurt all over, but the drug-induced fugginess has gone. I take a mental inventory of my injuries. The heavy bandage on my arm is now a straightforward dressing. My throat still rasps when I swallow, but my head no longer aches. The flowers next to me are wilting; I must have been here for days. A week, perhaps.

I hit the call button by my fingertips.

A nurse bustles in. 'Oh, we're awake. Feeling better?'

'Where's—' I cough, and try again. 'Where's Cate?'

'Don't try to talk, now. You've been very sick, you know, we nearly lost you—'

I struggle unsuccessfully to sit up. '*Where's Cate?*'

Her lips purse.

'Get me Dr Nicholson!'

The nurse stalks out.

I fall back against the pillows, trying to remember. I dredge up an image of the police car careering towards us, out of control; the young boy at the wheel, terror in his eyes; and then nothing until I wake up here. I thump the bed in frustration. What happened to Cate? *Why* can't I remember?

'Same old Ella,' a voice says from the doorway. 'Still giving everybody grief.'

William looks twenty years older than the last time I saw him.

'Doctors make the worst patients,' I say hoarsely.

He pulls out a chair and sits down without meeting my eye. 'Looks like I owe you for two of my children now, Doctor Stuart.'

It takes a moment for the words to register. 'Cate's OK?'

'They didn't tell you? Christ, Ella. Yes, she's fine—'

'Thank God,' I breathe, my eyes closing in relief. 'Oh, thank God.'

'Yes. And thank *you*.'

My confusion must show.

'You pushed her clear of the car, Ella,' William says quietly. 'Don't you remember? It didn't touch her. You saved her life. She sprained her wrist when she fell against the pavement, but that's it. You're the one who took the full force of the impact.' He swallows. 'You saved her life,' he says again.

'I don't remember—'

'I'm not surprised. You've been out of it for nine days. Cate says you were thrown twenty feet down the road. One of the nurses from the PPPA Centre came out and gave you CPR, or you wouldn't even have made it to the ambulance. It's OK,' he adds, seeing my expression, 'Cate told me why you were there. She told me everything.'

'I'm so sorry, William—'

'What on earth for?'

'I didn't mean to interfere—'

Tears clog my throat. William squeezes my hand, and I realize he can't speak either.

We gaze at each other across a landscape of pain and betrayal. For the first time in eight years, we're both free; and yet we're further apart from one another than we've ever been.

There's so much I want to say, I don't know where to begin.

'I know,' William whispers, as if I've spoken aloud.

We both jump when Lucy appears in the doorway. 'What's so urgent I had to— Oh. William.'

'It's OK. I was just going. I came to thank Ella.' He

stands and drops a quick kiss on my forehead. 'Keep in touch. Let me know how you're doing.'

No! Don't go, I urge silently.

'Nice flowers. Cooper?'

I stiffen.

He smiles sadly. 'Take care, Ella,' William says; and then he's gone.

My heart blisters. I turn away, so Lucy won't see my tears.

She twitches my covers into place. 'He's been here every day,' she says casually, 'waiting for you to wake up. He's sat here for hours at a time, reading and talking to you. Shakespeare, mostly. The first couple of nights, he slept in a chair next to you, wouldn't leave. We had to promise to call him the moment you came round, just to get him to go home and shower.'

> *Doubt thou the stars are fire,*
> *Doubt that the sun doth move,*
> *Doubt truth to be a liar,*
> *But never doubt I love.*

'I remember,' I say quietly.

'Ella—'

'Don't, Lucy,' I beg. 'Don't say it. Please.'

She busies herself with my chart. I don't point out that she's not my doctor, and that she shouldn't even be here. I know she's probably spent almost as many hours in the past week sitting next to my bed as William has.

'There's a TV news crew who want to interview you,' she says, after a few minutes. 'They've been calling every day. Someone got pictures of the accident on their phone and put it up on YouTube—'

'I don't want to talk to anyone.'

'Richard was very impressed,' she adds drily. 'Especially when it got him and the hospital all over the evening news. He's managed to persuade the Shores to come to terms with their loss in private, rather than have it all raked over again in open court. I believe he pointed out that it doesn't look good accusing an injured heroine of being a baby murderer.'

I'm not fooled. I know she must have pulled out all the stops to persuade Richard to do that for me.

She clips my chart to the end of my bed. 'I'm sorry, Ella,' she says suddenly. 'I know you don't want to talk about it, but William has sat here for nine days begging you not to die. All he wants is some sign from you. Why is that so hard?'

'That was for Cate—'

'He knows what you did for her,' Lucy says. 'Not just saving her life. He knows you were prepared to put his daughter before your career. Don't you think that says a lot to him? You've been given another chance. Don't throw it away. He's still here,' she adds, gesturing towards the window. 'Speak to him. If you let him leave now—'

'He'll leave anyway!' I cry suddenly. 'Sooner or later! He'll leave! He'll make me love him and then he'll leave! He'll break my heart and I'll be left with nothing! Don't you understand? I can't! *I can't!*'

Lucy stares at me for a long moment. I can't bear the pity in her eyes. I turn away, but she sits carefully on the edge of my bed, so that I have no choice but to look at her.

'Ella, love doesn't come with guarantees. There's no safe way to do it. It takes you hostage, it gets inside you and opens up your heart and means you're no longer in control.' She sighs. 'You think you're safe, you build a wall around yourself and you think no one can get in, and then one day, somebody does, and your life isn't your own any more. Love is a risk, Ella,' she says urgently. 'Loving someone means risking failure, but not loving someone is the greatest risk of all. Don't you see?'

'He'll never forgive me,' I whisper.

Her gaze doesn't flinch. 'Maybe not,' she says. 'But can you spend the rest of your life not knowing?'

I shiver with fear. And then, without warning, I'm in the middle of the worst panic attack I've ever known. Adrenalin zips through my body, instantly shutting everything down but the instinct to fight or flee. My heart pounds in my ears. I have pins and needles; I'm so dizzy I feel sick. My vision blurs. My mouth is dry, and my mind races. I can't breathe; my body is smothering itself. I hyperventilate, trying to pull in enough air. Oh, God, this is it. The big one. I'm going to lose control, it's going to win, I can't fight it any more—

What's so bad about losing control?

The thought slices like a laser through the static in my head.

Where, exactly, has being in control got me?

Alone. Widowed, rejected by my lover, pitied by my dearest friend. Cut off from everything that makes life worthwhile. The more I've tried to control my life, the more the chaos has taken over.

Fine. Have it your way.

I let go. And in that instant the panic stops.

The tightness around my chest loosens. I can breathe. My heartbeat slowly returns to normal. The dizziness has gone.

I probe gingerly, like a tongue prods an aching tooth. There is pain, yes, and loss, certainly; but the panic has dissolved like salt in water.

It can't be that simple. Can it?

Come on, Jackson says in my head. *Take a chance, Ella. What've you gotta lose?*

'Is he still here?' I ask Lucy.

She glances out of the window, and nods.

'Help me up,' I say.

'You can't get out of bed—'

'Why? Too much of a risk?'

'Can't you just phone him and—'

'He'll never answer. *This is the moment!*' I grab her hands. 'Please, Lucy!'

She lowers the sling cradling my ankle, and helps me stand. My head swims. I take a deep breath, and the room stops tilting.

It's only four paces from my bed to the window, but it feels like a thousand miles. By the time I reach it, I'm sweating and dizzy. I cling to the windowsill. Four floors below me, William is walking towards his car.

I bang on the glass, but of course he can't hear me.

'Help me open it!'

'This is mad,' she says, but pushes against her side of the Victorian sash window. I do the same on mine. It shifts a little, but still doesn't open. William is searching through his pocket for his keys.

We shove again. He unlocks the car.

The window opens. I lean out, and yell his name as loudly as I can.

My voice is carried away on the breeze. William opens the car door. Lucy yells with me, but we're drowned out by the scream of an aeroplane overhead.

I grab the nearest thing to hand and throw it at him.

Then I collapse into a chair, and wait.

It doesn't take long.

'What the hell do you think you're doing?' William shouts, storming into the room. Lucy discreetly leaves, but he doesn't even notice her. 'You could've killed me!'

'I needed to get your attention,' I say.

'Well, you've bloody got it!'

'Why didn't you return any of my calls?'

'Why d'you think, Ella?'

'William,' I say desperately, 'that day at the Chelsea Brasserie, I made a mistake. I said terrible things to you, things I shouldn't have said and didn't mean. I wanted to apologize, to explain—'

'Not necessary. You made yourself perfectly clear.'

'But you don't understand—'

'Ella, you saved my daughter's life. I'll always be in your debt for that.' He turns away, so I can't see his face. 'But we've hurt each other too many times. How can you trust me, knowing I'm capable of cheating on my wife for eight years? How can I trust you, after you got pregnant by another man?'

There'll always be a question at the back of his mind. Unless, somehow, I can persuade him otherwise.

I only have one chance to get this right. I search for the words that will persuade him to stay. Jackson had just died,

I was so scared of being alone, Cooper happened to be there, I'd had too much bourbon. It'll never happen again; it's in the past. All true. All good reasons.

I step out on to the tightrope, and say the only words that matter.

'I love you.'

His back shivers.

'Why should I believe you?' he whispers finally.

'Why would I lie?'

'What about – ' he waves blindly to the flowers – 'about Cooper?'

'Cooper came to collect some of Jackson's things, and give me some letters. He kissed me,' I admit, knowing that honesty is my only option now. 'I kissed him back. But then I stopped. I told him I loved *you*.'

Finally, he turns around. His face is white and twisted with pain.

'I saw you kissing him!'

'You saw me kissing him goodbye!'

'You were pregnant with his baby!'

'*One* mistake, William! Haven't you ever made one mistake?'

'How can I trust you again?' he cries furiously. 'How do I know?'

'The same way I trust you! The same way any of us trust the ones we love! By choosing to! By taking a leap of faith, William! What else is there?'

'I can't do this any more, Ella,' William says, his voice raw. 'I don't want this kind of part-time love. I want to fall asleep with the woman I love, to breathe the same air as she does, for hers to be the face I see when I wake in the morning. I want to be the most important thing in her life.

I want to know her inside and out, for there to be nowhere I can't go, nothing I can't ask. That's not you, Ella. It never will be. You're too independent, too self-contained—'

'Do I look independent and self-contained to you?' I cry. I force myself to my feet, ignoring the bolt of white pain that shoots up from my ankle. 'I'm so far out on a limb here, I can't even see the ground! I'm fucking terrified, William! I love you so much, I'm too scared to breathe!' My cheeks are wet. 'Don't you *get* it? I've loved you from the moment I saw you, and this is the first time I've stopped running away from the truth long enough to admit it!'

'For Christ's sake, Ella, sit down before you fall down,' William says sharply.

'William, please—'

'It's OK, Ella. I get it,' he says tiredly.

In that moment, I know I've lost.

I collapse on to the edge of the bed. I'm out of words, out of ideas. My ankle throbs. My head aches. I'm sore all over. Even my fingertips feel raw.

'Cate didn't lose the baby,' William says. 'They're both going to be fine.'

For a moment, I'm too stunned to speak. 'I can't believe it,' I manage finally. 'William, that's amazing. It's – it's a miracle.'

'So Lucy said.'

Our eyes meet. In the midst of all the loss and anguish we've inflicted on each other, this tiny new life represents hope, no matter the circumstances of its existence.

'What will Cate do?' I ask. 'Is she going to keep it?'

He sits next to me, close enough that all I have to do is reach out and touch. 'She knows she's not ready to become a mother. She's got so many plans and dreams – university,

New York, journalism. So much she wants to do. She's decided to give the baby up for adoption.'

'Oh, William. How hard. For you, too—'

'Cate wants to give her baby to us, Ella.' He turns to me. 'I told her there wasn't an us.'

His eyes blaze with intensity. My heart heaves itself into my mouth.

'Ella? Was I wrong?'

It takes a moment to understand what he's saying.

He pulls me into his arms, burying his face in my hair. 'Dear God, Ella, we've been so bloody reckless,' he says fiercely. 'We could have lost each other for good. I love you so much. I never want to take that chance again.'

I feel the pulse of his blood beneath warm skin, hear the oxygen flowing in and out of his lungs, taste the scent and feel and essence of him, and know that I will never be safe again.

I search his face. 'Why . . . why did you come back?'

Without letting go of me for a moment, he places a single grey alligator boot on the bed. 'Firstly, you threw this at me. I know how you hate to lose one of a pair.'

'And secondly?'

'Secondly,' he murmurs, drawing me towards him, his lips hovering a fraction above mine, we're surviving on each other's breath, *there is no life but this*, 'secondly, I hate it too.'

Visit **www.panmacmillan.com** to read more about all our books and to buy them. You will also find features, author interviews and news of any author events, and you can sign up for e-newsletters so that you're always first to hear about our new releases.